UNDERWORLD LEGACY

N GRAY

By N Gray

Blaire Thorne
Ulysses Exposed
Voodoo Priest
Butterflies and Hurricanes
Salvation
Underworld Legacy

Scout Thorne
The Secret Tomb
Murder of Crows

Shifter Days, Vampire Nights, & Demons in Between
Twisted
Lady Hawk and Her Mountain Man
Hidden Shifter
Wolf
Wolf Retreat
Night Hunter
The Fixer
Kai
Lee
Flynn
Jude

Vinci Books

vinci-books.com

Published by Vinci Books Ltd in 2025

1

Copyright © N Gray 2021

The author has asserted their moral right to be identified as the author of this work in accordance with the Copyright, Designs and Patents Act 1988.
This work is a work of fiction. Names, characters, places and incidents are the product of the author's imagination or are used fictitiously. Any resemblance to actual persons, living or dead, places and incidents is entirely coincidental.
All rights reserved. No part of this publication may be copied, reproduced, distributed, stored in any retrieval system, or transmitted in any form or by any means, including photocopying, recording, or other electronic or mechanical methods, nor used as a source for any form of machine learning including AI datasets, without the prior written permission of the publisher.
The publisher and the author have made every effort to obtain permissions for any third party material used in this book and to comply with copyright law. Any queries in this respect should be brought to the attention of the publisher and any omissions will be corrected in future editions.
A CIP catalogue record for this book is available from the British Library.
Paperback ISBN: 9781036702328

The EU GPSR authorised representative is Logos Europe, 9 rue Nicolas Poussion, 17000 La Rochelle, France
contact@logoseurope.eu

"The greatest legacy one can pass on to one's children and grandchildren is not money or other material things accumulated in one's life, but rather a legacy of character and faith."

-Billy Graham

Chapter One

Léon climbed onto the bed and pulled me into the curve of his warm, naked body. Usually, he'd be cool to the touch, but whenever we were together, he ensured warmth. He'd just fed on one of his many tasty treats who lived at the Labyrinth, but that's where it ended. He'd said he only wanted me even though he shared me with Sebastian, although never in the same bed.

He kissed my temple, then my cheek and down my neck. With one delicate caress of his fingertips, my body hummed for more attention. When he stopped, I moaned my frustration.

"You know what the doctor said."

I frowned and turned my angry glare at him. "Just that I had to be careful," I said and pouted.

"And we are. You already have one scar." He trailed a finger over my swollen belly and traced along the scar that ran from bellybutton down to my pelvic area. I had more scars, but he wasn't referring to those. Now that I had my memory back, I remembered that awful day when Scout was born. She had been in respiratory distress and they had to get her out immediately. The umbilical cord had wrapped around her neck, and if the doctor didn't get her out in those few minutes, she would've met her dad in one of the worst ways possible. It was a blessing she'd survived and one I wouldn't forget.

I groaned again. "You sound like Sebastian."

"As I should. We only want what's best for you and our son."

I folded my arms across my breasts, but they were so engorged I couldn't keep my hands there, so I rested them on my stomach instead.

The little guy kicked, and I gasped.

"He heard you." I grabbed Léon's hand and placed it against the side where the baby had just kicked. The little one was using my insides for soccer practice, but it made my men happy to feel him move around.

"I can't wait to meet him." Léon's smile reached his dark blue eyes as he considered me and caressed my side. "He's our miracle."

Tears filled my eyes.

We knew how it happened but didn't think it was possible, and would never question it. It was another gift from the Gods I'd gladly take. Léon and Sebastian were old and powerful hunters of the night. We never suspected either could make a child, so we never used protection. Me falling pregnant had never crossed our minds.

When I blinked, the waterworks started, and Léon kissed away my tears.

"I hope they're tears of joy. You know I hate it when you sad-cry." He pouted and gave me puppy-dog eyes. His expression was so endearing and strange all at once, because his facade was usually one of control and dominance.

I snorted, wiping away the remaining wetness from my cheek. "They are. I'm just emotional lately. And... I'm worried about you, Sebastian, Scout, and now this little fella." I rubbed my stomach.

"Ah, Scout. Have you told her yet?"

I shook my head.

"You need to tell her. The longer you leave it, the worse it will be for both of you. What happens if you only tell her the moment she's meant to leave."

"I only found out yesterday. I'm trying to decide the best way to tell her, but I know. I will speak with her today. She's coming with us on another case."

"Good, spend time with her before she goes. You only have two days left."

I nodded, and more tears flowed.

Léon tsked me. "I need to get your mind off everything making you sad." Before I could reply, he was between my legs with his magical tongue and powerful fingers. With one hand caressing a breast, he sent his velvety power into me and gave me what I needed... a small release to take the edge off that wouldn't endanger the baby.

Chapter Two

Ralph fetched us in his new Land Rover; it still had that new car smell, and I didn't miss the stench of his older one. I sat shotgun with Devan and Scout in the backseat.

We headed to a new luxury estate where neighbors complained about a disturbance.

Ralph parked beside a police cruiser; when the occupant saw us, he smiled and visibly relaxed. "Thank God you're here, Ralph. We don't know what to do," he said as he climbed out his car, pointing at the house looming up ahead.

"Dispatch said it was gargoyles—"

"No, gorgons."

"Gorgons? Shit—"

"Five dollars, Mom."

"When we get home," I smiled and grabbed my bag out the car. "Has anyone dealt with gorgons before?"

Ralph shrugged and Devan stared with wide heterochromatic eyes; his cerulean-blue eye darkened while his green eye bled into the white, making him appear blind in that eye.

"From what I remember learning at school, they can turn us into stone with their stare," Scout said in a sinister tone.

"Well, that would be inconvenient," Ralph grumbled.

"How can we reverse the process if we're turned to stone?"

"Not sure, Mom. Maybe we need to ask a witch to assist?"

"Sunglasses," Devan blurted as he reached for a pair inside his bag. "Wear sunglasses," he yelled with panic in his tone. "If you wear your sunglasses, they can't turn you to stone."

The officer darted back inside his cruiser and retrieved his shades.

Ralph grabbed his pair off the dashboard.

I already had mine on and handed Scout the extra pair from my bag.

The sound of glass shattering stole our attention; someone flung an object out of the top floor window and it crashed into the hood of the police cruiser. Loud music blared through the now broken window. A short, naked man bent over and showed us his derriere. When he turned around, we could see his features clearly; his eyes glowed green, his mouth in a tight line while his head slithered and moved as his snakes hissed at us.

"Good call, Devan. I think you just saved us all from turning into statues." I pushed my sunglasses up my nose. "How are we going to do this?" I asked no-one in particular.

"Not sure," Ralph stated, then turned to Devan. "Devan?"

Devan shook his head and closed his eyes. I felt hot air rip through me. Then it snapped as his power retreated. "They're upset," he finally said. He'd paled and licked his lips. He opened his eyes and glanced at me. "They drove them out of their homes. They stay in the forest, near the trolls, but something or someone has disturbed them." He white knuckled the car door, sweat peppered his face then licked his lips again. From his body language, I'd guessed he'd stay in the car while we sorted this out.

"Thanks, Devan. Are you okay?" I placed a hand on his shoulder to assess whether he was still breathing.

He gasped, slapped my hand off his shoulder and shook his head.

"Don't touch me."

"I'm sorry, I forgot." I cringed and stepped farther away from the car.

Devan grabbed the bottle of water, struggled to open it, but eventually twisted off the cap. He spilled the contents all over his shirt and sipped. "I'm sorry. I didn't mean to snap at you. But please, don't touch me. I've seen too much of *you* already and if you touch me again, I don't think I could handle any more."

I blinked wide eyes at him. "I'm really sorry." I hated myself for touching him. Devan was an extremely sensitive clairvoyant, and I knew better. I had to remember not to touch him but lately I was forgetful. "Are you going to be okay if we leave you here?"

He nodded, spilling more water over himself.

"I will stay here," the officer said, locking his doors.

I stifled a laugh. "I guess it's just us three." I hooked my arm through Scout's. "You ready for your first gorgon?"

Scout's smile reached her emerald-colored eyes and

nodded. "I can't wait," she shrieked, almost bursting my eardrum.

We followed Ralph to the front door of the double story house. Shards of glass lay strewn on the front lawn with ripped clothing. Ralph reached for the front door, then stopped. I peered around him and saw the problem. No door handle.

"Just kick it open."

"I'd prefer to let the occupants know we're here. They might be armed."

"Be quick, I need lunch." I rubbed my stomach for added effect. My stomach swirled as the little bean moved in his comfortable cocoon inside me.

"Did he just move?" Scout asked, her face beaming. I nodded. She placed her hand over my stomach, and he kicked. "I can't wait to be the big sister."

My heart dropped, along with my stomach, and an overwhelming sadness engulfed me. I yawned, trying desperately to stop the threatening tears. My emotions were a complete mess at the moment. I'd watch commercials and cried. Watched a happy couple kiss on television and I had to grab tissues. I'd glance at my baby girl, who was not so baby and more complaining teen, and I cried. I still hadn't told her she had to leave.

"Mom? What's wrong?" Scout pulled me closer and wiped away that pesky rogue tear. "It's okay," she smiled, and it brightened her face. She still looked her age as the weight of the cruel world hadn't crushed her yet.

"Oh gosh, not again," Ralph teased. "Do you need another moment, Princess?"

I burst out laughing. "No, I'm fine." I embraced Scout and for once she didn't fight her way out.

"Are you ready?"

"Yes."

"Knock! Knock!" Ralph yelled and banged on the front door. "We're from Ulysses Assassins and we will assassinate your gorgon asses if you don't behave." The door swung open, banging against the wall.

The entrance hall would've been beautiful, if not for the graffiti on the walls and the chandelier on the floor.

Hissing echoed from somewhere inside the double story home.

"We don't mean anybody harm." A voice boomed from somewhere inside the darkness. "Come on in." A short naked man strode past and entered the living room.

I attempted to cover Scout's eyes, but she'd already seen his naked ass.

"I hope he covers the front. If not, don't look at him." I arched an eyebrow.

"Mom! Gross!" she grinned. Her pink cheeks gave her away, she'd already seen the front of the gorgon.

Ralph entered first, followed by Scout and then me. The smell of burned hair, wet sand and alcohol assaulted my nose.

When the gorgon saw Scout, he covered his front with one hand. He leaned against the couch that was lying upside down, wearing only an angry expression.

"What's your name?"

"Jedediah."

"I'm Ralph, that's Blaire and Scout."

"Would you mind letting us know what happened here?" I asked.

The gorgon noticed my belly. Something registered in his eyes, and his scowl turned into a pleasant smile. "We are protesting."

"For what?" Ralph asked.

"They are building apartments in *our* forest. They are destroying our trees, our homes, and our livelihood. Don't they understand humans can't enter that part of the woods? That is our territory as it has been for decades."

Cries echoed behind us and the snakes on Jedediah's head hissed.

"Who is that?"

"The owner of the house."

"Did you hurt him?"

"Maybe," he said, averting his eyes. "It's his company destroying our forest. I had to make him understand what exactly he was doing to us."

More cries sounded, reminding me of a wounded animal.

"Would you mind if we looked?"

He sighed. "Fine," he grumbled as he stomped across the living room floor, grabbed an apron from the kitchen counter and tied it around his waist, then headed toward the basement.

The basement light was on as we descended the stairs. The bright fluorescent light revealed a game room, couches, a large television and a family. The crying man clung to his stone wife, on his other side were three small stone children.

"This is not good," I breathed.

"Don't get your stockings in a bunch, I can undo it."

I leered down at Jedediah and his green snakes hissed as their hoods lifted around their heads. I wanted to touch them.

"Which sister are you a descendant of?" It was most likely rude of me to ask, but I had to know. I'd never met a gorgon before and was curious since most only knew about Medusa; the most famous sister of the three.

"We are descendants of Stheno. Only one of my snakes

has a red stripe though, while my brothers and sisters mostly have red snakes."

"She's the dangerous one." From what I remembered, Stheno was ferocious and had killed more men than Medusa and Euryale combined. I'd heard how she lured men into her room where she had her way with them, before killing them.

Jedediah nodded.

Now that we knew who Jedidiah was, the power he wielded, and the situation we found ourselves in, hopefully we could assist the owner in resolving the matter.

"Okay, how can we solve this." I gave the owner of the house my attention.

"I've already stopped the construction. We've retreated from their land and won't go there ever again. You have my word. We didn't know anyone lived there. When we bought the land, we were told it was untouched. I'm truly sorry." The owner of the house cried into his hands. "I had no idea gorgons lived there."

"Who sold you the land?"

"We bought it on auction. They said the land belonged to Sterling Meadow, and they wanted to sell it."

"Give me a name or I'm going to leave Jedediah to turn you to stone."

"No, please." The man clung to his wife. "His name is Deacon Packard."

"Phone him and ask him to come here."

Jordan McCarthy owned a construction company while his wife owned a rental business. He would build the apartments or houses, while his wife would lease them at double the cost. Their business practices were dodgy, but I'd hoped what had happened here today may have scared the living crap out of them and they had reformed. I crossed my fingers. They had three young children under the age of ten and hopefully they didn't take after their parent's unscrupulous ways.

Using my *charm*, I asked Jedediah to bring the family back to life.

Jordan had agreed to the terms and even handed Jedediah the title deed as a peace offering.

We stayed to facilitate the smooth process, but if anything went wrong, I'd shoot Jordan or Jedediah myself.

Before Deacon arrived, Jedediah sprinkled a green dust-like substance over the family and they slowly morphed back to life.

Mrs. McCarthy was upstairs showering while the three kids ate in the kitchen when the doorbell chimed.

Jordan opened the door and greeted the tall, lean man. Deacon had black hair sticking out under a cap, dark hooded eyes, and pursed lips. He shook hands with Jordan, then wiped his hands on his jeans. They entered the living area where we sat patiently, eyeing the new guest.

"You!" yelled Jedediah and stormed Deacon, hitting his mid-section, but only creased the white dress shirt.

"I should've known you would seek the construction owner," Deacon laughed as he kept Jedediah away with one hand.

Jedediah backed up, then ran full steam ahead and rammed into Deacon. They collided into the opposite wall and crashed to the ground; fists flying and snakes hissing.

Deacon's cap flew off his head, along with the black hair, when Jedediah smashed into him. This sparked Deacon's snakes to rattle and spit.

"Get off me, cousin." Deacon elbowed Jedediah in his back, forcing a cry, and his snakes hissed and struck Deacon, but nothing happened. Deacon remained calm and pushed Jedediah off. "Calm down," he said, keeping Jedediah at arm's length.

"I can't believe you sold our land. The land we've lived on for years. Why?" Jedediah's voice broke as he spoke, stepped back and swallowed hard. "We are family."

"Family doesn't kick family out of the clan, Jedediah."

"We are not the ones who were wrong, Declan. Nice name change *Deacon*. Who pretends to be a Deacon, anyway? *Pussy*."

"Dickhead."

I sighed.

It was a gorgon family matter that had spilled out into the human world. They had to sort it out among themselves. This was a family affair we couldn't assist with.

Jordan and his family were going to be fine, even if their house wasn't. Jedediah had thoroughly trashed the place, but Jordan was confident his insurance would pay his claim to cover the damage.

Declan and Jedediah promised they would resolve their issues and leave the humans alone. And they guaranteed they wouldn't turn anyone else into stone—or we would pursue them and vanquish their asses. Not sure how though, but I'd think of something.

As we closed the front door, I noted the stone object Jedediah had thrown out the window when we had first arrived. The object reminded me of a dog. I yelled at them to take care of the poor pooch before everyone forgot about it.

"Well, that was boring," Scout moaned behind me as Ralph pulled into traffic.

"One doesn't always have to use brute force or send someone to Hell to have fun. Sometimes one only needs to listen to the issues and use words to work through it."

She grunted her displeasure.

"At least we have the afternoon to spend together."

"I'd rather go to movies with my friend—"

"No!" I snapped, turning in my seat as far as my belly would allow. "I need to speak with you," — I glanced at Ralph, who winked at me. My eyes flitted to Devan, who gave a stern nod, — "It's important."

"What now?" Scout eyed the men suspiciously and folded her arms.

"Nothing, it's just... I need to speak with you in private when Ralph drops us off."

Chapter Three

Ralph pulled to the curb of our home and we climbed out.

"Thanks Ralph." I closed the door, but then he opened the window.

"Let me know if you need help." He eyed Scout as she traversed up the path toward the front door.

"I'm sure it will be fine," I smiled but knew I didn't sound convincing.

"You have my number pregnant faerie," he winked, closed the window and turned up the radio. Poor Devan covered his ears as the music blared. I waved goodbye and turned toward the house.

Scout was already inside when a warm wind caressed my face. The air popped and a silky film surrounded me as the air sucked out of my lungs. I turned inside the bubble and there he was.

"I heard you the first time, Vic, I know. You are fetching her in two days' time."

"Why haven't you told her, yet?" he demanded. The

sound of his deep voice made my arms pebble, and I swallowed hard.

"Give me time."

He edged closer, closing the gap I did not want closed. "Do not make me the bad person." He arched a dark eyebrow. "I've given you three days to say goodbye."

I harrumphed my displeasure. "You make me hate you more and more. And to think I loved you with all my heart, until you crushed it, stood on it, and threw it away."

He exhaled. His chest rose and fell. He shook his body and dark blue feathers with a purple hue floated around him. "I had to leave, Blaire. You know I had to."

"You don't have to be so cruel, *Prince of Darkness*."

He grunted when I called him the nickname he hated.

"I've already agreed that once she knows who I am and has met *the family*, she can choose where she wants to stay. But you must tell her today. I don't want to get here, and she hates me because she's surprised. I don't want to start off on the wrong foot."

"Why now?" I stepped backward and crossed my arms, making my cleavage larger than it should be. Victor noticed but said nothing. "How did you know about her, anyway? I didn't tell you, and nobody knew you were her father."

He pursed his lips and flapped his mighty wings. "It doesn't matter. Tell her today, Blaire."

The bubble popped, my ears zinged, and a blast of wind hit me in the face. When I opened my eyes, I stood alone on the curb feeling confused and angry. It upset me Victor had known about Scout yet never reached out to her before. There was a reason he sought her out now, and not just because he's her father.

A car drove past with loud music and hooted as they sped around the corner.

Sighing, I approached the impending storm with caution.

Chapter Four

I closed the door behind me, and the smell of cocoa assaulted my nose, and my stomach grumbled.

"I made you some." Scout stirred the liquid and handed me a mug. "Not sure what we're having for lunch, though. I think we have leftover Thai."

I gagged. "No, no more Thai." I shook my head. The cocoa was warm, sweet and creamy. "Hmm, you added cream?"

"Just the way you like it." Scout picked up her mug and enjoyed a long sip. She stared at me over the rim of her mug. "Does he have a name yet?"

"No, Sebastian and Léon want to wait for his arrival before naming him. They want to see their little boy's eyes before deciding on a name." I wanted to roll my eyes but didn't, it was actually a sweet gesture on their part.

She giggled. "I still find it weird."

I glanced at her. "What?"

"That you have two boyfriends."

"Well, one day you'll meet the right one, and who

knows, it could be one or two: boy or girl. I'll never judge you." I took her hand in mine and squeezed. "Hun, there's something I need to tell you—"

The front door flew open, banging against the wall. Sebastian entered with Lee and Kai carrying an injured woman.

"Grab towels, water, and the first aid kit," Sebastian ordered.

Scout dashed to the bathroom for the first aid kit. I grabbed towels out of the closet and the bottles of water.

They gently lay the woman on the floor in the living room. She had a gaping hole in the middle of her abdomen, blood gushing everywhere. If I didn't know any better, she was dying.

"Mel's on her way, but we need to stop the bleeding." Sebastian glanced up at me. "Or heal her."

"I can try, but what happened to her?" I kneeled on the floor beside her and took her hand in mine.

"No!" Scout yelled as she carried the first aid kit. "The doctor said you can't be in a stressful environment. I'm sorry she's injured, but my mother's health and that of my baby brother comes first."

"You're right, Scout. I'm sorry. I should never have suggested it. We'll wait for Mel." Regret flashed in Sebastian's eyes when he glanced at me, before turning to Kai. "Find out where the hell she is and tell her to get her ass here now," he yelled.

"Who is she?" Scout asked.

"Her name is Viola. She's Anne's niece visiting from England. We were hunting when a wild buffalo charged her."

"Is she human?" I asked as I sat on the sofa.

"She's a leopard, but she hasn't shifted yet. She's only seventeen, and apparently a late bloomer."

"Mel is two minutes away," Kai said. "I'll wait for her outside."

"Why come here if you're hunting?" I asked, not understanding what had happened.

Sebastian and Lee glanced nervously at each other, then at me. "Our home was closer."

Did they think I didn't know their tricks? There's a reason they hadn't told me what had really happened. They probably did something they shouldn't have, and I needed to extract the information out of them.

"You say a buffalo charged." They nodded. "Was this some sort of initiation thing you were doing with her?" They glanced at each other knowingly. "Jesus, Sebastian—"

"Mom, swear jar."

I furrowed my brows and ignored Scout until she stomped her foot.

"Fine." I stood as gracefully as I could, grabbed a bill out of my purse and inserted it into the almost full swear jar. "There, are you happy?"

"It's for his wellbeing." Scout pointed at my stomach. "He can't have a mother who swears."

I pursed my lips and returned to the living area. I knew she was right, swearing was a nasty habit I'd started when I was a teen and knew I needed to *unlearn* it. I didn't want my kids to swear therefore I had to stop doing it.

"I'm sorry and I will try harder."

Scout smiled and retreated to her room.

Viola coughed and spluttered blood all over my carpet.

Mel burst through the door with Kai behind her. We all knew she'd do what she did best—fixed what Sebastian broke.

It took Mel about two hours to stop the bleeding and to stabilize Viola. She would make a full recovery and was now asleep in our spare bedroom.

Mel, Kai and Lee sat around the kitchen island eating a late lunch while Sebastian and I were outside.

"What were you really doing?" I asked, my anger reared its ugly head now that the excitement had ended. I was upset he had omitted information, as if I was too stupid to realize. "And don't lie to me."

"Don't be angry." He planted a soft kiss on the back of my hand and continued his butterfly kisses to my shoulder, then my neck and nibbled.

"Stop it, you know I can't be angry with you if you do that. Now tell me."

He pressed his lips against mine for a second, then sat back, his luscious smile lingering. I hated him when he did that; it made it harder to be cross with him and he knew it.

"I did the same for Ivy and Greg. They too were late bloomers, and to help them along I took them to the buffalo reserve. We'd play around, charge the animals, and eventually they'd shifted—"

"Out of sheer will or frightened into their change?"

"A bit of both," he chuckled lightheartedly. "It worked for them and thought it would work for Viola, too. And I thought with it being a full moon tonight, it would help her along. But this buffalo was different. He was mean with shaggy fur and his horns were larger than the others and he had the worst breath ever. We chased after him once, but Viola didn't want to do it again. She had a bad feeling. As we turned to leave, he charged and gored her. The animal dropped her and ran away. I wanted to pursue, but she needed medical care. I knew she wouldn't die, but she's a very slow healer until she comes into her full power."

"Does Anne know?"

"Of course, she asked me to do it. Viola was losing patience and needed help. That's why she came here. She needed Anne to help her shift into her beast. Not even the buffalo helped her shift, I guess she will have to wait until she's ready. It reminds me of your shift."

"Mine was out of anger—"

"And sadness."

I nodded. "And sadness."

Sebastian pulled me into an embrace and kissed the top of my head. "I'm sorry."

I glanced up at him, "For which part?"

His lips curved upward. "For all of it, I guess, but mostly because I asked you to help. We don't know what would happen if you used your healing powers and I don't want to. I don't want to risk your life, or our little one's."

"It's okay, but promise me you won't do anything this stupid again."

"I promise."

I sat between his legs on the pool lounger and rested my head on his chest. In comfortable silence, we stared up at our surroundings. Birds whistled in the distance along with the white noise from the street.

When I thought I had lost Sebastian two years ago, our bond had severed, and I had lost hope. When he returned to me, I didn't think we'd ever connect like we did when we still shared the bond. But I was wrong; my heart swelled with love we still shared, and we were stronger together without the vampire/leopard bond; we had our own special *Sebastian and Blaire link* that's a hundred times more powerful. When I had that strange feeling deep within my diaphragm,

I knew something was up with him. Like now. It wasn't my pregnancy, or what we'd shared before, this was something only we shared. A warm wind caressed cheek, followed by a cold stab of whatever—a sadness that didn't go away until I understood what was wrong.

"What else is on your mind?" I lifted my head to see his face.

"I'm worried about you."

"Me? Why?" I sat straighter, turned around and gazed into his green eyes with the golden sliver.

He jerked his chin in the house's direction, toward Scout's room.

I sat against him again, and he enveloped me with his arms and hugged tightly.

"I won't lie, it's going to hurt when he takes her. I understand where he's coming from and I would never deny her seeing him. But she's only been in my life for a short while and everything was going perfectly—"

"You will never lose her. She will always be your child no matter what age she is or where she's living."

"I know," I sighed audibly. "I know."

"Hey, Mom."

"Yeah?" I sat up.

"You wanted to speak with me?"

Chapter Five

I stared at my hands for five minutes and thought how I'd tell my daughter she had to leave. I could feel tiny insects crawling along the base of my skull as I looked vacantly at my fingers.

"What is going on with you? Is it the pregnancy?"

I glanced up at my *mini-me* and it was like I was staring at a much younger version of myself. Scout was only sixteen with a mind of her own, and powerful in her own right. I couldn't be prouder. But it meant she was old enough to do her own things and wherever she wanted to do them. And I couldn't stop her. She was so much like her dad; she just might enjoy his world and never return to mine. That awful ache I thought had gone was back, and I inhaled sharply, exhaled slowly.

I cleared my throat. "Your dad knows about you," I said quickly and waited for her response. When she didn't reply, I continued. "He wants to get to know you. He asked if you could stay with him for a while."

"When?" She scrunched her brows. "How?" Her hands settled on her hips, and she pursed her lips.

"I don't know how he knew, but he does and wants to get to know you. He'll fetch you the day after tomorrow."

"I don't want to go. Mom, he treated you like crap and left you—alone and pregnant. He didn't even know about me. Why should I care about him now?" she asked as she paced.

I approached her and opened my arms. She wrapped her arms around me, and we hugged until I felt her heartbeat slow down. Her anger seeping away. Her temperament was much like mine, yet she had no animal to shift into. I wasn't sure if it was a blessing in disguise. I smiled into her hair. She would most likely have the company of a spirit animal—like her father.

"He is your biological father, and his family dynamics were at play," I whispered. "They wouldn't have liked that I'm human. And if he had known, he would've taken you away from me soon after you were born. But now you're old enough to decide what you want, and where you want to live so you can speak your mind and tell him. One thing he can't do is make you do something you don't want to."

She pulled away and considered what I'd said. "Does he want me to stay with him permanently?"

"Like I said, you are old enough to say what you want to do. But he has asked if you wouldn't give his world a chance. You do after all wield his powers." And the same shape as his nose. But I didn't say that. She would see for herself when she saw him.

"I'm not leaving you like this." She glanced at my stomach.

"It's okay. He said he would bring you back when it's time for his birth."

"He wants me to stay by him for three or four months," she shrieked. "No," she said, shaking her head. "I don't want to go. Please don't make me go."

I hugged her tighter. "We can speak with him when we see him, okay." She nodded. "Perhaps he will agree to a couple of nights first before anything more permanent."

She nodded again and let go, but she wasn't happy about any of it.

I wasn't looking forward to letting her go again either.

Chapter Six

Sebastian rubbed my lower back; his powerful fingers massaged the areas where I had pain. I lay on my side with a pillow between my legs while he pushed on the pressure points that hurt the most. I had a busy day yesterday and a restless sleep last night which meant his sensual deep massaging was heaven sent.

"How does that feel?" he whispered into the shell of my ear.

My arms pebbled as I moaned into my pillow. "Good, it feels so good. Never stop." Sebastian used both hands and massaged my right hip, when he moved over my middle it sent waves of goosebumps up my back. "Stay with me?"

"As much as I want to," — he nipped the nape of my neck, — "I have things to do today."

I turned over. A *gah* sound escaped my lips with the uncomfortable movement and placed my leg over his. I draped my arm over his neck, my stomach pushed against his, and brought him in for a kiss. He closed the gap between us, and I rocked my hips. The little one kicked, and

Sebastian froze mid kiss. He pulled away and rubbed the spot where he'd felt him.

"I love it when he does that." He continued rubbing the spot while the little bean continued using my insides and ribs as his personal punching bag.

"And always when I'm trying to get some lovin'." I exhaled frustratingly and turned onto my back. He kicked again, and I rubbed the affected area.

"You're a high-risk patient." Sebastian traced the scar from my bellybutton to pelvis. "I don't know what I'd do if something happened to either of you."

"I know." I'd been wondering about that myself. The possibility of the umbilical cord moving around his neck was real, or some other complication. I was more human than Sebastian, and the thought of dying and leaving Scout without a mother left me ill. If I was immortal—like Sebastian, like Léon—then I'd be with them forever. But did I really want to live forever? I aged slower than humans, but not slow enough. If I lived forever, I'd watch Scout grow old and die.

I pushed the thoughts to one side, I'd figure it out when I was ready, and turned onto my other side. Leaning on my elbow, I pushed myself up slowly and swung my legs off the bed. "Come on, let's dress and eat before you dash off."

Viola was already in my kitchen making coffee. I should've felt relieved that someone else was making coffee, but I didn't. I didn't know this girl. She was prancing around barefoot in *my* kitchen like she lived here. Her porcelain skin with not a blemish and her features perfect. Even though her short brown hair stood up on all sides, she still looked gorgeous. When she heard me stomp around the corner, she shrieked, making me flinch.

"Blaire! I'm so happy to finally meet you. Anne and Sebastian couldn't stop speaking about you it feels as though we're already friends." One moment she was near the cupboards, the next she was hugging me. Her skinny arms were deceiving as her hugs were like a vise grip.

"Glad you're feeling better," I said and pushed her away without coming across as rude.

"Yes," she beamed. Her eyes flitted from mine to Sebastian beside me, then back to me. "If I don't see a buffalo again, it would be too soon. I still see that big, horny and fluffy monster charge me like I was dinner or something." She twirled and went back to pouring coffee in mugs. She had way too much energy for someone who almost died yesterday—it was almost annoying. "I've made you decaf, is that okay?" She returned with a mug of my favorite liquid.

I sipped and as much as I didn't want to like it; I did. She made a great coffee. I hummed my pleasure. "This is a good cup. Thanks," I mumbled.

"Please tell me you're joining us at the Leap for our full moon celebrations?" Viola's eyes sparkled as she spoke, but she looked at Sebastian when she asked.

Sebastian squeezed my hand. "I haven't asked her yet," he said, pulling me into an embrace and kissed the top of my head.

"I will think about it." I groaned inwardly. I loved the leap. I loved going there with Sebastian and watching the new fledglings take part in hunts while others enjoyed shifting into their beast. I enjoyed visiting with everyone around the bonfire, surrounded by nature while my beast roared to life. But since my pregnancy, my senses had heightened, and Mel had advised me not to change into my saber. If I were to attend and everyone changed, it could spark my change even though I didn't need the fullness of the moon to trigger my beast to life. There had been too many miscarriages because of the sudden change from shifting. I didn't want to take the chance, even though I controlled her. Besides, I was usually in bed by nine and the leaps celebrations only started at eleven. I'd be on a stretcher, fast asleep, and drooling before they even began.

I sat at the kitchen island beside Kai and Lee, who were full of jokes and smiles. Their arms were maroon from slapping each other. I had no idea what childish game they were playing before I entered the area, but they'd stopped now. They seriously needed to find themselves girlfriends to calm their boyish ways. It was endearing to watch their brotherly friendship, but only up to a point.

I glanced around and we were missing a person. "Where's Scout?" I asked the boys beside me.

"She left early to meet with Ralph," Kai said over the rim of his mug. The way he hid his face, one would've thought he didn't want to tell me for fear I'd be angry.

"Oh," I said and pulled out my cellphone and sent Ralph a message. *'Is Scout with you?'*

'Yes, I will bring her home when I fetch you for work. We have a raging buffalo we need to sort out.'

I showed Sebastian the text, and he chuckled. "I think the buffalo is back. Do you need help?"

"Yes, you started this. I think it's only fair you end it."

Chapter Seven

After I ate pancakes, two sausages, two eggs and a muffin, we met up with Ralph, Devan and Scout at a field near the only cemetery in Sterling Meadow. I was only six months pregnant, yet I already looked and felt like I was nine months. I'd grown larger and more quickly than the first time around. I waddled to the field, rested my hands on my hips and leaned backward, my back clicked, and the pain released.

"Everything okay?" I asked Scout when she joined us.

She ignored my question and stood on the other side of Ralph. I glanced up at him and shrugged.

He shook his head and mouthed, *Later*.

She was angry, and I the object of her misery. I felt her emotions vibrating from her in waves. Any parent with a teenager knew when something upset them; the scowl in their expression, the silent treatment, or just the ease with which they snapped at the slightest remark.

It reminded me of the time Scout was a baby. I'd just

get her to sleep, gently lay her down and made sure she was asleep before I dared move away. Carefully, I'd tiptoe out of her room. But the moment I closed the squeaking door, it was like a bomb had exploded and she'd cried for my return.

Only this time my child was older, could use her words yet refused to talk to me. But I was still in the wake of that explosion.

Then again, I was a teenager myself and would leave her alone for now. After we'd sorted out the rogue buffalo, I'd corner her and demand she tell me what's bothering her.

"There it is," Lee yelled and ran.

In the distance stood a large fluffy beast. Its colossal head hung down, its horns were huge, and it grunted when it saw us snorting out puffs of green smoke.

Kai, Viola and Sebastian ran after the buffalo while the four of us walked.

"It's not happy," Devan said under his breath and stopped. "Uh, I don't think that's a real buffalo."

His comment caught us all off guard, and we stopped beside him.

"What do you mean?" Ralph stepped forward to get a better look.

"It's a wildebeest, and it's angry."

"Yeah, so?" Ralph asked, still staring out at the animal.

The were-leopards neared the animal.

Devan closed his eyes. "Tell Sebastian to get back. Now!"

I called on Sebastian. I thought his name and sent out the warning into the surrounding air. I felt him hear my call and stopped. He yelled at the others to do the same and they backtracked.

The beast blew flames out of its nostrils and kicked up its front leg.

Sebastian and the others ran back toward us.

The wildebeest charged, its horns downcast and aimed at Viola.

"Mom, get to the car," Scout shouted and pulled on my arm.

I followed her to the car as the others joined us.

We'd never dealt with such a beast before and had no idea what it would do. "Is it powerful, Devan?"

"Very," he said beside me in the car.

Devan preferred to avoid all physical contact with everyone. Whereas I wanted to fight, but in the interest of our little peanut, I didn't partake in the action.

Scout closed the car door and ran to Ralph with her weapons drawn, a knife in each hand. Sebastian, Kai, and Lee neared, and I wondered where Viola was. As I searched for her, I saw she had stumbled and fallen. The wildebeest charged her, aiming his horns at her. He blasted flames out of its nostrils, opened his mouth and released a green gas. The green vapor covered Viola. Instead of goring her with his horns, the wildebeest ran past and disappeared.

Viola coughed violently as her body shook and vibrated. She fell onto her hands and knees again. I heard her bones snapping and muscles tearing from inside the car. At least one good thing about this encounter: she could finally shift into her leopard. But instead of turning into her leopard, she turned to stone.

"No way!" I opened the door. "Are you coming?" I asked Devan.

"Nope. I can see fine from here."

"That wildebeest was a gorgon animal?" I asked when I reached the others who had circled Viola.

Viola was a frozen chunk of stone. Her change had started while on her hands and knees with one hand mid-reach for her throat, as if choking on something we couldn't see. Her legs had started changing into her leopard, but that's where it stopped. Her shift into her leopard had worked, but now she was a statue.

"Now what?" Sebastian asked.

Jedediah arrived with Declan; one short, stocky man walking beside a tall lanky man. They reminded me of characters out of a comedy.

Declan wore a smirk on his face the moment he saw Viola. "Yeah, that's definitely one of ours." He crouched beside her and touched her hard cheek.

"An animal did that." I leaned against Sebastian.

"A fluffy wildebeest with large horns and able to breathe fire," Sebastian added, wrapping an arm around my shoulders.

Jedediah snarled at Declan and pointed at him as he spoke. "This is all your fault. If you hadn't sold our land, they wouldn't have broken the fence and one of ours wouldn't have escaped. You broke it, you fix it. I will wait for you in the car." Jedediah stomped away.

"Fine," Declan yelled, stood and pulled a pouch from his pocket and opened it. He grabbed a handful of something that resembled green dust and sprinkled it over Viola. He mumbled foreign words, and the dust sparked as it hit the stone. The wind snapped, and I felt the potency of his energy. Scout rubbed her arms while Ralph just stood and stared. Sebastian and the were-leopards stepped farther away, as if expecting an explosion.

The sparks flared and bathed Viola's stone-body in flames.

My ears popped, followed by a flash of light.

The sound of muscles snapping and pulling, then a low growl.

When the smoke had settled, a medium-sized fluffy snow leopard stared back at us with twinkling blue eyes.

"Perhaps next time you shouldn't use buffalos to help fledglings shift into their beast. It could be dangerous." Declan turned on his heel and left. "Au revoir."

"Thanks," I called after him.

"How are you feeling?" Lee asked Viola, who rubbed her head against his leg. He scratched behind her ear and it sounded like she purred. I guessed she was okay and unaffected by the incident.

"Now what?" I asked, pointing at her.

"Let's take her to the leap. It will be safer for her to remain there until tomorrow. I'm sure she's hungry and we have food for her there. It's too risky to stay out here." Sebastian petted the top of her head.

"Okay, you guys take her, and I will go with Ralph. See you later at home?"

"Are you coming to the full moon feast tonight?" Sebastian pulled me into the curve of his side.

"No, I don't think it's wise. I have all those beasts stirring within me, and I don't want my saber emerging. She's behaving herself for now, but who knows what will happen with an entire leap of leopards shifting."

"You're right. You don't mind if I go?"

I stopped walking to emphasize my words. "No, absolutely not. It's what you do, and I'd never tell you not to go. They're just as much family as you and me."

"Thanks, babe." He cupped my face and kissed me. His soft lips caressed mine, and I melted in his hands.

"I'll see you later." Our lips touched one last time before separating.

Just another day at the *office*.

Chapter Eight

I finally reached Ralph's Land Rover and noticed Scout already in the front seat, avoiding eye contact. I sighed and climbed into the back seat beside Devan. I sat lower on the seat which helped me not feel so squished with my stomach but with me relaxing I needed a bathroom.

"Can we stop somewhere and eat?" I asked.

"Sure, anywhere in particular?" Ralph was still as sweet as ever, especially since the pregnancy. Let's just say my taste had changed slightly, and I enjoyed a wider variety of food.

"I want some chili dogs."

"Ewe Mom, that's so gross."

"I gotta eat what I want to eat. You don't want me grumpy, do you?"

We parked and approached the establishment where they served the best hotdogs. If you could think of a certain hotdog, they had it, chili, mustard, diced yellow onion, or tomato and onion, neon relish, yellow mustard, or even one with sauerkraut. The tantalizing smell assaulted my nose before we reached the door. The smell of the all-beef frankfurter was heavenly, and my stomach rumbled, or little bean moved, either way I was famished.

A girl with dark purple pixie styled hair neared. She stared at the ground and didn't see Ralph. She was about to bump into him when he grabbed her by her arms before they collided. She glanced up at him and smiled sweetly; her violet eyes brightening her face.

"Sorry, I didn't see you," she said charmingly.

"It's okay." Ralph let go of her, allowing her to continue on her path. He glanced over his shoulder before entering.

I smiled to myself. Ralph was aging like a fine wine; he'd cut his hair short and neat on the sides, but one could still see the natural curl he had on top. With his hair shorter and not tied in a ponytail, it was cleaner for longer and you saw his handsome face. He still kept that all-year-round stubble, and he was a lot more agreeable in his *old age*.

"Ugh, I hate this smell. It reminds me of old food that's been in the pot for too long," Scout moaned beside me but followed us inside.

"Come on, you will miss it when you're gone." I bit my lip, but by then it was too late.

Scout pulled away to sit on the other side of the booth, folded her arms and sulked. "I still don't understand why you're allowing him to take me."

I sat down and scooted over into the corner and Devan sat beside me.

"Don't you want to meet your father? Meet your grandparents?" I arched an eyebrow.

"From the Underworld?"

I nodded.

"Where the dead go?" she grumbled.

"Yes, and depending on your religion, they have different names."

"What do I call my father?"

"He is the Lord of the Underworld. He is in training to take over from his father."

"And his name is Victor."

"Yes, that's the name he chose."

"Did you ever meet his parents?"

"Oh no, never…" I trailed off, reaching for the menu when I saw our server approach. I thought it best to end the subject by reading the menu and remaining silent. I was Victor's dirty little secret; but I dared not say it out loud. Vic had kept our relationship a secret, since his family had forbidden him from dating humans. We couldn't help ourselves. From the moment we met, we couldn't keep our hands off each other; our relationship was intoxicating, scorching, and deliriously fun. Those few months together meant the world to me, and I had loved him, and even though he wouldn't admit it, I knew he had loved me once, too. But we had fought a lot, and it wouldn't have worked between us. We were too different, and I wasn't submissive enough. And having Scout was the only good thing that came out of it.

We ordered our meals, then I politely excused myself to go to the bathroom. When I returned, our meals were ready.

"Why did you take so long?" Scout continued moaning. Even her tone was the same teenager monotone laced with disgust for me.

"I'm pregnant, it takes a while sometimes. You will understand when you have one of your own."

"No, thank you."

"Don't you want children?" I sat down and Devan sat beside me. I slouched slightly in the booth until I found a comfortable position. My stomach didn't press on my bladder and I could breathe easily.

"No," she said and sipped her soda.

"Wait until you meet the right one. You never know what your future holds."

"If it's anything like yours, I don't want any kids."

I froze with the hotdog near my face, but instead of taking the bite I craved, I placed my food back on the plate. "Excuse me? How dare you speak to me that way, Scout Thorne—"

"Okay, enough. I've listened to the two of you bicker all day long. You are going to say something you'll regret later," Ralph interjected, but his speech was for Scout. He pointed a finger at her and she physically shrunk in the booth opposite me.

I burst into tears and shooed Devan out of the booth again. As I scooted out, I knocked over his glass of milk. In slow motion the glass shattered into a million pieces, white liquid splashed everywhere and all over my new slip-on shoes. In that moment, it felt like my heart had splintered and crushed. The tears flowed harder, and I knew it was going to be an *'ugly cry'* as I ran to the bathroom. I tried not to look at the concerned stares following me to the restroom. Ralph said something to Scout, but I couldn't hear what.

Once in the bathroom, I locked myself in a cubicle, blew my nose and wiped my face dry. It was only a glass of milk, yet it felt worse. Like everything was spinning out of my control and I couldn't stop anything from changing. I couldn't control everything, but it was too much; the pregnancy... Scout... I flinched when someone knocked on my stall door. At least the tears had stopped.

"Mom?"

"Are you going to say something hurtful?"

"I'm sorry. I shouldn't have said that. I didn't mean it. It's just…" She leaned against the door and slid down to sit in front of my door. I watched her fidget with her clothing through the small gap under the door. "I guess it's this whole daddy thing." She exhaled audibly. "I don't want to go."

I unlocked the door and opened slowly; I didn't want her to fall backward. I reached for her hands and pulled her up and into an embrace. She was so much taller than me, I could now rest my head on her shoulder.

"Victor really is a great guy. It's just—"

"His family."

"Yeah, exactly." I scrunched my nose up. "His family is strange. He's told me so much about them it feels as though I've met them for real, even though I haven't. But from what he'd said, his mom, your grandmother, is really great. Just don't call her that. Even Vic calls her by her first name."

"What's her name?"

"As much as I want to tell you everything, I think your dad should. And I know…," I lifted my hand to stop her from interrupting me. "He hasn't been the best man or father. But I've forgiven him, and so should you. All I ask is you give him a chance. Visit with him until peanut is born. But if you want to come home earlier, just ask." I rubbed my stomach and smiled. A happy tear slid down my cheek and I hugged my *little* girl again. "And when I see you, you will be the big sister to a brother. How cool is that?"

She laughed. "Just promise me you won't say *cool* ever again."

"Cheeky," I said as we joined the others at the booth again.

"Everything okay?" Ralph asked when we sat down.

"All good." I glanced at my now soggy hotdog and picked at the pickles. I had a bite of sausage, but it was already cold.

"Can I order you another one?" Ralph asked with an arm in the air, already summoning the server over.

"Yes, please, I don't think I can eat it like this."

After an hour, I'd eaten a fresh hotdog and fries and drank a milkshake. I was full and ready to leave. When we stood, Ralph felt his pockets like he was searching for the Holy Grail. With panic etched on his face, he turned to look outside.

"That girl with the pixie haircut. She stole my wallet."

"No way. Did that little girl pickpocket you?" I laughed and handed cash over to the server. "You don't have to lie, Ralph, I don't mind paying."

"I swear, it was my treat today. The little wench stole my wallet." He felt his breast pocket of his jacket one last time before turning to the server. "Do your cameras work?"

The manager assisted us and showed us the video. They had a camera facing the door and filmed the entire wallet pinching episode. The young woman in her early twenties, with pointy ears, lavender-colored eyes, and a waterlily tattoo around her wrist—it was the emblem for the herd of faeries closest to the trolls. She had slipped Ralph's wallet into her pocket with no one noticing. And she was quick, too. There was no way Ralph could attempt getting his wallet back. The trolls, faeries, and now gorgons, didn't like humans snooping around that side of the forest and doubted anyone would help us name the girl, or show us where she lived. It was easier to just replace the items stolen.

Since we didn't have a case to solve at that moment, we accompanied Ralph to cancel his bank cards and to get a new set.

Then we waited in the car while he replaced his license at the DMV.

I closed my eyes for a few seconds when I awoke from a tsunami of butterflies. My little bean moved inside his safe womb, but it felt as though he was doing laps and knocking against my ribs whenever he turned. I rubbed the area to ease him when my cellphone rang.

"Hey, hun."

"Where are you?" Léon asked.

I glanced at the time on my cellphone, and it was almost five. We'd been driving around with Ralph to sort out his stuff for three hours.

"Outside the DMV. Ralph's wallet got pinched, so we're driving with him to replace all his things."

"I'm waiting for you at the doctor's rooms."

"Oh, shit!" I sat upright as Ralph opened his door. "I'll see you now," I said into the mouthpiece and ended the call. "Ralph, please take me to my doctor," — I glanced at the time again, — "we have seven minutes to get there."

Chapter Nine

I ran through the hospital hallways as fast as my body could handle. The others waited at the coffee shop while I went for my bi-monthly check-up. As I rounded the corner to the consulting room, Léon greeted me with a warm smile and a gaze that sent a pleasurable ripple through my body.

"You are late." He kissed me chastely. "Come, Désiré is waiting for us."

We entered the private room and found our doctor/midwife waiting patiently for us.

"Sorry we're late." I wheezed, catching my breath, and removed my jacket.

"I'm just glad you made it this time," Désiré said with kind eyes. Dr. Désiré Saunders was a general surgeon first and a witch second. She'd agreed to be my midwife upon hearing the good news. It was pure luck because she was busy specializing in gynecology and midwifery. It didn't bother me I was her first patient. She'd treated me and others several times, and nobody had died on her watch.

Désiré flicked her long raven hair out of her way and sat

down. She pressed buttons on the fetal ultrasound machine and lifted my shirt.

Léon sat beside me and held my hand, his eyes glued to the little screen.

Désiré squirted gel onto my skin and with the probe made circles over my stomach. The outline of our peanut's head came into focus and Léon squeezed my hand.

"There he is," Léon said with wonderment and a twinkle in his dark blue eyes.

"Where's Sebastian today?" Désiré asked in a pleasant tone. I'd been on the receiving end of condescension and casual disdain from others when they'd found out I was dating two men at the same time, and that they were brothers. But it was only those closest to us who had accepted the situation, and I knew there was no malice in Désiré's question.

"He has leap stuff to prepare for the full moon harvest tonight. Besides, it's Léon's turn to join me today." I winked at him.

"Ah, well, it's lovely to have you with us today, Léon. Now you can see and hear him." Désiré moved the probe left, then right, and started measuring his head circumference, the length of his body and a leg when she could.

Then we heard his heartbeat, and Léon almost broke my hand.

"Ow," I moaned and let go of his iron grip.

"I'm sorry, it's just—"

"You've never heard one before?" Désiré asked, and a smile flitted across her face.

"I can hear his heartbeat whenever I'm near Blaire, but never like this and where I can see *my* baby," he said as red liquid welled in his dark eyes. He wiped away his blood tears without glancing in my direction. I reached for his hand again, brought it to my mouth and kissed his palm. He was ancient and hadn't needed to go with a pregnant woman for a sonar before, and I suspected because the baby could be his, had made my Master Vampire a little emotional.

"Ours," I said jokingly.

"Yes, of course. Ours." He looked at me then and stood, cupped my face and kissed me with a heated enthusiasm that sent the baby squirming away from the probe and broke the sound of his heartbeat.

"Well, everything seems to be fine. His growth is on track and I can't see any underlying conditions. And his umbilical cord is right where it should be. Like I said before, we need to monitor you and him every two weeks. And if you feel anything strange, call me so I can have a look. You were younger when you had Scout. We need to take precautions—"

"I know and we are."

"Good."

"And you still can't sense anything?" I asked.

"Let me try again." Désiré placed the probe down and wiped my belly clean of the gel goo with tissue paper. She rubbed her hands together to make them warm and placed them over my stomach. I felt the faint hint of her energy hit and then disappeared as quickly as it had started. She shook her head. "No, I'm sorry, but I'm not picking up anything. Have you asked Devan to check?" She removed her hands and pulled down my shirt.

"Yeah, he says the same thing. Our little boy is going to be a normal, pure vanilla human. He can't determine whether he has any supernatural abilities or that he is anything but human." I sat up and climbed off the bed with Léon's help.

"I think the most important part is to keep you and the

baby safe. You can worry about his abilities once he is born." She smiled warmly, even though they held a hint of sadness.

"You've seen a lot at this hospital. Have you come across anything similar? I thought all babies born to supernatural parents had some kind of ability."

"Yes, it's true. But you need to understand, Blaire, your case is not like all the others. I don't mean to sound judgmental, but do you know who the father is?" She pointed at Léon.

I glanced at him and caught his facade slipping, then he recovered quickly. We didn't want to know who the father was. In our eyes, they're both the father. Our concern if we knew who the father was, the other might not like the answer. I loved them both—I could never choose between them.

"No," I said and pulled on my jacket.

An expression crossed her face I couldn't decipher.

"Also, *you* are very different. You were born with certain manufactured abilities, even though your mother was part-fae, part-witch. I've looked at your blood work and still don't know what you comprise. I'd prefer not to assume," she smiled, and it lit her face and reached her dark eyes. "Let's take it one day at a time?"

"Thanks, Désiré. Not only for now, but for everything you've done for us."

"Anytime," she said while cleaning the equipment. "See you in two weeks' time."

Once we reached the coffee shop near the entrance, Scout, Ralph and Devan were devouring a slice of cake each. I smiled as I watched them. Ralph was teasing Scout with his lemon meringue but eventually allowed her to cut a piece and savor the taste. My mouth watered as I watched in awe.

Devan was shy and reserved because of his ability, but since joining us he'd become used to us and had finally come out of his shell. Even though I worked with these two men, I'd considered them part of my family. I watched them share the three slices of cake and it made me happy to see my family bonding, yet sad that Scout wouldn't be enjoying this for a while.

I said a silent prayer that Vic would take good care of her.

"Mom, are you okay?" I hadn't seen them finish their treat and walk over.

"I'm fine."

Léon stared at me like I'd sprouted a fourth head.

"What?" I asked.

"I'd been speaking to you and you hadn't heard a word I said."

"Sorry, I didn't. Tell me again." I smiled sweetly up at him and fluttered my eyelashes.

"Construction at the Labyrinth is complete, and the pool is full. They started filling it at five this morning."

"That's great."

"Does that mean we can finally swim in a larger pool?" Scout's face brightened.

"Yes, and it's even heated for those cold evenings." Léon placed a warm hand on the small of my back. It sent a burst of yummy power that made me weak at the knees. He brought me in for an embrace, kissed my temple and near the shell of my ear he whispered, "And other things."

My arms pebbled at the thought. "Sounds wonderful."

"Can we swim now?" Scout asked with a moment's hesitation. I wanted to ask her if she was all right but decided against it. If she'd thought about leaving home in that second, I didn't want to upset her again. Upsetting her once was enough. "I just need to fetch my swimming costume from home."

Before I responded, Léon's limo pulled up with Elena in the driver's seat. She climbed out, opened a large, black umbrella and held it above his head. She nodded and waited for her boss's instructions.

"Do you want to ride with me? I can take you girls home to fetch your items." Léon's words were velvety and seductive.

I hooked my arm through Scout's and nodded.

To Ralph and Devan, I said, "See you guys tomorrow. Do we have a case yet?"

"We might have." Ralph opened his car door. "If there's anything I'll let you know."

It relieved me we had no case requiring our immediate attention, and I could spend the time with Scout.

Chapter Ten

Léon had added sections to the Labyrinth the last two years; a wing on one side with high arched windows and stained glass he'd imported from Italy. And he included the large pool where he'd hoped to host lavish night parties. Léon had become domesticated in his *old age*, but I wouldn't say it to his face or that I was the reason he had *calmed down*. If anyone found out the Master Vampire of Sterling Meadow had chilled, someone brave enough would try their luck. But he did it for me and my family. And now that we had a little one on the way, we'd use the pool area often.

The new wing boasted four bedrooms, each having a bathroom. My bedroom was different, as it had metal curtains to block out the sun for when Léon slept with me. Understandably he didn't want to burn with the early morning sunrise, even though he could withstand some heat. He had the metal curtains installed which ensured no sliver of sunlight touched the inside of the room. The only discomfort I had upon awaking was not knowing where I was in the heavy darkness.

Every time I stayed over, it smelled and felt like home away from home. And Léon was just another part of my life, and I shared my heart with him.

One bedroom refurnished for our baby boy. They painted the walls blue along with cute cartoon storks stuck on one side, and in the middle of the room sat a large white cot with a rocking chair in the corner. Léon had spared no expenses for this wing, constantly asking if there was anything else I required.

We traversed the large hallways that shifted every twelve hours for security reasons and entered our wing. Even after all these years, I still didn't understand the sequencing and required a guide to navigate the maze.

Scout closed her bedroom door to change, and I went to mine. Léon came in behind me, kicked the door closed and wrapped his hands around my belly. He kissed down my neck, leaving me a quivering, moaning mess at his tender caresses. I leaned into the front of him and felt his hard body against my behind, and I pushed my ass out.

"There's much I want to do to your body," he breathed into the nape of my neck.

"It's been over a month," I moaned my frustration and gripped his thighs; the hard quadriceps muscles flexing beneath my fingertips. I moved my hands over the curve of his ass and pulled him closer to me. The angle of my arms hurt, but it was worth it; to feel him like this was worth the strain on my shoulders.

His hands found my breasts, his thumbs grazing my sensitive nipples over the material. "These are more than a handful now." I felt him smile against my neck.

I moved my hands to the front of him and seductively gripped the bulge in his pants. He squeezed my breasts in response.

"Mom, it's time to take your vitamins. And hurry, I want to swim before it rains."

My arms fell to my sides. "Almost done," I yelled and stepped away from Léon. I turned around, finding him naked from the waist up. "Wow, I can't wait to get all of you naked. But I have to go."

"I know." Our lips touched, and the heat was still there, untouched and most welcomed. "Dress and take your vitamins. I have things to do and will meet you by the pool. Should I ask Elena to bring you some food?"

"Uh-huh, that would be great. I want ice-cream and fries."

He arched an eyebrow.

"What? He's hungry."

"You're eating for yourself, Blaire, not two, just you."

"I know, but it's what I feel like."

"Fine." He pulled on his shirt. "I'll see you in a short while."

Scout was already floating on her unicorn in the water. She held a juice in one hand and her cellphone in the other.

"How's the water?" I placed my towel on the lounger and approached the pool.

"It's warm once you get in."

I stuck a toe in first and it felt lukewarm; once I was knee high in the water, it warmed.

"Take your vitamins, Mom," she yelled without glancing up from her phone.

I groaned and walked back out, saw the bottle of vitamins and swallowed the recommended dose with the fruit juice. On the table beside my glass was a bowl of mints, I grabbed one and sucked on it, and climbed back into the water. Once the water reached my hips, I dropped into the cerulean liquid and sat at the bottom of the pool. When I opened my eyes, I noted the glass on one side of the pool. All these months they'd cordoned off the area, and Léon hadn't informed me of this detail. My vampire voyeur liked to watch. Grinning at the thought, I swam toward it and saw Léon wave up at me. I stuck out my tongue and came back up for air.

"Did you know we can see into Léon's office?"

"No way, he's such a perve."

"Scout!" I chastised. "He's your—"

"What Ma? He's my what exactly? He's nothing of mine. He's just a vampire you're banging—"

"Scout! Don't be rude." I swam to her black and red unicorn and pulled her to the shallow side. "I did not raise you to behave this way."

"No, Mom, you didn't. Mason raised me while you were too busy dating a vampire and a were-leopard. And now Mason is dead. He died because of you, and now the man who's supposed to be my dad is fetching me tomorrow—"

It was a reflex. I didn't mean to do it. It's something I'd never done before, and I hated myself for doing it. Scout was close to me and she spewed horrible words she'd never said to me before. She was mean and unfair. But she was too close to me and she had hurt my feelings. I didn't realize my hand was in the air until after I'd slapped her. I gasped after I hit her and covered my mouth with both hands.

"I'm sorry. I'm so sorry, Scout. I didn't mean to." I reached for her and she hit my arm away.

"That's it, I've had enough. Dad!" she yelled. "Come, fetch me. Now!" she yelled louder. "Call him, Mom. Tell him to take me away now. I've had enough already. Tell him to just come fetch me."

I froze and unsure what to do. I wasn't sure if that was how it worked. "I don't know if I can do that, Scout. Please, stay with me for another day—"

A blast of power blew me back into the water. When I surfaced, the tall dark angel of death extended his wings as he stretched his shoulders back, making his form larger than it was. I guessed that answered my question.

"What happened?" Vic asked me, then turned to Scout. "Are you okay?"

"She hit me."

"It was an accident."

"You still hit me, Mom." She sounded wounded.

"You were cruel."

"You didn't have to slap me."

I waded to the shallow side and climbed out. Vic handed me the towel, but I avoided his gaze. I could feel his judgement as I passed him.

"Are you sure you want to go now?" he asked her.

"Yes." Her chin trembled.

"Can I at least get one last hug?"

"No! Get away from me."

"Scout!" Victor demanded her obedience by saying her name in a deep baritone.

She flinched and nodded.

I hugged Scout and whispered how sorry I was. I had already forgiven her for what she'd said to me, now all I needed was her to forgive me. We couldn't part on angry terms. She relaxed in my warm embrace and nodded. She mumbled it was okay and broke free.

"I take it you know who I am then," Vic said once Scout pulled on her clothing over her swimming costume.

She glanced up at him and said shyly. "Yes."

He held out his hand. She hesitated at first, but took it. He covered her much smaller hand in both of his and stared at her.

I pulled on my gown and closed the gap.

"You look so much like your mother." That caught her attention, and she turned her green eyes toward his darker blues. He let go of her hands and turned to me. His raven hair blowing in the breeze while his large black and purple wings glistened in the dim lights. "Never strike our daughter ever again or I will punish you."

I swallowed hard at his words and nodded.

He turned to Scout. "If you really want to leave, we can."

She glanced at me with wide eyes, then back at him and nodded. "Let me change first." She picked up her towel and ran inside.

"Is everything okay?" Léon asked. One moment he was by the door, the next he stood between Vic and me. "You must be the sperm donor." Léon scowled at the dark angel. His stone features concealing his emotions, but the tone of his voice hid nothing—he did not like the man in front of him.

"I am her father and Blaire's first *love*. You must be the spare wheel in her pathetic love triangle," Vic said, waving his hand in the air and in Léon's direction.

I winced at the low jab—Vic definitely knew how to fight dirty.

"Keep our Scout safe, fledgling," Léon replied. His tone deep and commanding.

"Best you do not forget your place, *vampire*."

"Best you don't forget it is your father who runs the

Underworld, you are merely the Pitbull who ensures the dead do not escape."

"I am more powerful than you could ever be," Vic growled. His tone harsh and low. It made my arms pebble at the intensity of his words.

When Léon spoke, a warm wind blew in all directions, forming mini tornados in the sand.

"Your power is yet to mature, *fledgling*. It is your father who wields the power you so desperately desire. You're just a pretty *face* and gatekeeper," he hissed as the power snapped, and the tornados of sand filled the air and blew leaves off the trees. Small stones pelted the windows, and I had to cover my eyes.

"Consider this your only warning. Don't insult me or my power ever again or I'll bring you back to the hell you forsake to stay in luxury with the living. I merely have to snap my fingers and bring you back with me. Do. Not. Tempt. Me," Vic said between clenched teeth.

The wind whipped around us as the small stones, sand and leaves hit us and covered the pool in a brown glaze.

"That's enough. Stop it, stop it, stop it," I yelled, placed a hand on Vic's chest and the other on Léon's. The moment my hand touched Léon, a sharp pain shot through both hands, down my arms and hit my stomach. Flashes of my beasts doubled my vision; first my rat, then my leopard, my lion, my wolf, and lastly, my saber. My beasts flashed one after the other, forcing me to shift. I couldn't risk having my saber reveal herself while I was pregnant. She had remained hidden during my first pregnancy, and I didn't know what she'd do if she revealed herself now. I had to stop her. I doubled over, cried out in pain and coughed up blood.

"Jesus, Blaire!" Léon tried to grab my one arm while Vic reached for the other, but I pushed them both away.

The wind died down; the air warmed and my skin got sticky.

"Don't touch me. Get away from me, both of you. Whoever that was just stop already. You're both powerful. You're both pretty. Now please stop it." I sat on the ground and wiped my mouth with the towel—leaving red marks.

"You're bleeding," Vic said the obvious.

"I bit my lip when that blast of power pumped into my body. I felt my beasts come to life, and I needed to calm them down. Biting my lip was the only thing I thought of."

"I'm sorry." Vic stepped away. "I didn't think it could hurt you."

"Naturally, you only do what's right for you and never consider the consequences. Just promise me one thing. When you take my child tonight, you'll think of her needs first and not just your own."

"I will."

"Say it, say you promise."

"Okay, I promise."

I smiled inwardly. It was a small win to get Vic to promise something. To make him obey *me*. It was usually I who had to obey him.

"I'm ready," Scout said in the doorjamb. She wore jeans, sneakers, a t-shirt and jacket with her backpack. "How much clothing do I need? Or must I get more from Mom's home?"

"No," Vic said, approaching her with purpose. "There's clothing for you." He held out his hand for her. "Ready?"

"Yes, just one more thing." She ran to me and hugged like her life depended on it. "I love you, Mom. And I'll see you soon." She let go and went to her father.

Vic held out his hand for her and brought her closer. His wings extended, reflecting a purple hue, and then closed around them. The air snapped, popped, then they disappeared.

My heart fell to the ground and my breath escaped my lungs. The back of my throat ached as I swallowed the tears. I was grateful for the years I'd spent with her. But now she had to discover his world; one I could never be part of. But it was who she was now. She was old enough to be her own person. I'd taught her that much, and I was so proud of her.

Tears streamed down my face when Léon brought me into the curve of his body. I closed my eyes and held onto him. After a few moments, he pulled back and cupped my face. "You have swollen eyes, *ma chérie*." He kissed away the tears. "Come, let's get you to bed."

Chapter Eleven

SCOUT

The look in Mom's eyes as I stepped closer to my dad would haunt me forever. I was so cruel to her and had deserved the slap. It wasn't necessary for me to be so awful to her. I was hurting. She was sending me away again, and I wanted to make her hurt. It was the wrong way to go about doing it, but I wanted her to feel the pain I was going through.

I didn't want us to part angrily, even though I had asked her to call my father. I strained my neck glancing up at the man; he was even taller than Sebastian. His shoulders were broader with muscle mass I'd only seen on body builders during their training. He wasn't as large, but one could definitely see the definition through the black armor he wore. His raven hair cascaded around his shoulders, framing cerulean-colored eyes and a thin nose—like mine. I was definitely his child.

I stood close enough to my dad to feel his power pulsate. It was a low hum of pulsing electricity that if unleashed upon the world it could wreak havoc. Victor was a creature I'd never seen before. He was otherworldly and from what

Mom had told me, a deity of the dead. It explained why I sensed the dead near him. It wasn't a zombie feeling, but more ghostly—*souls*—like a dark fog swirling around his aura and mine.

His black armor reflected light, giving it a metallic shine, and solid to the touch. It covered his entire body, leaving his face and hands open. I wondered whether I too would get to wear such a body armor. But what caught my attention were the dark wings outstretched behind him. The sight of them left me dumbstruck.

I waved goodbye to Mom and Léon and swallowed my tears. My eyes stung and looked away. Father's wings closed in on us and at first, I felt claustrophobic, then the next moment we moved, and all my thoughts disappeared. My stomach dropped to my feet as we transported, and it felt as though time stood still as we travelled through a blackness so thick, I could taste it, like raindrops and dirt.

We *landed*, if that's what it was, in a dark room. It had no smell, but the air was fresh. There were no plants, windows or furniture, and dim torches adorned the walls. The longer I stared at them, I realized what they were, gargoyle heads. The monsters were grotesque in various stages of near creation; as if the creator had forgotten an important step for each. The one closest to me had a chain through its nose that came out its empty left eye socket. The chain snaked up the wall, connecting it to the next lamp; this next gargoyle's chain was through its head. In each gargoyle's head, the light shone through their open mouths and eye sockets, screaming in silent torment.

A shudder ran through me.

"Don't mind them," Dad said in a low tone that left me shivering. "They've been part of the walls since forever."

I reached out to the closest one, my hand an inch away,

and its head moved in my direction, snapping its jaw. I shrieked and jumped back.

A low rumbling chuckle came from Dad. "Just don't go near them. They're still quite alive and love to bite."

"They're alive? How is that possible?"

"Well," — he moved toward the archway, — "those who don't belong anywhere ended up as ornaments on the walls," he said it so casually, like it was something that happened often. It scared me. I couldn't image how it felt being stuck in a wall and becoming a light fixture. It was unthinkable and cruel.

"Why don't they belong anywhere?"

"It happens." He shrugged and entered the next room, leaving me gasping at the wall with the strange heads.

Not wanting to stay alone with the roving eyes, I ran after him.

"There are rules you need to abide by." He marched through the dim hallway, not bothering to look over his shoulder. It was like he didn't care whether I was following him, yet he knew I was there. "Do not touch the walls. Do not wander around. And do not open closed doors. Do you understand?" He didn't wait for my reply and continued speaking. "You've just witnessed that these walls are alive. If your curiosity gets the better of you, understand there are consequences, and I might not fetch you—"

"What does that mean? Will these walls swallow me up?" I stopped and glanced left, then right. The walls in this corridor were burgundy. I leaned forward to see the detail. The walls moved like snakes slithering just beneath the layer of paint.

"What did I just tell you?"

I stood straight and faced him, my cheeks heating.

"Do. Not. Touch. The. Walls."

I nodded, feeling like a six-year-old caught stealing a cookie. I wanted to sulk and run away, but that would leave a poor impression. "But the walls are moving. Are they supposed to do that?"

"Yes, now, come along. We can walk and talk."

I dashed after him, keeping my hands to my sides.

"Don't call me dad, father, or pops, or whatever it is kids call their parent these days. Call me Vic or Victor."

That was a strange request. I thought it best not to interrupt him, but I did anyway. "Why?"

"It's a preference."

We entered another room when barking erupted. I stopped in the doorjamb and peered around the corner toward the barking—careful not to touch the door frame.

"This is Caesar." Vic crouched to pet the creature that had similar features as a Rottweiler. "Caesar is my spirit animal."

"What's a spirit animal?" I asked, entered the dimly lit room but kept my distance.

"An animal that's an extension of your soul. You will know yours when the time is right." He opened his mouth as if to say something else but stopped, instead adding. "Come closer, allow him to smell you."

I wasn't sure what he wanted to say, and it made me wonder which was my spirit animal. I loved animals of all kinds and even better when I snuggled up to them. But... this animal... was different.

"Scout!" Vic demanded my obedience with the single use of my name.

I flinched. "He's *different*," I muttered as I slowly neared.

Caesar bounced on his paws and leapt forward, but the large collar and chain restricted his movement.

"Yes, he's our guard dog."

"But he's so small." Once on my knees, I showed Caesar my hand. He sniffed and licked, and his tail wagged viciously. Then the other head licked and sniffed, followed by the third. I scratched behind each ear, each coat coarse and unique to the other, as if they were three different dogs. When I pulled my hand back, it dripped in their saliva.

"If any intruders get this far, Caesar becomes the guard dog I trained him to be. Never, under any circumstances, enter their lair without me. They will maul you to death. They will recognize your scent and allow you a head start. Don't let the collar and chain fool you, they break easily."

I wiped my hand dry on my jeans and stood, corrected the bag slung over my shoulder until I was comfortable.

Caesar continued to bounce as the three heads groomed each other. They were cute in a sadistic way; a black dog with three heads were better than one.

I glanced at my watch and furrowed my brows. The hour hand moved quicker than the seconds, while the seconds hand moved at triple the speed. I'd learned in one of my science classes that a magnetic pull could affect your watch, but I doubted to this extent.

"Vic." Calling him by his name left a sour taste in my mouth; it sounded foreign and rude. I wanted to call him Dad or Father but that too sounded strange; perhaps they had bewitched those words and could never utter them in his presence.

"Yes?" he said with an edge of impatience. He held his hands behind his back, and it was only then I realized his wings had disappeared.

I lifted my wrist near his face so he could see my watch as the hands spun around. "What's going on with my watch? And I've noticed my cellphone doesn't work either."

One side of his mouth curved up, and he exhaled. "This

place has no time. We are neither here nor there." I felt my face scrunch up in total confusion; he wasn't making any sense. "You will not age here, nor can you die. Caesar may destroy your body, but the room will absorb your soul and you may become one of the light fixtures."

I swallowed hard. Sweat dripped down my back. "Is it getting hot in here?" I fanned my shirt.

Victor crossed his arms over his broad chest. "Do you understand what I am?"

I shrugged. "I don't know. Maybe? Is this Hell?" I glanced at the slithering maroon walls, it felt as though they were breathing and edging closer. I glanced up at Vic and swallowed the bile that had risen.

His smile stretched across his face and reached his blue eyes. "This is where you come when you die. And I ensure, by all means necessary, you don't leave. Here we have the Fountain of Souls." He entered the next room, and I pursued.

The vast living area boasted bright candles, sweet-scented air, and strange leather furniture. In one corner was a large marble fountain with flowing liquid, but instead of the constant motion of water I heard the endless sounds of moans and screams. My head hurt as my eyes danced across the various objects inside the room. Portraits hung on the walls, strange ornaments adorned on tables and against the walls, and flames blazed in the fireplace. This was nothing like what we'd learned at school, nor was it something from any book I'd read. What I'd learned so far would leave me a changed person.

"Humans know little about the Underworld and they offer information they think is correct. All they do is confuse everything. But in time you'll understand." He continued to educate me and crossed the floor toward the fountain.

"When you die, the Ferryman collects your soul and brings you here. Depending on the type of person or monster you were throughout your life, your soul may enter various realms within this world—"

"Like Dante's Inferno?" I said the first thing that came to mind.

"Something like that." He nodded once, adding, "Except the levels don't reflect their sins but of a space and time within and which I deem fit. And there, they'll stay for all eternity. You don't go to a Heaven or a Hell. This is Heaven and Hell in one. I control the dead and have powers like no other. But you will wield some of those powers soon."

It reminded me of how I could push someone's soul out of their bodies. I opened my hands and stared at my palms.

"Tell me, I sense you can *push* and *pull?*"

My brows had stayed in that confused frown as I glanced up at him again. "I've never heard of that term."

"You can push people's souls out of their bodies?"

I nodded.

"Did you know you can pull them back in?"

"Like a necromancer?"

"Close, a necromancer uses chanting, salt, and fresh blood to animate a corpse. You can bring them back with none of that."

My jaw dropped as I absorbed his words. It was freaky and cool, but it scared the crap out of me. I'd only done it once before, and even though I did it to save our lives, I was in shock afterwards. My arms pebbled as the memories surfaced. I glanced at Victor again, his dark gaze penetrated mine as if trying to read my mind. It was unnerving. I had to say something so he would stop staring at me. "I'd been studying my grandmother's book, and I could do her spells easily—"

"Now you know why." Vic raised his hands and extended them, palms out, then pulled his hands back towards his body. He repeated the action. "Push," — he pushed his palms out and away from his body, — "pull," — he brought his hands back to his chest.

I followed his lead and pushed, then pulled. The lights flickered as if a wind licked the flames. My body pulsed with a current and I laughed.

"That's it." He stopped and crossed the floor again and stood beside the fireplace. The flames raged angrily. "This is the Eternal Fire. It's hot, so try not to get too close to it." He pointed at the portrait on the wall that hung above the fireplace. "This is your," — he coughed into his fist, — "... grandfather."

The painting was a *man*; tall, muscular, and red. His skin tone a deep maroon, with black eyes that bore through me, leaving me uncomfortable the longer I stared at it. I had to avert my eyes.

"Yes, it does that to you. The painting is alive, of course."

That caught my attention, and I stared at it again. "Is he in the portrait?"

"Oh no, it's just his soul."

"Is he dead?"

"No, but he is somewhere... everywhere. Who knows what he's up to these days?" He waved his hands in the air. "But this is part of him. He changes his appearance when he is with mortals and reverts to this," — he pointed at the painting, — "when he's home."

The black armor he wore glimmered as if he was breathing in the portrait. The horns on his head were thick and pointy. My eyes flitted to Vic. "Do you have horns and are you red beneath the armor as well?"

"I do, and so will you. It develops the older and wiser you become. Well, hopefully." He winked. "Again, I feel I need to emphasize that you are not to touch it. What you see in the middle of the room you can use at your leisure. But anything against or on the walls, the fireplace, and the fountain are off limits. Do you understand?"

"My Lord."

I flinched at the sound of a man yelling as he rushed into the room, stopping dead when he saw me.

"What is it?" Vic replied, irritation laced in his words.

The man glanced at me, then back at Victor.

"Speak freely," Vic said without introducing us.

"Is she the newcomer?"

"What is it, River?"

"Apologies, my Lord. I have the signed contract you requested." River produced a golden piece of paper and handed it to Victor.

"Ah, good job. And yes," — he pointed in my direction, — "this is Scout. She is assisting me."

River crossed the floor quickly and stood before me with his outstretched hand. I hesitated at first, then reached for his hand, which was warm and firm. He shook once and slowly let go. His smile lingered before turning his attention back to Victor.

"My Lord." River stood with his hands behind his back, awaiting further instructions.

River was a head taller than me. His brown hair in need of a trim but otherwise neat and off his face, with a couple of days' worth of stubble on his jaw. He wore black cargo pants and boots with a loose-fitting white top with the sleeves rolled to his elbows. His features were pleasant enough as I watched his interaction with my father. Although, he kept stealing glances my way. My cheeks heated, forcing me to find a chair away from him and sitting.

"I have another errand for you," Vic said, producing a piece of paper. "I need you to get everything on this list."

River reached for the document and read what was on it. "These, my Lord?"

"Isn't that what I just said?"

"Yes, my Lord." River bowed slightly at the waist, turned on his heel and left, winking as he walked by.

"Who is he?"

"An apprentice of sorts. Come, allow me to show you where you can place your things. Then we need to be off."

"Where are we going?" I asked, but he didn't reply.

Victor led me through another dark hallway and stopped by a door. He eased it open with a long finger. It was one of the tiniest rooms I'd ever seen. It had a closet and a chair. There was no bed or bathroom.

"Where do I sleep?" I set my bag beside the chair and sat on it. "Do they all look like this one?"

"Right, I forget you still have lots to learn. One," — he started counting on his fingers, — "we do not need to sleep. Two, my room is bigger—naturally—because I'm Lord of the Underworld. Three, there's a bathroom next door, it's huge and it will satisfy your needs. Four," — he opened the closet, — "here are some clothes." He turned to exit, then stopped. "Freshen up, and wear something comfortable from here," he pointed at the closet. "You have an hour." He closed the door behind him.

I exhaled a nervous breath and sagged against the chairback. My stomach continued to twist as realization settled into my bones. My eyes pricked as I thought of Mom,

Sebastian, and even Léon. When the latest scan of my baby brother flashed before my eyes, I wiped away the tears. I missed everyone. I prayed I wouldn't miss my brother's birth; I wouldn't forgive myself if I wasn't there to hold the little guy. I knew Mom needed me to be there.

With only my thoughts to keep me company, I immediately regretted picking a fight with Mom. I still had a day to spend with her, and I had to do something so stupid and immature. Now I understood why Mom always said we should spend each day as if it were our last. Living in regret was a waste of emotions, yet that's what I felt.

I glowered at the open closet and all the neatly packed clothes, dresses of all kinds, t-shirts, pants, and underwear. I groaned, hoping Dad didn't buy them for me. I frowned. *Who bought it, then?*

I leafed through the various dresses, pulled out a stack of pants and shirts to pick something I liked. There were a handful of neutral colors to choose from. Since I wasn't sure what we were doing, I chose something comfortable yet practical, khaki cargo pants and a white vest.

Victor told the truth. The bathroom was enormous, larger than Léon's in the new wing. In the center stood a large white bath with a walkthrough shower with jets lining both sides. There were two sinks, and a toilet with a low divider separating it from the rest of the bathroom.

As tempting as the bath was, I showered instead. Once done, I grabbed one of the black bath towels from the shelf, wrapped it around my body and exited. The hallway was eerily quiet, but I heard a murmur in the distance. I entered my room and dressed quickly. Once I'd pulled on my vest, I grabbed my phone and noticed the screen was black—I'd forgotten my charger. I glanced around the room, not finding any electrical outlet. Cursing to myself, I remembered my phone wouldn't work here, so it was pointless trying to charge it, anyway. I threw my phone into my bag and slowly opened the door.

The murmurs continued. I entered the corridor, but instead of heading in the living room's direction, I went the other way.

There were two closed doors, both locked. Both dark wooden doors adorned with metal plates where the hinges were. I turned around, passed my door and stopped outside the door after the bathroom. They made the door out of ancient metal with a slot that slid open. I pulled the lever open and pressed my forehead against the cold door and peered through the glass. I blinked and a pair of yellow eyes stared back at me. I yelped and fell backward, landing on the cold stone floor. My heart hammered in my chest. Groaning sounded from the other side. I shook my head. Victor had warned me not to snoop, yet I couldn't help myself. Once I'd found my breath, I crept up the door frame and slammed the slot closed. The moaning ceased, but then nails scraped down the door. I shuddered at the sensation, reminding me of why I hated eating ice-creams off a stick. I thought it best to leave that door alone. The creature could be dangerous, and I should leave it be. *Why was it so close to the bathroom, anyway?*

The next door was wooden—similar to the other two I'd seen—with detailed carvings etched into it. Each carving depicted two people dancing in various poses. There were at least twenty carvings of the couple; it was romantic. As much as I wanted to open the door and look inside, I was afraid of what I might find; if it was like the other door with the creature, I didn't want to open it. This was not my place, and I did not know what was on the other side. Victor had already warned me not to go near the walls. Perhaps this was a test, and I shouldn't open any doors other than my own and the bathroom.

Peering around the doorjamb, I saw Vic and River deep in conversation. I couldn't make out what they were saying, but it sounded important by the expressions they wore. I noticed both had changed their clothing; they wore black pants with loose black shirts.

When I'd first arrived and walked through this room it had smelled like leather and candles, now, the aroma of food wafted around me driving my senses mad. My mouth salivated as I stepped farther into the room. The men stopped speaking, stared at me, freezing me to the spot.

"Help yourself to some food. We'll join you in a moment." Vic led River to the farthest corner to continue their conversation.

I was jealous Vic was speaking to River in that way; my dad had his hand on River's shoulder, and the expression he wore reminded me of a close-knit family. It was a glance a father gave his son when praising him; reminding me of how Mom smiled at me when she spoke of her day and how she wanted me to join Ulysses. It tugged at my core, and I hoped Victor looked at me like that someday. I ignored their rude behavior and picked up a plate.

There were trays displaying various eats I'd never seen before. The closest tray displayed crackers with a white crumbly blob and a green herb balancing on top. I brought one *cracker* close to my nose and threw it back on the tray immediately. The stench of sour milk lingered. I moved on to the next tray filled with brown goo. I did not smell it, but I pushed a spoon into it, and it moved about like slime. They filled the next bowl with a type of soup I could not explain. The moment I lifted the glass lid off the bowl, the rich aromatic flavors caught my attention. I grabbed the soup ladle, swished it around in the soup and poured some into a bowl. I spooned some soup near my mouth and had a tiny taste. The liquid was a burst of rich flavors and I tasted meat, yet none were visible. I finished the bowl and went back for seconds.

"I would not have expected you to eat *that*."

I spun around to find River staring at me with an expression I couldn't decipher. Normally I would ignore a comment like that, but what angered me was the slight upturn on one side of his mouth. Like he knew something I didn't.

"Why? What's wrong with it?" I set the bowl down and crossed my arms.

"For one, it has eyeballs in it. And two, it's the worst tasting dish." He swished the ladle around and came up with three white balls bobbing. One eye flipped over and stared back at me.

The soup repeated itself on me. I moved away from River and the table and threw up in a trashcan near the door. The soup came out of my nose and mouth; I shuddered. An icy shiver ran down my spine. I wiped my mouth with the paper napkin River offered.

"The first two dishes smelled and looked terrible, so I tried the third and it tasted okay. If I'd seen the eyeballs earlier, I wouldn't have,"—I swallowed hard, — "tasted it. Who made these dishes?" I pointed at the table.

"Well, to be honest, I've never met the chef," — then he whispered, — "and I don't want to." He winked. In a firmer tone he added, "In all the time I've worked for Victor, I'd only eaten here a handful of times and never saw the creature who made it. The only dish I ate was this one," — he pointed at brown balls that looked like cooked dough. "I'm not sure what you call it, but it's like a savory donut. Inside, it's loaded with vegetables and cheese. Those dishes over there," — he pointed at the one that looked like a strangled grilled chicken, — "skinned peacock with stuffed baby snakes. When you slice the bird open, the baby snakes gush out and slither into your lap. That," — he pointed at something brown and slimy, reminding me of fried livers, — "mashed mermaid brains. Those are pixie-stix." The tray he pointed at looked like a deep-fried frog dish with legs sticking in different directions. "And you know the eyeball soup over there, and that's the quiche Minotaur balls."

"All that is just gross. Doesn't Victor know we eat *normal* food?"

"I've never seen Victor eat. Besides, I don't think he cares what we eat. The *chef* made the delicacies according to what they eat."

I shuddered. I didn't want to eat *this* food but was still hungry. "I'd love a cheeseburger."

River offered me the tray with the savory donuts, and I took one, smelled it first, then bit off a tiny piece and he was right; it was only vegetables and cheese. I glanced at the gooey inside and saw a variety of peppers and melted cheese. I enjoyed a larger bite, and it went down better than the soup.

"This will have to do," I said with a full mouth while glancing around. "Do you know where Victor went?"

"He never stays."

"Then why the food?"

"The chef knows when there are new arrivals and always makes something that day." River loaded some savory donuts onto his plate, along with crackers and something that resembled seaweed.

"Does he ever host parties?" I wanted to know more about my father and suspected River could give it.

"Hmm," he hummed, shoving a cracker into his mouth. "Sometimes, but I don't stay. I'm only the help."

I pointed to the corner of his mouth and he swept his tongue along his lips to lick the seaweed that had stuck there.

"Does he eat anything?"

"Souls maybe," he laughed. It sounded genuine.

"Excuse me?"

"I'm just kidding. You should see your face." He pointed. "I don't know if he eats food, but he doesn't eat this."

I glanced at the table and my vision swam, or the food moved, I couldn't be certain, but it was unsettling. I didn't want my food repeating on me, so I faced River to get my mind off the food and asked him questions about what he did.

"What do you do for Victor?"

River chewed slowly. "Whatever he needs me to do."

I doubted he wanted to speak about it, so I didn't push him for more information even though I was dying to know.

"Well, he did say I had to keep you company," he grinned and a piece of the green seaweed stuck between his front teeth. I licked my teeth to feel if I had anything stuck, River noticed and did the same, removing the inconvenient plant.

Grabbing a handful of the savory donuts, I chewed slowly.

"Are you ready?" Victor's voice boomed throughout the vast room.

"Where are we going?"

"You'll see."

"Do you know?" I whispered to River as I set down my plate.

He shook his head in a manner only I could see, and it filled me with dread. River knew where we were going, and he didn't seem to like it—if I'd read his expression correctly.

I followed River to where Victor stood.

Victor had undone the top two buttons of his shirt, and I saw the metallic shine of his black armor underneath.

"Where are we going?" I asked again, hoping this time he would provide a proper answer.

"I need your help in retrieving an artifact," he said before touching my and River's shoulders at the same time.

The room disappeared. The thick darkness swallowed us, and I tasted sand on my lips; it was not salty sea sand, but hot desert sand.

Chapter Twelve

I awoke to the sound of my cellphone ringing and ringing. As much as I wanted to ignore it, it didn't stop. Léon was dead to the world beside me; his one arm was over his head while the other rested against his stomach. He was naked and beautiful; an ageless abomination, but to me a work of art. I kissed his cheek and answered my cell.

"Hello?" I said, not looking at the name of the person phoning.

"Where are you? I came home to an empty house."

"Sebastian?" Oh no! I'd forgotten to let him know where we were yesterday. I leaned back on the pillow.

"Of course, it's me. Where are you?"

"At Léon's."

He exhaled a shaky breath, and I felt his anger vibrate within me. I felt the whirlwind of emotions within him; anger, sadness, regret, but the emotion I felt the strongest—*relief*.

"I thought something had happened to you. I stayed over at the leap and when I woke this morning and checked my messages, there were none from you even though I'd sent you one last night."

"I'm sorry, so much happened last night, and it slipped my mind." I explained what had happened with Scout.

"Do you need me to take you anywhere today?"

"No, I had the scan yesterday—"

"The scan? You didn't tell me about that either." He sounded depressed.

"I'd forgotten about it until your brother reminded me. He was waiting for me at the hospital. I'm sorry." My apology sounded hollow, and I needed to make it up to him. "Maybe fetch me and we can spend some time together. How about breakfast?"

He was quiet for a heartbeat too long, then finally spoke. "Okay, I'll see you in half an hour." He hung up before I responded, and I knew I was in the kitty box.

I kissed Léon on the cheek, left him a note and got ready.

I waited for Sebastian at the entrance near the pool. I saw his car speed around the corner and almost missed the entrance. He backed up and hit the horn. I opened the car door and climbed inside. As I fastened the seat belt, Sebastian drove at a responsible speed.

"You're still angry."

He grunted but didn't glance in my direction.

"I said I was sorry. I'm a little forgetful lately," I said as I reached for his hand that was gripping the gear lever. He didn't pull away, instead he held my hand bringing it to his mouth and kissed my knuckles.

"I worry," he said, his words filled with sadness. "I can't lose you, Blaire. If anything had happened to you—"

"I know and I'm very sorry."

He nibbled my knuckles and let go of my hand when I giggled.

"Where do you want to go? What do you feel like eating?"

"Pancakes."

We stopped outside one of my favorite coffee shops. They offered a variety of breakfasts, scones, muffins, pancakes and coffee. I ordered a decaf coffee and pancakes while Sebastian ordered a meat breakfast—sausages, bacon, scrambled eggs, biscuits and gravy.

He told me about last night. When they'd arrived at the leap, they'd taken Viola to the cages where she stayed for the rest of the evening. When he'd said they'd given her a lamb for dinner, I almost burst into tears as I pictured a soft, fluffy animal. He ignored my gasp and continued with his story. Viola had settled down once her stomach was full and had slept. During the night all the were-leopards had shifted into their beasts, they hunted together and enjoyed the feast they had caught. Most had fallen asleep in their leopard form and by morning everyone, including Viola, had shifted back into their human form.

This morning they'd tested her skill; she'd shifted back into her leopard soon after turning into a human. She wasn't tired or hungry and shifted back into her human form without breaking a sweat. Sebastian suspected she might be as powerful as her cousins Greg and Ivy.

Her parents in England were ecstatic when she gave them the good news. They'd agreed she could remain here until the end of the month and return home before the next full moon.

Even though Viola had turned into a block of stone, the results had pleased Anne. She'd said Sebastian had shown leadership, and she was proud to have him share authority over the leopards. They wanted to make his and Greg's crowning official and host their celebratory dinner soon.

And tonight, they'd meet to discuss Viola's celebration. But Sebastian wanted to stay home with me.

"I don't mind if you go. It's your leap, and you need to be there. I love staying home alone and should anything happen, I have so many numbers on speed dial it's enough to make me vomit," I grinned.

"It's not funny."

"I'll be fine. I promise. When it's over, come home and tell me all about it."

"Okay."

As we finished breakfast, and about to pay, my cellphone rang.

"Hey, what's up?"

"We have a case," Ralph said breathlessly. "A kidnapping."

"Are you running somewhere?"

"This house has six floors, and no elevator. I'm walking up."

"Why didn't you fetch me?"

"It was near my house. I thought I'd check it out first, and I think we can help."

It sounded intriguing; I loved a good mystery.

"Who is our missing person?"

"All I know is he's a scientist. Listen, can you come? Devan should be here soon, but I need you here."

I glanced at Sebastian, who nodded. Those super sensitive ears of his could hear a pin drop two shops over.

"Sure, give me the address."

Chapter Thirteen

Sebastian dropped me off at the skyscraper of a house. Before we arrived, I'd Googled the scientist's name as I'd never heard of him and neither had Sebastian.

Dr. Craig Avery was on a revolutionary discovery. He'd been studying vampire DNA and how to manipulate and use it to fight cancer cells. Even though turning into a vampire removed all known cancers and illnesses, most humans didn't want to become the undead and live forever; they still wanted to die, just not so young or in pain. Some believed Dr. Avery was close to some sort of breakthrough. Others thought he was crazy and needed to be institutionalized. Dr. Avery had won many accolades and well respected within the scientific community.

As I entered the foyer of his six-story house, I almost bumped into the back of Devan. He stood like a statue in the middle of the entrance, staring up at the atrium. My handbag collided with his back as I tried not to touch him, but my bag moved and my palm grazed his shoulder blade when I lifted my hands, protecting my face.

"Please don't touch me, Blaire." He jumped out of the way, colliding with the staircase and fell to the floor.

I raised my hands. "I'm so sorry, but you were standing in the middle of the room and I wasn't looking where I was going." I flinched. "Did you see anything?"

"You know it doesn't take much for me to see *you*."

"I'm sorry." I cringed. "Do you want to share what you saw?"

He clucked his tongue and shook his head. After a brief pause, he finally said, "You know it's better for all if I don't." He exhaled and shuddered. "It's okay," he said and stood, dusting the back of his pants.

"Have you been up yet?" I pointed at the staircase.

"No." He violently shook his head. "No, this is where I stay." He pointed at his shoes. "There's too much going on I don't know where to start."

"Do you think you can try? I'd love to know your thoughts."

He continued shaking his head. "I'm sorry, but... there's just... something dark and dangerous about this place," he said through clenched teeth and shivered.

"It's okay, Devan. Maybe stand outside or sit somewhere you won't be in the way—"

As I spoke, men in uniform descended the stairs. They removed their blue gloves marked with maroon liquid. One man paled and held on to the banister.

"What's going on?" I neared the steps.

"Whoever took the doctor liquidized his cat and dog." The officer who spoke I'd seen before at multiple crime scenes. When he stopped on the last step, I saw his name badge—Officer Blackwood—I repeated his name over to myself, so I didn't forget it again.

The information Ralph had given me wasn't much. We

Underworld Legacy

rarely took missing persons cases, but Ralph had thought we could still assist. With Officer Blackwood stating how they had killed the animals, I wanted to understand more.

"Is there anything else you could tell me?"

"Perhaps you need to see the crime scene and the scientist's research yourself. There's a lot happening up there," Officer Blackwood said, pointing up. "With your trained eye you might find something we didn't" He threw his gloves into a white plastic bag that stood near the front door.

"I'm going outside." Devan hurriedly exited, not waiting for my reply.

"Which floor should I go to?"

"Sixth," Officer Blackwood breathed, cupped his hand over his mouth and ran to the bathroom.

The other officer joined Devan outside.

I wanted to get a sense of who the scientist was and explored the house before going to the sixth floor.

I entered the living room on the ground floor first. Two couches faced each other in the middle of the room with a large coffee table between them. On the walls hung large portraits, and large arched windows brought in enough natural sunlight. The room boasted high ceilings and lavish furnishings. There was a door to the side, but it was only a closet filled with coats and boxes on a shelf.

The large kitchen and open planned dining area with a flat screen television on the wall sat on the other side of the foyer.

The first floor was the doctor's study and library.

The next two floors had two rooms and two bathrooms each, which I suspected where guests stayed.

The fifth floor was the doctor's bedroom with a large king-sized bed, walk-in closet, and a portrait of an old gentleman wearing sixteenth century clothing adorned his wall above the bed. I felt his eyes on me as I crossed the lavish bedroom and entered the marble bathroom with a large clawfoot bathtub standing in the middle, with a shower and toilet. The walk-in closet kept men's clothing and a safe.

"The crime scene isn't in the doctor's closet."

I flinched at the stern voice behind me. I spun around, coming face to face with a man my height, shaved hair and eyes the color of coals.

"I know," I smiled sweetly. He'd caught me with my hand in another man's closet and needed to play nice with whoever he was. "I wanted to get a feel for Dr. Avery." I thought it best to be honest. I was too pregnant with porridge brain to worry about lies I had told.

"Well, everyone is upstairs," he said and turned to leave.

"And who are you exactly?"

"Benjamin Curie, I'm Dr. Avery's assistant." He stopped near the doorjamb.

"No relation to Marie?" I asked and my sincere smile was back on my face. Poor Benjie seemed a little frazzled around the edges. His creased clothing was missing a button on his collared shirt. At least his pants zipped to the top, and he wore the same color socks.

"No relation," he said, and headed for the stairs.

"Before you dash off. Can you tell me when last you saw the scientist?"

"Yesterday afternoon when we finished for the day and closed the lab upstairs. He said he wanted to do one last round of testing before ordering dinner. This morning I came in the usual time and found his lab in a state and they had slaughtered his animals." He choked on his last words and I pictured those poor animals and the back of my throat ached.

"Thank you, I'm sorry you had to walk in on that. It's this way?" I pointed up.

"Yes, your partner is waiting for you. He'd asked me to look for you when you hadn't arrived."

"Thanks, let me go up to the scene."

I found Ralph hunched over a red mess with brown fur I assumed belonged to the cat and dog. Red lumpy blotches painted the walls, floor and the doctor's desk. The coppery stench wafted in the air as a strange sensation washed over me, causing me to step back over the threshold and into the passage.

Ralph glanced up at my arrival. "What's up?" He stood and approached.

"I don't know. But I understand why Devan doesn't want to come inside the house. There's something strange emanating from this room." I pointed at the lab.

I couldn't help Ralph solve the case from outside and stepped back into the room. I closed my eyes to shake the bad feeling, but the sensation remained. Once I opened my eyes, I shuddered and hugged myself.

To understand what had happened, I needed to concentrate on my surroundings and not the vile feeling that lingered.

The doctor's glass desk stood to the left of the door with papers strewn everywhere, with a handful of pages on the floor near his chair. On the wall behind his desk hung three portraits: sixteenth-century paintings of two men and one woman. They were pale with ruby lips and wore clothing fit for royalty. The rest of his lab had steel tables, pipettes, Bunsen burners, freezers, incubators, coolers, stirrers, and fume hoods.

As I traversed deeper inside the lab, I passed two glass cells. That's what they looked like; glass walls with two glass doors. Inside each *cell* were chains, shackles and a toilet.

"Ahh, Ralph, why are there two cells in the doctor's lab?"

"I know, it's creepy. I asked Benjamin, and he said it's for their test subjects," — he rolled his eyes, — "they needed actual vampires in order to perform their experiments and I suspect they couldn't have them bite them."

"Is this even legal?"

"They had the subject's permission. All documents signed and filed." He handed me a manilla folder. Inside documented contracts for at least fifty test subjects who were each paid a handsome sum of money to be poked and prodded.

"We need to find out if they're still alive."

"We're already on it. Officer Blackwell is tracking them down."

"Okay, he looked a bit green around the gills, so hopefully he can be of use to us," I grinned.

"Let's give them a chance to help. You know he enjoys working with us and he actually does a superb job. But this," — he waved his hands around, — "will make anyone ill."

"Except for us."

"Except for us."

"What else do we know?"

"Dr. Avery devoted his life to his work. He won a few awards for his work in DNA. He never married and had no children. The only creatures he looked after were his cat and dog. Unfortunately, they'd killed the animals in some sort of ritual, although I don't see any markings on the walls to confirm that."

I glanced at the walls. Dried blood marked a few areas

and had left the portraits untouched. I lifted the frame of the first portrait, then the second. When I saw the third, I asked Ralph to take it down; at the back was a symbol reminding me of Egypt and the three crystals.

"We need to ask Léon if he recognizes this or someone who would."

"It reminds me of that time," Ralph said as he snapped photos of the symbol and portrait; it was a painting of the same woman in a different pose to the one behind Dr. Avery's desk. Ralph checked all the portraits, but the markings were only on the one.

We continued our investigation of the lab, but there was nothing else. The area was neat apart from the blood and dead animals.

After three hours of standing on my feet, I felt exhausted and sat behind Dr. Avery's desk. His chair was comfortable, and I leaned back and stretched my legs and feet.

"His house was grand and his lab immaculate. He'd documented everything he did, yet disappeared into thin air. Why did they slaughter his animals?" I spewed my thoughts as I stared at the ceiling.

"Maybe he has a competitor? They discovered he was close to a breakthrough and wanted the glory for themselves."

"That's a theory." I pulled open the top drawer and found notepads, pens and blood. "Ahh, Ralph, come look here." I pointed at the droplets left behind no longer than twelve hours ago.

Ralph pulled the scanner from his sling bag, pressed the button and the light illuminated. The blood had a purple hue to it, which told us one thing…

"Vampire blood," we said together.

Chapter Fourteen

SCOUT

The heat was suffocating. The sand irritating as the dust storm receded over the horizon. I was grateful for the clothing I'd selected, but if we stayed here overnight, I might need a warm top. More importantly, I was glad we had missed the sandstorm.

Victor had brought us directly to the first step of an ancient Egyptian temple. At the top of the stairs sat pharaohs carved out of the mountain on either side of the large, closed doors.

When we had *landed*, Victor had let go of us. Disorientated I had stumbled backward, mis-stepped, and crashed onto hot sand that seared my ass. I jumped up the moment I felt the fire on my butt. River and Victor roared with laughter at my expense.

"Next time, please warn me before we travel through space," I moaned and climbed the steps, leaving them at the bottom. "And where are we, anyway?"

"A short distance from Cairo." Victor's voice was right

beside me, then the next he stood at the top of the stairs. He had cheated and teleported his way to the top.

River took two steps at a time, winked as he passed me.

I stomped the rest of the steps to the top. "Why didn't you just teleport us all to the top?"

"I needed to see the top of the stairs to teleport. I can't conjure up pictures and hope for the best. I need to know exactly where I'm going, and I only knew of that spot." He pointed a long finger toward the bottom of the stairs.

"And why are we here?"

"Scout, I've brought River with us to help you inside." The way Victor said that left all the hairs on my body standing on end. "He is to guide you, and where necessary, protect you."

"Why? What will happen to me inside?"

"Nothing will happen while you are inside. River joining you is only a precaution."

"You aren't coming with us?"

"I'm forbidden to enter." He thumbed behind him at the doors. "This is as close as I'm allowed, unfortunately."

"Why?"

Victor pressed the bridge of his nose and exhaled. "They stole an artifact from me, and I need it back. The person who stole it has brought it here, and I am forbidden to enter. If I enter, I'm stripped of my powers, rendering me human... and mortal."

"I don't understand." My brows furrowed. "How did this happen? I thought nobody could get into your... *home?*"

"I don't have the luxury of time to explain, Scout. Now, please, will you do this for me?"

"Sure, but—"

"Enough!" Victor pressed the bridge of his nose again, and I was sure he was counting to ten.

My eyes pricked at his outburst, and my cheeks heated by his intimidation. I leaned against the stone wall, the cold centering my burning body.

"You've killed before, correct?"

I nodded, not trusting my voice yet. I wasn't sure why he needed to confirm *that*, and the thought left me swallowing hard. It felt like I'd swallowed sand. I needed water. If I'd known I was coming to the desert, I would've packed refreshments.

"Good, you may need those skills here," he said and disappeared.

I gasped at his departure and just as I was about to ask River what was going on; he reappeared.

"Before I go, River has provisions should you need it and can answer questions you may have." And then he left.

"What the hell? Now I know why my mom swears." I approached River. "I need water. And do you know what's going on?"

River let go of a frustrated breath and shook his head slowly. I didn't know River very well, but the look he wore told me he wasn't enjoying himself either. He handed me a bottle of water from his backpack. A *backpack* I hadn't noticed until he removed it from his shoulders.

"I know little more than what he has already shared, only that I know what we are looking for—"

"Which is?"

"It's a golden scarab."

I glanced at the large doors behind me and cast my eyes to the desert before me. All I saw was a sea of sand and sun. Which meant there were lots and lots of snakes, danger, and heat. The safest and coolest place to stay was here.

"It's not that I don't trust him, but is it even his to take?"

River's lips turned up at the sides. "Yes, it's his."

"Do you know who took it?"

He nodded but said nothing else.

"Well, who?"

"That I cannot say. What I can tell you is, Victor has a limited time in which to get the golden scarab or he will lose."

"What will happen if he loses?"

"As he said before, if he enters the place, he will become mortal and forced to roam the earth until he dies. If the item isn't found before the time has passed, the same will happen."

I stared wide-eyed at River. It was as Victor had already said, but when I'd first heard it, I didn't register what it really meant. The consequences of not retrieving the item fell on my shoulders, and immediately I didn't want to do it. *What if I failed? What if I couldn't do this on my own?* And the man I'd only recently come to know as my father was about to be destroyed by my hands.

"Why me?"

"I don't know. I can't answer all your questions. But I will do everything in my power to help you succeed."

River's amber-brown eyes shone with warmth and honesty. His words felt genuine. He was telling the truth. But there was something else he wasn't saying, and it was important; not directly to the task at hand, perhaps with him. I didn't know River very well, but I'd recognized his expression anywhere. It was one beseeching me to ask no further questions.

"Fine." I spun around to face the large doors. "Let's go inside before I lose my nerve."

The doors were tall and ancient. There were no keyholes or handles, only dents in identical places on both doors. Dents, I assumed I placed my hands to push open the doors. I pressed both palms against the dents, but it didn't budge. I kept pushing against the doors when a flame flared to life at one end and started outlining my hands. I got such a fright I pulled my hands back.

"What the…?"

"Do it again," River said beside me. "You're the key." He sounded as surprised as I felt.

"How can I be the key?" I had no idea what was going on or how I could be the key for something Victor had lost. None of this made sense. "How did they get my fingerprints?" I stared at my hands, then at the doors. The flame wasn't hot and didn't burn my palms. I did as River suggested and pressed my hands in the same position as before. At least this time I knew what to expect. The flame started again at the same place, outlining my hands like a fuse of dynamite without the explosion. Once it finished outlining my hands and ended where it began, the doors clicked and cogs turned, opening the door.

A blast of cold, sandy air hit us, blowing me backward and into River.

"Sorry," I mumbled the moment my back hit his front.

"Are you okay?" He held my shoulders, steadying me.

"I'm good." I quickly moved forward so he'd stop touching me. "Let's go see what's inside."

Chapter Fifteen

Ever since the whole Shannon debacle and his subsequent *disappearance,* the monsters had stood together to stop the killing of their kind. The supernatural's in Sterling Meadow were stronger together through the Were-Animal Alliance and a force to be reckoned with. There had been no more attacks on the shifters, and no stranger dared entering Sterling Meadow unless vetted by a specific animal group. Not to mention Léon and his vampires who readied themselves to vanquish anyone who tried—with the blessing of the Council.

The alliance now included the faeries, trolls, and even the gorgons if they were so inclined.

When the new governor, Thomas Sellect, replaced Shannon, we knew he was different. He had accepted all supernatural's and wanted everyone safe and not only humans.

He had come from a humble background and had studied law. He worked his way to the top and jumped at the chance to govern Sterling Meadow.

Thomas was a tall man with dark curly hair, chocolate-colored eyes and a thick mustache. He had a wicked sense of humor but always remained professional.

When Thomas discovered how Shannon had tried to disband the police force by stopping funding and ensured no supernatural crimes were investigated. Thomas wanted to change the perception of the police. He had pumped funds into the force by giving the right men the correct weapons, training on supernatural's, and even kept assassins such as Ulysses on retainer. Hence, whenever there was a case that an officer or detective couldn't handle, they had the authority to call us in to assist—and paid us handsomely.

Ulysses Assassins was a well-known establishment and received most of the calls from the police. The other organizations were smaller, and thankfully none had tried to get in our way. We suspected it could be our ties to the supernatural beings and the fact that I was one.

After Ralph and I found the vampire blood at the doctor's lab, we brought it to our labs for testing ourselves. We entered the precinct and headed toward the office we shared with one detective who was currently on vacation.

Detective Georgina Carson had relatives who were of different flavors and didn't mind working with us on cases she couldn't handle with her colleagues. She reminded me of Michonne from The Walking Dead. Apart from the physical characteristics, I'd seen Georgina with a sword and had to step backward or I'd end up in meaty cubes. She had also become close to everyone at Ulysses, and we welcomed her as a friend.

Our office had no windows instead there were posters on the walls of forests, trees and the beach. Ralph and I shared one desk and one PC, which Ralph operated. I slouched in the chair across from him.

"I just need to write the report, then we can head to the lab, and then to Léon. He should be awake by then?"

"Uh-huh." I sat in my chair and allowed it to swallow me. The soft cushion of the seat and backrest was heavenly against my aching body.

"Are you struggling?"

"I don't remember my first pregnancy being so hectic. I'm tired all the time and constantly hungry."

Ralph chuckled lightheartedly. "It's almost over. I'll just be ten minutes then we can drop off the vampire blood."

"Is anyone reviewing the camera footage for the doctor's house. I forgot to ask at the scene."

"Blackwood found the hard disc drives, but there wasn't a company sticker to call for assistance. He's taken the entire thing to their IT department to decrypt. He said it should be ready in a couple of days."

The lab where we sent supernatural specimens to was only a short walk from the precinct. Eloise McGibbon was one of six supernatural forensic pathologists working for the police force. Thomas Sellect ensured there were enough staff able to assist the police and speed up investigations. The last thing he wanted was to keep innocent vampires in a cell, or a guilty troll set free on a technicality. Governor Sellect was a straight arrow who made sure everyone received a proper investigation.

We entered Eloise's lab and the sparkling fae greeted us. She was part-dwarf, part-faerie, and always welcoming. I felt like a giant in her lab. They had made her tables and shelves specifically for her, which came up to my knees.

"Hey guys. What do you have there?" she said, reaching for the sample in Ralph's hand.

"We're investigating a missing scientist. You'll get more specimens to process but we found vampire blood at the scene after the tech's had left. We need to know if it's in the system?"

"Give me some time and I will call you with the results."

"Thanks, Eloise."

"How's the baby?" she smiled sweetly.

"He's good, growing well."

"Still normal?"

"Yeah," I said, rubbing my stomach. "There's nothing supernatural about him."

I didn't know why, but that's what pregnant women did —we rubbed our stomachs. It was comforting and soothed the baby within. If anyone spoke to us about how the pregnancy was going, we rubbed our sides. Luckily, nobody had touched my belly, wanting to feel him move. That annoyed me in my first pregnancy. People didn't understand what personal space meant. I guessed in today's times things had changed and I was grateful for it.

"Don't worry, he might still *turn*." She raised an eyebrow.

"You think?"

"Maybe." She smiled sadly and headed toward the machines. "I'll call you when I'm done."

Léon was in his office. Eden, his new club manager, sat

beside him on the couch. They both looked up when we entered.

"Blaire, what brings you here?"

"We're busy with an investigation and we need your opinion on some markings we've found."

"What makes you think I could be of use?"

"They look Egyptian and reminded us of the three jewels."

"Ah," he said as he stood. "Eden, would you mind if we continued in thirty minutes?"

"Sure." Eden nodded, buttoned her jacket as she stood, and both men gawked at her. The slit on one side of her mini skirt stopped near her hip bone and showed her entire leg. She picked up her folder and held it near her body, but all it did was flatten her breasts, improving her cleavage. "Are you joining us tomorrow night for the new lineup?" she asked me.

"I'm not sure. I'll see how I feel. I don't think you guys want a pregnant woman there, anyway."

"Nonsense, all body types frequent our nightclub."

"You mean Léon's nightclub."

"Yes, of course, Léon's club." She placed a hand on Léon's shoulder, adding in her sultry voice. "I'll grab a coffee and see you in thirty."

Once Eden had left, I sat on the couch feeling slightly grumpy. "Sorry for cutting your *important* meeting short," I said sarcastically.

"Nothing we can't finalize afterwards." Léon sat beside me. "What did you want to show me?"

Ralph pulled out his cellphone and showed him the pictures he took of the crime scene while I explained what had happened.

Léon scrolled through the pictures of the frame with the

symbol. He paused at the photograph of the woman. He enlarged the photo and caressed the glass over the woman's face.

"Where was this found?" He stared at the picture.

"At Dr. Craig Avery's lab. Do you know who they are?"

Maroon tears welled in Léon's eyes and an uneasiness settled in my stomach.

"Yes, it's our Penelope."

"Who is Penelope?" I asked, yet the expression he wore I knew it was someone he'd loved. Léon's usual marble stature crumbled before my eyes, and I didn't know what to do. "Are you okay?" I shifted closer to him and touched his elbow. He sat motionless and stared at the woman in the picture. Her soft blond locks, porcelain skin and cerulean-colored eyes.

Léon wiped his eyes dry and cleared his throat. He handed Ralph his phone and stood without answering me. He grabbed his desk phone and spoke to someone in French. When he placed the handle back, only then did he give me his attention. But he didn't respond. He just stared at me. His stone facade was back, and a chill ran through me.

Jean-René burst through the doors and held out his hand. "Give it to me, I need to see it," he commanded, ripping Ralph's phone out of his hand—not giving him a chance to respond. "I can't believe it." He shed an ichor tear. "Where did you get this?"

"There are portraits of her with two other men. One looks vaguely like a relative of Dr. Craig Avery's and another man. They're dressed in similar fashion to her. Who are they?"

Jean-René handed Ralph his phone and sat in a chair near the desk. "We loved her when she was human," he murmured as he stared at Léon. "She was one of the kindest people you would have ever met. She had a heart of gold. But, one day she changed. Someone took her away, they bit her, and it changed her in more ways than the obvious. She went from being kind and precious to sad and despairing. Her new power dampened our relationship so much it forced us to give her up."

As Jean-René spoke, I watched Léon. It was hard for him to listen.

I now remembered who she was, Sebastian had told me about her, but I'd never asked Léon for details. It was personal and his choice to tell me or not. He seemed torn knowing her portrait was hanging in another man's house or reliving those years with her.

"Penelope became mean and calculating. She was not the same woman we'd fallen in love with." Jean-René cleared his throat.

"Do you recognize any of the men?"

Ralph searched for the correct photo and handed his phone to Jean-René again.

Jean-René grunted his displeasure. "We used to be friends with them." He handed the phone to Léon, who clucked angrily.

"If I ever saw those two men again, I'd kill them. Is one of them your missing doctor?"

"I doubt it. Our doctor is fifty-six years old, so he's not a vampire. But, if I look at his picture and the portraits, I'd say close relatives to one of them."

Silence filled the room as the two vampires regained their composure. I'd never seen them this angry-sad before. I could understand why—it was over a woman they'd once loved and lost.

"Hand me the phone again," Léon said, reaching for

Ralph's phone and sat across from me. "I have seen these symbols before and yes, they relate to the jewels you keep safe. I don't understand how they relate to Penelope or your doctor, though. But they relate to Apep and the Underworld. I've told you the story of Apep, the god of darkness, who created men just like him by infecting them with his bite. Apep caused chaos in the Underworld and they sent his nemesis to destroy him, Ra—the god of light who created the earth, the sky and the Underworld. Every time Ra visited the Underworld, he and Apep would fight. Eventually, Ra decided upon the creation of three jewels of immense power, with which he hoped to destroy Apep. By keeping the three jewels together, it harnessed enough power to control the vampires—or kill them. It would strip vampires of their powers and leave them at the mercy of the one holding the jewels."

Léon's words sent cold vibrations into the room and my arms pebbled. He spoke with emotion; his anger lay below the surface as he reflected upon a time when I'd almost destroyed him. It was a time I'd wished never happened, but grateful it did because I'd met him and Sebastian. But it was also a time where my true colors had shown, and I had almost destroyed his empire.

And he spoke of the Underworld; a place where Scout was because her father ruled there. Victor's ancestors, Apep *and* Ra, where their offspring had joined hands, had children and ruled the Underworld together. Victor rarely spoke of his family and what each of his siblings did, but I knew they were powerful. It relieved me I still had the three jewels. If Victor knew they were in my possession, he'd want them back and might use it against Léon. I should destroy them.

Léon's starless eyes penetrated mine. His power rippled

through me and it wasn't lust or a velvety caress I was used to; this power stung like scarab beetles crawling under my skin. Like tiny bites into my muscles.

"Léon!" I yelled and darted out of the seat as quickly as I could. "You're hurting me." I closed the gap between us and cupped his face; smooth, pale skin beneath my fingertips was cold as ice. His eyes darkened and glowed crimson—something I'd never seen before. His power swirled around us and I doubled over, hugging my belly. "Stop, Léon, please," I said through gritted teeth.

"What are you doing?" I heard Ralph's voice in the distance, and movement followed by a hand hitting skin. The air snapped and sucked out of my lungs, and I breathed again.

Léon's arms draped around me as he whispered his apologies. He kissed my neck tenderly and that velvet smooth sensation swarmed me and cradled me like a warm blanket.

"I'm so sorry, I don't know what came over me. I think everything from those times came rushing back, even though I'd forced myself to forget. I would never hurt you. Can you forgive me, Blaire?" he asked with pain etched on his face.

"It's fine," I said with my cheek against his chest. "I'm okay." I felt his heart beat against my ear, and it slowed as he calmed down. His skin cooled beneath my touch and he flinched, causing me to stare up at him.

"I need to feed." He hissed and let go of me. "I can hear your heart race and all I can think about is drinking from you. Not until after our baby is born."

Jean-René made a strange noise from the base of his throat as he glowered at me. I did not think he approved of this pregnancy, nor did I care what he thought.

"Who are the two men?" I asked before Jean-René left.

"They were our friends," Jean-René added as he communicated an unspoken language with Léon. They stared at each other as Jean-René relayed their story. "Léon and I had bumped into them decades before. The three of us had been together for years when we met the two men again. At first, they were only visiting, but they extended their stay multiple times as they grew fond of Penelope. Hugo Wright and Richard Cook had simply fallen for her as hard as Léon and me. And it is they who had turned her into the mean vampire she became. After her change, we never saw them again." He exhaled and the silent conversation they were having ended. "Until now."

Chapter Sixteen

SCOUT

Once the dust had settled, we entered the cold, ancient temple. The inside was just as glorious as the outside; two rows of huge carved statues of pharaohs stood side by side, forming a path for us to walk through. They reminded me of guards warning off intruders. The air was clean with an earthy undertone the farther we traversed inside, and on the walls behind the enormous statues were hieroglyphics.

"Can you decipher any of that?" I pointed at the wall.

"No." He stared fixedly at the walls, then the large structures. "But they don't matter. What we're after is down there." He pointed ahead of us.

As anxious as I was to get this over and done with, the splendor of the temple we were in entranced me. The two pharaohs we past had both arms crossed over their broad chests. Their colossal forms towered over us as their eyes followed us. I had the distinct feeling of being watched, and I didn't think it was the statues. Or perhaps the room only radiated a silent warning to those who wanted to desecrate the temple, and somehow, I sensed it. Or the dead roamed here, which was plausible. We were near Cairo—a place famous for their ancient mummies and curses.

The next two pharaohs had their right hand crossed over their chest, their fists near their hearts. They seemed to stare at one another. It was unsettling; like they were conversing with each other. I shook off the feeling and continued forward.

The next two pharaohs had their hands crossed at their wrists, pointing downward.

And the last set of pharaohs had their arms by their sides, reminding me of soldiers.

If any of these statues moved, I would crap myself. I doubted any power I wielded would assist us in escaping. I glanced at River and hoped he had some sort of power, but I sensed nothing, although he was *something*, I just didn't know what *it* was. Unless he was only a warrior and here to defend me in battle.

The moment my foot crossed the threshold into the next cavernous room, the sensation of being watched faded. I glanced over my shoulder and found the last two pharaohs staring down at us. I quickened my step farther into the next room and stopped dead. I took in the room's emptiness. It was clean and smooth, almost medical, and advanced for its time, except for the blocks on the floor. Each block had a symbol on it.

"Come on," I groaned. "Is this the part where I stand on the wrong block and an arrow comes out of the crack in the wall and kills me?" I glanced at either side, but there were no cracks or crevices. There was nothing. The sandy-cream color walls were smooth.

River chuckled beside me. "How old are you, anyway?"

"I'll be seventeen in a few months." Actually, only next year, but he didn't have to know that.

"You look younger." He wiped his brow with the back of his hand. "And you watch way too much TV." He crossed the floor, walked on the blocks, on a crack, then on two different blocks at once. Nothing happened. "Come on, we don't have all day."

I was so sure there were booby traps. There had to be. A room like this would've been perfect for them. I imagined an adventure with action as I crossed the floor and dodged arrows or a large ball. Instead, I felt embarrassed. I huffed and followed him.

The next room was a long, narrow hallway. I found similar hieroglyphics on these walls as those I'd seen at the entrance. I traced my fingertips over a symbol of an eye, beside it three crystals, then another symbol in the shape of a scarab.

"We're here," River called at the far end.

I hadn't realized I was so far behind and jogged to catch up.

The next room was bright, and it took me a moment for my eyes to adjust. I stared and felt my jaw slacken.

In the center of another vast room stood an obelisk, a much smaller, four-sided, narrow tapering monument which ended with a pyramidion. Balancing perfectly on top was a shiny object.

"Is that it?" I narrowed my eyes at the object in the distance. There were stairs leading down to it, reminding me of a Greek amphitheater. Adorned on each step lay golden treasure scavengers would kill over, coins, jewels, golden frames, swords, goblets, and so much more. No wonder the room was so bright. "Is this a joke?"

Glancing over my shoulder, I found River just as mesmerized at the display before us. I grabbed his elbow and shook him. He blinked, closed his mouth and swallowed.

"My Lord said…" — he coughed into his fist. "Touch nothing other than that," — he pointed at the golden object on the obelisk. He shook his head and whistled, — "I sure could use a pocketful of these, though." He cupped his hands over the side of his head near his eyes like one would a horse, blocking his view of the treasure, and focused on his feet. He mumbled as he descended the steps.

"What would happen if we took something other than the scarab?" I reached for the jeweled necklace when a hand grabbed mine.

"Don't even look at it, Scout." River chided harshly. "Victor will kill my m—me." He tugged on my arm, forcing me to follow him. "We are here to do one thing, and one thing only. Please do not let us fail."

I stared daggers into the back of his neck as he traversed down the stairs. I didn't appreciate being manhandled.

"You didn't have to hurt me," I grumbled behind him.

"We can't afford to get distracted. If we disobey Victor, his punishments are severe. I don't understand why you're here or why you could open that door, but, somehow, you have a role to play in whatever this is." He waved his hands in the air. "Let's get that thing and get out of here."

I didn't think River knew Victor was my dad, nor did I want to tell him. Victor had said nobody could know, so I would keep that information to myself. If he needed to know, Victor could tell him.

I followed River down the stairs, avoided the gold that kept catching my eye, and we reached the bottom without incident.

Before us was the item we wanted. We climbed the two

steps to the obelisk. The scarab balanced carefully on the narrow pyramidion.

"Now what?"

"Take it."

"Me?" I brought my fists to my chest. "What will happen if I take it?" I surveyed the room again, but it was only us and the treasure.

River pulled a knife out of the sheath strapped to his ankle and the gun from behind his back.

My eyes widened. "I... what are those for? Do you even know how to use that?"

A strange sound came from the back of his throat. "Of course. I wouldn't be here otherwise if I didn't."

"Is that what you do?"

"What?"

"Fight?"

He glanced in my direction. His amber-brown eyes hid secrets he did not want to share.

"My mom kills monsters. She's prepared like you," — I pointed at his weapons, — "I thought that maybe you're like her."

"I don't even know who your mom is." He glanced around, as if searching for something.

"Never mind! All I'm saying is you look like you could be a hunter or an assassin, that's all." I faced the golden scarab, wishing I'd brought my knives with, but I was in a hurry to pack and didn't think I needed them. Slowly, I reached for it; my hand hovering just above it. Sweat trickled down my back, causing me to shiver in anticipation.

"Do it already."

"Do you mind?" I brought my hand back to my side. "You're distracting me."

"Yeah, I get that all the time," he smirked.

I scowled at him. "This isn't a nightclub, River. Anything can come from anywhere and attack us."

"What exactly can you do, anyway? And why did Victor ask if you've killed before? You're too young to have killed anyone."

"Long story. Now shush. I need to concentrate."

"Just grab it, it's not that difficult." He sounded irritated, but so was I.

My dad had asked to spend time with me to get to know me, but instead of doing that, I'm running an errand for him that could cost me *my* life. Did he even care about me or was his only reason to *spend time* with me so I could do *this* for him? He didn't even have the audacity to explain everything to me, instead he dumped me in an unknown place with a *boy* I didn't know. Now I understood why Mom swore when she got angry. I felt like screaming swear words at the top of my lungs.

I shook my body, inhaled sharply and flexed my fingers. I just had to get this over and done with. It was right there for me to take.

In one swift motion I grabbed the golden scarab and crouched down, expecting the roof to rain down on us, but nothing happened. I stood, pocketed the jewel in River's backpack, and slung it on my back. We were going to be okay. The room didn't crash down on us. Nothing broke when I removed the item. The ground didn't crumble beneath our feet. My smile reached my eyes when I caught River's glare.

I spoke too soon.

Screeching echoed around us.

I froze.

River turned toward the loudest scream. He widened his stance, muscles flexing, and his jaw twitched.

I glanced around. There were four paths leading down from four exits at opposite ends. At the top of the stairs on each path stood... a man, a mummy, a *something* wrapped in cloth. They neared. I stood closer to River.

"Keep the backpack on you. When you have a chance, run up the same set of stairs we used before. Whatever you do, don't look back. Just get out of here."

"What about you?"

"Don't worry about me. Just as long as you get out of here. Do you understand?"

I nodded and moved behind River. We stepped slowly toward the stairs we'd used earlier. Screaming sounded behind me. I spun around. The creature reached for me; long bony fingers aimed for my face. The creature was so quick I hadn't heard it move down the stairs. River moved away from me as more screaming sounded to my left. The creature advanced. It snapped its teeth, crunching sounded as it pulled a chewed bone from its jaw and discarding it to the ground. If I had to take a guess, we had interrupted its meal and now it was angry—or still hungry, either way we had to get rid of them or become their next meal.

Its eyes had sunken into its socket, its cheeks were gaunt, but behind those pale green eyes I sensed it was still *human*. I didn't think it was the undead, but it reminded me of a ghoul—a desert demon. Whatever it was, it ate flesh, and it was hungry. Unfortunately, it wanted to eat us. The demon neared. I didn't have a weapon. I couldn't protect myself. I swallowed the frightful lump in my throat as I thought about being mauled by these creatures. I imagined it tearing muscle from my bone with blood everywhere. I pictured my body on the ground with the creature digging inside my abdomen for some soft juicy bits.

You've killed before? Echoed in my mind, reminding me of

what I was capable of doing. His voice reminding me I had his blood running through my veins. I was not *just* a human. I had deity ichor coursing through my body, and I could use it to my advantage—or to save my ass.

I screamed and closed the gap with my monster. It stopped, dropped its arms to its sides and glanced around. If I didn't know any better, that was confusion on its face. I lifted my palms and smashed my hands into its chest. It croaked as if its soul had travelled through its windpipe to get out. Its soul flew out of its body. I grabbed the nearest object on the floor near my feet and smashed its head. Nothing happened; its body stayed upright as its soulless head lulled to one side, resting on its shoulder. The golden plate bit into the soft skin between my thumb and index finger, letting me know it was sharp around the edges. I didn't have time to grab anything else and could use the sharpness to my advantage and advanced again. This time I sliced into its exposed neck. With a pop, its head flew off. Blood splashed around me, narrowly missing my new sneakers. Its soul howled in silent torment. I dropped the golden plate, and it clattered to the ground. I wiped my hands down my pants, but some of its dark sticky blood remained.

A squawk caught my attention. At the very top, a murder of crows sat on golden trinkets. Five black birds stared down at me. Their dark gaze penetrating mine. They were more unnerving than the creatures attacking us.

"Scout!" River cried, bringing me back to the fight.

I spun around in time as another desert demon descended upon me.

River was fighting his demon, who was now missing an arm and a leg. River aimed his gun at its chest, pulled the trigger, obliterating its heart. It crumpled to the ground in a heap of meat and bones.

I gaged then focused on the one trying to kill me. The demon neared, and I struck him with my palms. My power vibrated through my hands and into it. Its soul tore halfway out of its body, scowled at what I did, and returned to its vessel. I had only angered it. I moved backward, tripped over the step where the obelisk stood and fell to the ground. The creature advanced. I backed away on my butt and hands. As quickly as I could, I maneuvered away from it. When my hand found a slimy, cold substance, I froze. Glancing quickly over my shoulder, I saw it was the other demon's blood. The plate I'd used was close. The creature jumped onto me, baring its sharp teeth. My left hand grabbed its throat, preventing it from biting me. Its soul shuddered from my clasp around its neck, but it didn't leave its body. I reached over and fell onto my back. The plate was at my fingertips. I heard River fighting the fourth creature. The one above me snapped its teeth, pushing down on me. I couldn't continue holding its weight—it was freakishly heavy. My elbow strained. It neared my face. It gnashed its teeth. Its breath was foul. I touched the plate. With my index and middle finger, I pulled it closer, grabbed it and as hard as I could I brought it down on the demon ending the attack.

I crawled out from under it, my top and pants soaking with its foul-smelling blood. I didn't remember the other one had such an awful stench; it could've been the adrenalin helping me forget.

Glancing down at the mess, I'd lodged the plate into its skull, splitting its head in two. Its sunken eye had burst upon impact, leaking puss. I gagged again, turning away, grabbed hold of the backpack to ground me. Knowing I still had the golden scarab was comforting, we didn't endure this in vain.

The ghostly figure of the ferryman rowed past in his

phantom boat, scooped up the souls and continued on his merry way. His eyes glaring at me from the back of his head. I shuddered and glanced away.

River sat on the step to catch his breath. One side of his mouth twitched upward. "That was intense. Are you ready to get out of here?"

Gasping for air, I sat beside him and breathed, "Absolutely."

Chapter Seventeen

We left Léon and Jean-René in the office so they could discuss what we'd found with the Vampire Council. They thought it best to advise them of the portraits and symbols, in case of further developments.

As we rounded a corner, Heath and Sawyer approached. We greeted them, and I wondered what they were up to. Heath stayed at the Labyrinth while his band, Envision, took a break. I guessed vampires needed a break from each other as well and being in the same two vampires' company for months could become a bit much.

I still couldn't get over the fact that Heath's nose hadn't straightened after he had turned, but vampirism affected each new fledgling differently. I glanced over my shoulder and they stepped inside Léon's office.

"It's getting late. Are you staying here, or do you need a lift back to your place?" Ralph opened the exit door.

"Mine please, but before we go there, I need food."

We stopped and ordered a deep-dish pizza—*mine*.

Ralph had a date with a mystery woman he didn't want

me to know about. He'd actually blushed when I asked too many questions.

"I will tell you about her only if we go on another date. Until then, my lips are sealed." Ralph wasn't one to keep the same woman longer than a month. He'd said he preferred to end things while they were still perfect. Usually after the second month things got serious, and he wasn't ready for that. I said a silent prayer for Ralph and hoped he found love. It wasn't easy being alone for so long—and he wasn't getting any younger—he needed to find someone he wanted to keep around longer than just a month.

"Ah, you're no fun." I opened my front door and flicked on the light switch. "Do you want coffee or are you heading out now already?"

"No thanks, I have about forty minutes to get to the venue. You sure you going to be fine alone?"

"I'll be fine thanks. Enjoy your date."

I only finished two slices of my greasy pizza; they were heart stoppers, and I couldn't eat any more. I browsed the tv channels and watched a thriller series about a woman sleuth named Dana.

I laid on the couch and stared at the TV, but all I thought of was Scout and hoped she was okay. If anything was wrong, she would've made a plan to contact me. Or she would've made Vic contact me. Besides, she'd only be gone for a few days. That could turn into a month or two. I could live with that.

I rubbed my stomach and the little guy kicked; reminding me he was still here with me and wasn't going anywhere soon. I kept thinking about the type of person he would become. If he was a plain human, there were various avenues we could try, but we would educate him on the various supernatural's. I didn't want him to fear us, but he had to know everything about us, and we'd protect him. It would be difficult, but I could do it. I had to. The little guy was my flesh and blood, and Sebastian's, and Léon's, even though we didn't know who the sperm donor was. As I kept saying, it didn't matter—they came from the same cloth and our son would be *theirs*.

The faint chime of a lullaby brought me out of my slumber. I was still on the couch and wiped drool from my mouth. My cellphone was still ringing. It was Ralph.

"Hey, what's wrong?"

"There's been another abduction, this time there're witnesses."

Ralph fetched me soon after he called. Officer Blackwood had interrupted his date, requesting our immediate help.

We arrived to chaos. Police cars surrounded a building in town with hordes of people standing around.

Ralph parked beside a cruiser, and we approached the crowd. A police officer near yellow tape recognized us and allowed us through. Officer Blackwood stood to one side interviewing a witness. In the center of the yellow tape was a large pool of blood.

We walked around the large puddle toward Officer Blackwood and waited patiently for him. While he was busy, I scanned the crowd. A woman with a layer of sweat on her face and eyes as big as saucers chewed relentlessly on what I assumed was gum or the inside of her cheek. The gentleman beside her had paled and stared at the maroon liquid splashed on the sidewalk, rubbing his nose. A few pale onlookers with an air of authority stared down at us hungrily. It looked like they wanted to lick the maroon liquid. It was a crowd of humans and vampires, but none looked suspicious; sometimes the assailant liked to return to the scene of their crime to watch, but doubted our attacker was here.

The building behind us was a club. It must've been new, as I'd never heard of it before tonight. Since being pregnant, I hadn't felt the need to go out clubbing, and I'd heard a few new ones had opened.

"Thanks for coming."

I flinched at Officer Blackwood's words.

"Sure, what's going on?" Ralph shook his hand.

"Witness statements describe a red cloud swooping down and picking up the victim. Within seconds blood sprayed over there," — he pointed at the mark, — "and whatever it was took the victim with it. Every person we've spoken to said the same thing. It's a red cloud of something taking, and we're assuming, is killing people."

"How many crimes are similar?"

"It's my first one like this. When I arrived, I knew I had to involve you guys. We don't know what monster did this and we need your help."

I'd never heard of a monster doing this. Ever. It reminded me of Shannon, who enjoyed dabbling in human and monster DNA. He enjoyed creating his own brand of monsters, and I wondered if this creature was something Shannon had produced.

"Are you sure it's a cloud?"

"Some say fine mist, others say it looked like a red cloud. I don't know." He pointed to a camera. "We are waiting for the footage." As he spoke, another officer ran toward us with a tablet in his hands.

"See this, it's crazy." The officer held up the device for the three of us and pressed play.

People traversed the sidewalk at leisurely paces. Others came out of the nightclub. People huddled in a corner, laughing. Then a fine mist obstructed the view. All I saw was red liquid moving like mercury, without the thickness. The mist moved like a flock of birds as it darted over the heads of those below it. It curved around a couple as if it was searching for someone. It moved up and circled back. A tall man with a brown leather jacket exited the club. The mist darted for him. It surrounded the man like a dark cloud lifting him up. Blood sprayed the mist and man ascended into the night sky. The camera didn't rotate, so we could only assume the mist had travelled upward.

"I've never seen anything like this," I said while covering my mouth. It was terrible.

"Who can we ask about this?"

"Send me a copy, we can ask around."

Chapter Eighteen

SCOUT

We waited for Victor at the top of the steps outside the ancient temple. The sun blazed, the hot air made it difficult to breathe, but we'd found shade near the double doors. We decided against staying inside the temple in case more of those things descended upon us.

The wind had picked up, changing the landscape once more. I sighed as I leaned against the hard rock, wondering if Mom was okay back home. Squawking sounded, bringing me out of my thoughts. I glanced up to find five crows perched on the large pharaohs carved into the mountain. Their black beady eyes focused only on me; no matter where I moved. Their staring left me unsettled. Crows had never behaved this way around me before. I'd seen them devour a dead animal left on the side of the road but never had one, let alone five, following me.

"I think they like you." River leaned against the limestone wall and retrieved another bag that had mysteriously appeared out of nowhere.

I furrowed my brows. "Where do all these bags come

from? And what is with those crows?" I mumbled, leaned against my side of the wall until I couldn't see them anymore and folded my arms. I felt as grumpy as I sounded.

"You need food." He threw a smaller bag my way, it hit my hand and fell into my lap.

"Thanks," I muttered as I tore open the bag.

"Do you have your spirit animal yet?"

"Huh?" I ripped open a packet of chips with my teeth. Some landed on the ground and I shoved a handful into my mouth. Salt and vinegar. It was divine. I hummed in satisfaction.

"Your spirit animal?" He leaned forward, considering me.

"I don't know. Victor mentioned it briefly but no, I don't think I have one."

He thumbed up. "These guys could be your spirit animal."

I harrumphed. "They're scavengers, and gross." I shook my head. "No way. I'd much prefer a dog or a wildcat." I thought of Sebastian and regretted it; I wouldn't want a large kitty to be my spirit animal. Watching Sebastian with Mom was gross enough as it was. Never mind the vampire. If I ever dated anyone, they would be plain human—I didn't want anyone who could do *anything* special. I would never share my blood or do anything *physical*. Yuck. Girls my age were already dating older boys, but I was so not ready for any of *that*. Perhaps I would wait until marriage. No, before I did any of that stuff, I wanted to travel the world. I glanced around and my mouth curved upward—at least I was traveling.

River spoke, bringing me back to our conversation.

"Well, you never know. When a dog followed me home

one day and didn't leave my side. I realized she was my spirit animal."

I spied the crows again, but they knew I was watching them. The dark orbs for eyes hadn't shifted their gaze away from me. I sat back, pressing my spine against the cold building. If they were my spirit animal, what would that mean for me?

"What kind of dog?" I would much prefer asking him about his animal than about crows.

River whistled. The melody was soothing; a tune I'd associate with a grandmother showing affection for her grandchild—endearing and beautiful. The air swirled around us and produced a dog. I frowned and shook my head. I had a long way before I became accustomed to the trickery and magic of the Underworld.

"This is Luna." He scratched behind her ears. She sat down so her hind leg could scratch near her ear. "She's my protector and friend."

Luna stared up at River with big brown eyes and so much love.

I giggled. "She's so cute. What kind of dog is she? I've never seen one like her before?"

Luna was black and hairless, except for her mohawk. She turned in my direction as she sniffed the air and snarled at me.

"Easy, Luna, she's a friend." River rubbed her body to sooth her, then continued to scratch behind her ear. Luna stopped growling, licked her lips and her tongue fell out her mouth as she enjoyed his attention. "She's a Mexican hairless dog, and one of the oldest breeds. I'd just met Victor when she found me."

"Oh, how long have you known Victor?"

"Uh," he hesitated, as if thinking whether he should

disclose anything. When Luna fell into his lap, he rubbed her stomach and chest while he ate a sandwich with his free hand. "Let's just say I met him when I was at my lowest."

He didn't offer more information, and I couldn't leave it I had to know more. "Why were you at your lowest? Did something happen?"

A strange grunting sound came from him, and he swallowed. "My mom was ill."

"Is she okay now?"

He nodded.

"What does your mom getting ill have to do with Victor?"

"Do you always ask this many questions?"

I grinned and shoved the last handful of chips into my mouth and tore open the sandwich bag. "This is good," I said with my mouth full. "Thank you."

"I can't tell you. It's between Victor and me."

"Oh!" His answer was even more cryptic, which only prompted me to ask more questions. "Did Victor help her recover?" My dad was Lord of the Underworld. It was his birthright and apparently mine; one day I might rule. He controlled the dead. He was the Soul Keeper. And River's mom was ill. "Was she dying? And Victor didn't take her soul."

"That's enough!" River flew up. Luna growled at his sudden movements; I think she'd fallen asleep in his lap. He descended the stairs, then ran back up. "I can't tell you," River yelled. "Please stop asking questions." His voice croaked as he stared down at me with watery eyes.

"I'm sorry, didn't mean to upset you," I whispered. I didn't want to anger him any further and ate the rest of my sandwich in silence. From his behavior, it was apparent my dad had done something. River's mom was ill, but still alive.

Which meant Victor didn't take her soul. I glanced at River; his face was still a bit blotchy from his outburst. He'd stopped eating, but Luna was consoling him with her wet kisses. I smiled at the affection she afforded him.

Once my bag of snacks was empty, I downed the rest of my water. We'd been waiting about an hour when I realized I didn't know how we were going to get back. I wanted to ask River, but he was still brooding in his corner. I asked anyway. "River?"

He glanced up; his amber-colored eyes filled with kindness again.

"How are we getting back? I don't know how to call Victor to fetch us."

He smiled sadly. "I've already called him. He should be here soon."

"Thanks."

"Sorry for yelling at you. It's not directed at you, but more the situation—"

"It's okay, you don't have to say anything else," I smiled, hoping he would understand I meant it. "How did you *call* Victor? I didn't hear you."

He pointed to his head, opened his mouth to respond when sand blasted our faces. I lifted my hands to shield my eyes. Dark storm clouds circled above us, and my ears popped. Speak of the devil, and he'd arrive. I chuckled. I didn't even know if he was the devil. There were so many questions I needed answers to and hoped Victor would help me understand before I went back home.

"Children…" Victor's voice boomed above us like God was speaking.

River and I stood at the same time while Luna barked. Sand whipped my face, my long hair twirling around my neck.

"Do you mind?" I yelled, but doubted Victor heard anything other than the angry wind he conjured.

As quickly as the wind had started, it stopped, and Victor stood before me. "Hand it over," he said with an outstretched hand. His black nails long like claws.

I removed the backpack, unzipped it, but before I retrieved the item River placed a hand on mine, stopping me. "What the—"

Cackling interrupted me. The vision of Victor flickered as if he were a hologram. River pushed me behind him. Confused what was going on, I did as he suggested and stayed behind him.

"You must be his little lapdog," the hologram said. "And that makes you his daughter."

"His daughter?" River glanced over his shoulder with a questioning look.

I smiled sheepishly.

River didn't respond.

The hologram flickered again, and a man appeared with a similarly shaped nose as Victor, and as me. The same raven hair framing pale features. But instead of Victor's glacial-blue eyes, they were emerald green. Even his voice sounded like Victor's.

"Brother!" I flinched at the deep rumbling voice echoing from the other side. Victor appeared above one of the pharaoh statues, imposing and spine-chilling. "You don't fight fair. She has the item you seek. Now let this game end."

"Oh brother, you know how I love a little competition."

Victor grunted. "This is not a competition you seek, but the end of me."

"Hand it over," the other man demanded. The three-dimensional picture glimmered when an actual hand emerged from it; reminding me of a portal I'd read about at school.

"Give it to him, Scout," Victor ordered.

I glanced up at him. He nodded, answering my silent question. I retrieved the scarab and slowly gave it to the outstretched hand.

"Thank you, my dear." The man pulled back his hand. "Remember little brother, you must collect two more by the end of the week," he added before the hologram winked out like a bubble popping in our faces. It caused River to step backward and into me.

"Are you hurt?" Victor asked beside us. "Apologies for my tardiness. At least I got here in time."

"What is going on?" I screamed and slammed my fists into his chest. Before I could hit him again, he grabbed my wrists.

"Calm down and I will tell you. But first, let's get out of here." Victor grabbed River's forearm and the dark nothingness surrounded us again as he teleported us back to the strange living room in the Underworld.

Chapter Nineteen

When I called Léon to ask him questions about what we'd seen in the video, Eden had answered and said to meet them at the new club. After two years he had a string of nightclubs and this was his newest addition; a snack bar for vampires.

Ralph and I entered the dark hallway; reminding me of the caves we'd explored when we were searching for Sebastian. I didn't understand why Léon had this built. When I'd first asked, he said vampires wanted something darker, and this was what he'd come up with. I wondered if Sebastian had approved or if Léon even cared it might affect his brother.

The narrow hallway opened into a cavernous hall with torches on the sides. The dim light easy on the eyes and the soft music soothing. Sections cordoned off where vampires could *eat* in private or on display for others to view. The only humans allowed inside were those who'd passed the screening two days prior to entrance and escorted inside with a vampire. Léon had mentioned the tight security was to ensure peace and calm. And if the vampires weren't on the guest list, no entrance either.

This club was the most exclusive club in Sterling Meadow with a hefty monthly membership fee. The person managing the club for Léon was Eden. She glanced over her shoulder as we entered, and one side of her mouth curved upward. There was a twinkle in her eye not meant for me. I glanced up at Ralph, who stared longingly back at her and smiled. I elbowed his side.

"Oof. Ow."

"Was she your mystery date?" I wiggled my eyebrows.

He flinched at my words and pulled on his jacket. "What? No." He cleared his throat, but a smile lingered on his face. He couldn't tear his eyes away from her.

"Blaire," Eden said my name, but she stared at Ralph through thick flirtatious eyelashes, and it flabbergasted me.

I elbowed him harder.

"So you're the mystery woman Ralph doesn't want to tell me about?"

"Blaire," Ralph moaned.

Eden blushed and nodded.

"Now that I've solved one mystery. We have another one. Where's Léon?"

"He's in the back." Eden thumbed behind her.

Ever since I'd known Ralph, he had always only dated human women. He liked them delicate and needy. Eden was the complete opposite. She had moved to our little town from England when she managed Envision—Heath's alternative music group. While Envision were on a break she'd asked Léon whether he had any positions available for her and he offered her this gig. At first, I was jealous; she had flowing chestnut hair, big brown eyes and a killer body. But she knew her boundaries and never stepped over it. I'd first assumed she enjoyed the company of other women, but the seductive stare she and Ralph shared told me otherwise.

I was happy for them.

I left Ralph to continue his date with Eden while I spoke with Léon. I found him in his office. This was the only office I hated. He had dark leather couches, stone walls, and his grotesque desk; it looked like a giant's ribcage. He had it made especially for this club. The room was gloomy and sinister.

"Hey honey," I said and sat on the soft couch.

"Shouldn't you be in bed?" He peered over the papers he was reading.

"Yeah." I stifled a yawn.

"Everything okay? Eden said you were looking for me, again. I don't mind seeing you, it's just a little strange I've seen you twice in one evening."

"Yeah, we have a problem." I sat up and pulled out my cellphone. I found the video footage of the blood mist and held it up for him. He came around his desk and sat beside me to watch.

After he watched it, he watched it a second time. He was eerily quiet when he handed back my phone.

"Well?"

"I don't like this case you're on, Blaire." He turned to face me. "I've only seen this once before..." he stood and went to his safe and opened it. "I move this around as often as I can because I don't want anyone knowing where it's kept." He handed me a leather-bound journal.

"What's this?"

"I documented my travels over the years. Near the middle you will find a story of a vampire who tormented town after town. A mist of blood swooping down to collect its victims, never seen again." He sat beside me again and helped me find the right spot. The aged pages smelled of ancient ink. The writing was his and beautifully written.

Léon opened the journal at a section where he had seen the mist himself, and together with Alex they had vanquished the blood mist vampire. Alex was on the Vampire Council and could manipulate the elements, earth, fire, water and air. He had brought down judgement on Roland and had pulverized the naughty vampire. I could only imagine what he'd done to *this* vampire.

"We believed the one who had made our kind had created the mist vampire; his potent powers destroyed everything in its wake. Alex and I had chased the rogue vampire until we came upon a deserted town, where he hid within. We called other master vampires to assist. We killed him, and his body cross bound in a sarcophagus."

Léon's words sent an ominous shiver throughout my body. They had killed that rogue vampire, yet we were seeing someone with similar abilities.

"Where is this town?" I took his diary out of his hands and paged through it. But there were no names. Only a description of the mist and the destruction it had caused.

"I did not write it down for fear someone would want to retrieve what remained of his body." He took the diary out of my hands and returned it to his safe.

"Why didn't you destroy his body?"

"It's precious. It would be the equivalent of destroying all human artifacts. History lost and forgotten with no-one to shed light. Only Alex and I have something similar, along with those sitting on the Council. I will need to inform them of this, or at least Alex."

"Where's the town, Léon?"

He remained quiet for a very long time, hopefully considering my request. Then he snapped out of his statue like trance. "I'll only take you. No-one at Ulysses may know about this place, and that includes Ralph. We can leave tomorrow at sundown."

I sighed. "Okay." I scooted to the edge of the couch and pushed myself up in one heave. "Must I pack a bag or is it a night trip?"

He held out his hand for mine, "It's a night trip. You will be back before bedtime."

Chapter Twenty

Ralph and Eden huddled in a dark corner near the bar, whispering sweet nothings to each other. I made sure they heard my shoes against the floor as I stomped closer. Ralph distanced himself from her and neatened his shirt. Eden pulled down her top.

"Are you ready?" I asked with a knowing smile.

Ralph cleared his throat and coughed into his hand. "Yes, where to next?"

"Home, I need to sleep."

"What did Léon say?"

"There are things we need to confirm first before I can comment." I wanted to see the town first before I told anyone about it. It could just be a coincidence that there was another mist changing vampire, although I didn't believe in them. If it was the right town, someone had known about it and had found something belonging to the dead vampire, or it was just another vampire with the same abilities, which I highly doubted if the first vampire created the original mist vampire.

"Like what?"

"I will tell you when Léon and I get back."

"Oh," he said, sounding hurt. "Just the two of you are going?"

"I can ask him if you can join us?"

Before I could open my link to Léon, he whispered, *'Oh, alright, he can come,'* into my mind.

The closer we became, the stronger our bond. It was almost as powerful as the bond I'd shared with Sebastian when bound to him.

'Thank you,' I whispered back to him.

"Léon says it's okay, you can join us."

"I can't get used to the fact you have these telepathic abilities. It's great, don't get me wrong, it's just freaky."

Ralph parked outside my house when his phone rang. "Don't go," he yelled. "It's Officer Blackwood."

"I'm tired," I moaned as I leaned back into the seat.

Ralph nodded as he listened to Officer Blackwood on the other end. "Buckle up, cupcake." He pulled away from the curb with my door open. "They found the victim."

I moaned as I closed my door and buckled my seatbelt.

I enjoyed a power nap while Ralph drove to the scene of the crime. When the car went over a bumpy road, I awoke. Red and blue lights flashed before us.

"Where are we?" I wiped sleep out of my eyes and yawned. The clock on the dash read it was almost two in the morning.

"We're in the middle of nowhere. There's nothing here but sand and rocks. I doubt the shifters come this way either." Ralph parked and climbed out.

We traversed the path toward the six police officers surrounding a lump of something on the sand. There were six bright lamps on stands highlighting the crime scene with the standard yellow tape. As we approached the mess, I noticed an arm sticking out, bent at the elbow. A leg was beside the heap, still attached to the hip. The abdomen was beside the one leg with the scalp draped over the other arm, layers of skin and ribs covered it all.

"Jesus." Ralph stepped backward. "What the fuck?"

"I know," Officer Blackwood said behind us. "I've asked Detective Carson to cut her vacation short and join us. She needs to be here," — he pointed at the lumps and bumps of limbs, — "hopefully soon."

Someone gagged, followed by quickened footsteps and then that glorious sound of retching. Luckily, I'd seen my fair share of gore and this was no different.

"We may have a lead," I said. "We are checking it out tomorrow night, or rather later tonight. Once we have confirmed if it's connected to this, we will share our findings."

"Okay, that's great news," Officer Blackwood sighed with relief. "This is a cluster fuck of momentous proportions. After some digging, I couldn't find anything similar to what we saw on the video. I called everyone I knew, and nobody had heard of anything like this. I really hope your lead pans out."

"Yep, so do I." I crouched as low as I could to get a better view. "Whoever did this drained our victim. There's no blood anywhere apart from what's on the body parts. They flayed and ripped him into chunks. Do we know if the victim still has his organs?" I said, covering my nose and mouth with both hands but it didn't deter the stench of raw meat.

Officer Blackwood paled under the soft lights of the lamps and cruisers. "His organs are intact, except his heart."

"Okay, our bad guy needs hearts," I said more to myself than anyone else. "Have there been any other abductions?"

"No—" Officer Blackwood's radio crackled, cutting his words off. He excused himself to answer.

We waited in silence

When Officer Blackwood returned, he said, "We have another victim. A woman." He turned to another officer, asking him to get to the fresh crime scene to establish a perimeter and contain the evidence until he arrived.

By the time we arrived at the newest crime scene, it was almost three in the morning. The mist had grabbed a woman as she exited the twenty-four-hour diner. She was a server coming off her shift when it happened; she didn't have time to call for help.

The footage of her legs kicking as it lifted her into the air was disturbing. I couldn't see the rest of her body, just her legs dangling in the air as it snatched her up.

Officer Blackwood was still at the other crime scene, helping to collect evidence.

We met Detective Carson at this crime site, and she looked great; she seemed relaxed and fresh off the vacation train, but that would change shortly.

She shook her head as one of her subordinates informed her of the details about what had happened the last twenty-four hours.

"We need more detectives in my department," she said.

"At least I stayed away for five days this time. Previously, it only took two days before they called me back."

"Ralph and I don't mind taking over for you. Then you and the family can continue with whatever you were doing."

"It's fine, thanks Blaire. I think a week at home is too long, anyway." She winked. "Okay," — she glanced at my stomach, — "you probably want to get home and sleep?"

"No, I'm fine now."

"There isn't much you can do. My guys are collecting evidence from the body for processing and until you've confirmed your lead, there's nothing you can do. We'll finish up and log what we need to. I'll call with any developments from the lab."

"Sounds good."

Chapter Twenty-One

Léon had arranged for our transport to the town where he and Alex had killed the mist vampire. The vehicle he had arranged was huge and reminded me of a military vehicle —it was larger than a hummer, yet smaller than a tank. I thought Léon was a lunatic when I saw the monster of a vehicle parked outside the Labyrinth. They upgraded the military vehicle with luxury furnishings and bullet proof armor.

The ride was smooth, and I barely felt the bumps. "You still haven't answered me why we need this kind of vehicle?"

"You will see when we get there," Léon said as he continued working on his laptop. He took care of business during the ride that couldn't wait until he returned home. To witness Léon working on his laptop like any regular *guy* was strange yet comforting. He was the Master Vampire of Sterling Meadow and instead of being a badass mob boss, as one assumed he'd be, he's a business*man* making a fortune. Léon owned many companies, from shipping, to entertainment, and accommodation. If I made an educated guess, I'd say he owned most properties in Sterling Meadow, which meant this was *his* town.

But looks were deceiving. He was still a deadly vampire who wouldn't think twice before killing you.

I settled into the back seat and closed my eyes.

I awoke—three hours later—when the vehicle stopped. The atmosphere inside the cabin was eerily quiet. Léon stuck his head through the small window and whispered to Sawyer and Marc, who sat up front.

Ralph gawked at something outside his window. While on my side, I only saw the face of a rocky mountain.

"What's going on?" I mumbled, still confused to our surroundings. I wiped my eyes again.

Ralph pointed at something. I scooted over to his side. My jaw slackened and my throat went dry. A blessing of black unicorns stood to one side, close to our vehicle, and stared. They were all black with different colored horns to match their mane; some were red, gold, blue, or purple. Some had long fluffy coats, while others had short, sleek coats. But all their eyes glowed red and at us.

I wanted to say something when our vehicle rocked. Another unicorn galloped into us and the vehicle moved backward and to the side. Another strode casually to us, stared at Ralph, opened its mouth and breathed fire. The flames licked the window, yet I didn't feel the heat nor did the glass break. Another unicorn hit us on the side and our vehicle moved in the opposite direction. I couldn't see any dents in the vehicle, and no windows had cracked.

"Now I know why we have this vehicle," I whispered to Léon, knowing he'd hear me even though we weren't sitting next to each other.

Léon crawled to me, bringing me into the curve of his body. He smelled like the ocean and the French soap he used, with a hint of him. I breathed deeply and nestled into him.

"They protect the town, and we need to ask their permission before entering. They are hostile creatures and don't like company. I thought it best to be prepared."

Léon let go, waved Ralph away and took his place near the window and opened it. He pulled an old piece of paper out of his breast pocket and waved it out the window.

A unicorn approached with a purple mane and horn. The closer he got, I saw him clearer; his horn seemed to move like purple mercury. His eyes glowed red as he took the piece of paper between his sharp teeth and ran back to the others.

A couple of minutes passed when a unicorn neared with a flaming red horn and mane, and his eyes bled back to black. He cleared his throat, coughed. "Welcome, Léon. It has been a long time."

Léon chuckled lightheartedly, and swirls of his power danced across my skin, causing all the hairs to stand on end. He opened the car door; I grabbed his arm and shook my head.

"It's okay, I know this one," he said as he climbed out.

Léon greeted the unicorn by rubbing his head while asking for permission to enter. "How have you been keeping, Allan?"

Allan? I frowned. Allan was a boring name for such an elegant creature. A deadly creature, but they were still mystical. I'd always wondered where they were, and now I knew. I glanced at the sign outside my window—Nowhereville—how appropriate. If anyone asked me where I went, I'd say to Nowhereville with a straight face because it's true. I'd never heard of this place. I surmised Sawyer and Marc had used a magical portal or something similar to get us here, as I doubted anyone could follow a map and drive here.

"We had an intruder last week," Allan said through his enormous mouth and a flame licked his bottom lip.

I was afraid the fire would enter the vehicle, so I closed the window slightly because I still wanted to hear what they were discussing.

"Did you see who it was?"

"It was two men. They breached the perimeter during the shift change. It only took two minutes, but they knew the routine. We realized someone was here when we found their footprints, followed them to the other side of the land, then came across tire tracks. We couldn't trace further than the outer boundary. You know what happens when we try to leave."

"I do." Léon continued to rub Allan's body, and I wondered if his fur was soft and if what Léon did was comforting. "A man has disappeared with murders committed by the mist…" Léon left the last word hanging, and plumes of smoke erupted out of Allan's nose.

"They are stupid. They have no idea what they have unleashed," Allan said as flames continued licking the sides of his mouth. Léon had to stop rubbing him and stepped backward. "Sorry friend, but it's upsetting they've done this. You need to destroy this abomination."

"I will, that's why we need your permission to enter. We wish to destroy what's left, ensure nobody can come here again."

"Yes, of course." Allan turned to his blessing and a faint whistle sounded, followed by all the unicorns rising on their hind legs and kicking their front legs out. "You are welcome to enter." Allan leaned his large head against Léon's then retreated to follow the rest.

Léon climbed back in the vehicle and instructed Sawyer to drive forward slowly.

"They ruined the land." Léon leaned against the back seat and stared out at the night sky. "There's an angry volcano beneath this land with smoke emitting out of the crevices." He pointed at the mountain on my side. "That's where it starts and it surrounds this land, protecting what it holds."

"What does it hold?" Ralph asked as he leaned forward to listen to Léon.

"Hopefully, the mystery around the mist that enjoys killing," he said and closed his eyes.

Ralph glanced at me and shrugged, and I shrugged back. I had no idea what he meant. But this place might hold the clues to what's happening in Sterling Meadow.

Chapter Twenty-Two

SCOUT

Victor had grabbed my wrist and then River's forearm, and we landed with a thump; I fell onto the couch and the food I'd eaten threatened to repeat itself, lurching over the arm of the couch in case, but it was unnecessary. Swallowing hard, leaving a sour taste in my mouth.

"The more you do it, the easier it becomes," Victor said, his voice a monotone of sarcasm.

Tears streaked my cheeks. I wanted to go home. I wanted my mom. Even though I was a mature sixteen-year-old, I was still only sixteen. This was too much for me. I wasn't a treasure hunter who travelled the world, and I wasn't ready to fight creatures on my own. I might have told Mom I was ready, but she knew I wasn't. Not yet, anyway. She protected me from so much, and I had Ralph guiding me when I joined them on their cases.

Here, I had no mentor, no mother, and no guidance. This man, my *father*, didn't bother to teach me anything. He didn't care about what I wanted or how I felt. He only needed me to do something for him... for selfish reasons. For a game, he played with his brother.

River sat beside me and squeezed my knee. It was a friendly gesture, trying to reassure me. I wiped my tears with a tissue from the box on the table.

Victor's shoulders dropped. His concrete expression softened for only a second as he stared at me. "What's wrong with you?" he demanded.

"Take me home!" I yelled. "I want to go back to Mom."

"Not yet, there's still two more artifacts you must retrieve."

"No!" I folded my arms across my chest. "You aren't interested in knowing me. Instead, you only want me to get stupid stuff. All because you and your brother are having a competition. Do you always play with mortals? No wonder Mom didn't want to stay with you."

"That's enough! How dare you speak to me that way." Victor's dark form towered over me. The lights flickered, casting demonic shadows on his sharp features. His black armor rippled over his body and shone like a dark and dangerous metal yet to experience. His hands extended and claws emerged. Two horns grew out the sides of his forehead and his ears at the top grew into points. He hissed, revealing sharp fangs. He looked like his father in the portrait.

I hugged my knees. The tears flowed quicker than before. I hid my face between my legs, waiting for his wrath. I was sure he was going to smite me into one of his levels.

"That's enough, Victor!" River said with an air of authority. I was grateful he stuck up for me, but I didn't know what Victor would do since River didn't say, *'my Lord'* like he always did. "Why didn't you tell me she was your daughter? I could've protected her better. Explained a little more."

"I don't have to share anything with you. Best to remember you're under my hand, not the other way around." Victor threatened River with unspoken words—making me flinch at his tone.

I glanced up at River. He clenched his jaw as he readied to fight. My eyes flitted to Victor who was scary as hell and I knew he would win this fight; River didn't have a chance at survival. I grabbed River's forearm and shook my head when he turned to me.

"Don't," I said to River, then turned to stare Victor dead on with the expression Mom said she hated. "*Dad...* please stop." I wiped away the last of the tears, crossed my legs underneath me and sat straighter. I needed to exude confidence, helping me feel better. Now I needed Victor to understand that if he wanted me to help, he couldn't go around hurting people. "Nobody has to get hurt today. Please. All I wanted to know was what's going on, and for you to act like a father."

Victor's hard expression softened as his features returned to his human form. He pursed his lips then finally said. "You're right." He pointed at me. "Do not mistake my kindness for weakness," he said to River with a finger pointed at his chest. "Utter to anyone that she's my daughter and I will end you."

"After everything I do for you and you still don't trust me," River said and his jaw ticked. He sounded hurt, but I doubted Victor cared much.

"I'm at war with my brother. He is much older and painfully competitive, and he despises me for what I've done..."

"What did you do?"

"That, I do not have to share." He crossed the floor and stood near the fireplace, leaned his elbow on the mantlepiece as he spoke into the flames. "Anyway, he has hidden three items belonging to me and if I don't get them back within the allotted time frame, they will strip me of my powers."

"How is that possible?"

"Our father has joined in on the competition. He has allowed my brother to do this." He stared up at the portrait of his father with hatred.

"But why involve me?"

"This is their game, Scout. And they play it however they choose to." His gaze met mine. His eyes glistened and his gentle expression hardened. He cleared his throat and went back to staring into the fire. "They have sought to punish me and are using you as the key. It was a trick, you understand. They didn't think you would want to help me." His cerulean-colored eyes flitted to mine once more. "If you do not wish to continue, I will not hold it against you. But understand, I will lose everything."

As much as I hated this game, I couldn't allow them to do this to my father. He was a shitty father so far and hadn't been around for most of my life. It didn't mean I had to behave like him. I wasn't like him. I only held similar powers, and that's where it ended. I could help him and when I retrieved the last two items, and I needed a favor— he would have to help me.

"It's fine, I will do it. But... only if you allow two things?"

He perked up at my response and the corners of his mouth twitched. "What?"

"Prepare us. If you can't enter the place, you must tell

us everything before disappearing. I don't want to set foot in another temple and have our heads chewed off."

"It's a simple request, consider it done. What's the other?"

"If I ever need you for something and I ask you for a favor. You will do it, no questions asked."

He narrowed his eyes at me. He glanced from me to River, then back again. "It's only fair."

"One last thing."

"You said two things."

"Do you need my help or not?"

He grunted in frustration. "Depends, what is it?"

"I don't know what hold you have on River, but when we're done, you fix it."

"Did you utter a word?"

"No, my Lord." River turned wide eyes in my direction. The vein in his forehead throbbed, and he clenched his jaw. "I didn't tell her anything."

"Then why has she asked this?"

"She," — they were speaking about me as if I wasn't here, — "sensed a reason River had to work for you." It was strange speaking about myself in the third person. "Anyway, say you will pardon him, or whatever it is you need to do to free him from your service." And River stopped addressing Victor as *'my Lord'*. I wanted to roll my eyes. We were in modern times and calling him Victor should suffice, shouldn't it? But I didn't say any of that, instead I averted my eyes as Victor's eyes glowed crimson, and I felt heat beat against my skin. He, like River, was unhappy with my interference. They'd have to get used to it because that's the person I was.

"I cannot." Victor neared. "It's already written in

blood." His eyes flitted between River and me. "But I'll see if anything can be done."

"Thank you." I stood. "That is all I ask. If River is going to put his life in danger to help me," — I pointed at Victor, — "and you, then he needs our help too."

"Fine." Victor's shoulders dropped slightly, and he exhaled. "If you wish to freshen up, do so quickly. We need go to the next destination."

"Already? My feet ache." I fell back onto the couch.

"Time is of the essence, Scout. The sooner we get all the items, the sooner you can see your mom. I sense the little one may arrive much earlier than we expected."

Chapter Twenty-Three

Sawyer drove the monster military vehicle slowly through a ghost town long forgotten. The wooden structures had weathered and torn, with nothing living around it; no trees, plants, or even insects I could see. It was dark, but nothing moved between the eerie buildings.

The winding road descended a cliff, then reached a dead end. The dark air moved, and the wings of large crows flapped near my window. A sense of dread filled me as I stared at the five crows. They hovered beside my window, flapping their wings and staring at me as if they were trying to communicate. Their dark orbs for eyes glowed metallic, then bled back to black. I thought of Scout. I couldn't explain why I thought of her, but as I watched the crows fly away, I tried to reach out metaphysically to her, but it was never something we shared—but I tried, anyway. The dread I'd felt disappeared and replaced with calm. She was okay. There was nothing to fear, it was only a mother's concern.

"Is this the place?" Sawyer reversed and parked.

"Yes, I need you and Marc to carry the flamethrowers."

I swallowed the lump in my throat, and for the first time in my career I hesitated getting out of the protective vehicle.

"Do you wish to remain in the vehicle, *ma chérie?*" Léon asked with concern and squeezed my knee.

"No." I lied. "I want to come with."

"Remain between the flamethrowers and me, and you'll be fine," he said and exited.

"What are we expecting to see here?" I scooted off the seat behind him.

Ralph followed and stood close to Sawyer.

Léon brought me in front of him and whispered near the shell of my ear. "Vampire bats."

"No!" I groaned and my shoulders sagged. "You're kidding? Oh gods, at least you will feel right at home." I teased.

Léon pinched my ass and led me forward just as I heard a noise to our left. A large opening of a cave moved in the black night. My arms pebbled, I closed my jacket and tied my hair in a low ponytail.

Léon let go of me and approached the mouth of the cave. He sliced his wrist and blood drops fell to the ground.

I stood beside Ralph as we watched... waiting for something... I wasn't sure what.

The ground moved. Leaf-nosed bats approached the blood on all fours. The white-winged bats neared the blood and lapped it up. I shuddered and felt Ralph shiver beside me.

"At least they aren't mole-men." A few years ago, a mole-man had followed us when we were cave searching and Ralph had shot it. They were one of the ugliest things with their skinny bodies covered in fur. They had features like a small human mashed together with a star-nosed mole.

Ralph snorted in response; no doubt relieved there wasn't one.

"Come." Léon waved us over and entered the dark cave.

Ralph and I stayed in front of Sawyer and Marc while they lit our way with the flames. The heat at my back was comforting. It was the cave we were heading into that freaked me out. As we crossed the threshold, the walls moved, and thousands of bats flew out of the fire's way.

"Light up there." Léon pointed a finger to the right. A cauldron of bats flew away as the flames reached them.

Sawyer and Marc had to duck, or risk being flown into.

I cowered behind Léon with Ralph crouching beside me. I shuddered when one white-winged vampire bat walked on all fours toward me.

"Don't kick it," Léon said, anticipating my move.

Instead, I walked around it and followed Léon down a narrow corridor. Sawyer and Marc turned off their flamethrower to navigate through the passage. Once we were through it, we entered a large, cavernous burial chamber. In the center stood a stone sarcophagus with markings similar to what we'd found at the scientist's lab. As we neared, I got a better view; the lid of the sarcophagus was not closed properly with the surrounding dust disturbed.

"Oh no," I said as we reached the coffin. "They were here—"

"Yes." Léon prevented me from getting closer. "Stay here, Blaire." He glanced at my belly. "Ralph and Sawyer help me move the lid. Marc, you stand guard and burn anything that moves." He glanced up at the high ceiling.

Marc stood to one side while the men removed the lid and placed it gently on the ground. I rocked onto my tiptoes and peered into the coffin. The husk of a man remained. His severed head wrapped in a cloth. Each of his limbs wrapped similarly. They had opened the cloth around his head, revealing the hole in his forehead. Someone had drilled into his skull and had removed samples of what remained.

"I should've burned his body when we had the chance."

"Why did you preserve his body? And why leave it here?" I asked as I stepped closer.

"Alex had just joined the Vampire Council and had sought their recommendation. Unfortunately, we had to do this. But," — he grinned — "I'm going to destroy it."

"Without their knowledge?"

"No, of course not. Alex should arrive in a couple of minutes. It was his suggestion to burn the body, but he has to perform a ritual first—"

Before Léon finished his sentence, wind howled through the cave. Everybody froze in anticipation.

Alex stepped through the opening of the narrow passage with a smile.

"Friend," he said and approached Léon with open arms, and they hugged. "It has been too long. Why is it the only time you contact me is when you want something destroyed?" He winked at me, referring to Roland.

"You know you are always welcome anytime."

Alex gave a curt nod, then came to me for a quick embrace. "I couldn't believe it when Léon told me," — he glanced at my stomach, — "we should celebrate when this is over." His stone demeanor brightened and then quickly disappeared. "Now," — he rubbed his hands together, — "what have I missed?"

"Nothing yet, we just arrived." Léon approached the sarcophagus.

"Good." Alex clapped and all the hairs on my body stood up. I thought Léon and Salvador were powerful—

Alex was something different. I'd seen him extract Roland's body fluids, flinging his remains across the room and into a blue flame until there was nothing left. I didn't know the extent of his powers, but knew he could manipulate the elements; earth, wind, fire, water and air and that I shouldn't interrupt him.

He ran his hand through his short hair and his green eyes glowed like emeralds. He removed an old vial of liquid from his pocket and opened the lid. The stench wafted in the air and I stepped back. The rotting fumes filled the cave, and Marc and Sawyer gagged. Léon held out an open palm to assist Alex while Ralph stared in wonder. I sighed. Humans were lucky creatures; there were things they couldn't hear, see or feel.

"Don't be alarmed by what I'm about to do," Alex said to no-one in particular.

A brown substance dripped slowly from the vial as Alex chanted in French, then Latin. A fine smoke expelled from the corpse. The smell of dry blood and rotten flesh filled my nostrils, and I gagged, covering my mouth. I watched as fine smoke materialized into the shape of a man glaring down at his body. Alex continued chanting, which reminded me of witches, and I frowned at him as I wondered if he had learned of spells or if he was something entirely different—and not just a master vampire.

The ghostly figure glanced at his surroundings and laughed silently at Alex.

The chanting echoed in the hollow spaces between us, and my arms pebbled. A snap of air shook the ground and the ghostlike figure dissolved, then animated before us. Vampires were classy creatures who rarely chipped a nail doing tasks. Yet, a faint red glow covered Alex's pale skin as he perspired. I watched in awe but remained concerned. I wanted to know if he was okay and reached for him.

"No—" Léon tried to warn me, but it was too late. I touched Alex's shoulder and his power coursed through me like a tuning fork, but it didn't hurt. It felt like warm insects running across my skin. The smell of hair burning caused me to look in Sawyer's direction as he blasted flames in a corner where a dark figure loomed. Marc's blowtorch was on and pointed down the narrow passage we had used. Ralph stood like a marble statue.

"Léon! Alex! What's happening?" I asked with panic in my voice, unable to let go of Alex.

Through gritted teeth Alex said. "Someone placed a spell on his corpse after we had bound him, and I'm struggling to vanquish his remains." His body shook. "We need help," he breathed.

The vibrations coursed through him into me, and I felt the power surrounding the corpse. The ghost continued to hover above us, laughing soundlessly. The pull of air whipped past my cheek and I felt liquid drip down my face. When I wiped my cheek, I came away with blood on my fingertips. Léon's eyes widened. He'd seen what had happened. His soulless eyes flitted from mine to the cut, at the delicious liquid, and in an instant was holding me while I was still holding Alex's shoulder. I knew what my blood did to them, but I also knew he would never hurt me. He sucked in air over his fangs as he breathed me in and closed his eyes.

"Your blood is exquisite and enticing," he murmured into my neck, near the cut on my cheek. "Allow me to stop the bleeding." His lips found the wound and kissed gently.

It didn't hurt, but it sent a pleasant quiver through my body.

"There, all better." He kissed me chastely.

I stood transfixed on Léon; the way his one hand rested on the small of my back and the other on my belly. How he looked at me as if I was the only person in the world, and my heart fluttered. One side of his mouth curved upward, and I wanted to melt into his arms. He still had that effect on me after all these years together.

When he blinked, so did I, realizing I'd completely forgotten where we were, and what we were trying to do. I was still holding onto Alex and the intense force he emitted in the cave and into me.

When Léon let go, I felt everything; an energy so great my chest ached. I had to let go. I had a baby to protect.

"It's too powerful, we have to stop," I yelled as my body shook, clenching my jaw. I knew I had to stop touching Alex, but I couldn't let go. "Help me, Léon."

He nodded, understanding what I meant, and lifted one of my fingers at a time. The moment my hand left Alex, a blast of hot air pushed us across the room. Alex flew into the other side of the cave. Sawyer and Marc fired their flamethrower at any shadow that moved, and screeching cries echoed around us. The ghost disappeared and Ralph crumbled to the ground. I'd crashed into Léon and was grateful for my soft landing. He was fine, but Ralph wasn't. I crawled on my hands and knees to Ralph to assess the damage caused to him. He was human and breakable. He was breathing, but unconscious.

Léon climbed to his feet and shook his head. "We need a witch to help you. But we cannot risk leaving this area unattended." He glanced at Sawyer, "Call Désiré."

Chapter Twenty-Four

I sat in the reclined front seat of the vehicle, pushed it back for leg room and placed a calm hand on my stomach. Our little man was busy after Alex's failed attempt at destroying the mummified vampire. Léon had left Sawyer and Marc to protect me and Ralph, who lay unconscious on the backseat. Léon and Alex had left us to seek permission from Allan for Désiré to enter.

It was nearing eleven o'clock, and it exhausted me. Relaxing into the seat, I closed my eyes and easily drifted to sleep dreaming of viridescent trees and crystal lakes. I swam through clear cerulean waters that were just the right temperature. The blue moon cast its lustrous shine on the rippling water. The farther out I swam, the larger the waves. I floated over a wave, waiting for the other, but there wasn't. The water flattened out and I washed to shore.

"Wake up." A voice echoed inside my head. "Wake up, Blaire." It said again.

I flinched at the soft lips against my cheek and opened

my eyes to meet Léon's. "You're back." I smiled lazily and stretched as best I could.

"How's our little man doing?"

"He's fine. Is there a bathroom somewhere nearby?" I asked. Once the words were out of my mouth, I realized I desperately needed to go. Dreaming of all that water didn't help matters either.

"We can take you to the old buildings up the hill."

"Please." I sat upright and glanced over my shoulder; Ralph was still fast asleep and would most likely remain that way for a few more hours.

"Hey, Blaire," Désiré said near my window. "Didn't I tell you to take it easy?"

"I'm just driving with; they're doing all the heavy lifting," I said with a smirk.

"Good, I'll see to Alex before we begin."

"Don't start until we return," Léon said.

"We won't."

Marc entered the cave with Désiré and Alex while Sawyer climbed into the back with Ralph. Léon drove us up the mountain and stopped at the first decent building. Sawyer had his blowtorch ready in case he needed it and entered the building first with a halogen spotlight. The light was bright enough to light our way; we didn't need our own, but I brought a smaller flashlight with for emergencies.

The shop we'd entered was a pharmacy. They had cleared the shelves of its contents with broken bottles and medicine littering the floor. The smell of dust and spilled spirits assaulted my nose, but there was another foul smell I couldn't quite place. A thick layer of dust covered the shelves and floor with a patch of dark substance in the far right-hand corner. I nervously glanced at the dark corners, but thankfully nothing moved.

Underworld Legacy

Sawyer led the way. He stood over six feet tall, with broad shoulders and enough muscles to scare any human away, and I hoped it would scare the critters away too. He approached the back of the pharmacy, their shelves void of any drugs, toward the only other locked door, which we assumed to be a bathroom.

"Stand back." Sawyer readied his weapon, his tattoos peeking out of his clothing which ran down both powerful arms. He knocked on the door and yelled, "Hello, is anybody inside?"

Silence. Then scratching sounded behind the door, followed by crying.

Léon and I stepped farther back as Sawyer kicked in the door. Groaning continued from inside the dark bathroom. The strange smell from earlier was stronger as it was coming from inside the dank room. The grunting grew louder as the walking corpse slowly approached Sawyer.

Sawyer blasted the living dead with fiery flames, but it kept advancing. The rotting meat on the corpse melted off his bones, but he kept pushing forward.

I pulled out my weapon when Sawyer did, and we fired. His head rocked backward, but it did little else. We pumped bullets into him; one hit his eye, and it exploded with white puss dripping down his face. When the last bullet hit his chest, he crumpled to the ground in a burning heap of rotting meat and haunted bones.

"Gross." I shuddered and pinched my nose. "Sawyer, shine your spotlight on it."

When the light touched the mess, his meat and skin shone green and his bones yellow. He'd been rotting inside the moist bathroom for a very long time.

"Look at his clothing." Sawyer trained the light on what remained.

"How long ago were you here?" I asked Léon.

"Centuries," he said dryly.

"I don't understand. They built these structures in eighteen hundred, yet his clothing is from much earlier." I pointed at the linen collar and breeches.

"Alex and I were here in sixteen hundred and buried the devil mist in his tomb. But we didn't close the town. Although it was void of people then, it seems some returned and modernized it. Unfortunately, we heard others say the town was haunted and later deserted again. With Alex's help, we protected the town from outsiders and allowed the fire breathing unicorns to take refuge here. They were desirable creatures in need of a place to hide, so they took care of the town for us." He pointed at the rotting zombie at our feet. "I don't know how he came to be, though? A necromancer maybe?"

"Do you still need the bathroom?"

"Yes, but I don't want to go there. That thing lived here for who knows how many years, and it stinks. Can we try the next building, please?"

The hardware store next door had no living dead to scare the bejeezus out of me. Dust covered the tools and counters like a fluffy blanket and the bathroom was neat; all I had to do was clean the seat. Once I'd relieved my bladder, I felt much better. One irritating thing about being pregnant was the frequent urination. It was something men couldn't comprehend but were sympathetic.

I opened the bathroom door to darkness. Neither Sawyer nor Léon were waiting for me like I'd asked.

"Hello? Where are you guys?" I called out into the blackness.

"We're over here, but be quiet," Léon whispered.

"There's more of them outside. The noise we made must've brought them out."

Luckily, I had my flashlight and turned it on. I pointed it at the floor to guide my way to them. I found Sawyer and Léon hiding behind a metal locker filled with tools near the window. Groans and grunts came from the hoard of walking corpses outside, dressed in similar sixteenth century fashion to the one we'd killed.

"Are you scared of the walking dead, Léon?" I teased.

"It's not my life I fear, but you and our unborn child. If we make a noise, they'll charge this place to get to you. And I don't want to risk taking you up in the air with me."

That sobered me up quickly. I hugged him from behind, and he pulled me in closer, but my belly got in the way.

"What do we do?"

"We wait them out. We've already informed Marc they might head their way and we can only leave here once it's safe to do so."

We waited almost two hours. The painfully slow walking pieces of meat and bone shuffled one foot at a time, and eventually all sixty-something had past through the town. Léon gently nudge me awake and helped me to my feet.

We arrived back at the opening of the cave and Ralph awoke, slightly groggy. But he'd be okay. We entered the cave, and it was empty.

"Where did they go?" I peered inside the coffin at the husk of a corpse, still there and in pieces.

"They read the text message I'd sent them," Sawyer said as he shone the light in every corner and between the rocks.

Léon walked along the wall of the cavern while Ralph

and I walked on the other side. With my small flashlight, I checked everywhere we walked.

"It reminds me of our little adventures," Ralph said behind me.

Footsteps echoed in the cave and we spun around at the same time as Alex, Désiré and Marc surfaced behind Ralph.

"Where were you?" I asked.

"When those things shuffled past the cave, we hid. They are harmless if left alone, and I didn't think it necessary to fight them," Alex said. "Right, let's finish this." He removed the vial once more and opened it, sprinkling the contents onto the corpse.

Désiré removed items from her bag and started the process with Alex. She poured salt around the sarcophagus and burned herbs that smelled like lavender and something else. She lit a black candle and placed it near the head of the corpse. I'd known necromancers who used salt as a protection wall the soul they were trying to raise could not penetrate. But I wasn't sure if that's what she was doing.

My visits to her had lessened since Scout was back home, but I tried to visit as often as I could. She'd given me lessons on potions and spells, but I'd tried none of them. I wasn't a witch per se, but I possessed certain qualities, I just didn't home in on any of those skills. My true powers were that of a healer, and shifter of my saber animal. I didn't want to dip a toe in witch's brew, so to speak, and would leave that to the professionals. I had even brought Scout with on various occasions, which delighted Désiré because she had an actual student with powers. Scout had a direct line to the undead and powers that made me afraid. But Scout was a good girl and hadn't used her powers for evil or to enrich herself.

Léon held my hand, and I held Désiré's while her other

hand in Alex's. We stood at the head of the sarcophagus, while the others watched.

Alex and Désiré chanted in Latin and the air snapped as it did before, but intensely. The candle burned brighter, and the smell of the wick assaulted my senses—a potent thyme and rosemary essence mixed with something stronger. The wind was hot, and I wanted to reach for my cheek again, but I kept my hands in theirs.

The ghostlike phantom rose from his body parts.

Their chanting increased in speed and louder in tone. Hot air blew my hair back. I wanted to get away, but they gripped my hands. Sweat peppered my forehead and dripped down the sides of my face. Désiré seemed as affected as I, but Alex and Léon were still pristine creatures of the dark.

The spirit rose and glowered down at us. He was not happy.

Désiré's body started vibrating, and those vibrations travelled through us. The spirit of the blood mist vampire grew larger and then evaporated into a cloud of mist—the blood droplets rained down on us. His wrapped limbs dissolved until there was nothing left of them, leaving behind indentations into the material below.

The air felt thick and stale.

The smell of rotten herbs surrounded us, and when Désiré and Alex let go, the air snapped.

Chapter Twenty-Five

It was Saturday, and I slept most of the day. We only got home around six in the morning, dropping me off first. I wanted to spend time with Sebastian, but when I awoke early afternoon, he hadn't come home and had left no messages.

"Hey, babe," he said sleepily.

"Where are you?"

"At the leap."

"I thought you were going to come here last night," I asked as a sliver of nervousness slid down my spine.

"Who's that?" a woman asked in the background.

The sliver of nerves became a raging inferno of heat, and I ended the call. I behaved childish but to hear a woman's voice ask who he was speaking to upset me. Sebastian meant to come home after his meeting and didn't. The thought of him with another woman didn't sit well with me.

My cellphone rang, and I shouted when I answered. "What?"

"Why did you hang up on me?"

"Who are you with, Sebastian?"

"It's only Viola."

I grunted my displeasure upon hearing her name. She was young, fragile and a were-leopard. Everything I was not. Sebastian had helped her adapt to her new animal. What if he was doing something *more*?

"Why didn't you come home, Sebastian?" I choked on my words as the back of my throat ached.

"I thought you would stay by Léon. I didn't think you would come home."

"I sent you a text message letting you know where I was. Didn't you see it?"

The silence stretched for too long.

It was only a matter of time when one of us strayed, but I didn't think it would be Sebastian. I thought Léon would be the first to leave our little love nest. Everything had been going so well between us. We had a way of managing our feelings and who did what and when. But I didn't want to admit to myself that it wouldn't last.

I didn't think we'd last as long as we did. But we did… until it didn't.

"I only saw it now," he whispered. "I'm sorry, I thought I would get an early start here."

"But it sounds as though you just woke up."

He stammered into the receiver.

If he wanted to expand his wings and leave but didn't know how, I'd help him make that decision.

"Fetch your clothes from my house." I ended the call.

He tried phoning again, but I kept cancelling his call. I only answered Ralph's call.

Ralph fetched me, and we went back to the scientist's house. They'd solved the password and could review the recording of his lab the night he had disappeared.

When we arrived, his assistant, Benjamin, was waiting for us. "They're waiting for you before they review the footage," he said as he entered the house first.

I was out of breath by the time we reached the sixth floor, where Detective Carson waited.

"Morning," Georgina said. "You're just in time." She tapped Officer Blackwood's shoulder and continued talking. "We couldn't review the footage at the precinct, so we've had to come back here. Benjamin helped us set it up once we had the key code and knew how it worked."

Officer Blackwood pressed play.

The television screen flickered to life. Dr. Avery dismissed his assistant with the wave of a hand while peering through the microscope. Benjamin left the room.

"Were you leaving?" I asked.

"Yes, by that time it was already dark, and I needed to feed my cat."

"What was Dr. Avery so engrossed with?"

"The blood of our latest test subject. He was testing to see how the blood attached itself to cancer cells and how they regenerated to create a normal vampire cell. He was hoping to eradicate the cancer without the human patient turning into a vampire. It worked to a point, then as the cells mutated and changed, vampirism absorbed all the human cells and the human turned."

"I read he was on the verge of a breakthrough?"

"Yes, because of that." He jerked his chin at the screen. "The latest subject held promise—the human cells remained human with no cancer detected. But it became unstable, the vampirism dissolved as the cancer returned."

That got our attention. I glanced at Benjamin. When he noticed me staring, he turned away.

Glass shattered, and I focused my attention back on the screen.

The doctor stood and backed away from the microscope. Another glass shattered as the lab shook. The doctor fell to the floor, his coat covering him, and steam rose off his body. He clawed at his face as he yelled. He scratched his skin and yanked off his coat. Next came his tie and work shirt. He sat naked from the waist up. His head moved, not his neck or his shoulders, his head only. His head turned one hundred and eighty degrees and stared at the camera.

I pushed my chair back. It felt eerily as if he were staring straight at us. At me. And now.

"What is happening to him?" Georgina asked.

"He's changing," Ralph said beside me. "Somehow he got infected with something. Where did you get the sample from?"

When I turned, Benjamin had left. I stood and looked around the room.

"Where did he go?"

Everyone stood from their chairs and searched the lab.

Georgina sent an officer to search the rest of the house and to send a squad car to his residence.

The lights flickered off, leaving us in a blanket of darkness. Chaos erupted. Chairs overturned. Glass crashed to the floor. The only light came from the screen. Dr. Avery stared at us with black orbs and pale skin. The video played. Dr. Avery turned the rest of his body to match the angle of his head and continued to glare at us. In a wink of an eye, he splashed to the floor in a pool of blood, then rose from the tiles in a fine red mist.

Chapter Twenty-Six

Ralph turned on the lights from the master switch for the doctor's lab. It was a confusing task because this house was six floors, and each floor had its own electrical box.

Georgina spoke with the officer who had searched Benjamin's apartment. When she finished the call, she turned to us. "He says we need to go there. It seems Benjamin was doing his own experiments at his apartment. We must tread carefully as we don't exactly know what he's been doing. And if my suspicions are correct, he may have infected the doctor without his knowledge and created that." She pointed at the screen where Dr. Avery's blood had splashed on the floor.

"We need to find him," I stated. "Before he infects others."

"I've ordered a BOLO and we're monitoring all roads leading in and out of Sterling Meadow."

"And the forests?"

"That's where we need your help with the shifters."

"Right," I mumbled and didn't feel up to contacting

Sebastian; definitely not after the last conversation we'd had. He sat at the head of the WAA with other leaders, and the next best person to contact was Shawn—King of the werewolves.

When I pulled my cellphone out of my pocket, Sebastian had left fifteen missed calls and nine text messages. I ignored them and called Shawn to inform him of the fugitive. When he asked why I didn't go straight to Sebastian, I told him I couldn't reach him, and this was urgent. It was the best lie I could come up with under pressure.

"We should go to the apartment," Ralph said as we descended the stairs. He was reading the report from the crime scenes where they'd found the other bodies.

"Anything interesting?" I asked when we reached the ground floor.

"Just what we already know." He closed his manilla file and handed it to me. "There's one thing we didn't know, they found gold residue around the neck area."

I stopped walking. "Gold residue? The real deal?"

"Yep. Gold dust around the neck before the beheading."

I shuddered. We continued walking. My cellphone vibrated in my pocket; I saw it was Sebastian but ignored it.

"Aren't you going to get that?"

"No." I climbed into the passenger side and buckled up.

I thought about the gold dust they'd found on both victims and which supernatural used gold. Gold could harm Anubis, while a banshee could die if gold struck their hearts. And gold attracted dragons and leprechauns, while one could use gold to summon the Reaper. I didn't know which used dust in this manner.

"What do you know about gold?" I asked.

"What do you mean?"

"You can summon the Reaper with gold. Dragons and

leprechauns want gold. And you can kill banshees with it. Which supernatural being uses gold dust?"

"Gorgons make gold dust."

"Shut up!"

"I'm serious. After our encounter with the gorgons and the animal, I researched them. Didn't you?"

"No, I've been busy," I said defensively. "I know little about gorgons. I only knew about the three sisters."

Ralph chuckled. "One point for me, zero for pregnant fairy over here."

"Huh." I considered his words. "Well, we only know two gorgons and I'm hoping they can help us." I sent the gorgon cousins a text each hoping they could assist. I wanted to know who had asked them for gold dust or if their extended family had used dust the last couple of days.

Jedediah responded first.

"Now I'm just confused."

"What did he say?"

"Jedediah responded with a text saying they have a shop. When I searched for it, it's only a few blocks away from the scientist's home—"

"That means he bought it there."

"Sure, naturally, but Jedediah says it's been closed this week while they've had to sort out their housing problem."

"Someone broke in and stole it."

"Exactly, so it could be anyone and not our doctor."

I sighed frustratingly. This did not help our case.

We arrived at Benjamin's apartment building. The elevator had a sign reading *'Broken'*, forcing us to use the stairs. We stepped over broken bottles, trash, and even feces. Some steps had cracked, and others crumbled beneath our shoes. It was a miracle we arrived on the fourth floor without injury. I told Ralph to go ahead, I'd be taking my time. My lower back was killing me, and I wore slip on sneakers because I couldn't reach to tie my laces. My stomach felt as though it had grown bigger since last night, and I rubbed the sides he'd kicked as I slowly ascended.

I finally arrived at the open apartment door where three officers collected evidence. Ralph was speaking to the officer first at the scene.

"Come look," Ralph said when he saw me. "Officer Harris has preserved this part of the apartment for us." He pointed at the various vials of maroon liquid.

"Blood?"

"I think so." Ralph picked up a notebook from under the table. "He left in a hurry and forgot this one. He wrote his findings in here. He's been pricking humans with needles tainted with vampire blood." He flicked through the notebook, stopping at scribbles and markings and what looked like blood splatter. He turned to the end and read the last entry. "*'Craig's obsessed with one DNA strand he can't explain. The sample we extracted from the forbidden mummified remains holds clues to the answers we seek, yet he still only focuses on the cancer cells. What he doesn't realize is we could sell our formula to the military and make tons of cash. Just imagine the type of soldiers who dissolved into mist before releasing their wrath on the enemy. Or we could sell it to the highest bidder. Imagine a villain who robbed banks and disappeared before the cops came. I need to find the right time to share this with the doctor. I hope he listens this time.'*"

"Well…" I cleared my throat. "It doesn't look as though the doctor listened. Instead, Benjamin infected him to force him to see what was possible. I'm amazed the doctor didn't kill Benjamin first."

"Maybe there's an order to those he's killed already."

I hadn't considered that, and slapped Ralph's shoulder. "Not just a pretty face, heh?"

"I'll ask Georgina if the victims have any connection to the doctor. If I remember the footage we'd seen, he was waiting for each target. He ignored all the people on the sidewalk. He only wanted those specific people."

We continued searching the apartment, but Benjamin had already taken the incriminating evidence with him.

Georgina found nothing linking the victims to each other or to Dr. Avery. The sun had set, my feet ached, and all I wanted to do was lie down. There hadn't been another crime scene, and Benjamin was on the lam. And now that we knew Dr. Avery was our killer mist vampire, we'd stopped searching for him as a victim but as a murderer.

"I'll call you if we get a hit for any of them. Get some rest and I'll only see you tomorrow if we need to, otherwise I'll see you Monday," Ralph said as he parked his car.

"Although I might see you tonight?" I climbed out his car.

Ralph feigned ignorance. "What do you mean?"

It was the opening of Léon's newest club, which Eden managed. We were all going to attend, and I silently hoped Sebastian wouldn't. I didn't feel like bumping into him. I think I was still angry at him.

"Your little girlfriend will be there," I said, batting my eyelashes.

"Bye, Blaire," he responded and drove away.

I giggled and strolled up the path toward my wing at the Labyrinth and flinched at his voice.

Underworld Legacy

"I've been calling you all day," Sebastian yelled.

I felt my blood drain from my face when I saw him. He stood at the open door with his arms crossed, and the muscles in his jaw ticked. Even his eyes glowed scary and vivid. I was in trouble.

Chapter Twenty-Seven

"Where's your girlfriend—" I retorted and stepped past him and entered the large foyer. But I didn't get very far. He grabbed my elbow and all the anger and resentment I'd been holding on to all day dissolved on my tongue and I forgot the rest of my sentence. I relaxed in his embrace and I hated him for it. I pushed him away. "I hate it when you do that."

"Your anger is not safe for the baby." His harsh words made me swallow my words. "What do you think I did wrong?"

After a moment, I finally answered. "You didn't come home. You didn't read my texts. And some woman asked who you were talking with. And you hesitated, Sebastian. Never hesitate when you speak with me. I'm sensitive." I broke down into a fit of sobs and he pulled me into the curve of his body and held me tightly.

"I was sleeping in the lounge. I'd given Viola my room at Anne's, and she'd walked in and heard me. She only asked a question. Everybody had a late morning. We hunted for most of the early morning and we just needed to rest. And I'm sorry I didn't respond to your texts." He cupped my face and planted delicate butterfly kisses all over my face and wiped away the tears.

I hated that he knew me so well. And he was right. My anger was not a pleasant emotion to blast around the house and in my *condition*. And I didn't want to glow white and change into my saber; it could be catastrophic.

"I'm sorry," I mumbled in our kiss. "I just thought our beautiful bubble was going to burst, and I wanted to get it over with."

"I love you, Blaire. I loved you from the moment I picked you up off the cement in that ghastly alley and I love you still. You are carrying our baby and that makes me love you more. You care for everyone and I know you don't want us to get hurt, but a brief fight nudging me in the right direction is healthy. It doesn't mean I've done anything wrong; you need to remind me I need to consider other situations as well."

I nodded into his chest.

"Come, you need to get ready or do you want to lie down."

"I need a power nap. What time are we leaving?"

"In an hour."

Léon caressed my cheek and planted soft kisses along my temple. I opened my eyes to his starless ones, and he smirked.

"Hey cheeky vampire. Are you my wake-up call?"

He helped me sit up. "Oui." He walked to the bathroom and opened the shower sprayer, "Your water is ready."

"Thanks." I undressed as I walked to the bathroom and stepped into the shower that was at the right temperature. The jets hit my tense shoulders, and I relaxed. "This feels good," I said and washed my body with the luxurious French liquid soap.

"Sebastian told me about your little fight."

I groaned. "Does your baby brother always tell you everything?"

He chuckled lightheartedly.

"Who's talking about me?" Sebastian entered the bathroom wearing a broad smile, and his eyes hinted at mischief. "I brought your dress."

That caught my attention. "I'm pregnant. There are only so many styles of dresses I can wear, a long tent dress or a short tent dress. Or maybe preggie pants with the fat elastic and a low-cut shirt that shows off the *girls*."

Léon burst out laughing. "She's all yours. I'll see you later." As he kissed my cheek, his head and shoulders got wet. "I have things to finish."

Sebastian slowly removed his shirt and threw it on the floor. I stopped washing my body. He unbuckled his pants, opened the buttonhole and unzipped. My hands fell to my sides as I gawked at him; he was so deliciously yummy—tanned skin with rippling muscles and powerful hands as he slowly removed his clothing. He kicked off his pants and dropped his boxers. A strange noise came from the back of my throat and I closed my mouth. His muscles moved beneath his skin with such fluidity I couldn't wait to get my hands on him. He entered the shower and slowly turned me around.

"I'll try to be gentle," he whispered into my neck and a shiver ran through my body, a tiny shudder of pleasure as I felt him behind me. His hands slid around my sides and he stopped.

"What's wrong?" I asked with concern and spun around.

"You've grown," he said as his brows knitted together. "I don't mean you're getting fat, but he has grown."

"I thought the same thing earlier, but I dismissed it. Do you think it's possible for him to grow so much since yesterday?"

"Désiré measured you the last time?"

"Yes, it was only a couple of days ago."

Sebastian climbed out of the shower, wrapped a towel around his body and left. My body sagged at the sudden loss of heat, switched off the shower and climbed out. By the time I had my gown fastened, Sebastian entered the bathroom again.

"I can't wait to have my way with you, but I won't lie when I say I'm concerned." He glanced at my belly. "Désiré will join us at the club tonight. She wants to check on you again in Léon's office. If she's concerned then we can go to the hospital, if not then we enjoy our evening." He kissed my temple and climbed back in the shower. "Give me ten minutes and I'll be your handsome, charming date," he grinned seductively and washed while I ogled frustratingly at him.

Golden balloons filled the club's ceiling, and each cordoned off area showcased a vampire with their *guest* as they performed various acts.

Blood dripped down a human's neck. Her vampire host licked it off her while she levitated off the ground.

Another vampire threw blades at a human target. He strapped her to a device that spun in circles—she came off a little dizzy and a scratch on the inside of her thigh. Her vampire host licked the blood clean before she collapsed in a puddle of orgasms.

Other vampires protected their human company from the hungry. Even though the club's members were a certain class, there's always those who took a chance.

Léon and Eden tended to business at the bar, where they only served the red liquid at varying temperatures. Léon had tried to get a liquor license, but they denied him because he had so many already. He decided this club was strictly for wealthy vampires wanting something *different*, and they only served blood and cold drinks for humans.

Sebastian sat with me in Léon's office while we waited for Désiré. There was a soft knock on the door, and she entered with Kai carrying her equipment. Kai opened the portable bed and set the monitor beside it.

"You came prepared," I said with a smile, hoping she didn't pick up on my nervousness.

"I want to make sure you two are doing okay." She tapped the bed, "Hop on."

Kai left us while Sebastian stood next to me holding my hand. Not feeling too scared, but I was alarmed something was wrong. I'd grown since yesterday and my imagination had run away from me; I pictured a growth on the side of the baby's head, the umbilical cord wrapped around his neck, or his head exploding. All these terrible images flashed through my mind and it would only stop once I knew what was really going on.

I had removed my dress and pulled on the paper gown Désiré had brought with her. She stared at my larger belly, but kind enough not to say anything. I suspected she too was curious what was happening.

She switched on the machine and added the gel to the probe and moved it around on my belly. I flinched at the coldness but got used to it quickly.

Sebastian squeezed my hand as he stared at the black and white grainy picture of our son.

Our baby still had both arms and legs. His spine was still straight. His head was average size. But... he was just *bigger*. He'd grown as if a month had passed in only a day.

"You might birth sooner, Blaire," Désiré finally said. She kept going around on my belly and measuring him; she measured his head four times then spoke again. "These three or four minutes his head had grown a millimeter." Her tone was solemn and a nervousness I hadn't felt earlier overcame me.

"Should I worry?" I squeezed Sebastian's hand.

"No, but prepare yourself. If he continues to grow this rapidly, you might meet your boy by next week."

"Are you serious? She's only due to give birth in three months' time."

"I guess we were all fooled. Your boy is not that human after all. Especially if he's growing so quickly." She wiped the probe clean and handed me a tissue to clean my stomach.

Sebastian helped me clean the areas I'd missed and helped me dress. My hands shook as I picked up my slip-on shoes—my body felt like an ice bucket had just toppled over me and I started crying. My emotions were a bundle of raw nerves being prodded and hearing I would have our baby so much sooner left me shaken. I hadn't prepared for him yet. And to hear that he may in fact be supernatural should've left me elated, but it didn't.

"It's going to be okay, Blaire." Désiré placed a calm hand on my shoulder. "I would like to spend more time with you the next couple of days to monitor his growth. I'd advise against working. You should be resting. As in bed rest."

I shook my head and snorted. "No, I can work less, but I won't stop. And you shadowing me all day long, will feel claustrophobic. How about I just get you on speed dial and promise not to leave town?"

She sighed. "You're so stubborn. Fine, but I'm going to let Mel know about the situation and you need to carry a baby bag with the items needed to help you give birth."

I nodded. "That sounds reasonable." My tears had dried, and I'd felt better. We had a plan. Sometimes I just needed someone to guide my thoughts instead of leaving me to think of the worst and freaking myself out. "Thank you, at least now we know he isn't completely human."

It was a relief, but worrisome—what flavor monster would he be…

Chapter Twenty-Eight

SCOUT

We stood outside another set of locked doors. I pressed my palms up against them, filling the dents in the doors and the fuse lit outlining them, similar to the temple doors. When the door clicked open, the cogs turned opening the doors slowly then stopped half-way. I pushed against the doors, but they didn't budge. Luckily, it was wide enough for us to squeeze through.

"This is where I leave you." Victor stepped backward as if bracing for an explosion or something.

Warm air greeted us with hints of citrus, reminding me of fruit trees.

"You know what to expect and are comfortable for me to leave you alone?" he confirmed.

"Yes, we should be fine. River will call you when we're done."

Victor didn't say goodbye, he just disappeared in a blast of hot air, making my ears pop and then they closed. I yawned, trying to open them with no luck.

"I hate it when he does that." I stretched my jaw wide and finally my ears popped a second time, opening them.

"It's because he stands so close to you when he teleports. I'm so used to it already."

"Can you do it on your own?"

"Yes, but not with another person." River scratched behind Luna's ear. She leaned her head against his leg as if it was too heavy for her to hold up. "I barely feel it anymore. Let's go inside." He ruffled her mohawk, and she walked ahead of us.

I squeezed through the opening and entered a completely different world to the one we'd just left. Outside, we'd stopped in a dark and dreary cemetery in Scotland somewhere. The doors led us to a bright garden filled with insects, bees and warmth. The instant I entered, my arms pebbled, sending a cascade of gooseflesh throughout my body. Above, the sun warmed me down to my bones, so I removed the jacket and tied it around my waist. A breeze caressed my skin, and it felt good.

Luna barked when a butterfly landed on her nose, and she tried to catch it.

River stood beside me and whistled. "This place is stunning." He reached for the fruit dangling near our faces, but he didn't pick it. "It is tempting isn't it. Now I know why Eve couldn't help herself," he smirked and ran after Luna who had ventured to the left of the path.

"How do you know that's the right way to go?" I yelled after them, quickening my step.

"I don't but I trust Luna," River yelled back. "Luna! Wait! Halt!" he called after his dog and she listened, sat beside a strawberry bush and another fork in the path.

"Now what?" I asked when I caught up to them.

"I brought her leash." He snapped it onto her collar. "Easy, girl. Now which way?"

Luna stood and casually walked, sniffed at a corner, turned her head and went in the opposite direction.

They had crafted the maze out of tall, thick hedges, trees, and leafy brushes. Victor had hinted at a sacred garden no human had entered after that *one* time. It was closed off to everyone, but his older brother, Seth, had seduced Mother Nature into allowing him to use it for his little *game*. It made me wonder what Seth had promised her for this *little* favor.

Victor had mentioned he didn't know what creatures lurked around the corners, but we had to remain vigilant. And the moment we entered, the clock started—giving us twenty-four-hours to reach the center of the maze or we'd lose. Victor didn't know what would happen, but if the rumors were true, it would swallow us within, and we would become part of the maze ourselves. Neither River nor I wanted to remain here, and the only recourse we had, was to follow Luna.

Squawking sounded above my head. Glancing up, I saw five crows circling. "How did they get in here?"

"Spirit animals can go where their owner goes. And if they are here, they are definitely your spirit animal. I'll admit, it's impressive to have five of them."

"But crows? Really? Of all creatures they are the ones attracted to me?" I scrunched my face as I stared up at them, the sun shining brightly and momentarily blinding me. I rubbed my eyes and stared down at Luna until my eyes adjusted again.

"We don't choose them, unfortunately. They choose us. And they are awesome. Just give it some time, maybe they will introduce themselves to you soon."

Victor and River each had a dog for their spirit animal. Victor's had three heads, nevertheless, they were a dog. I sighed and followed the Mexican mutt with River gripping the leash.

Luna was fast; she sniffed, barked, and started running. We passed through the tall hedges of the maze with no end in sight. We heard insects, saw butterflies and hummingbirds, and smelled fruit. An abundance of fruit enticing us to take one, but unfortunately, we couldn't eat or drink anything from the garden. It was a test of will just to stand here. My stomach ached as the sweet smell of the fruit filled the air and the water I heard in the distance was soothing. I moaned as I sat on a rock near a spring that ran under the hedges. It wasn't the first stream we'd seen, there were multiple streams throughout reminding me of veins in our bodies; it seemed to connect everything—the lifeblood of the garden.

"Please, can we sit and rest for a bit?"

"We don't have time to waste," River said, but stopped to wait for me, anyway.

"I only need five minutes." I drank the cool water, quenching my thirst. "You sure you don't want any?" I offered the flask to River. He drank a sip, cupped water in his hand for Luna to drink, and handed it back to me. I stuffed it in the backpack and stood, feeling slightly better.

A bell chimed twenty-three times in the distance. We had twenty-three hours left in which to retrieve the object. When Victor had told us what object we had to recover, I laughed.

"I'm dead serious," he'd said with a straight face.

"*The* half-eaten apple?"

He had nodded and continued to explain our role within the garden.

I couldn't believe we had to retrieve Eve's apple. It was unbelievable. I'd thought they made the story up to keep men in line—a book filled with stories scaring the living crap out of anyone who *sinned*. It was mostly real. I would have to read my old Bible again to refresh my memory.

"Let's go." River walked in the direction Luna had taken him.

We passed a cherry blossom tree with a birdhouse stuck in its trunk. Someone must've placed the house there while the tree was still young and the tree grew around it, holding onto the birdhouse forever. A bird sat inside with bright orange and white feathers. Luna stopped at a fork in the path and went right, barked, turned around and went the other way. When she reached another fork, her barking continued and again she went right, then turned around to go in the opposite direction. Her barking seized, she stopped, glanced up at River with sad doggie eyes and whined.

"Go, Luna."

Luna didn't budge. She sat and stared up at him with big brown eyes and continued her whining.

"Are we lost?" I walked farther ahead and saw the same cherry blossom tree with the same birdhouse sticking out of the trunk with the orange and white bird inside. I walked back to River and Luna and her whining had stopped. "We just went around in a circle. That's the same blossom tree." I pointed.

"What?" River approached but stopped when the leash pulled on his arm. He handed the leash to me and walked ahead to see for himself. "Crap, now what, Luna? You got us lost, old girl."

Squawking overhead let me know the crows were nearby. I glanced around looking for them, saw four sitting on the cherry blossom tree with one flying a short distance to the right of it. Taking a chance, I followed the one. "Let's try this way."

The crow either sat or flew near the path we had to take and squawked at us if we were lagging. We followed it through the maze, making great strides in a short amount of time. We didn't have to turn around or retrace our steps since *my* birds were helping us.

We finally reached a waterfall that had iced; the magnificent cerulean blue and white of the frozen water was mesmerizing. I exhaled and saw my breath before my face. I untied my coat from my waist and pulled it on, River did the same. Snow covered the hedges, reminding me of Christmas.

My crow screeched, flapped its wings and sat on a hedge near us. The bells chimed again. We had twenty-two hours left. I stared at the crow and passed it, stopping when I reached three paths. I glanced up at the crow. "Well, which way should we go?"

The crow squawked and flew away.

"Bad crow!" I yelled. "Now what?"

"Are you up to helping again, Luna?"

Luna barked and stopped beside me.

The sun barely touched this side of the maze, leaving the three paths in dark shadows. An uneasiness settled in my bones as I stared out at each of them. They were identical; scary, dark, and covered. If we got lost, there was no way to ask my birds for help.

"I don't want to split up, but maybe we must—"

"Absolutely not. Victor will kill me if I let you out of my sights. How about we take the middle one?"

"Fine with me."

Luna preferred this path anyway. She wagged her tail, tongue hanging out of her mouth as she panted.

We traversed the middle path and for a moment I didn't think it would go in any other direction but straight, but it veered to the right, dipped down and continued downward. The height of the hedges towered higher as our path descended lower. The air was harder to breathe. It was colder. The path had thick layers of hard snow as it crunched beneath our feet. I couldn't smell anything as my face chilled and cheeks burned. River's teeth chattered. Even poor Luna was shivering.

"I don't th-th-think this is the r-r-ight path." I stuttered, hugging myself for warmth. My jacket was thick, but not thick enough as the crisp wind seeped in and stung my flesh.

"What's th-that?" River pointed at a dim light up ahead.

I squinted at the light in the distance but was too cold to shrug. River wrapped an arm around my shoulders.

"H-hold on to me f-for w-warmth." He squeezed my shoulder.

I hesitated at first. I'd never *hung* onto any guy before; let alone someone I hardly knew. But it was freezing, and we were the only two people around. I let go of myself and wrapped my arms around River. I felt his muscles move beneath his clothing as he walked, and my cheeks heated. His honed body would look great in a swimming costume. I felt awkward, but it was a necessity, and nothing else. Even though I'd hugged men before, they were more like family. Whereas River was a stranger. My heart fluttered in my ribcage just thinking about him; he was good looking and sweet, but it still felt weird. River brought me in closer to his body, squashing me against his side, and I could smell him —the softener on his clothing, his fresh cologne, and him. I squeezed my eyes shut with the hopes we found warmth soon, and before he saw how embarrassed I was.

At first, River was cold to the touch, but then I warmed. It wasn't a lot warmer, but it was better than hugging myself. We clung to each other and traipsed the path.

Poor Luna continued to tremble, then she barked and didn't stop. Something had rattled her. Her barking became erratic, and she ran ahead, pulling the leash out of River's hand.

"Wait!" River yelled but didn't dash after her. If he did, we would lose each other's heat.

Her barking continued as if she was trying to tell us something, egging us on.

"We need to walk faster."

"Why?" I tried to look over my shoulder, but I was too cold to move my head.

"Quicker."

We quickened our steps. The dim light brightened the closer we came to it. Finally, warmth kissed our faces, and I felt my cheeks thaw and sting. Luna bounced near the source of the light—lamps on the hedge. Against one side stood a stack of firewood with a fire pit. River stacked firewood and lit it, warming us quickly. Where the heat touched, snow melted, revealing greenery.

I had to admit it was strange having a fire pit here, but it felt like a prize for making it this far and staying alive. But then a strange sensation washed over me. I didn't know if it was the warmth at my front or the cold at my back or a combination of the two, but something felt off. And River felt it too. We turned to see if anything was behind us. The path we'd travelled through had iced over. We hadn't let go of each other yet, and I squeezed his side. The ice advanced, moving over the hedges, freezing everything in its way. I pushed River closer to the fire pit until we stood right beside it without burning.

He gasped when the ice tendrils reached for our feet. Frozen fingers neared our boots. One touch and I was sure we would become icicles. We shuffled backward out of its reach.

"What the hell?" River mumbled.

"It's alive! Whatever that was, if we were any slower, we would've frozen to death."

"Good girl." River scratched behind Luna's ear and picked up the leash. She barked again and continued up the path, wagging her tail happily.

"I guess we lit the fire in time."

"Yep." River jerked his chin in Luna's direction.

This maze was alive. Nature could either cure or be cruel, and I suspected this corner of the maze to be ruthless. Whether the moving ice would've approached if we had gone down one of the other paths, we'd never know.

But it relieved me that we were quick enough to get out of its grasp.

Chapter Twenty-Nine

Léon had reserved the front row for his VIP guests, including myself, Sebastian and Désiré. There were some from his kiss who had joined us, and I sat beside Jean-René because neither Sebastian nor Désiré wanted to. These last few years I'd made a conscious decision to be nice to Jean-René, and so had he. He hadn't been snippy or insulting while I treated him with respect. If Jean-René was happy, Léon was happy, and vice versa. They'd whisper like a couple of schoolgirls at a boarding school when I wasn't around. They'd been friends for centuries; I didn't want to come between them.

On the other side of Jean-René sat Alex, then Charlotte. She used to be Léon's lover until I came along and ruined her chances at a permanent place beside him. She now dated Ian. Esther had moved out shortly after I moved in, I guessed she couldn't tolerate me at all and would rather take her chances with the Master Vampire of New Orleans than to stay anywhere near me. I didn't care either way—she'd tried to hurt me with Ian's help, but it was only Ian who'd begged for forgiveness.

On stage was Salvador and his human partner. They were the star performers for the evening. I still thought it strange that Salvador and his two sons looked like they could be brothers instead of father and sons. I wondered if Sebastian and Léon felt uncomfortable seeing their father in such sexual positions, and on stage.

Salvador held the jute rope carefully in his hands as he neared his partner. He was forever elegant as he approached her like a predator. She seemed elated by his demeanor with a smile across her face. He grabbed the jute rope and bound his partner; she gasped in surprise when he tightened it. His delicate fingers caressed her breast and her mouth parted in illicit pleasure. He fastened the jute around her breasts and made a beautifully intricate knot against her umber skin. Once bound, he kissed her with a tremendous fervor that made most of the audience members shift in their seats. I grabbed Sebastian's hand in anticipation.

"Don't you feel awkward seeing your father do this?" I whispered near Sebastian's ear.

He turned to face me with a sly smile. "No, not at all. We have shared partners before."

My eyes bugged at that confession and smiled sheepishly. "Oh." I felt my cheeks heat.

Sebastian moved closer so I could feel his warm breath against the nape of my neck. He nibbled my earlobe then said. "But I would never share you with anyone—" he seemed to have forgotten about his brother and added quickly. "At the same time that is." And kissed my temple before squeezing my hand.

I rested my head on his shoulder and continued to watch in awe.

Salvador threaded the jute through a metal ring and hoisted her up. Her expression reflected utter peace as she swung gently in the air. Salvador raised his palms and the light show accompanied by soothing music was astounding.

Everyone clapped, but somewhere in the back a slow, forceful clap made everyone stop and turn toward the insulting audience member.

A man in the back row continued clapping slowly; clap—two seconds passed—another clap.

Léon stood from his seat and approached the man. He said something to him I couldn't hear.

"Fine!" the man yelled, jumped off his chair and stomped toward the exit. He was a little person with fiery red curly hair and a bushy mustache to match.

Léon called a server over and asked her to clean the seat—from my view the rude man had spilled liquid.

"Apologies for the disturbance," Léon said in that sweet seductive tone. "Please continue."

Salvador finished the show, and it was spectacular. He carried his partner to the back and joined us a few minutes later.

Once the guests were out and in search of other, more intimate, entertainment, I asked Léon if he knew the man who'd disrupted the show.

"He's one of our newest members. I had Eden search for his details and he's just a miserable vampire. I suspect he and Salvador crossed paths once, and now he's back to show him his displeasure. Either way, we've revoked his membership. We don't allow such crass behavior."

"Are you ready to go?" Sebastian wrapped his arms around me.

"Yeah, I'm feeling tired."

Sebastian greeted Salvador.

Ralph stayed to spend time with Eden.

Désiré wasn't ready to leave either as she'd found herself a tall, dark vampire to keep her company.

While Sebastian and I went home.

My head just touched the pillow when my cellphone vibrated on the bedside table.

"Don't answer it." Sebastian pulled me closer to his body as I reached for the phone. Unfortunately, he was quicker than I and I couldn't pick it up in time. Then it chimed, letting me know the caller had left a voice message.

"I have to answer it."

"Do you remember what Désiré said?"

"Yes, but I'm not going anywhere. I'm just going to listen."

Sebastian let go. I crawled to the end of our bed and listened to the voice message. "That was Georgina. Another person has gone missing, but still no sign of the scientist or Benjamin." I explained the rest of the detail. "She just wanted to let me know and asked us to come in tomorrow to review the evidence they've collected and processed from the victims of the other two scenes. Ralph sent a text; he'll fetch me after ten."

"Good, that's tomorrow's problem. Right now, we're cuddling."

Chapter Thirty

SCOUT

Luna was such a goofball, but I was grateful River had brought her with. And I was glad he was joining me on this little adventure, even though the chance of us getting hurt was high. If Mom found out what I was doing, she'd release her anger on Victor, and I didn't want to be around when that happened.

We trailed behind Luna and the snow and frozen hedges became less and less the farther we traversed.

We arrived at a drinking well we couldn't drink from it, but we had our own refreshments.

"I think it's safe to rest here for a few minutes." River let go of me and sat down.

It was comfortable walking right beside him, and I shivered from the heat loss. If I was on my own, I doubted I would've made it through the winter tunnel. I would've succumbed to that ice that seemed to kill everything in its path.

I joined him on the soft grass with Luna between us. It

felt like we were at a park having a picnic instead of a maze that could kill. I gave him the backpack with our refreshments; he handed me a bottle of water and a sandwich. We ate in comfortable silence. It was comforting to know we had made it this far, but neither of us wanted to discuss what had just happened—which I didn't mind. I watched River give some of his food to Luna and cupped water in his hand for her to drink. What she didn't drink, he threw in the flower bed near the hedge and scratched her stomach. She lay on her back, her tongue out of her mouth, and made that sound dogs made when their human owner showed affection. I smiled at their interaction.

I glanced up at the crows, *my crows*, perched on the hedge near us. If they were my spirit animal, would I have a relationship similar to what River had with Luna? I shook my head, doubtful. I couldn't see myself scratching their feathered bellies or feeding them parts of my sandwich, but I threw crumbs to one side. At first they glared down at me. Shortly thereafter, they flew down and ate the crumbs. I ensured there was enough for all. I didn't know if bread was good for them since they were carnivores, but they seemed to enjoy it.

The bells chimed, letting us know we had twenty-one hours left. We finished our meal and stretched our legs. My body ached all over. Even though Victor had said I didn't need to sleep, I wanted to lie down. Everything hurt from walking, running, and fighting. The last time I felt like this was when I trained with Ralph and never again. I couldn't move properly for a day because it was so strenuous.

My crows followed us and sat on the hedge Luna directed us to. When we approached another fork in the path, the crows sat on the hedge to the left, and Luna followed. At another fork in the path, the crows perched on the hedges to the right and Luna followed their direction.

I realized we could feel and see the sun in this part of the maze; they filled it with flowers, bees, and hummingbirds. The hedges were greener, the grass taller, and the streams flowed faster under the hedges.

"I prefer this season," I said as we neared another drinking fountain filled with fish. It felt like summer in this part of the maze; the sun was upon us and the garden came alive with fauna and flora. River seemed to like it too as he lifted his face toward the sun, reminding me of a sunflower.

Unfortunately, I'd spoken too soon.

The ground vibrated. The leaves shook. Hissing sounded. Luna barked, and my crows squawked, flapping their wings vigorously in the air above our heads. A loud cry sounded, shaking me to the core.

"What's that?"

"I don't know, but I don't want to hang around for it. Run!"

River ran with Luna while I followed closely behind. He held out his hand for me to grab, which I did. I glanced over my shoulder as the hedge opened its leafy mouth, revealing a garden snake; a snake made of branches, leaves and flowers. Its yellow eyes swirled around like liquid gold and held a predatory gleam. Small blue and purple flowers bloomed across its long body as it lifted its hooded head and rattled its tail. The garden snake slithered along the path behind us and hissed, its forked pink tongue smelling us. It was quick, and it was getting closer.

"Run faster!" River yelled.

River scanned our surroundings and pulled on my hand. He mis-stepped and crashed to the ground, taking me with him. We climbed back onto our feet as my crows continued screeching. They sat near the correct path we were to take, with Luna running ahead of us. Another wave of shaking ground knocked us to our hands and knees. River fell hard against rocks near the hedge and hurt his knee while I tried to pull him by his hand.

"Go!" He pushed me away.

"No! Not without you, now get up." I grabbed his hand again, yanked him to his feet and wrapped my arm around his waist, half carrying him. River had hurt his ankle and hobbled the rest of the way. Luna barked. Our strides slowed.

The monster raged behind us. My crows screeched and flew toward the snake and violently flapped their wings near its face, forcing it to stop. The snake hissed as my crows squawked and nipped at its leafy face and body. The snake had no way to bat them away as they slowed it down.

Ear-piercing cries sounded as the crows continued biting the garden snake. I saw bits of branches, leaves, and flowers fly around as they continued their savage attack. I was grateful for their help in slowing the creature down, but we weren't safe, not yet. The snake could animate itself again and come after us. What concerned me the most, it could have a deadly venom and if it bit us, we had no anti-venom to counteract the poison.

Luna had brought us to a path deep within the maze; we no longer heard the snakes' cries, but I kept turning back to see if it was approaching.

"I think your crows saved our lives."

I gasped for air, my lungs burned from the run and nodded. "They did, didn't they?" I said with pride and sucked in a deep breath. "Are you okay?"

"Yeah, I'll be fine." I helped River sit to tend to his ankle. "Where are we?"

"I don't know." I glanced around. It was a large area with four more paths to choose from. At the mouth of the first path, I heard sounds and songs. As I passed the second path, the sounds clashed with the path on either side of it. I couldn't make out what the sounds were, so I entered the first path to listen closely; it was a soft whistle of a tune I'd never heard before. Inside the next path was a delicate lullaby. The third path had a sharp melody from a harp. While the last path had nothing; an emptiness so great it hurt my ears to stand there. It was a sound I couldn't describe, yet painful to hear. If we avoided that path, I would be happy. Nobody in their right mind should enter that path; it felt like a warning.

I walked back to River. "There are four musical paths, and we need to choose one." I glanced up when my crows returned from their fight with the snake. None of them were bleeding, but it ruffled their feathers. I smiled my appreciation. But when they sat on the hedge near the deadly silent path, I shuddered and shook my head—I did not want to go down that one. That was the only path I didn't want to use, yet my crows seemed adamant.

"How are you feeling?" I asked River as I neared him. Perhaps if I took my time before going anywhere, my crows would change their minds and pick a different path.

"It will be okay." He pulled a medical aid kit from thin air and bandaged his swollen ankle.

The ground vibrated again. I glanced up, expecting the snake to return, but the sky was clear. A shadow appeared from the side. I turned in that direction and met a hedge closing in front of me—separating River and me. It happened so quickly I didn't have time to react and cross the threshold to be on River's side.

"Scout!" River yelled.

I watched everything unfold in slow motion, and I couldn't move fast enough. River stood as Luna ran to me. Then the tall hedge came between us, blocking my path. I pushed my arm through the hedge to reach him, meeting thorns instead. I pulled my arm out with three cuts on my forearm. Wincing at the pain, I wiped the blood away with my shirt. There was green residue left on the wounds that I couldn't wipe off.

"Are you okay?" River yelled.

"I cut myself on the thorns. There's blood and a green substance on the wound."

"Use this." He did something on the other side, then an object fell behind me.

I picked up the first aid kit and cleaned my wound. "Thanks," I said as I removed a solution and gauze. I winced at the sting but pushed through the pain. The welts raised red and painful. "Now what?"

"We can't climb over and it's too thick to climb through it. And if there are thorns, it would make our climb more difficult. We have to continue on our own paths."

"I don't want to go on my own."

"You have to. Besides, your crows will help you. I'll find another way to reach you."

"But—" My chin trembled. The nothingness sounded behind me and I turned in its direction. It seemed to pulse with each of my breaths.

"You can do this, Scout. This was something you meant to do by yourself, anyway. Don't worry about us, we will see you soon."

"Will you be able to get out of here?" My heart sank to my toes. "What if you can't get out?" *What if I couldn't get out?*

"It's a maze, there is more than one way to the center."

"I hope so," I said, and knew I didn't sound convincing. I stared at the path the crows had suggested, winced at the throbbing wound, and finished wrapping a bandage over my forearm. "Be safe," I yelled, picked up the bag and stood.

"And here, this is for later." River threw over another bag filled with food and drink.

"Thanks." I picked it up, placed the first aid kit inside and slung it over my shoulder. "See you soon."

I took one slow step after another toward the path and the crows. I stood just outside and listened again. *Nothing*. But that nothingness had a sound, and it felt like a loud boom inside my ear drum.

"I hope you are right," I mumbled to the crows. They squawked and flew away.

I exhaled a sharp breath and entered the path. The nothingness stretched on. The soundless tone vibrated within my chest. I clutched my clothing near my heart—it beat so fast and so steady. My breath hitched in my throat. I glanced at the hedge that had closed in on me and it was still there, with River on the other side. I turned back to face the new path and entered with a heavy heart.

The winding path went on forever. Nothing happened. It was just straight, long, and boring. I was grateful, but wondered whether I was going nowhere... slowly.

During the time I'd been by myself, the bells had chimed twice, even though it hadn't felt like I was on it that long. The path veered left, then right. I was sure it went in a circle only to come back onto a straight path again. I didn't know which direction I was going in. There were no shadows, no darkness, just light on a path to guide my way; one long nothingness.

I was alone, and I hated it. Being an only child was

lonely, and now the maze had separated me from my partner, and I missed him. River had kept me company, and we helped each other if we needed to.

If I ran into trouble now, I'd have to do it on my own.

I didn't like that very much.

Chapter Thirty-One

Before we met Georgina at the lab, we drove past the doctor's house and headed for the gorgon shop that sold gold dust. Apparently, it was a thing to use gold dust on everything; food, cakes, face and body creams, makeup—anything and everything you could think of—they used gold dust. I didn't know the monetary value of *genuine* gold, but it was still pretty pricey. And based on Jedidiah's last message, their shop had been closed all week.

Jedediah stood on the sidewalk with one foot tapping, and his arms crossed. "I thought you'd never show," he mumbled as he opened the front door.

"Sorry." I followed him inside.

Jedediah stopped in the entrance and gasped. Ralph and I almost walked into him. Someone had thoroughly trashed the place. It looked like the Tasmanian devil had fought with the dust devil. They smashed the counter glass. Gold dust covered the floor. The golden frames cracked and thrown to the ground, and a stale stench wafted in the air from lack of ventilation. The windows remained closed and the air conditioner off.

Jedediah ran inside.

"I won't bother asking what's missing."

"Our golden fountain is missing," Jedediah yelled from a room. He stuck his head out and added. "We use it to make the dust, but whoever took it must have our gorgon quartz as well."

"Do you know who'd do this?"

He shook his head as he stared at us with misty eyes. "I do not know who did this." He pulled out his phone and dialed someone's number and entered the small room again.

"I feel bad for him, I really do, but now we know where the gold dust comes from." Ralph pointed at the dust on the floor.

"Mitch is back from vacation. Take a sample for him to test against the residue found on our victims."

Ralph scooped some gold dust off the floor and into a Ziplock bag. Some particles floated in the air and I backed away; I didn't want to inhale any of it. I wasn't sure if it could damage the baby, even though others consumed it.

"Jedediah, we're going to go," I yelled as I approached the hallway to the small room. He was sitting at his desk, that was lying on its side. They had destroyed the manager's office too; files strewn on the floor; the desk lay on the opposite side with coffee messed everywhere.

"You sure you didn't piss off someone?"

Jedediah wiped away tears. "That was Declan. He asked the others, and they'd seen a stranger rummaging near our homes earlier this week. I'd been so busy in the city I'd forgotten to call home. One youngling saw the back of a man leaving and from her description he wore a white coat with light color hair. I can't understand it," he cried. "Why?" He buried his face in his hands and wept.

"Is Declan coming over?" I asked. I didn't want to leave Jedediah alone. What had happened to them was awful and would most likely affect their livelihood.

"Yeah, he'll be here in twenty." Jedediah sounded defeated, which I understood. They'd lost so much, and it felt hopeless.

We stayed with Jedediah until Declan arrived. The cousins embraced and cried over the loss of income they would face. From what Jedediah had told us while we waited, the money earned from this shop was enough to feed their entire village. They all worked together to ensure it continued running while others created the gorgon quartz. They had to find a way to make up for the loss.

I didn't know how they made it, but we didn't have time to watch.

"What do you think?" I asked Devan. "You've been extremely quiet this morning, more so than usual."

He blinked slowly and shuddered. "I don't like the monster that was inside there. I'm not talking about the gorgons; this is something else." He smacked his lips together as if tasting something. "It leaves a sour taste in my mouth."

I didn't like the sound of that, but at least we had confirmation that the mist vampire was here, at least we were on the right path. Now all we had to do was figure out why he needed gold dust.

"We have to help them," I said to Ralph as he parked in our reserved spot at the precinct.

"We have to find the doctor. Justice will ease their minds. I think they will be fine." He locked the car. "They seem like they'd come together and make it work."

"I hope so," I said as we entered the building.

We found Georgina in our shared office. She was typing on her keyboard with a pencil stuck behind her ear and three cups of half empty coffee scattered on her desk. I wondered if she had stayed overnight after the discovery of another missing person. The office was dim, but her corner had a well-lit lamp.

"You're just in time." She downed the coffee from the closest cup, removed the pencil from behind her ear and stood. "Mitch is waiting for us."

We traversed the hallway, exited out the back door, crossed the courtyard and entered the back of the building where the refurbished lab accommodated the latest technology to help fight crime.

The building was bright compared to the precinct. The fluorescent lights reflected off the white walls and stainless-steel counters, momentarily blinding me. Even Ralph blinked rapidly to adapt to our surroundings.

Georgina entered the room first, where a lab technician hunched over the counter. Mitch peered through the lenses of the microscope and made notes. The gills on the side of his neck opened and closed as he breathed. Some thought Mitch was the link between anthropoid and creature; he breathed underwater and on land. He looked like a man, walked like a man, and spoke like one; for all intents and purposes, he was a man. A bald man with no hair or a tan, but he was still a man. I didn't know what was between his legs, and I would never ask. He had a girlfriend though; and again, I wouldn't ask.

They'd found Mitch washed ashore on a remote island

near the Bahamas and the Bermuda Triangle. Some speculated he came from a crater within the seabed and had swum his way to the surface. He remembered little of his life before being *discovered* and didn't wish to pursue it. He'd said if it was a place he was trying to get away from, it was better left alone. He was making fresh memories, and that's all that counted.

"Hey, you made it," he said and smiled. His large lips curled at the ends, brightening his pale-gray face. He grabbed the glass of brown water beside him and drank it down.

"Did you watch the game last week?" Ralph asked. "The Shift Crusaders whipped your Were-Packs."

"That's only because they benched my favorite player. If he was playing, he would've wiped your favorite player's ass all over the scoreboard," Mitch laughed; it sounded like music you heard under water. His Adam's apple bobbed up and down as he laughed, and his gills flapped open and closed. Some drops of the brown water he'd drunk splashed to the floor. I doubted it tainted the evidence, as I knew he was careful. As I was about to question him about it, a little machine appeared, cleaned the mess and went back to its hiding spot in the wall.

Mitch wiped his mouth with a handkerchief and handed us documents. "Elouise gave me what she'd found before returning to process human evidence. The blood samples you found in the lab match the sample you gave us from the cave," he said to me. "Either it's the same dead vampire in the cave, or it infected a human with his blood and ultimately *becoming* him. Like a clone. I found similar DNA markings and characteristics that match one-hundred percent."

"At least it confirms it's him, or it's turned a human into

him. I'm just relieved it isn't another monster we need to be aware of."

"Exactly." Mitch glanced at his notes and then at Georgina. "The only fingerprints found at the lab belonged to the doctor and his assistant. It's safe to say whatever happened in there was caused by one or both of them. The footprints out back were too small to be theirs. I'm thinking there's a third party, but they touched nothing. Or they cleaned after themselves. I compared the indent of the small shoe print and am confident when I say the other person may be a child or a little person. The red strand of hair discovered on the couch doesn't match Benjamin's and since the doctor has gray hair, we can rule him out as well. The third person is short with red hair and has small feet." He set the paperwork down and picked up another pile of paper.

I interrupted him before he continued.

"Mitch, did you do all these yourself?"

He smiled mischievously and nodded. "Elouise only started on the blood work, but I finished it. The equipment does most of the legwork for us. I only need to ensure it's correct and I compare. I run everything twice. If anything seems off, I run it a third time. Governor Thomas has ensured we have the best and we use it to its full capacity." He flipped through the next pile. "Now for the victims, if we can even call them that. We processed their remains in the chamber. That machine makes the biggest difference. You stick the body in there and the machine does the full autopsy for us. We can do an X-ray, MRI, and a scan simultaneously, and it comes back with the what and how. They bled the first victim, then skinned and chopped him up into a mangled mess. His organs were intact, but they removed his heart. They found the second victim similarly; skinned and chopped. Her heart remained in its bone cage, but they removed her spleen, kidney and liver."

"Gross." Georgina scrunched her face in disgust. "I love how you help us, but you always go into the gory details."

"You need to hear it, darlin'," he drawled, handing her all the reports.

"I will admit, I love how you can get things done so quickly."

"Thanks, I love my job." He faced the microscope and added another specimen slide.

"Oh, before we go can you see if this is the same gold dust taken off our victims." Ralph handed him the sample.

"That's right, the gold dust. I forgot about that." He took the sample and laid it down. "I can tell you now it's gorgon gold."

"How do you know?" I asked.

"I read up on it yesterday. We have access to an online library with samples from around the world. I will however check this one to confirm which gorgon made it. They have similarities, but each flake is unique per gorgon."

"Wow, I did not know that."

Mitch smiled again and his entire face lit up. The ends of his sharp pointy teeth stuck out when he did so, and his gills flapped open and closed. He clapped his webbed fingers and went back to the microscope.

We entered our office again, but Devan stayed just outside.

I turned to him and shrugged. "What's up?"

He shook his head. "I don't know if I'm having an off day or it's this case."

Underworld Legacy

Ralph and I approached him but kept our distance. "What do you mean?"

"That's just it, I don't know. It could be the original mist vampire I'm channeling, or it's the new one, or it's the monster and the gold dust. But... I don't know." He took a step farther out into the hallway. "I'm going home. I may just need some time out."

"Okay, let us know if you need anything," Ralph said with concern.

"He looks a little frazzled today, doesn't he?" I said after Devan had left. "He's always jittery but today more so."

"I'll check in on him later today."

We turned when Georgina cleared her throat. "Sorry to interrupt, but they found the third body on the roof of an apartment building." She read her notes and sighed. "It's even in the same vicinity where we found the second body."

"And you're sure there's no connection between any of them?"

She shook her head, "No, there's nothing." She handed Ralph a folder because he was closest to her. "This is what we have."

Ralph handed me the folder.

"I'll look while you drive us." I messaged Sebastian about our plans later before I got stuck in the information.

Chapter Thirty-Two

SCOUT

When the bells chimed a third time, it was too much. I plonked down on the grass and cried into my hands. Removing the bag River had given me from my shoulder, I dug inside, pulling out a packet of chips, a chocolate, and a sandwich. I ate slowly, stretching out the time, and hoped my situation would change. I'd been on this godforsaken path for three hours already, and it didn't feel like it was going anywhere. The nothingness was a pain, but at least the ear-piercing sound had stopped unless I was used to the constant buzzing of nothing.

One of my crows flew back and stood on the grass near me. Slowly it stalked toward me, as if ensuring I was okay with its approach. Its dark orbs staring into my soul. It was unnerving, and I wanted to shoo it away, but I didn't. I stopped eating and gave it my attention.

"Hey there. Are you finally introducing yourself?" I felt stupid for speaking to a crow. If I was at school, my friends would've thought I'd lost my mind. Maybe I had. This maze had shown me a few things that wouldn't have happened in the real world. Perhaps I was in a hospital, strapped to a bed and heavily sedated. I chortled at my silly thoughts.

The bird jumped up and landed on my knee. I gasped and leaned backward, not wanting to disturb it at the same time.

'You know you shouldn't make jokes like that. People might take you seriously.'

I glanced left and right. "Did you just speak to me?"

Squawk. *'Yes.'*

I blinked wide eyes at the bird. A strange, strangled laugh came from the back of my throat as I gazed at the bird that had *spoken* to me. Still not believing what I'd heard. I glanced around again. "How can I understand you?"

'We don't have all day, Scout. Stop your pity party, finish your meal, and continue on your path. You're almost there. We can get to know one another later, but right now you must finish. You're running out of time.'

"Okay." I nodded absentmindedly at the bird. He made sense. I had to get going. I needed to find the center, find River, then get out. Sitting and moaning wasn't helping my case. At least I had birds to help me. They were talking to me, but they were *my* birds. Maybe I was losing my mind, and this was a way to cope with everything.

'I'm really speaking to you, Scout. You aren't losing your mind.'

"Okay, thanks for clearing that up. Can you read my mind?" I yelled, sounding irritated.

Squawk.

"Fine, I get it."

I finished my sandwich, spying the bird sitting on my knee. Its black eyes silently judging me. "Do you have a name?" I asked with a mouthful of food.

'You can call me Jake. The others are my brothers and sisters.'

"Why did you choose me?"

'It was fate. Now get moving, it's coming.' The bird flew off my knee toward the hedge, egging me on from there.

I didn't know what he meant by *'it's coming'*, but it made me determined to finish.

"Fine, I'm up." I winced as I collected everything off the grass and slung the bag over my shoulder. My forearm hurt but I would redress it when I found the center.

"Let's go."

I literally took ten steps and entered a large area of the maze. "Is this the center?"

'Yes.'

"Oh, thank goodness." I was so close to the end I could've kicked myself. Instead of pushing through, I sat, sulked, and mumbled. Meanwhile, I was already here.

I crossed the garden and headed toward the center where the statue of an angel stood. She was otherworldly. Her expression was peaceful and serene. Her hands pressed together prayer-like with the item I needed to retrieve wedged between her hands. The object was the half-eaten apple Seth had stolen from Victor. The chewed apple was red and fresh—as if they picked it only moments ago instead of many, many years. It had a golden shine to it, which I attributed to the fact that the gold had most likely kept the apple *fresh*.

I surveyed the sizeable garden for anything untoward. There were rose bushes, daisy's, and vines creeping up the hedges surrounding the area.

"Is there anything I need to look for?" I asked Jake, who hopped along the edge of a water fountain.

'Don't know.'

"Thanks for nothing, bird," I mumbled and closed the distance with the angel.

I reached for the apple, but before touching it, I glanced around. My crows sat nearby, all those beady black eyes on me. I would've felt self-conscious, but I was already used to having them around. A couple of butterflies fluttered near a rose. Water flowed out the top of the water fountain; the sounds were soothing, hypnotic. The sun shone above me. If I knew one thing, nothing was as it seemed; *something* lurked nearby, ready to kill me. Not knowing what that something was, but I had to face it alone, well almost. Jake chirped, reminding me he was still here.

The calm before the storm...

What creature would I face once I removed the apple?

I had to do it and couldn't wait for River because I didn't know if he would even get here. I hoped he was all right.

Sucking in my breath, I removed the apple. I braced myself for what came next... nothing. Slowly, I opened an eye, then the other. I grinned and pocketed the apple in the backpack.

"Now what—"

They cut my question short. My crows flew away. The water fountain stopped flowing. The butterflies dropped dead. Grey clouds covered the sun, bathing me in sinister shadows. The hedges neared; their form shifted and twisted into leafy limbs. An arm made of branches and covered in leaves joined the upper *body* of another hedge. Another leafy arm connected to the other side, the branches twisted and connected like veins. The legs of the garden beast were next as they helped it stand frightfully taller. And last, on its shoulders, balanced the head of the angel. Its body rippled as the branching veins and leafy muscles connected to soil *tissue* to form a giant garden creature.

I stood with my jaw slackened and my body frozen. There was no way I could defeat *it*—whatever it was.

It roared, fisting its chest with its large claw-like hands. It reminded me of King Kong. Slowly, I stepped back until I reached the outer edge of the garden. Not wanting to make any sudden movements, I scanned the area out of the corner of my eyes. There was only one way out. Unfortunately, it was behind the garden creature. I hoped I was quicker.

The creature roared again, glowered down at me with its soulless eyes and licked its leafy lips.

"You look tasty." It spoke. Its voice was low and frightening, making my arms pebble.

"You don't want to eat me. I'm all skin and bone."

"Even better." It stomped toward me. It was so large it looked like it walked in slow motion, yet scary because I was its destination.

I had to get out and the only way out was behind it. Digging my shoes into the dirt, I kicked away and headed straight for it. I screamed, raised my fist, but instead of hitting it, I slid between its legs, narrowly missing its fist as it smashed its hands into the soil. The ground rippled beneath me. Climbing to my feet, I tasted freedom but stumbled over a root sticking out of the ground. I managed to stay on wobbly legs instead of crashing face first into the dirt and ran as fast as I could.

Behind me I heard the creature growl in frustration, then I felt its footsteps. It shoved hedges out of its way and flung trees in my direction, missing my head. My crows flew overhead, directing me where to go. I sprinted until my lungs burned and my legs ached. But I wouldn't give up; I was so close to getting out I couldn't allow this creature to win because I got tired. The creature snarled and snapped its jaw behind me. Up ahead, I saw a hole in the ground.

"I can't make that!" I yelled at my birds. Even from where I ran, I could see the gaping pit in the ground. I was angry my birds had brought me on this path with no way of jumping over it.

'Jump, we will help you.'

"I can't!" I cried in disappointment.

'Trust me,' Jake whispered in my head.

In my heart I could trust this crow, but it was my head that thought otherwise. I was afraid of not making it. I was afraid of falling—of failing. My father would lose his powers and become *human*, but the thought of becoming a part of this garden made me a little ill. What creature would I turn into? If I stayed, I would never see my mother again, or get to know my brother. They were my only family. I shoved the negative thoughts down and focused on the large hole closing in on me, and my crows.

'Now!'

"I'm trusting you, Jake. Don't let me fall," I screamed as I neared the pit. I sped up as much as I could, pushed my toes into the ground and leapt into the air. My five crows were by my side, like Jake had said. Their sharp claws grabbed my arms and shoulders, and I felt the pull of their power course through me as I soared through the air with them. Glancing down, I saw the deep pit below with a river of lava, and I squeezed my eyes shut. I felt the heat beat against my body as I flew over and opened my eyes in time to see the ground on the other side, not believing I'd *flown*.

'With our help!' Jake squawked near my ear, reminding me it was them who'd helped me.

I laughed nervously, glanced over my shoulder as the

creature leaped into the air. It was going to make it. When it landed on this side, it would kill me. A foot touched the edge, the ground gave way, and it started sinking into the pit of lava. It was too slow to reach out with its other foot as it leaned forward with outstretched arms. I crawled on my hands and knees to get out of its grasp. It grabbed my ankle; branchy digits curling around my leg. I turned around and kicked at its wooden tendrils. It continued sinking deeper into the pit. It cried. Its branch-arms tried to find a way out of the pit from Hell. The angel head disappeared below, but its hand still held onto me. I pried its branchy digits away from my leg until there was one left, which I broke off. The creature cried in *pain*—if that was possible—before descending into the scorching depths of darkness.

I laughed in celebration as happy tears streaked my face. *I did it! I defeated the garden monster.* My crows squawked with happiness; I think.

Then something hit me on the side of my head, and darkness swallowed me.

Chapter Thirty-Three

I still found it strange working *with* the police instead of running away from them. There were still the odd—much older—officers or detectives who didn't want us around, but with more and more monsters coming out of the woodworks, they needed us. As much as they hated that, they needed us more. And working with and becoming Georgina's friend had been a breath of fresh air.

I read over the notes and reports in the folder she'd given Ralph and couldn't find any connection between these victims.

"I don't know," I said, closing the folder. "There's something we're missing."

"Maybe it's just random. The mist vampire is thirsty and needs blood." He swallowed hard. "And organs, like he's collecting them to either consume or for something else."

"Maybe..." I glanced over the reports again and slapped Ralph on the shoulder. "It's their blood type, Ralph! They are the same."

He smiled at me.

"No, don't do that. You look goofy."

His smile disappeared.

I burst out laughing, and he chuckled.

"It has to be their blood type. It's the only thing that's similar." I flipped through the pages to make sure. The victims shared the same rare blood type; Rhnull. "I've never heard of Rhnull before. Have you?"

"We can confirm once we have this victim's blood type." He jerked his chin at the road.

I nodded.

Ralph slowed the car. When I turned to see where we were, he'd stopped outside an apartment building.

Georgina stood outside speaking with an officer.

Sebastian hadn't read the message I'd sent him thirty minutes ago, and I wondered why he was taking so long. He never took so long to respond. He knew I was a high-risk pregnancy, and something could've happened to me.

Unless…

Unless he was with someone else.

Unless he didn't want to answer me. Maybe he'd changed his mind about our son—about me. What if he didn't love me anymore? He'd found someone younger, prettier, and a were-leopard.

I silently cursed myself for the upsetting thoughts and tried to push them back from where they'd come from. I was thinking up stuff that was stupid. It was crazy talk.

Sebastian loved me, he cared for me and wanted this baby. It must be all in my mind. I expelled the thoughts, but they were still there… lingering.

We followed Georgina through the double glass doors into the apartment building and I had to cover my nose and mouth. A vile stench hovered near the entrance.

"What is that?" Georgina asked another officer.

"It's the body, ma'am." He pointed to the ceiling. He looked gray as he shook his head. "It's on the roof."

"But it smells like it's coming from here."

"It gets worse the closer you get to it." He crinkled his nose.

Georgina stared with wide eyes and pressed the up button for the elevator. While we waited, I glanced at the dirty floor and empty envelopes strewn near the post boxes for each apartment.

The elevator pinged and opened, but we didn't climb inside. Crumpled dirty clothing was in one corner with a naked man lying in the center of the elevator.

"Officer, please can you take care of this." Georgina pointed at the man and kept the elevator doors open with her foot until the officer neared. "Can you take the stairs?" she asked me.

I nodded. "Yep."

I lied. I could not take the stairs. When I reached the second floor, I used the railing as a guide to help me up. I told them to go ahead, I'd catch up; taking one slow step at a time, rubbing my belly with one hand while the other gripped the railing. I didn't know why this pregnancy affected me so badly—it could've been that I was in my forties and once women reached *that* age, their bodies *changed*. Ugh. Although, I'd felt no different until I fell pregnant. But the evidence didn't lie; my body wasn't happy carrying another life, excluding the beasts within. But I'd do everything to push through.

I finally reached the tenth floor after ten minutes and out of breath. I rubbed my aching left hip.

"You're a monster, Blaire. You're supposed to be immune to everything," Ralph smirked.

I harrumphed. "Not funny, Ralph." I pushed him out of the way and the stench made me stop in my tracks. "Oh no, that's awful." I removed my jacket to cover my nose and mouth.

"Yeah, it's pretty bad," Georgina said while an officer gagged and ran past us. She laughed, then sobered when she glanced at the heap of flesh, skin and bones poking out from the mess.

"He looks minced. Or she?"

"Male with dark hair." Georgina pulled on gloves, pinched the scalp between her fingers and lifted it up for us to see. "He has a receding hairline."

"I'll stay over there," I said into my jacket.

"I'll let you know what I find," Ralph said and conversed with Georgina.

I found a couple of chairs farther away and slouched in one of them. At least the air was slightly better here, and I didn't need to use my jacket as a mask.

"Why does he do that? What is the point?" I yelled at them.

Ralph waved me away—silently telling me to shush. I showed him a *sign*—but he had already turned away.

"Fine!" I yelled and folded my arms under my breasts, but that became uncomfortable. The little bean pushed on my bladder and I bolted upright, which only made it worse. Standing as quickly as I could, or I'd go right here. I hurried to the exit and down the stairs. I banged on the first door until the occupant opened.

A girl had opened her door and allowed me to use her bathroom.

When done, I found Ralph and Georgina waiting for me near the stairs, both a little green around the edges.

"Are you finished?"

"The ME is with the body now. We didn't want to stay for the show. He has a large plastic box to scoop the victim in, it's gross. I can't believe he looked like that." Ralph shuddered.

We descended the steps and again I took them one at a time. When I reached the bottom, an officer had placed an air freshener near the entrance. It was a slight improvement. Ralph and Georgina waited outside. He leaned against the side of the building while Georgina smoked her cigarette a short distance away.

"Where's my hundred?" I approached Georgina with my outstretched hand. She tried to flick her cigarette away, but I'd already seen her and sighed. She picked it up off the sidewalk and pinned the filter between her lips while she retrieved money out of her purse and handed me the note.

"I couldn't stop." She puffed on the cancer stick. "It's so hard."

"Well," — I stuffed the note into my bag, — "I don't mind, I get money out of it," I grinned.

"Ralph and I were discussing the case while we waited for you." Georgina said while killing the cigarette, then threw it away. "I asked Mitch to check the victim's blood like you suggested and he will test our latest victims when he gets it," — she pointed at the apartment building, — "to see for similarities. If they are being targeted because of their blood type, we need to reach out to the others and keep them safe. Mitch is working on a list for us along with where they are. I'm going to finish up in there, then go to Mitch. Do you want to meet me there?"

I nodded.

She entered the building while Ralph and I climbed in the car.

Chapter Thirty-Four

SCOUT

I opened my eyes to raging flames when the blackness ate at me again…

A ball of fire fought the angel. The skull attached to a body was alive with angry flames. I suspected I had a concussion and was seeing things. My eyelids were heavy, so I closed my eyes for only a second…

The ground shuddered, waking me. I opened one eye, and the skeleton dressed in men's clothing burned brightly. My head was heavy, and I couldn't focus on him. He neared. I couldn't defend myself. I slept…

I moved; someone had picked me up. The blazing skull stared down at me. Panic-stricken, I glanced at my body, but I wasn't burning. My head hurt from the sudden movement and I whimpered.

"It's okay, Scout. We're almost at the end," the Fire-skull said.

The bells chimed. We had an hour left to get out of the garden, or stuck here forever.

"Who are you?" I managed to say through thick lips and

swallowed hard.

He didn't answer. A dog barked behind me. I glanced over the man's burning shoulder and saw a dog on fire; it looked suspiciously like Luna. My eyes flitted back to the man, and that action sent a shooting pain through the base of my skull. It couldn't be River, could it?

"River?"

He stared down at me, dark orbs and bony jaw licked by fire. His hands raged with flames too, orange, deep blue with yellow and red. It was beautifully scary.

"It's me." His voice was deeper and hair-raising.

"How can this be?" I reached for his face, but he pulled away, not wanting my touch. I winced as I brought my hand back. "What did Victor do to you?"

Luna barked and ran ahead—a ball of bouncing flames happily leading the way. The exit came into view. River quickened his steps. The heat from his body receding as he swallowed the flames consuming him and his human form returned. He crossed the threshold of the garden with a groan, alerting me someone had injured him. He laid me down gently and fell beside me with a grunt.

I stared down at him, not sure what to say or expect. A moment ago, I'd just seen him engulfed in flames, now he was skin and bone—back to being the human I'd only met a couple of days ago. I didn't understand what he was.

"I know what you're thinking," he said into the ground. He laid face down and had somehow known what was swarming inside my head.

I assessed his wounds; a strapped ankle, but there was another wound on his side. Blood pooled beneath him. In a panic, I grabbed the first aid kit out of the backpack. Then I watched in awe how his blood seeped back into his body and he stretched his ankle around. I felt a sudden surge of power during the *procedure* and I shuffled away from him.

"What just happened?" I asked with panic laced in my voice.

"I didn't want to show you *him* unless it was necessary. And to save you I had to change." River sat up on his elbows and considered me, his amber-brown eyes warm and friendly—no longer black and surrounded by flames. "To save my mother's life, I gave mine to your father. I work for him, but in order for me to accomplish what he needs, I become… *that*."

"A raging ball of angry fire?" My brows furrowed, and I stepped farther away from him.

"I can't hurt you if I don't want to, Scout." He sounded hurt. He sat up and moved to sit on the far opposite side of the entrance, and away from me. "And yes, only once I've fulfilled my contract do I get my life back."

"When will that be?"

"To be honest, I don't know; I didn't read the fine print. And I'll stay like this until that happens."

"And that's why you didn't like it when I asked Victor to let you go?" He nodded. "Do you think he will take your mother then, if he cancels your contract?"

"I don't know. I didn't even know I would turn into that thing when I signed. He made it sound like something I would love. He made it sound alluring like those awful vampires out there, but what I have, is nothing like it. I scare everyone away." His voice trailed off and I couldn't help but feel sorry for him and ashamed for what my father had done.

"I'm sorry my father did that—"

A burst of light shattered my words, and I cowered

Underworld Legacy

behind my hands. The hologram appeared, shining in all its glory. Seth stared down at us with an expression I hated—smug, superior, and extremely pleased with himself. His large form imposing but it was only a reflection of him and at first glance I thought he wanted to be God—he even wore white. Didn't he realize he was already a type of God? I exhaled and reached for the apple.

Victor appeared behind the hologram and floated closer. "Well, done! You two did very well," Victor beamed at us. "Go ahead, hand it over."

"Only one more, brother." Seth grabbed the apple out of my hand, almost yanking my arm out of its socket.

I groaned in pain and pulled my hand back.

Seth chuckled darkly and threw the apple between his hands, not caring if it fell and destroyed. I got the distinct impression he felt the same way for mortals or anyone *beneath* him. We were all expendable. Then again, I got the same feeling from my father.

"The next game will be far worse, my dear," Seth said, basking in all his glory. "You must understand, the next game is extremely difficult, and you might not make it. Are you sure you want to give your life for my brother's?"

My eyes flitted between the two forms. "Of course," I whispered. "My father would do the same for me." I glanced at him, but he averted his eyes.

"She's so sweet, Victor, and trusting," Seth said. "Little do you know who your father really is, little one." With a blast of power and angry wind, he left.

"What does he mean?" I stood taller as I faced Victor. River stood beside me with Luna between us. My crows sat on the entrance behind us with Jake perched on my shoulder.

"You have your spirit animal," — Victor pointed at Jake, — "already?" He sounded shocked, yet pleased.

"Answer my question, Victor. What did Seth mean?"

"It's nothing. Come on, let's freshen you up before the last game."

"No! Tell me now or I'm not doing it," I groaned, standing my ground.

Victor didn't answer me. He was so quick I hardly had time to push him off me as he grabbed River and me at the same time and with such violence. He sent us through the black portal so quickly we teleported back to the living room in the Underworld with brute force.

I fell from the ceiling and crashed to the ground with a loud and painful grunt.

River flew against the wall and poor Luna yelped as she landed on top of him.

My birds flapped vigorously, then finally settled on the mantlepiece.

I wiped blood from my mouth as I slowly climbed to my feet.

Victor stood by the fireplace with his arms crossed over his black armored chest. It rippled in the dim light, and his dark wings shimmered in soft purple and blue hues.

I wanted to help River, but was still unsure of him; would he hurt me with his fiery touch? I picked up Luna and rubbed behind her ears, and Jake flew to my shoulder and rubbed his head against my cheek. I scratched his feathers and coughed.

Victor didn't look at me. He stared daggers into the fire as it raged angrily; blue, yellow and red flames licking the sides of the furnace trying to get out. The same flames that engulfed River when he turned into the skull thing, I didn't know what he was, but he looked exactly like the Eternal Flame now that I thought about it.

"You have half an hour to clean up, then we have to go to the next game," he said and disappeared.

Chapter Thirty-Five

We arrived back at the lab after the ME had dropped off the body. I ate before arriving, which, in hindsight, may not have been the best idea. We were about to view the victim, and even though I'd seen my fair share of bodies, this one might be the worst of them.

The blob of meat sat in the chamber for scanning and processing. Mitch was near his microscope and spoke while he worked.

"Same blood; the golden type."

"Why is it called that?"

"It's incredibly rare." He stood an entire head and shoulders taller than Ralph. "This type of blood has healing qualities that's unique. Almost perfect, even though it's missing an antigen. I wondered why this mist vampire was after this blood type and only came up with one answer; to strengthen himself. We processed all the blood samples from the doctor's lab, and only two were the golden blood. One an unknown candidate, while the other belonged to our doctor—he shared the same Rhnull blood type. Benjamin had most likely infected him with the mist vampire's blood by consumption and in effect turning him into the mist vampire. But from the vampire's behavior, he may have been too weak to change completely and needed to consume more blood to gain strength. I found a list of people who shared the golden blood and only six lived in Sterling Meadow; three are dead, one infected, leaving two who may be in danger."

"How do we know this? Is there a place where people can go for testing?"

"When you are born, they draw blood where it's tested and catalogued. The government uses this to determine how many are human and who have mutations. It's a way the government monitors humans and how many become vampires or a shifter or whatever, and who remains human. It's quite important, especially if your blood group is unique—such as this one."

"I'm seeing a connection between gold dust and golden blood," Ralph said. "But I don't know why."

Mitch nodded. "Agreed, but you know my theory about it needing the blood to strengthen him, perhaps start there."

"It's an excellent theory," Georgina said behind us. "I might just steal it." She smiled through tired eyes. "What does the new arrival tell us?"

"Still processing, but so far, the results are the same as the others; murdered, drained, and has the same blood type. The only difference is they extracted his spine and nervous system. That's why it looks like a blob of flesh." He thumbed behind him. "I wonder." He turned and pulled folders out of a tray and opened them. "Do you think he's building a new body, or just consuming the parts he needs from the victims?"

"We don't know," Georgina said. "Can you give me the two names?"

Mitch handed her a piece of paper.

"Thanks, I think they'll need protection immediately."

I slouched in the passenger seat to get comfortable. We were on our way to the first person's home while Georgina went to the other. She had officers call them ahead to expect our visit. My side ached as if my skin stretched.

"Everything okay?"

"Yeah, just a little tired."

"You sure you don't want me to take you to the leap?"

"When we're done here, you can."

Ralph parked beside the police cruiser. Officer Blackwood kept the door of the mobile home open and I wondered why he wasn't inside. The moment I approached, the heat from inside the home stole my breath. A bald man wearing a stained vest and boxers sat in a weathered chair with a beer in one hand and a cigarette in the other. He had a long sip from his beer can, exhaled, and his vest rode up his enormous stomach. Streams of yellow light cascaded between the off-brown curtains with dust and smoke particles dancing in the air. Empty cartons littered the floor, an open pizza box lay on the kitchen counter with flies buzzing around it. The stench of mold, sweat and rotten food assaulted my senses, making my eyes water. I removed my jacket again and covered my face. I didn't care about proper etiquette this man was disgusting, and I doubted showing a little hostility would go a long way with him. He barely registered I was here.

"You can't be serious," Mr. Banks said as he puffed on his cigarette, blowing smoke rings.

"We are very serious, sir," Officer Blackwood said with some irritation rising.

"Fine, let me pack a suitcase." Mr. Banks rocked off the chair, slammed his beer can on the counter and flicked his cigarette in the general direction of the kitchen; it hit the wall and fell into the sink. I wanted to spray water on it, but too afraid to touch anything in this home.

"Can't we just leave the mist vampire to do what he needs to," I whispered and jerked my chin in the direction Mr. Banks had disappeared down.

Ralph flicked my shoulder, and the lines between his brows deepened. "We can use him as bait," he grinned.

I winked darkly.

The other potential victim was a half-breed; she was half-fae, half-human. They couldn't reach her at her grandmothers, but when Georgina took over and with enough prodding, they located her in the fae side of the forest. Since Mr. Banks was secure and on his way to the safe house, Ralph and I thought we'd join Georgina in the forest.

We arrived within the hour and approached the house when chaos erupted. Georgina yelled, followed by a gunshot. I crouched low and stood back while Ralph entered the house with another officer.

"Go back to the car, Blaire," Ralph yelled and entered.

I used the wall as my guide, stood slowly, and waddled to the car. As I climbed inside, a girl with dark purple pixie styled hair exited the house with her hands behind her back. I narrowed my eyes at her. Ralph exited the building and walked beside the girl while Georgina held her arm. Another officer opened the back door of a cruiser and helped her inside.

I climbed out of Ralph's car and pointed at her. "I've seen her before. Isn't she the one who took your wallet?"

"Yep." He raised his hand, holding something. "And I found everything still inside except the cash. It was a pain in the ass going through all that, and for nothing." He pocketed his wallet.

"Negan said she had to do it."

"What? Steal wallets?"

Georgina nodded. "Her cousin made her do it," she said as she read from her notebook. "Apparently he flew in from Ireland a week ago."

Ralph and I glanced at each other.

"What?"

"Don't you think that's coincidental. We have gorgon gold dust on victims, golden blood which she has," — I pointed at Negan, — "and let me guess, her cousin is a leprechaun?"

"How did you know?"

"It's the gold, Georgina. Somehow, she is part of this mist vampire murder spree. Now we just need to figure out how everything fits together."

It took Georgina seconds to understand where we were going with this, and finally she gasped. "Oh, my gods, but I don't really understand." Her brows furrowed.

"Me neither, but Negan must tell us what she knows. Do you think we can speak with her now instead of at the precinct? I'm eager to put my feet up and rest."

Georgina opened the back door again. "Negan, are you aware of the vampire going around killing people?"

She stared at Georgina with frightened violet eyes.

"He kills people with similar blood type as yours. Do you know how rare and special your blood is?"

Again, Negan just stared at Georgina.

"I don't think she's going to say anything."

Negan's eyes flitted from Ralph to me, then back to Georgina. "I'll only speak to the pregnant one." She pointed at me, then faced the front of the car. "Alone."

Georgina opened the front door and helped me climb inside. I twisted my body so I could see her through the protection glass.

"Hi, Negan. I'm Blaire." I rubbed my stomach and smiled at her. "Baby is due any minute now." *Literally*, I thought.

She exhaled audibly.

"I see there's a lot you want to say. How about you get it out of your system, and I'll ask Ralph not to press any charges against you for stealing his wallet?"

Supernatural's, monsters, all of them made it difficult for the police force to hold them in a normal human jail cell. They had to build special prisons in various secret locations throughout the world, in the ocean, in the desert, and even in space. The type of materials used to keep the monsters locked up was indestructible. I suspected it was something similar to what had kept Sebastian locked in his cage. Therefore, the police didn't have to kill first and ask questions later. They arrested supernatural's for questioning and they went through the usual process like humans would. There were incidents where police officers had killed one or two monsters on sight—usually giants and daemons—but those stories never reached the public.

Negan was still young, and I doubted she wanted any criminal charges on her record or worse, end up in one of those prisons. If I told Negan there may not be charges against her, it could entice her to speak freely about everything.

"It was Benjamin who threatened my life. He had a list of people with the same blood type as me, and he wanted me hurt. I didn't have any friends and few family members here, so I called my cousin, Brian O'Connors, to help protect me; he's a *fixer* in Ireland and knew I could count on him. At first, he protected me, but then he got all weird and stopped replying to my texts. I found out he'd been helping the vampire all along." She cleared her throat and swallowed hard. "They only wanted their blood. I don't know the details of what they did, and if one is to believe the newspapers…" she shuddered. "Two days ago, I followed my cousin and watched him help the vampire in locating the people and received gold dust for his services. He's an accomplice to murder," she said solemnly. "My cousin promised they would leave me alone, but after the third death I panicked and hid here. Only my gran knew about this place," she said the last sentence with a hint of anger. She was most probably upset her gran had given the details to Georgina.

"Detective Carson is going to take you to one of their safe houses. There's only two people left in Sterling Meadow who share the same blood type, and we'll do everything we can to keep you two safe until we catch them. Do you have a number where we can reach your cousin?"

She opened her mouth to say something but closed it again. The expression she wore told me it conflicted her, but she needed to assist us.

Finally, she said, "When he arrived in the country, I gave him my old phone to use. It has a tracker app I'd installed in case he ever got lost. You can use that."

I'd told Georgina what Negan had said and promised

her we'd keep her safe. She'd remain in her own safe house while Mr. Banks would be in another. And with the GPS tracker activated on Negan's old phone, they had located Brian in one mausoleum at the cemetery.

"Thanks for your help, Blaire. But let us handle the rest. It's a Sunday and I'm sure you want to spend some time with your family. Go home and I'll call if I have any news or see you tomorrow."

"No problem, let us know how it goes."

We climbed into Ralph's car and I checked my phone; after four hours with no response from Sebastian. What could he be so busy with that he couldn't answer me?

"Will you take me to Léon's?"

"Sure, but aren't you going to the leap today?"

"I don't feel like going."

Chapter Thirty-Six

SCOUT

I sat on the chair beside the bath and pulled the towel tighter around my body. I wanted to savor the moment, which included hiding away in the bathroom. The moment I left the bathroom, Victor would bang against my door to hurry. I didn't want to go anywhere or do anything for him.

I stared at the bath taps, at the pretty engravings etched into it. They engraved the feet of the bath with a similar pattern I'd never seen before, nor could I describe it.

Knocking sounded, followed by River's loud voice on the other side. "Scout? Victor says you must hurry."

I sighed audibly, leaned against the chairback and yelled. "I'll be right out. Tell him to give me a few more minutes to finish up."

"He isn't pleased," he whispered.

"I don't care," I mumbled my response.

I folded my arms and continued to stare at nothing. My mind reeled from the events of the last few days—if it was days. I had no concept of time here even though we had been in the garden for twenty-four hours; it didn't feel that long. I wasn't tired, but I needed to rest my aching body and I got hungry. Perhaps my hunger was a way to gauge time. And somehow River always *produced* food from thin air. *Who did that?* It was most likely his *condition* he could do that, and Victor's dark power rubbed off on him.

I thought of Victor and the stupid games he played with his brother Seth, and I wondered whether Victor had always known about me but didn't care to seek me out. Perhaps that's why he had left Mom; he'd found out she was pregnant and didn't want to play *house* or take care of a newborn. He wanted nothing to do with me. That thought alone tugged at my heart. But it was only when Victor needed something did he look for me. It wasn't because he wanted to get to know me, or to make amends for years lost. It was so he could play a stupid game and to save his hide. A strange strangling noise came from the back of my throat. I had to stop thinking these negative thoughts, but it was impossible not to.

I heard women's laughter as they passed the bathroom, and how they flirted with River. *Was he still waiting for me?*

I climbed to my feet, unlocked the door and saw River standing against the wall. "Victor says we mustn't lean against the walls."

"These walls can't do anything to me he hasn't already done himself," he said bluntly. "You need to wear the armor on your bed, then you can pull your normal clothing over it." He pointed toward my room.

"Why? Where are we going this time?" I narrowed my eyes.

"Be ready in five minutes." He pushed away from the wall and headed in the living room's direction.

"Fine," I grumbled. I felt miserable and slammed my bedroom door, then locked it.

A black armor—similar to what Victor wore—hung over the chair. I pulled on underwear, then the armor. Once on, I felt vacuum sealed as it molded to my body without squeezing the life out of me. I knocked on my stomach and it sounded solid but without the ache. I wondered where we were going, since I had to dress for war. A shudder ran through me. *War.* Was I about to battle something and needed the armor to survive?

I continued moaning to myself along with a few swear words Mom would be proud of. This was a cruel joke. I was suiting up for the unknown and possibly my death.

I stretched my shoulders and crouched low, testing the elasticity of the suit, and it seemed to manage against my body like a second skin. I pulled on black cargo pants and another black vest over the armor.

Once dressed, I entered the living room. On the floor were four half-naked women at Victor's feet. I immediately looked to the ceiling when I saw one brush against the other's breast. They reminded me of snakes as they moved around him, making me shudder with disgust.

"It's about time!" Victor pushed away the two women attached to his legs and stepped over the third, standing on her hair as he crossed the threshold. "Hold that thought ladies, I need to get these two out of here first." He motioned for me to approach, but I remained steadfast in the doorjamb. "Come here, Scout," he said, the threat in his words rang true and powerful.

"You're sending me to war while you lounge in the safety of this room, doing who knows what." I pointed at the ladies who waved back at me. I rolled my eyes.

"I cannot go where you're going, Scout. Besides, you are the only one able to do this."

"You still haven't told me everything." I pouted and crossed my arms.

"I don't have to explain everything. Now come here." He raised his hand and extended his fingers. Instantly, I hovered above the ground and moved through the air toward him. I stared with wide eyes, trying in vain to get away, but I was swimming in air; no amount of arm movement stopped me from getting closer to him.

Victor touched my shoulder, then River's, and the thick blackness swallowed us.

Chapter Thirty-Seven

"What are you doing here? It's Sunday," Léon asked from his comfortable office chair, leaned against the soft high back and the little lines between his eyes flashed. He'd only been awake for half an hour and on the wrong side—he was grumpy and snappy.

"Don't you want me here?" I placed my hands on my hips for effect, but my pout wasn't as effective as it usually was. While I stood, I massaged my gluteus muscles from climbing steps.

"It's not that." He stood, walked around his wrought iron desk and approached. "I love having you around, but today is Sebastian's day. You need to go to the leap." He cupped my face and pressed his lips to mine. "I will ask him to come fetch you. We can tell him you forgot which day it was." He took my hand in his and led me to the sofa. "I don't know what's going on with you two, but it has to end. You are pregnant with our baby, yet you're acting like a spoilt child."

I sank down into the soft sofa as it enveloped me in its

downy cushions. If Heaven was a sofa, it would be this one. It was the best sofa made with the finest fabric, a blend of Egyptian cotton, silk and velvet. It always reminded me of Léon's touch—I shivered in anticipation.

He arched an eyebrow. For a night creature etched in stone, he was showing more expression than usual and I smiled. He lifted my foot off the floor and removed my shoe. He massaged my foot as he spoke. "Talk to me, Blaire. Why don't you want to go to the leap?"

I sighed. It was childish. I knew I couldn't keep it to myself for long. Léon would want to know what was bothering me or he'd listen in on my thoughts like he sometimes did. But perhaps I needed to get my frustration out with words.

"Fine. Sebastian and I had a little tiff, and I told him to fetch his clothes from my house—"

"Yes, he spoke to me about that, but you made up." He pressed hard into the soft part of my foot.

"Ow!" I pulled my foot out of his clutches. "Not so hard."

"Sorry." He beckoned me to bring my foot back and continued massaging but softer. "Why don't you want to see our third?"

I sighed louder and leaned my head against the soft cushion. "He hasn't answered my texts today even after we've discussed this, and he said he would."

"Tsk, tsk. He doesn't answer my texts immediately either. You don't see me sulking. This is not you at all, Blaire. You have never been the jealous type. What's really going on?"

"The reason I told him to fetch his clothing was because a woman spoke on his end. I thought the worst. He says he did nothing, only offered her his room while he slept in the lounge, but... I don't know. I don't feel like seeing her there today. And then today he didn't respond to any of my messages and I just don't want to go there."

Léon carefully placed my foot on the ground and lifted the other one, removed my shoe and massaged my aching foot. I slouched down the sofa and closed my eyes. His touch sent tiny spikes of warmth up my leg forcing me to relax; to climb out of my anxiety filled mind and into a thoughtless meditation. His thumbs kneaded the arch of my foot, then the soft padding near my toes. A combination of sensations travelled through my foot, up my shin and into my thigh. The current of pleasurable vibrations sent me to a place, making me weak in the knees, putty in his capable hands. His delicate touch travelled up my leg, and I gasped when he pushed my knees apart. I kept my eyes closed and smiled at what was next. He nibbled the inside of my thigh through my pants, each sensual bite a stroke of ecstasy and a whimper escaped my lips. His powerful hands moved under my ass and pulled gently so I lay down on the sofa. Léon left a trail of kisses up the inside of my thigh until he reached the apex of my legs, and I tensed before the wave of satisfaction washed over me. He continued kissing up to my hip bone and another passionate, yet gentle, orgasm hit me. He leaned over me and I opened my eyes when he stopped.

"You're so beautiful." His eyes communicated his desire and frustration. His body hummed between my legs with pent-up passion. He moved to lie beside me, pulled me into the curve of his hard body and kissed the nape of my neck.

I reached behind me to return the favor, but he stopped me. "I will wait for you, *ma chérie*. I want all of you, not your hand," he said into the shell of my ear, sending a cascade of goosebumps all over my body. He knew what I wanted and when. We shared special moments like these often. He knew I needed extra attention, and I loved him for being so in tune with my needs—as painful as I was at the moment.

"Can't I stay here with you?" I moaned. I didn't want to go anywhere else.

"No, I do not wish to fight my brother. Things have been going well between us, things are working. You need to sort yourself out and not be so *sensitive*. Our Sebastian will have a good reason for not responding at your every whim."

A knock on the door brought us out of our little world.

"Come in."

Elena entered and smiled like she caught us red-handed. "Sebastian is here."

As she said the words, the door swung open, hitting the wall loudly. Sebastian stared down at me with glowing, angry eyes. Léon cleared his throat, kissed my temple and stood. He helped me to my feet. I slipped on my shoes and ambled around the sofa.

I felt Sebastian's eyes on me, and I knew I'd messed up. I shouldn't have been so sensitive; thinking up things that weren't true—especially after he had already explained himself. And I shouldn't have come here. It was his day to spend with me, but I'd come here—to Léon.

I stood before him and felt so small, so child-like. I sighed and my eyes slowly raked up the length of his body; his dark blue jeans, his black t-shirt straining against his body as he hummed with power—with fury. When I stared into his dark golden eyes, they bled back to their emerald shade when he saw the apology in my eyes.

We stared at each other for what felt like minutes, neither looking away. I wasn't trying to defy him. I wanted to say *I'm sorry* but didn't know how.

"What's going on?" he finally asked, breaking the chilly silence.

I glanced at Léon.

"Don't look at him."

I flinched at his words. They were hard and hot, like a branding iron against my skin, and I exhaled sharply. "I'm feeling insecure and didn't want to go to the leap today. I want to spend time with you, but I didn't want to spend time with anyone ar*ound*."

Sebastian grunted. I almost saw smoke. "Blaire, this is not like you. You've never, ever been insecure. Where is this coming from?"

Shrugging, I finally said, "I don't know." I dusted a rogue tear from my cheek. "I feel vulnerable." I lifted my arms and pointed at my stomach to show what I meant. "And… I guess… you two will live forever. I won't. I'm getting older. You still look twenty-eight. You are meeting younger women… I guess… I would rather let you go now then have you force yourself to stay with me as I age."

I watched Sebastian's Adam's apple bob up and down and his hard face softened. "Blaire…," his whisper caressed my cheek, and I wanted to lean into it. "I can't talk for him," — he pointed at his brother, — "all I want is you. Now and forever, and I will still love you. And, if you don't want us to turn you, then bind yourself to me. You will age *much* slower than you are now. You already age slowly because of your saber and the other animals you carry, but if I give you both marks, you're bound to my life. For as long as I live—so will you."

"We should ask what would happen if we both bind her."

Sebastian nodded. "Good idea."

My eyes widened, and my mouth opened. I imagined

my life with him, with both of them. I imagined staying young forever and sharing my life with them. But was forever too long? I didn't know whether I was the kind of monster who would want to live for centuries. Perhaps it was time I decided. We'd spoken about this before, but I wasn't ready. I wasn't sure. I might be sure now. I loved them; I did. I wanted to spend the rest of my life with them, but it would only be a few short years compared to theirs. I'd age and grow old; my body and mind withering away...

I swallowed cotton balls and tried to swallow again. Léon handed me a glass of water and I hadn't seen him move. I smiled. I loved that they still surprised me. Another tear slid down my cheek.

"I feel like an emotional wreck. I love you so much." I glanced from Léon to Sebastian. "I want to think about it. Maybe after he's born?" I rubbed my stomach.

"Whatever you want, babe. Just knowing it might be something you want is enough for me." Sebastian pulled me into an embrace. He moved, and I felt his body jerk. "You were just holding her. Give us some space," he said jokingly, then opened his arm and brought Léon into the fold.

After a moment had passed, Léon spoke in our group hug. "I've received word from the Council. Plans have changed. Alex is hunting the mist vampire. He hopes to have found him either by tonight or tomorrow. Should the humans encounter him first, they are not to approach; Alex will handle him." Léon let go of me.

"Is he going to destroy him?"

Léon shook his head. "No, Alex and his men must capture him and take him to the Council."

"Why?"

"It is not for me to question their actions, but to help carry them out."

There was something more to the story, but I didn't think Léon wanted to talk about it, nor did I want to pursue. The Vampire Council had their reasons for doing things, and even though the mist vampire was dangerous, there was another reason they wanted to capture him instead of destroying him.

We arrived at the leap as the moon cast its silver shine. It wasn't a full moon, but the leopards were celebrating. Viola stood in the center of the field wearing a long white dress with flowers in her hair. Surrounding her were logs of wood and I froze.

"Is the leap going to burn her at the stake?" My twisted sense of humor hoped it was true, even though I knew it wasn't.

Sebastian chuckled. "No, we're celebrating her change, her right into womanhood."

"I've never heard of the leap celebrating someone's change like this before."

"She's like royalty among the leopards. Her family heads up the England pack while Greg and I share the crown here. And when a natural born change into their beast, we celebrate."

"Oh, and that's happening now?" I asked nervously.

"Don't look so worried." He pulled me closer to him and rubbed the small of my back. "I won't leave your side. If you get tired, let me know and we can leave. But I have to stay for a short while as I am their leader."

"Is this what you were busy with?"

He nodded. "Yes, we had lots to prepare."

Guilt struck me like a bullet wound to the heart. He had

enough on his plate, but instead of supporting him, I was complaining—me and my delicate emotions.

The leopards circled Viola and the wood. Anne greeted me while Greg stood beside Viola and said a few words of encouragement.

Sebastian asked Kai to bring me a chair. Relieved to be off my feet, I rubbed my stomach while Sebastian stood behind me with his hands on my shoulders. I couldn't see their faces, but heard Greg speaking. He called Sebastian to say a few words. He kissed my cheek and joined his *brother*.

"These last few days have been wonderful, and it's been an honor getting to know you." Sebastian's voice drifted as if he said something only she heard, then he spoke loudly again. "We are all proud of how you have changed from when you first arrived, compared to now, how you stand before us as one of us. You've blossomed into a beautiful were-leopard who would become a powerful asset in any leap. Welcome to our family."

My stomach dropped at the words for Viola, and they felt—*intimate*.

I watched Sebastian kiss and hug Viola through the gaps of those standing in front of me. I expected a quick peck on the cheek, but she kissed him on the lips and for much longer than necessary. And it wasn't a quick hug and let go either. It was a cherished hug that lingered.

Something in my chest broke. I was being silly, especially after what Sebastian had said at the Labyrinth. But... the way she ogled him, and how he allowed her to do it, brought that green monster to the surface. I glanced at Anne and she was frowning.

I pulled on Anne's hand, and she crouched to face me. "What's wrong?"

"Is this something that typically happens?"

"A celebration like this?" I nodded while she shook her head. "Not really, but we thought it would be nice for her, you know, to make her feel welcome and part of the family."

"Is she still leaving at the end of the month?"

"No, it sounds as if she's extended her stay," she smiled, but it seemed forced. "She said she liked the air here better."

I peered through the bodies in front of me, my eyes darted to their handholding. When Sebastian saw me, he quickly let go of her hand. I stood. He whispered something into her ear. I greeted Anne and walked toward the house. I felt Sebastian's eyes, then I heard his quickened steps behind me.

"Where are you going?"

I turned around and slapped him. "Don't insult me, Sebastian. You just flaunted your affection for her while she reciprocated. I'm pregnant, not blind."

"What are you talking about?"

"That delicate kiss that lingered. The intimate hug. The holding of hands. You only let go when you noticed me staring at you." I pushed on his chest, but he barely moved.

A sharp pain ripped through my side, forcing me to double over in pain. A lightning bolt of discomfort coursed through my mid-section. I felt my stomach grow in that second and cried out in tortuous pain.

"Let me take you inside."

"Get away from me. I'm calling Léon. You can go play with your new girlfriend."

"Christ, Blaire! Enough already!" he yelled. "There's nothing going on between her and me. Please let me help you," he said the last part gently as he reached for me.

"Get away." I pushed him again.

"Stop it." He grabbed my wrists to stop me from hitting him and pulled me to his body. "There is nothing going on. All that was just to comfort her. She was nervous. Why can't you believe me?" he said into the shell of my ear.

"It's hard to believe you when I just witnessed that up there." I pushed him away, pain seared through my abdomen and I cried out again.

He grunted his frustration, picked me up and dialed Mel, then Désiré's number as he carried me to Anne's house. When he ended the calls, he pocketed his phone and set me gently on Anne's bed.

"I'm going to get the kit Désiré gave us. Don't go anywhere."

"Where do you think I'm going?"

My heart thundered in my ribs. Sweat beaded down my face and back. The shooting pain ebbed around my stomach. Our little bean kicked and punched my insides; I saw his movements. It was like he was trying to punch his way out of my womb. I turned onto my side and steadied my breathing. Sucking in air in two quick successions, I exhaled slowly. I placed a calm hand on my stomach and tried to relax my body and mind.

The punching slowed. The kicking stopped. He settled down.

Sebastian returned with the kit and came around the bed. "How are you feeling?"

"How do you think?"

"You aren't as pale as you were earlier." He placed the towels on the bed and opened the kit. "Are you still in pain?"

I shook my head.

He rubbed my stomach.

"Don't touch me." I pushed him away.

"There's nothing going on between Viola and me. I wish you would stop thinking that there is. You are turning small things into big things. You are putting his life and yours at risk. What would have happened if you changed into your saber?"

I didn't want to answer him. I might still be angry. I closed my eyes to rest for a second.

Chapter Thirty-Eight

SCOUT

We traveled through space and time, and it was a longer *ride* than before. I had no idea what lay before us, and it was unsettling. I stared blades at Dad, my arms still crossed, and my brows furrowed. It was the equivalent of a tantrum for teens. But it didn't help, Victor continued ignoring me, but he glanced at me out of the corner of his eyes with a playful tug at the corner of his mouth. If he smiled, I would hit him in the face, father or not. Mom told me violence solved nothing, yet she seemed to manage just fine.

We finally *landed* on a black rock. My world tilted as the ground moved beneath my feet. I turned and doubled over as I fought the nausea.

"Where are we?" I asked as I slowly stood straight and cast an eye at the scenery. It was a wasteland where nothing grew. There was no smell in the air, no sounds of birds or insects—there was nothing. Only mountains and mountains of black rock lay behind and ahead of us. Nothing but dark, ominous rocks surrounding us.

"There's no limit on your time here. All you have to do is retrieve the golden egg."

I burst out laughing. "Golden egg? Are we in a children's book?" I quickly stifled the laugh when I caught sight of Victor's stern expression.

"This isn't funny, Scout."

I mocked him. "It is to me. You aren't the one doing all the hard work, *my Lord*," I said sarcastically and curtsied before him. Yes, I was being childish. I was a child, after all.

Victor's features morphed as his anger flared, but he didn't change into his devilish appearance and remained in his human form. But he wasn't happy. "It's the last one, Scout. When you have completed this task, I will see about setting River free," he said, then abruptly left.

His words hung in the air even after he had gone. I stared at River, who blinked in response. I wasn't only doing this for Victor, but for River as well. If I retrieved the golden egg, River would be free of whatever curse Victor had placed on him.

My shoulders sagged as I exhaled. I still wanted to go home. I didn't want to do this. But as I stared into those amber-brown eyes filled with sadness, I knew I had to continue. River and Victor counted on me to finish. With the heaviness on my shoulders, I couldn't give up. Not now.

"Don't do this," River said with a mix of emotion.

I was sure my doubt was visible on my face.

"Let me call Victor and tell him to take you home. It's not fair for him to do this to you. None of it is your fault and you shouldn't be the one doing any of it."

It made me happy to hear him say that. He cared enough to push his selfish wants aside in order for me to go home. If only Victor had done something similar, then maybe I'd be willing to do it without hesitation.

A thin smile crept up my face as a small burning desire ignited, making me want to help River. I wanted him free of my father's hold, but in order to do so I had to help Victor get his egg back or his brother would win this stupid game.

I exhaled sharply and held my head high. My smiled broadened. "Thank you, River, I needed to hear that. I don't want to go home. I've decided to help you. Now," — I rubbed my hands together, — "can you tell me where we are?" I scanned the wasteland again.

"We're still in the Underworld, somewhere. I have no clue which creature or creatures lie here. Your guess is as good as mine."

I arched an eyebrow. "I thought you had to help me; you seem to know just as much as I do—which isn't a lot," I said. He shrugged sheepishly, and I rolled my eyes. I surveyed our surroundings again and saw in the distance smoke curling up in the air. I pointed at the obvious area. "That way?"

He squinted in that direction and nodded solemnly. "Yep, must be." He whistled and Luna appeared at his side.

"How can you do that?"

"From what I've gathered, she's tied to me—spiritually and physically—so wherever I go, she's able to go. It's as if these animals have a power of their own they used to seek us out and come to us when we need them. Like now, your crows aren't here. Call them and let's see what happens."

"Okaaaay." I had nothing to lose by trying, and at least I would learn something since Victor wasn't sharing any information with me. "Jake?" I shrugged as if calling the crow by his name was a swear word, and it felt strange calling for a bird to magically appear.

The air whooshed beside me, and wings flapped. I smiled when I saw the five crows.

'You called. Are you in danger?'

"No, I wanted to see if I could summon you. Is that what it's called?"

'It is. Where are we?' Jake flapped his dark wings. The white light in the sky beat down on us and cast his feathered body in a silver hue. It was magical and beautiful. I never knew they shone like that, unless they always did, and I never noticed before.

"I don't know where we are, but I'd feel better if I knew you were nearby."

He squawked and the five crows flew higher and in the smoke's direction. *'We're going to check it out.'*

"I guess we need to go there."

The terrain was rough with sharp rocks pointing in all directions. The smoke we'd seen was quite a distance away, and I was grateful we didn't have a time limit forcing us to hurry.

Luna climbed the mountain near River's side while my crows were nowhere to be seen. I'd only hoped they went to the smokey area to determine whether it was safe for us to approach and not do anything unsavory.

River climbed down the face of a rocky area first. He showed me where to grip when it was my turn. We didn't have any equipment with us and could only depend on our own strength and each other. I followed in his footsteps—*literally*—I'd place my feet exactly where he'd placed his feet and gripped the rock where he had placed his hands. My legs strained to keep my balance while my arms and hands ached from gripping onto the rough rock. We were slowly scaling down the mountain.

We were almost to the bottom and excitement grew within me. The next stretch we could walk at a leisurely pace with hardly any climbing. I gripped a part of the rock without looking. It moved beneath my fingers. Flinching at the sensation, I lifted my hand even though my other hand had barely gripped the rock. The foothold I was standing on was narrow, and I almost lost my balance. I quickly gripped the rock and glanced up to see what had moved beneath my other hand and it hissed. *Snakes... again!* I moaned silently, trying not to attract any attention from them. Luckily, they were only babies, but where there were babies there was a mommy.

"River!" I whispered. "Help me."

River stared wide eyed and motioned for me to come to him.

I steadily gripped the rock as I tried to move away from the baby snakes. My eyes flitted from the nest to where I needed to go. I shuffled my feet on the narrow ledge and came across loose pebbles and sand; it was slippery under my feet and one false move and I could fall.

"Go slowly," River cautioned. "Move your left hand here and with your right hand take its spot." He directed. "Lift your left foot and bring it up here. That's it."

I glanced quickly to the area he had said I should stand, and my eyes darted back to the black snakes. They were up, all six of them, their hooded heads open, yellow eyes on me, and tongues out. They rattled and hissed as they rubbed their heads against each other, no doubt calling their mother.

"Now move your left hand farther up."

I did as instructed and slowly climbed away from the snakes. River kept directing me where I needed to move to as he slowly moved with me down the mountain. When the air was void of any noise apart from our footsteps and my beating heart, I glanced up at them. The black snakes had stopped hissing. Only one stared back at me—its yellow eyes eerily disturbing.

"Now jump."

Glancing at my feet, I noticed we were near the ground. I jumped and landed with a soft thud on the ground.

"Hurry."

I followed him. Then I glanced over my shoulder and saw a huge black snake scaling down the mountain toward her babies. She did not look happy. She curled her body around the nest, and it looked like she was counting them, then turned her beady yellow eyes in our direction and hissed loudly. A warning from her which I would gladly adhere to. There's no way I would harm any of them.

I walked faster and passed River. "How long had she been there?"

"From the moment you disturbed her nest."

"Crap." I darted, sweat dripped down my back and squished against the armor. "She had ample time to slither down and bite us, scare us, or knock us to the ground."

"Probably."

"Crap, crap, crap. Let's get away from her."

Luna barked when we reached her. River scratched behind her ears and her tongue lulled out of her mouth. Her mohawk stood up between her ears and with the few loose stray hairs along her body it made her look a little goofy. She was a welcomed comedic break. I ran my fingers through her mohawk, and it was surprisingly soft. She licked my fingers, then pushed her head into my hand for more scratches.

We walked alongside the flattest part of the dark mountain. It was also the straightest path toward the smoke we'd seen earlier. I saw the faint fumes billowing into the sky, but it was behind another black mountain. I groaned just thinking about the various reptiles or creatures we would find there.

The sand between the smaller rocks was black, reminding me of coal. I bent down and picked up some. It rained through my fingers; soft and warm.

"Is this volcanic rock?"

"No, it's nothing you would've seen on earth, perhaps the mountain, but not the sand. It's warm, isn't it?"

I nodded. "Yes." I dusted my hands clean on my pants. "And soft." I rubbed between my fingers to remove sand stuck there.

A warm blast of air whipped past us. I fell onto a rock while River landed beside me. Luna backed as she jumped up and down, trying to bite the little whirlwind. It was a tiny tornado whirling around us, then disappeared as if it never happened.

River sat up and laughed. "That was strange."

I sat beside him when a giggle tore through me, desperately needing to laugh as well, and it felt good.

We cut our laughter short when movement caught our eye. We swallowed our happiness and stood abruptly.

River's hands morphed into his skeleton and held a blue and orange ball of flame. The rest of him stayed human, but I stared at him in wonder.

Something moved again. I stepped onto a rock. The black sand beneath our feet moved as if someone was shaking it.

River stepped beside me.

Luna growled.

There was something just beneath the sand. It moved and brought the sand up with it.

"Luna, get up on the rocks," River yelled, and she ran up to stand beside him.

"Not another snake, please. I don't think I can handle another one." I groaned and glanced up at the mountain we'd just climbed. The black snake was still there with her babies. "Do you think this is the father?" I asked, still staring at them in the distance.

"I've given up guessing. Anything can happen here." River walked across the rocks, careful not to touch the sand. "Follow me." He jumped on the rocks that stuck out of the moving black sand.

I stepped where he did and glanced around. I wanted to make sure the creature wasn't following us. The farther we moved away from the sand, the less I saw of it, and I didn't feel the vibrations.

Luna stopped growling and ran up ahead.

River's hands were no longer on fire, and the tension between my shoulders eased, but only slightly. I didn't want to be caught with my guard down again.

Surveying the area before taking another step, I noticed something dark had climbed out from under the black sandy blanket. It sat near the rocks where we'd first stopped, and it stared back at me. It was just sitting there. Staring. I couldn't make out the shape of its body, but I knew it sat like a frog with its legs bent and its body between its legs. I didn't know what creature it was, but it was black and smooth—almost oily. I swallowed the lump in my throat.

I faced forward to take another step when I felt its gaze upon me. It was like blades cutting into my spine. I spun around and the creature had gone. I quickly caught up with River and made our way around a bend and out of sight.

This was the Underworld, which meant anything could happen.

Chapter Thirty-Nine

Birds chirped and the bright morning sun splashed over me, leaving me feeling warm and safe. I opened my eyes slowly and rubbed the sleep out. It felt as though I'd slept for days; my body felt stiff and my head cloudy.

"Morning." The bed dipped as Sebastian climbed behind me. "How are you feeling?" He nipped at my ear.

"Good." I turned around to face him and smiled. "Surprisingly very good."

"You ready to eat something?"

I nodded.

I sat at the kitchen table and ate a bowl of mixed fruit while Sebastian made me an omelet. I still felt small and childlike—especially after my tantrum yesterday. "Where did Anne sleep?"

"She shared Ivy's bed, and I slept in the chair in her room. I didn't want to disturb you. You looked so peaceful sprawled on the bed." He placed the plate in front of me. "There wasn't any space for me to sleep," he smirked.

"Hmm, this is delicious," I said, and had another mouthful. "I'm sorry about yesterday. I'm seeing things that aren't there." I shook my head. "It's not like me, is it?"

"No." He gently took my hand in his and kissed it. "And I'm serious when I say I want to spend the rest of *my* life with *you*. *Only* you. If you bind yourself to me, we can do that."

I chortled. "That's a lot of years, Sebastian. Are you sure you want to be with *me* for so long?" I placed the fork on the plate to give him my full attention. "You will be with the same person for years and years, and many more years after that."

He shrugged. "I'm willing if you are," his smile reached his eyes. His leopard pushed to the surface, sniffed the air as he waited for mine to join his, along with my saber—they loved his leopard as they scent marked each other in the metaphysical realm. "I love it when they do that."

"Yeah, me, too."

"I think let's leave last night behind us. We need to concentrate on your health and our little man. Désiré monitored you while you slept, and he grew another two centimeters yesterday. I'm worried—you need bed rest. I don't think you should work until he's out. And from what Désiré had said, could be in a day or two."

"Me, too. I hope Georgina and Ralph find Brian, who can lead us to the vampire. And if that happens, hopefully Alex can get to our mist vampire before he strikes again—"

"Which reminds me, Georgina sent you messages, but I didn't want to wake you. I think you overexerted yourself yesterday and needed the rest." He handed me my cellphone.

There were a dozen messages from Georgina and a

couple from Ralph. "Brian wasn't there when they entered the mausoleum, and they found Benjamin. He sought refuge with another kiss on the other side of town. I need to ask Léon about them."

"Léon and Alex are down for the day, Blaire. Send them a message they can read when they wake. But you are staying here with me all day every day until he is born. I don't want you running around."

I sulked in my chair, but I knew he was right. I needed to focus on the little one. "Okay," I said and forked another piece of omelet into my mouth. "You get to spend all day with me." I wiggled my eyebrows.

A strange sound came from the back of his throat and I didn't know if he was happy or sarcastic, but I didn't want to start another fight and let it slide.

I continued reading the rest of the messages while he cleaned the mess he made in the kitchen.

"Okay, I should've just read the rest of the messages. The kiss is new to the area—"

"See, you're so quick to jump up and investigate. Maybe now you will be a little more proactive from the chair. You have another person to think about and not just yourself."

"Okay, I get it. Enough with the chiding." I sounded as grumpy as I felt.

Ralph sent another text letting me know Sebastian had contacted him and he would keep me updated with the case.

I hated this. I wanted to be there to solve this, but I couldn't, and I wouldn't.

Sebastian was right; Ralph could assist Georgina with the case while I assisted from here.

Ralph sent pictures of the location where the kiss had been hiding out—a small house on the outskirts of Sterling Meadow. It's a wealthy area, but this house was plain compared to the mansions built there—as if they were trying to hide in plain sight. The kiss had been asleep when SWAT knocked down their door earlier, killing one vampire when they opened the curtains. *Oops*.

There was another picture of Benjamin cowering in the corner; pale faced and wide eyed. He still wore the same clothing we'd last seen him in. They petrified him. Ralph had taken pictures of all the sleeping vampires, and I recognized two of them—the males from the portraits that hung in Dr. Avery's lab. The men who had bitten Penelope, turned her, and had taken her away from Léon and Jean-René. But I didn't see any pictures of anyone resembling Penelope. I was sure Léon and Jean-René would want to speak with the two men, but with Alex in town, he would most likely handle the situation.

While I waited for another update, I stared at the show on the television screen. Sebastian held meetings in one room but checked up on me every half an hour. My body ached from sitting and lying while standing hurt my lower back. No matter what I did, I felt miserable.

Two hours later, I finally received an update. The vampires were still dead to the world, but they had questioned Benjamin—who sang like a little bird. He had said the kiss was the original mist vampire's following; in today's term, we'd label them a cult. They wanted to resurrect the mist vampire and needed a worthy candidate. There were two vampires who headed up the cult; Hugo Wright and Richard Cook—the two men Léon and Jean-René would love to get their hands on.

The mist vampire's blood type was *golden* Rhnull and

Underworld Legacy

therefore required similar blood types to gain strength. Hugo and Richard had directed Benjamin to seek employment with Dr. Avery, who was a long distant relative of Hugo's. They had known Dr. Avery shared the same blood group as the original mist vampire.

Then, once Benjamin and Dr. Avery had gained the blood sample of the original mist vampire, Benjamin created a concoction as directed by Hugo and gave it to Dr. Avery with tea. Then Benjamin injected it into the doctor to ensure it worked.

The moment Dr. Avery turned into the blood lusting mist vampire; Benjamin helped him source the victims with the help of Brian O'Connors. But to ensure Brian kept to his side, they offered him the gold dust as payment.

Unfortunately, Benjamin didn't know where Dr. Avery or Brian was at the time of his arrest. He'd said they'd gone on their own. They had left him and the kiss out of the loop for the last twenty-four hours.

As the evening took over, my patience was a little thin and my anxiety high. Sebastian kept telling me to relax and to lie down.

Eventually my phone pinged.

Georgina had tracked Brian to another house when the phone he carried had switched on, alerting them to his location.

When the sun had started to set, they had notified Alex of Brian's location as Georgina suspected Dr. Avery might be there. If not, Alex could question Brian.

Ralph had a body camera strapped to his shoulder, and I watched it unfold as if I were right there. He was such an outstanding partner to do this for me. I'd hug him when I saw him again.

SWAT yelled and stormed the house. Screaming

followed and shots went off. Ralph followed in behind Georgina.

I watched Alex swoop inside like the hungry shadow he was, and within seconds he'd cornered the mist vampire with a silver rope and had nailed Dr. Avery's hands to the walls with more silver; ensuring he didn't turn into the blood mist and disappeared again.

Ralph surveyed the area.

Georgina checked left; Ralph checked right. They secured the lounge while Alex and another vampire busied with Dr. Avery.

Ralph entered another room. Hunched over a table was a short man with curly red hair—he had to be Brian. Brian held a straw to his nose with one hand while he raised the other and showed his palm at Georgina. Brian leaned over the table, the straw in a nostril, and hovered over the gold dust to snort the line.

"You've got to be kidding me?" I gasped as I watched.

"What's wrong?" Sebastian entered.

"Nothing." I waved him away. "There's lots going on. They finally have Brian and Dr. Avery."

"That's good." He sat beside me. "Wow!" he said as Brian came up for air and grunted, followed by that stomach turning sound as he swallowed whatever stuck at the back of his throat. "Gross."

"Okay, thank you, you can go now." I elbowed him.

"Call me if you need me." He squeezed my thigh, kissed my temple and stood.

I continued watching the action on my small cellphone screen.

Brian leaned on the table to stand but collapsed onto the couch in a fit of laughter. A layer of sweat covered the parts of his body I could see, and he had sweat stains on his clothing. His eyes rolled into the back of his head. He kept dipping in and out of his euphoric state, followed by giggles.

Georgina groaned beside Ralph and asked two officers to handcuff Brian and to carry him out.

Ralph continued searching the home; he found a bag of gold dust in a closet along with a stash of cash, luxury watches and diamonds.

"If I had to guess, while our vampire needed blood, Brian robbed everyone," Ralph said as he opened another closet with the gorgon golden fountain inside. He called an officer over to show him his findings. He walked out the room and headed toward the kitchen. "And did you see him snort the gold dust?" The camera shook as he laughed. "I had no idea it was a drug. Makes you wonder what it did to you."

I couldn't answer Ralph, but his points were valid. I ended the video and called him. "Is that it then? We've got everyone?"

"Looks that way."

"What about the cult?"

"Alex is handling them. The Vampire Council ordered their coffins delivered to them. They don't want to risk them escaping so they've cross wrapped all of them. And they want the mist vampire—alive." He sighed.

"What's wrong?"

"I don't get it. The two men heading the cult are the same ones from the portraits. The ones Léon and Jean-René recognized. But where's the woman—"

"So?"

"Why the secrecy? There are at least six other vampires with Alex to handle Dr. Avery. Which, in case you didn't see, looks nothing like Dr. Avery."

"What do you mean?"

"He looks like the man from the cave. Like he was being transformed into the original mist vampire."

"Maybe that's what they were trying to do. Bring him back from the dead using someone else's body."

"But Alex got rid of him in the cave. There was nothing left of his body…"

My brows creased. "I don't understand. What's your point?"

"What if Alex intentionally brought back the mist vampire and had a reason for not killing him?" he whispered. "Instead, he was canvasing for a new body with a similar blood type. The vampire was replenishing what he'd lost. All that blood, the organs, the spine, and nervous system. In the cave was the original dismembered body while the other one grew stronger. What if there's a larger reason the Vampire Council wants the cult and Dr. Avery shipped back to them?"

"We don't mess with the Vampire Council, Ralph. We did our job, and they have the bad guy. Besides, Benjamin already said it was Hugo and Richard running the cult and orchestrated everything. And there's no way I could've stopped him, let alone kill him. And neither could you without their help. We could've asked Léon and his kiss to help us, but I didn't want to risk it. He'd done enough. We needed them to do this. Now please, swallow your conspiracy theories."

"I know. You're right." He still sounded unhappy. "How's the little one doing?" he asked, changing the subject.

"I'm incredibly uncomfortable and miserable. I can actually feel him growing at the moment." I watched my stomach move as he punched and kicked, trying to get out.

"Jeez, okay. It's good that you're resting then. How about I come over to keep you company?"

"Don't you have Eden to bother?" I said and smiled.

"Yeah, she should be up by now," he chuckled lightheartedly. "I'll see you later." He ended the call.

Chapter Forty

It relieved me the case was over. My body ached, so I napped on the couch. Unfortunately, my mind raced and visions of Scout flashed in my mind. Slowly, I sat without hurting him or myself. I didn't know how to contact her when it was time to give birth and guessed I'd have to bother Victor. But I'd only call him when I was ready.

I allowed the couch to comfort me again when I heard raised voices down the hallway. Then they started singing. My brow crinkled, but I didn't move—I was way too comfortable.

The soft melody of their singing was soothing until they entered the lounge. Anne entered with a mischievous grin, her pixie hair sticking in all directions like someone had ruffled her feathers.

Ivy came in behind her mother, the blond streaks in her chestnut hair framing her face, and a wicked twinkle in her honey-colored eyes.

I narrowed my eyes at them and slowly sat up. "What's going on?" I asked when more of the were-leopard women entered, circling the couch I'd squatted on the entire day.

"Since you are here," Anne said with a naughty smirk. "We thought we would host a baby shower for you."

I shook my head. "I already said I don't need one. I've already bought most of the things, but thanks anyway."

"Too bad, don't care. You're having one," Ivy said and produced a gift wrapped in a cloth diaper. "Mine first." She held it out for me.

The women gathered around me, sat three to a one-seater while others pulled up dining chairs to sit on, and a handful stood. Anne sat beside me on the couch. Ivy sat on the coffee table gawking at me.

I unwrapped Ivy's first; a tiny brown newborn outfit with a hoody like a mane—reminding me of a lion. I doubted there were leopard outfits for babies, but this was just as cute. Included in the gift was a dummy and body cream. I held up the tiny outfit and all the women said, *'Aah'* at the same time. It's hilarious and adorable at the same time.

Viola handed me a gift. She smiled sincerely and sat beside Ivy. A pang of guilt hit me, I'd been so jealous of this young lady and it was all in my head. She was sweet and innocent—so incredibly young—she had her entire life ahead of her. I'd most likely given off *bad vibes* because she seemed a little meek and reserved around me, and I mistook it for guilt, which fueled my silly suspicions. I didn't blame her; I was sure I came across as aloof.

"Thank you." I unwrapped the gift, tearing off the animal print paper and found it was a gift for me, massage oil, slippers and chocolates. "I can't wait to wear these," I grinned. It was a pair of black leopard slippers with green eyes.

I felt something against me and glanced up. Sebastian smiled like the Cheshire cat, then left the room again. I would get him back for this evil trickery. He had most likely planned this yesterday as well; just another reason Sebastian didn't answer my text messages. Another pang of guilt hit me, but I shook it off. I needed to appreciate what the women had done for me and give them my full attention.

One by one, they each handed me a gift. They were all similar; various outfits for a newborn, lots of disposable diapers, creams, shampoo, and soaps. Another woman entered with a pram and car seat, while another held a travel cot. It was very sweet of them. I felt appreciated and part of the were-family. Their gifts warmed my heart and bursting with love for these women who had accepted me into their world even though I was not a leopard per se. I hugged and thanked each of them and waited for them to leave.

Only one woman remained: Anne still sitting patiently on the couch beside me.

She handed me her gift and whispered. "I can't let the others see what I'm giving you," she said with a wink.

"Now I'm worried." I opened one side of the tightly wrapped box and saw the erotic device. "Anne!"

"That's for after the birth, and something for you and Sebastian to play with." She winked again, leaving me blushing. I giggled as I packed it inside one of the larger bags.

I heard low voices in the direction Anne had gone, then Sebastian entered with the biggest smile I'd ever seen.

"I take it she told you what she bought us?"

"Yeah," — he shook his head, — "she's so naughty." He sat beside me and pulled me into the curve of his body.

"There's nothing else I have on today, so we could head to our place. Order in some food and take it easy."

"Okay."

"They want to host a celebration for Greg and me tomorrow night." He sighed.

"Are you serious?"

"Yes, they want to do it before…." He glanced at my stomach.

"Oh, okay." I leaned against his shoulder as our fingers entwined.

I closed my eyes to relax, when the door burst open with Ralph and Negan in the doorjamb.

Chapter Forty-One

"What are you doing here?"

"She's scared. She cornered me after I left Georgina at the precinct. I didn't know what else to do with her."

Negan stared up at me with sad, innocent eyes.

"You should've taken her into the precinct to Georgina, not bring her here." I narrowed my eyes at her. "Did she steal your wallet again?"

Ralph's eyes widened, and he checked his pockets. He held out his hand, palm side up.

"Sorry," she mumbled, handing it over. "It's a habit."

"Why didn't you take her to Georgina?" I repeated my question.

"She felt unsafe, and she'd heard Brian made bail. I phoned Georgina, and he hasn't but it still scared her."

"And the vampire might still come for me. Or even that assistant. The two officers in charge of babysitting me weren't that wonderful either—"

My phone rang. "It's Georgina." I hit the green button. "Hi."

"Negan escaped."

"Don't panic, she's with us. She found Ralph, and he brought her here."

"Why? She has nothing to be afraid of."

My eyes darted from Ralph, then to Negan. "Perhaps get one of your best to take care of her. If the other two allowed her to escape so easily, you shouldn't use them again."

Georgina sighed. "I will fetch her myself," she said, and ended the call.

"There isn't anything to be afraid of, Negan. Georgina is on her way and will take you herself. I'm sure they will arrange better accommodations for you."

"I still don't trust them." She folded her arms and leaned her hip against the wall as if trying to anchor herself to the house.

"The Vampire Council extradited the mist vampire and the rogue kiss. Benjamin is human and will remain in custody until his trial. And they caught your cousin red-handed with gold dust up his nose. He has at least six charges against him, and one of those is an accessory to murder, which he'll get at least ten years for. There is nobody else after you."

"Can't I stay here the night? Please," she said after a brief pause. When she found her voice again, she glanced from me to Ralph, then to Sebastian, who stood behind me. "I won't be any trouble, I promise," she mumbled and stuck out her bottom lip.

I sighed audibly. "We were actually on our way home."

Her chin trembled.

I wondered if she was lonely and in need of friends, if we were the first people she came to for help.

I leaned against Sebastian and glanced up at him.

"If you want to," he said, knowing my thoughts without having to say anything.

I sent Georgina a text. "Fine, you can stay the night but no stealing or I'll have you arrested."

She shrieked and jumped up and down.

"How old are you?"

"Seventeen," she said with a playful smile and bright lavender eyes.

She was only a year older than Scout. If Scout was in any danger and I wasn't around, I'd want someone to take care of her. I hated when kids pulled on my heartstrings.

"Why are you not with other fae or your gran?"

She averted her eyes, and her expression became a storm cloud of emotions. "My gran is old, and I don't want her getting involved in any of this. I hate troubling her. And the others... well..." she sighed. "The others said it was my fault my parents had turned to stone." She seemed to shrink back into herself. "They think I caused their demise, but it was an accident. They opened the man's wallet I'd stolen when green powder blasted in their faces and they turned to stone."

"Gorgon dust?"

She nodded.

"Where are your parents?"

"My gran takes care of their statues."

I grinned. This was going to be easy, and I was in high spirits.

I called Jedediah and Declan to help. Ralph took Negan to her gran, where they met the two gorgons. Ralph switched on his body camera for my viewing pleasure and I watched her parents come alive; their statues were solid, and they even had chips from being carried from one place to the next. Her parents slowly came alive within an hour;

at first it was only an eye twitching, then a wiggle of their nose. Because they had been stone parents for more than a year, it took them well over three hours before they were back to their usual selves. Ralph stayed with Negan until her parents were finally free and moving.

Before Jedediah and Declan had left, they gave Negan instructions on what to feed her parents; a green paste made specifically by gorgons to assist in the regeneration of cells and tissue. After the fourth hour, Negan's parents were whole, healthy, and couldn't stop holding their daughter.

While that was going on, Sebastian and I went to our home. He connected my phone to the television, and we watched everything play out like a movie.

Chapter Forty-Two

Ivy pulled the elegant cerulean dress over my head and allowed it to cascade down my body to the ground. The sleeves were a fine lace with a silk bodice.

"Nothing but the best," Léon had said when he had handed me the gown.

"Are you ready?" Sebastian stopped dead in the doorjamb, his mouth wide open, and his eyes raked up my body. "Wow!" He licked his lips.

"Almost," I smiled as I took him in slowly from head to toe; a white dress shirt straining against his honed body— the top two buttons left undone, so I caught a glimpsed of his powerful muscles underneath. With slim black slacks outlining his ass and legs. Strong. Powerful. Seductive. All I wanted to do was rip off his clothing.

"You look ravishing." He closed the gap. The gold sliver pulsing in his green eyes. He winked wickedly and kissed me, stroking his tongue along mine, and I flicked the tip of one of his fangs and a low growl sounded from his throat. He pulled away and licked his lips.

"We have to stop, or we'll shred your dress."

"And he must come out first."

"Uh-huh." Our lips touched one last time, then he took my hand in his. "You ready?"

"Yep."

He held his arm out for me to take and we walked down passages in Anne's house, then outside where everyone waited. They had decorated the trees with white flowers and a bonfire in the middle of the open space. All the leopards were there.

Jeremiah nudged Kai and Lee; the three were-leopards stood straight yet respectful of their leader. Jeremiah was the youngest, but the power vibrating from him made my hair curl. He had shaved his soft brown curls, and his soft cheeks now defined and sharp. He winked at me, which earned him an elbow jab into his chest from Kai.

"What?" He feigned ignorance.

Lee held his elbow out for me to take and led me to my chair; adorned with the same white flowers and a soft cushion.

Lee, Kai, and Jeremiah stood behind my seat.

Sebastian and Greg stood together in the center and watched their mother. Anne wore a black dress; she always wore shorts and a t-shirt, and my jaw almost fell to the floor. She was in her early sixties and hardly looked a day older than forty-five. Her smile was broad and even though her eyes looked tired, she held up the facade. She was ill and wanted to ensure the two men reigned together peacefully, and she wanted to be present for this. She couldn't wait until next year when they'd originally planned it.

She kissed each man on the cheek and motioned for everyone to sit. "Thank you for joining us on this momentous occasion. As you all know, my time has come. I have ruled the leap for many years following the murder of my husband and your leader, Rick..."

Nobody knew it was me who had murdered Rick, and I would keep it that way. He was not a nice man. He had cheated on Anne with my mother and had murdered my Ma when I was young. I'd vowed to kill the man responsible, and I had.

"... and some might argue I have many more years ahead of me. But, unfortunately, my body did not recover from the bout of silver poisoning that killed one other and hurt me..."

Last year Anne had mistakenly drunk a cocktail from another leopard who had poisoned the concoction. Anne had shared it with one other who had died soon after ingesting it. No amount of shifting eradicated the silver, and it had slowly been killing Anne. Mel had advised her she might have a year left; *maybe*. They had found the leopard responsible and had destroyed her and her home. While they had searched her home, they had found the reason she had poisoned Anne, *jealousy*. Rick had dated this leopard the same time he had dated Anne, but he had chosen Anne as his wife. This woman had held onto that grudge until she couldn't anymore; her reason had filled her with anger, and she had come undone.

Grudges and revenge were a dark black virus. It ate you up from the inside and did nobody any good. Except for me. I'd felt great after I'd killed Rick. The corners of my mouth curved upward as I recalled what I'd done. Then Anne's words brought me back into the present.

"... but I will fight every day until it takes me. And the real reason we're here is to celebrate my two sons and your new leaders. They'll work cohesively and I'm sure this leap will ensure that," — she grinned, — "and we all love a little celebration."

Sebastian and Greg thanked everyone and opened the festivities.

The leap clapped hands, some whistled, others started singing. The atmosphere sent a powerful jolt of electricity through my body and tears escaped. The field thrummed with the leaps power, a constant beat against my body. It was exciting with the potential energy radiating off the were-leopards. Some tore clothing from their bodies and ran into the forest to hunt. The waning crescent moon with its silver shine splashed on all the heavenly bodies.

My leopard came to the surface and roared, followed by my saber. I gripped the armrest until my nails hurt. I did not want that to happen. They needed to behave. My leopard rippled beneath my skin, and again, my saber did the same and it made me wonder if they were competing to come to the surface. My leopard had never won, I'd never shifted into her before—it had only ever been my saber.

A low trickling growl came from the back of my throat. Kai glared down at me. Jeremiah roared loudly beside me as he ripped off his clothing, rippling muscles moved like liquid metal as his body changed. His hands became large black claws, he fell on all fours as a wave of fur covered his body.

My heart thundered in my chest. Sweat dripped down my back. I was confident I'd be fine here tonight, but I knew I had to get away and reached for Kai, who helped me stand. "Get me inside!"

Gripping Kai's hand helped me maneuver through the sea of changing bodies. The smell of the kitties was alluring yet intoxicating. It drove my leopard crazy as she fought to climb out of me. I honestly couldn't say who was more eager to escape, her or the baby.

One hand held my rippling stomach while the other clung onto Kai. He moaned as I dug my nails into his skin and the smell of his blood assaulted my nose.

I screamed as I collapsed to the ground, my knees breaking my fall. My joints ached as my stomach pulled, and I was sure something tore.

Kai helped me to my feet. Once I regained my balance, I took one step at a time and on the third step, liquid dripped down the inside of my thighs.

"Sebastian!" I yelled through gritted teeth, sucking in deep breaths. Pain tore through my abdomen, blurring my vision. But Sebastian couldn't hear me over the roars and shifting from the other kitty-cats.

Kai yelled Sebastian's name.

Another wave of electricity shot through my stomach and I yelled louder. Blood poured down my legs, which was an instant party killer, especially for hungry were-leopards who wanted to hunt.

Sebastian called out my name above the loud murmur of everyone. I heard him running, digging my nails deeper into Kai's hand when another ripple of pain smashed into me, and he screamed with me. The other leopards gave us space even though they smelled the fresh blood. They knew I was not food, yet it was still tempting. I felt hands grip my sides as Sebastian picked me up.

"Get Mel and Désiré here now," he yelled and carried me inside.

Chapter Forty-Three
SCOUT

We sat on a mountain ledge for a well-deserved break. The armor hugging my body was comfortable even if it didn't look it. I sat cross-legged while I took in the scenery—it was breathtaking considering it's the Underworld. There was no sun, only a bright light that shone everywhere in the *sky*. It reminded me of an ever-present wasteland that never changed. The atmosphere was at a pleasant temperature and kept us comfortable. It was only the rough terrain we navigated that was unsettling.

We had climbed another mountain to get closer to the smoke, and my crows were nowhere in sight. As we sat on the ledge, we saw the smokey area clearer, which emitted from a crater in the ground with an outer circle.

"What do you think the other stuff is?" I pointed at the outer circle. From where we sat, it reminded me of shards of broken glass sticking out in every position.

"Not sure, but look how light reflects on the surfaces," River said as he broke off pieces of his sandwich for Luna.

She greedily gobbled it up and begged for more with her big brown eyes.

Depending on how I moved my head, different colors reflected, strangely, they were all light colors, pinks, greens, blues, and oranges. They were serene and comforting colors, not what I expected.

When I'd first read up on the Underworld and what to expect, it was all dark reds and black, followed by heat, lots and lots of heat. Just thinking about it made me hot. I smiled knowingly. But this Underworld was different, yet strangely majestic. I only wished Victor was here with me, taking me by the hand to show me the ropes. Instead, it felt as though he'd dunked me in the ocean of lava and told me to swim to a shore that kept shifting farther away from me.

River jerked his chin at me. "That's probably why you're dressed like that." He raised both eyebrows. "Perhaps it's something you need to do alone."

"Or you could burn it with your fire," I joked.

He bumped his shoulder into mine. "Maybe," he smiled.

I exhaled a shaky breath. "How long do you suppose we've been here? It feels like it's been at least a day."

"I gave up trying to understand time *here* or anywhere Victor sends me because no matter where I end up, it always baffles me. It's constantly changing. But," — he considered his words, — "it might feel like a week here, but back in the real world, it would only have been a few days."

"Really?"

He nodded.

I sighed.

"You miss your mom?"

"Yeah, I do. I didn't like how I left things before coming here."

"I'm sure she knows you love her."

"I know." A pang of guilt struck me. I was homesick and wished this was over so I could go home.

We finished our *picnic* and continued on our journey.

I hadn't heard my crows and was becoming concerned. I hoped they were okay. Then a thought crossed my mind.

"If our spirit animal gets hurt, does it hurt us in any way?"

"No, but it leaves you with the grief of losing a loved one. There may be a sting, but we won't die."

"Oh, okay. I suppose I would've felt something if they injured my crows?"

"Uh-huh," he smiled reassuringly and took up his place in front, leading the way.

The climb down the mountain was smoother than the previous one. I was happy there were no snakes hissing near us. We only stepped on the rocks and avoided the sand completely; we did not want to summon the sand serpent again. I didn't know what it was or what it would do if we walked on the sand again, but I didn't want to tempt it either.

We neared the area from where the smoke came from, the puffs of black fumes wafted in the air above us. There was no smell, debris or ash.

"Do you smell anything?"

River shook his head. "No, it doesn't smell like anything is burning here."

"Huh." I stood with my hands on my hips as I absorbed what lay before us.

The large *glass* spikes we'd seen from the mountain ledge

were ominous now that we stood in front of it. Huge crystal-like glass protruding from the ground near our feet. The light reflecting off the crystals was a delicate pink, almost tender—probably deceiving—but it was stunning and reminded me of the color salmon or a pink rose.

"How can we test whether it's safe for us to climb through it?" The crystals stood at odd angles, circling the smoking area with no way to climb over, under or around it.

"We could use Luna—"

"No!" I grabbed River's arm and shook my head. "What if she gets hurt? Maybe throw a stick at it, or a pebble."

He picked up a pebble and threw it at the crystals. It bounced off the surface creating a pleasant *ping* sound, then it *plonked* to the ground. I didn't feel any power radiate from the crystals, nor did I feel anything when the pebble hit the ground.

I picked up the same pebble and threw it, again it made the same *ping* as it struck the crystal, then a *plonk* when it landed on the black rock.

"It makes sounds," I beamed and picked up a handful of the black sand, but not before scanning the dark dirt for the sand creature. I threw the sand at the crystals and they made delicate *ping* sounds, reminding me of a feather dancing on piano strings—it was soft, yet audible.

"Perhaps it's safe for us to touch." I swallowed the lump in my throat and reached for the crystal. My arm trembled. My mind and body afraid of what would come next.

"Don't," — River lowered my arm, — "let me try."

Before River did anything, a wave of hot air pushed us back a few steps. Victor stood behind us in all his splendor; his dark wings spread out and shimmered with rays of purple and blue. They closed behind his back and tiny feathers danced in the air between us.

"Your mother has called on you, Scout. We need to go now."

I glanced at the smokey crater and crystals, then back at Victor. "What about your game?"

He stared with tenderness in his blue eyes and for the first time a spark of fatherly love. He surveyed his surroundings and exhaled. "We have more than enough time to complete the task. Your mother needs you more, and I don't think she can wait."

To hear him speak of my mom with that tone told me there was hope for him yet. Perhaps we could connect after all. To me he wasn't as dangerous as I had first thought, even though I hardly knew everything about him. To remedy that, I needed to spend more time with him. This was a game he couldn't play and needed me to help him, but when Mom needed me, he didn't think twice to fetch me. For that alone, my heart swelled with love and I took his hand.

Chapter Forty-Four

Mel lifted my dress as Désiré packed towels.

"Do you still want to go natural?" Désiré asked, ready with the epidural.

"Yes," I nodded. They advised me against going natural because of the previous procedure I had, but I wanted to try, regardless. I was in good health despite his rapid growth. Sweat dripped down my neck and I pushed wet hair out of my face. "But you are ready to cut... in case?"

"Yes, I've got my kit here." She pointed at her trolley with medical supplies. "And I have lots of drugs." She held up another syringe.

"Let's get the epidural done." I wanted a natural birth, but I also wanted to move around if I needed to. With the epidural, I wouldn't feel the intensity of the contractions.

Désiré nodded once and proceeded with the low-dose injection into my back. I didn't feel a thing. Then she helped me lie down.

I gritted my teeth when another contraction tore through me; it was intense as it felt as though my insides were being shredded. I did the breathing thing and felt the contraction subside.

"I want him out," I breathed, and another contraction hit, harder and more painful. "Noooooow!"

Désiré and Mel got to work.

When they told me to push, I pushed.

My first pregnancy was an emergency caesarian section where they had to perform a vertical incision on my uterus, and although this delivery was an emergency too, I didn't think another caesarian was necessary.

It felt like forever though, but it was only two hours of pushing, stopping, grinding my teeth and blood. Désiré had me on an IV to replenish lost fluids, but it still left me exhausted.

I sucked in air and pushed one last time. This had to be it. I couldn't last another two hours. Either he came out now, or Désiré would cut him out. The pain ebbed and dissolved. The drugs worked, but I still felt as though my insides were being shredded.

This had to be it...

Désiré told me to push, and I did; one last soul crushing push and there he was. Out.

I cried when his cries echoed mine. The loud, heart shattering, ice melting burst of joy of his voice sent my heart fluttering. He was out, alive and well.

He was perfect.

"Do you want to hold him?" Désiré wrapped him in a white blanket.

"Uh-huh." I wiped sweat and tears off my cheeks.

She handed me the bundle, and my heart stopped. Golden eyes stared back at me, reminding me of Sebastian's green eyes with the golden sliver. He had a full head of dark hair reminding me of Léon, and he reached for me. I gave him my free index finger, which he grabbed and pulled toward his mouth.

"I think he's hungry."

"For milk or blood?" Mel asked beside me.

The door swung open. Sebastian flew inside the room with tears streaking his face as his eyes adjusted to the scene. Shock registered on his face first when he saw the piles of blood-soaked towels and me on the bed with blood everywhere. But then his eyes darted to the white blanket in my hands and he visibly relaxed. He gently sat beside me, kissed my cheek and temple, and then looked at our son.

"Are you okay?" He cast his eyes toward the blood-soaked towels again.

"Uh-huh, he has yellow/golden eyes."

"I think it's safe to say he's yours, even with the dark hair." Mel reached for his shoulder and gave him a squeeze. "He wouldn't have been this calm if he was a vampire."

His smile reached his misty eyes. "He might still change."

"Perhaps," Mel replied nonchalantly.

"You want to hold him?"

He nodded.

I lifted him up, and he took our son, swaddling him tightly, and brought him to his chest.

"Ah, how lovely. I get to see my grandson before I die," Anne said as she closed the door.

Sebastian showed him to her, and she stole him out of his hands.

"What's his name?"

I shrugged. "We still have to think of one." I jerked my chin at Sebastian.

Sebastian sat beside me, placing his arm around me. "You sure you okay?"

"I'm just tired." I lay against him as we watched Anne hold and speak to our son. It was magical. She stood near the window and described the trees he would climb when he was older and about nature. It was a marvelous sight to behold.

A thought crossed my mind. It felt as though an ice bucket dunked over me. "Scout!" I sat upright. "I have to let Scout know."

"Did you arrange how that would happen?"

I leaned into Sebastian again. "No," I said and closed my eyes.

'Victor!' I thought his name.

Silence echoed in my ears.

'Victor!' I thought again. *'Are you there? Please bring Scout to me. Her brother has been born and I need her.'*

Seconds passed, then minutes and still nothing. Victor didn't respond, and there was no other way I could reach her. Sadness tugged at my core. It was the birth of my son without having my daughter present, even after Victor had promised he would bring her. I'd have to figure out another way to reach them.

I glanced at the window as the air stilled.

A black bird had perched on a branch, motionless.

Anne froze as she kissed him on the cheek.

Désiré and Mel stood stuck in time as they cleaned the room.

Sebastian arched an eyebrow and turned when the air snapped.

The baby cried.

Victor and Scout walked through the wall with another person in tow.

A smile splashed on Scout's face. She hugged me first, then approached her baby brother.

Flames and smoke bellowed behind Victor as his dark armor rippled from its hard outer shell to reveal his skin. His muscles flexed with an intensity, but it was for show, nobody was challenging him. His shimmering black wings closed and faded behind his back.

Victor snapped his fingers, and everything returned to normal.

Anne's shocked expression softened when she realized it was only Scout's hands over hers and handed the boy over.

Désiré and Mel gasped when they saw the dark figure looming over them.

I asked them and Anne to excuse us for a moment.

Sebastian helped me sit upright.

"Scout, come here. Tell me how everything is going?"

Scout rocked the baby as she closed the gap between us. Sebastian stood to give us space, but his eyes didn't leave Victor's; I didn't think he trusted him.

"He's beautiful. Those eyes." She glanced at Sebastian, then back at him. "I take it he's a leopard."

I shrugged. "We don't know, but he's definitely leaning more toward Sebastian's wild side. I guess we'll see if he craves drinking blood more than the hunt."

"Hmm," she said and lifted him up. "Is it just me or is he growing?"

"I haven't even held him properly to answer that."

She handed him to me, and she was right. At first, he was tiny in the blanket, I could wrap him up twice in it. But he's grown a few centimeters since I'd last held him—which was only half an hour ago.

"I think he's going to age quickly like Sebastian and Léon did. We will see if he stops at twenty-eight."

"No fair," Scout groaned beside me. The lines between her eyes deepened. "He's going to be older than me."

I laughed at her protest, but I needed to know how she was *really* doing. "Tell me, how is everything?" I jerked my chin in Victor's direction, hoping she would understand the extent of my question without me having to spell it out.

Victor still eyed Sebastian—it looked like they were trying to outmaneuver each other with their penetrating gazes. All I needed was for someone to bring out the measuring tape.

"It's okay…" she glanced over her shoulder at the other young man, then whispered. "I'll tell you everything when I get back. But I'm glad I came to see him," — she squeezed her baby brother's foot, — "but we must get going. I'm helping Victor locate something and must go."

"Okay." I lifted my free arm for a hug.

Scout hugged and kissed my cheek. "Love you," she added, "and I miss you."

"I miss and love you, too."

In a wink they disappeared, leaving Sebastian and I alone.

"I don't like him," he grunted, still staring at the spot where Victor had been standing.

"He's gone. Come, tell me about the names you were thinking of."

Chapter Forty-Five

SCOUT

Victor teleported us back to the wasteland in the Underworld, but he didn't leave. To my surprise, he'd brought us back to the same spot he'd fetched us from.

With the sudden impact of moving through space and time, I doubled over when we landed, spewing my guts between two rocks. The sudden change in scenery and motionlessness was too much for my mere mortal body to handle.

River and Victor were irritatingly fine.

"So that's your mom?" River said from a distance, perhaps afraid I'd mess on his shoes.

"Yeah." I wiped my mouth with my sleeve.

"What did you mean by you think it's Sebastian's?" he furrowed his brows as he watched me.

"Enough with the chit-chat. You need to retrieve the golden egg," Victor yelled with a bony finger pointed at the crystal barrier.

"Why are you still here? Usually, you just drop us and

go." I sipped some water and felt better, my stomach no longer twisting with knots.

Victor harrumphed and stepped backward. He seemed conflicted over something. "Fine! I'll leave then." The air snapped, and he vanished, leaving baby black feathers dancing in the air near my face.

"What was that about?"

"Not sure. However, I saw he and Sebastian doing some serious eye thing back at your mom's place."

"Ugh, why? He left my mom before I was even born. Why would he care if she had another child?" I clucked my tongue. "Anyway, where were we?"

"You were about to tell me who the father is. You know, your brother's dad."

"Oh, right," I groaned. My mom could do as she pleased and date anyone she wanted to. But sometimes it was a headache explaining it to someone who might not see it that way. Some were a little judgmental, and I wasn't sure how River would handle it if at all, but he asked, and I would tell him. "She's dating a were-leopard and a vampire. They wanted to wait until after his birth to see if he developed powers showing who the actual father was."

River was quiet for a few minutes as he thought it over. "Sometimes family dynamics get complicated."

I nodded, not sure what to say. I shouldn't really care what he thought about my family anyway, yet I still wanted to know his opinion.

"My kid sister has something similar. I haven't met them yet. She told my mom she's dating two guys at the same time; both are vampires. That was like two years ago, and we haven't seen her since. But she phones our mom at least once a month to check in to see how she's doing and to let her know she's still alive. She seems happy," he shrugged. "So, who am I to judge."

"Cool. People find love in the strangest places."

"What about you?" he asked, then his cheeks flushed a healthy shade of red. It was the first time I'd seen him embarrassed about anything. Usually, he was so calm and collected.

"I'm only sixteen, River. I have no interest in men, or women, or whatever. And besides, I want to finish school, then join my mom's business."

"The hunter?"

"Assassin. She co-owns Ulysses Assassins with another guy, just a friend before you ask. But yeah, and they have a clairvoyant who works with them. He's cool, too, a little weird, but he's super awesome to have a conversation with. Anyway, Ralph, the guy who owns it with my mom, is showing me a few things about the business—"

"So you're like an apprentice."

"Yes, exactly."

"Wow, you've got your entire life set out already. When I was sixteen, I was playing basketball and chasing girls." He blushed again and I couldn't help but smile.

"How old are you, anyway? You speak like you should be thirty, but you still look so young."

He cleared his throat. "I'm twenty-two. But I must add, I've been twenty-two since I started working for your dad— I mean Victor."

My brows furrowed. "How long ago was that?"

"Twenty-three years ago."

My jaw dropped. "What? You're lying."

"I swear."

"That means you're like in your forties then." Ew, gross. He was as old as Mason was.

"No, I will stay twenty-two until Victor releases me. Then I will continue to age like everyone else."

I didn't know what to say. Victor had put River's life on hold to do his bidding for him. I didn't know if Victor was selfish or generous, but River had a long life ahead of him. At least he was still in his early twenties, his adult life was just starting.

"Does it bother you that you haven't aged or that you're doing all this for Victor?" I lifted my arms and pointed at our surroundings.

"No, not one bit. He saved my mom. She would've died a painful death, but he took the hurt away and she's doing well. Apparently, he will only *collect* her soul when she's passed a hundred," he chuckled lightheartedly, but it still sounded hollow.

We fell silent for a moment. I didn't know what to say. I was grateful he was helping me, but sad he was, which only made me feel selfish. He could do other, more important stuff instead of babysitting me.

I cast an eye around and noted the crystals now held a delicate orange hue to them.

"Shall we?"

River reached for the crystal and paused an inch away from it. Beads of sweat peppered his forehead, which he wiped away with the back of his other hand. He neared the barrier.

My heart fluttered inside my ribcage. My armor clung to my body.

River had offered to test the crystals to see what would happen. We didn't know what to expect once he touched it.

Would he melt, burn, or just collapse? I hoped nothing happened and we could climb through it to get to the center.

He touched the crystal with his index finger and started convulsing. He jerked and twisted as his body shook. The crystals must have some sort of electrical current running through them. And now he was being electrocuted. His face twisted in pain. I screamed. He screamed. He pulled his hand away and stood straight, then burst out laughing.

"Not funny." I hit his shoulder with my fist, but the action hurt my hand.

He rubbed the area I'd hit followed by an, "Ow."

"Serves you right. That's a terrible prank to play on me, especially now and here of all places," I groaned as I crossed my arms.

"I'm sorry," he said, but the sheepish smile still tugged at the corners of his mouth. "I couldn't help myself. I thought we needed some comedic relief."

"Not funny." I hit his other shoulder, harder this time, but I came away whimpering as I cradled my injured hand. "That hurt."

"Admit it, though, it was funny." He rubbed the other shoulder.

My emotions deceived me as I smiled, then tried in vain to force it away, but it didn't help. I burst out laughing. It was funny to see him jerk around like a fish out of water.

"Yeah, it was funny."

Our laughing fit continued, then when our eyes met the laughter faded. The comedic break was something we sorely needed, but we still had so much to do. We didn't know what lay ahead or if we'd come out alive.

"At least we can climb through it," I finally said. "Did you know it wouldn't affect you?"

"I took a chance. Come, let's go through." Then he turned to Luna and ordered, "Stay."

We climbed through the crystal bars at the same time. The surface was cool to the touch and smooth. There were no dents or chips I could see or feel. It was an obstacle course of proportions. I had to lift my foot one way, pull my body up and bring my other leg up and over. There wasn't enough space to put both feet down at once, I had to find another foothold to rest. I climbed over, under, until eventually I met up with River on the other side.

River's clothing clung to his body as sweat dripped down the sides of his face.

I tugged at the armor; it felt suffocating, and I wanted it off.

"Don't," River warned. "You might need it later on. We don't know what will happen when we reach the center."

I continued pulling on the armor until it gave way at the collar, and I felt the cool air against my chest. I froze. *Cool air.* There shouldn't be cool air or even warm air. Ever since we'd arrived here, the temperature was perfect; not hot, warm, cold, or cool—it was perfect. I exhaled and saw my breath before me. I glanced up and the usual yellow sky had turned blue. *Cold.* It was getting colder by the second. The smoke had stopped. The gray fumes were no longer emitting out the center of the crater. Something had changed the moment we crossed through the crystals.

As if reading my mind, River's eyes widened. He grabbed my hand when the ground tilted sideways. We skidded down over a flat surface, heading toward the center. The thick darkness swallowed us as we reached the middle.

The ground had shifted creating a funnel and had lifted on all sides then stopped moving the moment we hit the center. River had found a foothold to stand on and clung to the narrow opening. He'd caught me and helped me stand beside him. I held on for my life. Sweat dripped down my back, and my arms quivered as my hands ached from gripping the opening.

"Look down," River whispered. "It looks like a soft landing."

"Whah?" I slowly adjusted my head and did as suggested. In the center of the large, dark room was water. I burst out laughing. "This place is so weird." The sparkling blue water was inviting, and I swallowed, my throat dry, and it felt as though I was back in the desert. A drink of water was a welcome refreshment, and below was all the water I could drink.

A shadow moved over our heads, blocking the light. We glanced up when the earth closed completely above us, swallowing us in darkness once more. I wasn't sure if the water had risen or if the ceiling had dropped, but I felt the water lapping at my feet.

This world felt strange the moment we arrived, and I wondered what would happen next. The water slapped against my ankles as the levels rose. The dark walls closed in. I was about to drown in a sea of darkness, when a light glowed from below, highlighting the depths which seemed to go on forever. The water continued rising, closing in on us. Soon we wouldn't have enough air and would need to swim somewhere. I wasn't a wonderful swimmer and couldn't hold my breath for long. If the water reached the ceiling of this cave—or room, or whatever it was—I doubted I could last long on one breath.

"We have to go in," River said with panic laced in his

tone. "We have to go under and follow that tunnel. I'm sure we'll be able to come up for air somewhere." He squinted as he stared into the water.

I followed his line of sight and couldn't see much of anything. "There has to be another way," I said, and my chest tightened just thinking about not being able to breathe.

"Down there is the only way. It looks like a tunnel we need to swim through."

The water rose to my hips and would reach my shoulders soon. My chest heaved and my breath hitched. Tears streamed down my cheeks. The water rushed.

"We have to go." River reached for my hand and squeezed it. "Trust me, let go."

I shook my head. "I can't."

"You must." He sucked in his breath and exhaled. "One… two… three," River said, then jumped underneath the rising water.

"No, wait!" I yelled, but it was too late.

I whimpered as River continued sinking into the abyss. His eyes widened. I couldn't make out what he was pointing at because there was nothing behind me.

I squinted, struggling to see him through the waves. I could've been mistaken, and he wasn't pointing at all but telling me to jump in. The dark water swallowed him as I struggled to see where he was going, and then he disappeared.

My heart sank as realization sunk in, I was alone in the dark with nowhere to go but down. I had to swim after him. I couldn't stay here. The water would reach the ceiling and I'd still drown.

The water reached my neck, and I had to let go. I sucked in one last breath, closed my eyes and let go. A strange sensation washed over my body as I floated down; a feeling of weightlessness and flying, yet sinking at the same time.

I could only hold my breath for a few seconds at a time. I wasn't used to swimming underwater for long periods of time, and I already needed to breathe.

My lungs burned as I continued sinking, and both ears popped at the same time. I desperately needed to breathe and felt my heartbeat slow down. I blinked vigorously, but my surroundings remained blurry.

I moved my arms and legs to swim, but something was pulling me down. Bubbles escaped my nose and lips. I had to breathe, and now. My pulse thumped in my ears. Just as I was about to open my mouth to breathe, I pursed them. I would drown if I did that. I whimpered and felt no tears escape as the water continued its hold on me.

I had to breathe… now…

I closed my eyes—I wasn't giving up, but I couldn't hold my breath any longer. I couldn't, I needed to relax, and concentrated on not trying to breathe in the water.

Something moved around my body and my eyes shot open. As if feeling my body struggle, the armor rippled against my body and *spread*. It moved up my neck and around my head, then covered my open hands—cocooning me in.

I closed my eyes as it sucked the water out of the suit, and I no longer felt wet. Slowly, I opened my eyes and looked through the bubble now formed over my face and I exhaled into my suit. It didn't fog up the glass, nor did I feel my air being restricted. *Air*. I had air and could breathe normally.

I wanted to laugh-cry with happiness, but my wonder was short-lived when the water rushed against me, dragging me farther into the darkness. I couldn't see anything around me. It was dark with an uncomfortable blackness. I felt blindfolded and on a water slide. I was grateful I could still breath and thankful I had this armor on; and silently thanked Victor for giving it to me.

When another water current hit me, it twirled me around and around. I went tumbling upside down until my head broke through the surface. *Surface?* I opened my eyes. I'd reached the end of the water tunnel and came to another open area. My armor creaked open when it hit the air, and I waded into the deep water.

"We're in another cave." Came the familiar voice.

I smiled as relief washed over me. "You made it? Where are you?" I squinted in the dim light as I swam in a circle, searching for him.

"Here." He stepped into my line of sight and reached for me.

I swam toward him. "I have no idea what just happened," I said as I grabbed his hand, and he pulled me to shore. "I flipped and turned around, only to enter an upside-down world. If that makes any sense." My legs wobbled when I stood beside him. He continued to hold me until the trembling stopped.

"I wish I had a suit like yours." He winked.

"And you held your breath the entire way?"

He nodded. "I used to be on the swim team," he smirked as he led me to a path on the far side of the cave wall. "And I still train on my *off* days."

"Of course." River seemed equipped to do a lot of things. "If my armor didn't morph into a breathing swimsuit, I would've drowned. I'd just held my breath when I needed to take another one. There's no way I would've survived the current without the suit."

"It's as if Victor knew." He eyed me suspiciously.

"Now that you say it, he did, didn't he? He knew what I would endure, and he made sure I didn't die. How thoughtful of him, or sneaky." I wanted to be mad at Victor, but I couldn't. He had helped me by giving me the suit. Then a strange thought gnawed at me; he knew what was coming. He knew as if he had planned it. I felt my brows deepen and shook the thoughts away. We needed to finish this first, I'd ask questions when I saw him. "What's next?" I sighed as I followed River.

"This way."

With no torches on the walls of the cave or natural sunlight from above, there was only the glow of the water to our side. It reminded me of pure fresh water; wholesome and beautiful. I'd never seen that color blue before; near the shore it was a little darker but lightened toward the middle —it was crystal clear, bright blue, and stunning—all the color blues at once. And it was our only source of light. The soft blue hue guided us to the far side of the cave, to a hole surrounded by stalagmites. River went first, using the protruding rocks as a ladder to climb down. I followed him, my legs shaky and my arms straining. It exhausted me.

My breathing came in hard and shallow as I descended the rocky steps into a dark room. My fingers overworked and aching, my shoulders burned and my legs unsteady but kept me up. When I reached the bottom, I landed with a loud thump and collapsed.

"Please, can we take a break? I'm exhausted." I searched for River while my eyes adjusted to the darkness.

"Shh," he replied from somewhere to my right, then I felt his hand on my shoulder. "She sleeps," he whispered near the shell of my ear, sending a cascade of goosebumps down the right-hand side of my body.

He touched my chin and tipped it down and to the right. I saw the outline of a resting creature and recoiled. Too afraid to make a sound as I stared, feeling numb. I didn't recognize *her*, but she was large. I could make out the silver outline of her body in the dim light as her skin shimmered.

When my eyes finally adjusted, I saw her clearer. The outline of her face seemed soft with something similar to a large beak, but I couldn't be sure. She had wings at her sides and a thick tail tucked beneath her wings with the end resting under her chin. She was not a dragon or a griffin—but something else entirely.

She stirred, kneading her bed to make it soft before lying down again, reminding me of a cat.

"Where's the egg?" I whispered.

"She's lying on it."

Great, how were we supposed to get it? I reached for River's hand and stood. "How are we going to get her to move?" I whispered near his ear.

"I don't know." He grabbed my hand and pulled me to walk with him. "But I have an idea."

We approached the sleeping bird-cat-like-creature carefully. Once my eyes had adjusted to the black of the cave, I saw a faint shimmering outline on everything as if coated in a glow-in-the-dark paint. The rocks protruding out of the wall were a similar shape—oval—like an egg. We stood and watched the creature sleep. Its body crested and fell as it breathed. The surrounding air was warm, and it smelled like a farmhouse; hay and animals. The ground at our feet was smooth, nothing to trip us up as we closed the distance.

When River had said he had an idea, I didn't expect what he had had in mind. He had caught me off guard when he let go of my hand and told me to stay. Then he disappeared to the other side of the creature. My eyes singed when a ball of flames ignited, his body alive with hot, angry fire. Somehow his clothing remained intact through the flames.

The creature awoke from its slumber, its fury made known by the soul-piercing cry. It rose, towered over us with its large pachyderms' feet—like an elephant. It stomped around its nest to face the flames and opened its wings, preparing for battle. Its sharp beak snapped at River while he screamed to hold its attention. Its leathery tail whipped from side to side as its wings spread wider, showing its dominance over the little man bathed in fire.

River yelled something, but I couldn't hear him over the sound of my heart beating in my ears.

"Scout!" River yelled again. "The egg!" he shouted as he ran down a tunnel I hadn't noticed. The creature stomped heavily behind River, leaving her egg.

River's flames were so bright I didn't think she noticed I was here. It would devastate her when she realized I'd taken the egg, but we needed it. The golden egg lay peacefully in its nest, waiting to hatch. The light River had offered now gone, and it plunged me in thick blackness. My eyes adjusted once more as I felt my way toward the nest. My hands touched sticks and branches and I knew it was the nest and climbed inside. The faint outline of the egg was reassuring as I crawled on my hands and knees to the lonely object. When I reached the egg, I slowly picked it up, ensuring I had it in my grasp and crawled on my knees to the edge. Still holding the egg, I climbed out and headed in the direction River and the creature had gone, although I no longer heard them.

The egg wasn't heavy and about the size of a large dog. It wasn't uncomfortable to carry, but my arms were already straining from the mountain climb and swim. As quickly as I could, I hurried down the dark tunnel.

I'd been walking for a while when I stopped, desperately in need of a five-minute break to catch my breath. The tunnel seemed to stretch on forever. My body ached as I rested against the rocky wall. I placed the egg near my feet and sat beside it. My tongue sticking to my pallet as I craved a drink of water and possibly an energy bar or something, but River had the backpack with all the refreshments.

I glanced in the direction I had traversed, then up the way I still had to go. The tunnel seemed to go on forever, and all I knew I couldn't give up. I had to stand, pick up the egg and continue. If Mom was here, she would've told me to put on my big girl panties and get going. I shoved against the wall, picked up the egg, and walked.

One step in front of the other, I continued on my hike through the dark—never ending—tunnel. Every muscle in my body ached. I was thirsty, hungry, and my energy drained, but I continued—one slow step at a time.

I ambled through the dark tunnel. Closed my eyes a few times but continued taking one step in front of the other. The movement was soothing and ritualistic. One foot, then the other, breathe. One step, then another, inhale deeply, exhale.

The air was hot and stuffy; I licked my chapped lips and came away with dirt on my tongue, but swallowed the dirt down, anyway.

I opened one eye then the other and saw darkness and more of the tunnel.

I groaned frustratingly, but I couldn't give up.

My breathing labored; my chest burned. Every couple of minutes I'd suck in a deep breath to stay awake.

The walk continued on and on, one foot then the other, breathe.

The egg nestled uncomfortably in my aching arms, and I needed to find a position that didn't hurt as much. I lifted the egg slightly and held it in such a way I entwined my fingers and rested my head against the egg as I strolled.

One foot in front of the other, breathe.

Not sure what came first—the sounds or the light—I stopped walking and slowly opened my eyes. I stared at the dim red light up ahead and wondered if it was real, reminding me of a mirage in the desert. My vision tilted, the ground lifted, and everything blurred at the edges.

"Scout," said the familiar voice.

Large hands gently tugging on my shoulders, waking me. My eyes fluttered open, and we were back in the room where the nest was, where the creature slept.

"What just happened?" I asked sleepily, stood and added. "I was just in the tunnel." I pointed at the dark area where we'd just gone through.

"I know," River whispered. "I was running ahead of the creature, then I woke up back here. When I realized where I was and glanced down, I saw you asleep. It took a while before you came to."

I felt disorientated and the dim cavernous room wasn't helping. I held onto his forearm to steady myself.

"Now what?"

"We obviously failed and must try again."

I groaned my disappointment.

River slowly approached the sleeping creature before I could protest. I watched him stealthily move toward it. Before the creature was a hybrid of animals, this time it was only a hawk. He approached it from the side. It stirred and ruffled its feathers. I was unsure of the plan but wanted to help and followed him.

Water cascaded down one side of the cave walls. Water filled open holes in the ground, creating puddles I had to step lightly into, or I'd make a sound. The stalagmite and stalactite were sharp and coarse, reminding me of a monster's mouth. I furrowed my brows; I didn't recall seeing this before.

My lungs burned as I controlled my breathing. A faint fog blew in from the tunnel we'd used earlier, filling the cave and making it harder to see. I'd lost sight of River. My armor rippled over my skin as if sensing danger. The fog thickened its hold around me. The outline of the creature was a comfort as it lay in its nest, still asleep. River was nowhere.

"River," I whispered. My voice travelled through the cave and bounced off the walls—echoing his name.

My breath hitched; I froze when a deep rumbling near the nest began. It reminded me of a kitten purring, except this was a large hawk and hawks didn't purr. I kept watch on the shape in the nest. It didn't move, but the tonal fluttering continued. I was only a few feet away, yet so close I felt its warmth. Keeping an eye of the creature as I moved around it. I mis-stepped and landed in a puddle, splashing water everywhere. The eyelid opened. I kept my other foot mid-air. The golden iris with flecks of green and a soulless pupil zeroed in on me.

"Run!" River yelled.

The creature shot up in one swift motion. It breathed fire over my head. I headed for the tunnel. River came around in his blazed glory; his skeleton engulfed with his angry flames. The hawk returned the banter with another breath of fire. I was almost at the tunnel and saw light. As I reached the threshold, a ball of fire struck my side, blasting me into the other side of the wall.

I jerked awake and fell off the rock I'd been sitting on. River grabbed my arm to stop me from falling into the pool of water beside me. He cupped his hand over my mouth to stop me from screaming and only removed it when I'd calmed down.

My chest heaved as my heart thundered in my ribcage. I groaned. "Again?"

"Yeah," River whispered near the shell of my ear. "Although this one might be easy."

He stepped back so I could see what he meant. There was no creature in the nest. I leaped to my feet, not believing it. In the center lay the golden egg; it seemed to glow in the darkness—an invitation. I grinned.

"Let's get it."

"Hold on." He grabbed my upper arm. "Look." He pointed at a corner.

I squinted at the dark shadow trying to make out what it was; round like the rock nearby with pointy tips. It moved, I jumped back. It continued moving down the walls.

"What is that?"

"A snake."

"Not again," I moaned as we moved in the opposite direction to where the snake was heading—and away from the nest. "How are we going to get out of this time-loop?"

River let out a harsh breath as he pushed me into a corner. "Let's wait and see what happens. I have an idea."

We watched with bated breath, unmoving and transfixed on the snake now curling up in the nest. Its shiny body settling down, resting with its tongue flicking out of its mouth. It knew we were here; I was sure of it. What it would do was another story.

Collectively, we approached the sleeping serpent. I didn't want River to do this on his own and leave me alone —a lonely prey for the hungry predator. The snake's eye had closed by the time we were halfway to the nest. We stepped quietly but quickly. The closer we got, I caught sight of the golden egg. The snake had curled its body around it, exposing it.

River pointed at the egg, motioning he would grab it while I ran. I shrugged and mouthed, *to where?* He pointed to the hole we'd used to come down here.

I nodded my understanding. Of course, no matter what we had tried to do down here, we kept repeating the same mistake and kept getting caught. The tunnel led to nowhere, and we kept dying and had to start over again like some sick game. There's no way out of this place, except to go back the same way we came from.

I cursed myself for not thinking about it sooner. It was so obvious, but not.

Carefully, I backed away from River while he slowly neared the egg. The snake didn't stir. I stopped and watched, too afraid of stepping in a puddle and alerting the snake to my whereabouts. River had the egg in his grasp. The snake's skin shimmered in the dim light. River slowly lifted the egg. The serpent moved, tightening its hold on the egg. River's face shone with perspiration as he strained to keep hold of the egg.

What came next happened so suddenly neither of us had time to react. The snake awoke, raised its hooded head and bit River, then it came for me. River collapsed to the ground. I ran away, but too slow. The snake was out of its nest, its body gliding across the floor, and magically appeared before me with its mouth wide open.

I shot up, hitting River under his chin as he bent over to help me stand. We moaned in pain; I rubbed the top of my head while he rubbed his chin. We smiled, then mine faltered when I realized we were still here and still had to get the egg.

River spun around and I stepped beside him. The nest now filled with golden eggs; there were at least twenty of them. Which one was the correct egg? There was no way we could take all of them.

I glanced around the dark room, no shadows moved and no sounds apart from my breathing and pulse thumping in my ears.

"Well, you don't see that every day," River said.

I shook my head, still stunned by the events leading up to this.

"Come, let's see which one is ours."

"How do you know?" I asked, joining him near the edge of the nest.

"We shake it." He turned to face me and smirked in the dim light.

"What are we looking for?"

"We won't know until we try."

Once we were both inside the nest, ticking started and we froze. We glanced around but saw nothing heading our way.

"Maybe we have to be quick," River stated. "Start looking."

Not knowing what to look for, I picked up the first egg near my feet. I struggled to see what was inside except for the outline of the creature that lay there, waiting to hatch.

"Oh gosh, I don't know what they are but what if they

hatch." I carefully placed that egg down and picked up another.

River worked at a quicker pace than me and had already checked three eggs.

The next egg I picked up wasn't heavy, and I lifted it higher. I tried to see the outline of the creature, but there was nothing.

"I think this is it." I shook it and my shoulders strained.

"Let me see." River took the egg carefully out of my hands and stared at it. "You're right. Let's go before they hatch."

I'd just climbed out of the nest and River offered the egg to me when a crack sounded. River froze and glanced around, followed by another crack. Then something falling.

"Get out!" I whispered and walked away from the nest with the egg in my hands.

More cracking sounded, following by chirping, hissing, rattling, and even a tiny roar.

River jumped out the nest and ran. The sounds increased as more baby creatures emerged from their eggs. Each a different creature and if I didn't know any better, they were hungry.

I was by the hole, placed the egg on the ground and climbed up. River reached me as I got to the top and reached down for him to give me the egg. He lifted it up and placed it in my hands. I brought the egg up as River climbed the rocky ladder. Sounds of angry babies filled the room below us.

River was out, but pulled back down again. He kicked at something below and escaped. He climbed out as I turned to run with the egg toward the water. River kicked a beak, then a blacksnake slithered through. He grabbed the snake and threw it down the hole. He waited until I was in the water before abandoning the hole.

The water rippled violently the moment I entered and swam to the middle. Water splashed against the sides as opposing currents formed a whirlpool. River dove into the water and joined me near the vortex.

Nineteen baby creatures entered the room, each as noisy as the next. Each creature a combination of two different ones, and they were ravenous.

The vortex rippled angrily and sucked us down before the babies climbed in.

The violent water swirled around and around as it pulled our bodies down. My armor rippled over my skin to protect my body and allowed me to breathe underwater. River held the egg with me as we travelled through the water current. It sucked us deeper into dark depths of the abyss. River gripped my forearms as we kept the egg in place between us, when a sudden force pushed us out.

We popped out of the hole from which we'd originally entered like water out of a blowhole. We flew, and I watched as the hole grew smaller and smaller until we crested and started our descent. The ground approached, and we'd land with a painful thud if someone didn't miraculously save us.

My crows squawked nearby, and I smiled. I'd thought they'd left me, but they were here the entire time, waiting for us. Three of my crows grabbed my shoulders while two latched onto River. They flapped their glorious black wings and slowly brought us gently to the ground on the other side of the crystal barrier. Luna barked when she saw us, her tail wagging happily. I thought her tail was going to sprain from excitement as she licked River's face.

I lay back on the ground, relieved we'd made it out and in one piece.

We had retrieved all three pieces for Victor and his brother. It would spare Victor the torment of becoming human; with our victory, he would remain as powerful as he was now and would release River.

"Are you going to call him?" I asked as I stared up at the *sky*. My body numb, while my head buzzed.

"He's on his way." River collapsed beside me with Luna nestled in his arm.

My crows sat nearby—our saviors. "Thank you, crows. You saved us from splatting on the ground."

'It was a pleasure.'

I smiled.

The air snapped, and black sand blasted our wet faces. I wiped mud out my eyes and sat up. Seth stood beside Victor and I could clearly see his features; he no longer hid behind the hologram or flickering picture. He was as graceful as his brother, slightly taller and broader, with similar features. They looked like brothers, cut from the same cloth.

"Well done, brother," Seth said as he held out his hand for the egg.

River and I lifted it together, handing it to him.

"This was fun. We should do it again."

I chortled sarcastically. "Just as long as I'm not involved, you two can knock yourselves out."

Seth glowered at me, and his eyes glowed red. "Control your offspring. She is rude."

"I will do no such thing. Now end this. I've had enough

and have more important things to attend to." Victor pushed Seth aside and held his hands out for River and I to hold. Once our hands touched, we teleported.

Chapter Forty-Six

SCOUT

I soaked in the enormous bathtub for at least an hour. Right before the water cooled down, I filled the tub with boiling water again. I did this five times before deciding to wash and get out. I sat on the chair with the towel loosely wrapped around my pink body as steam filled the room.

Knuckles rapped lightly on the door, followed by, "Are you okay in there?"

"I'm fine thanks, River. Am I needed?"

"Dinner is ready."

"I'll be right out."

When I heard his booted footsteps move away from the door, I stood, stretched my aching muscles and pulled the towel tighter against my body.

Once inside my room, I dressed in casual wear over my armor and left my knotty hair loose around my shoulders. There were no power plugs and doubted there was a hair dryer and it hurt brushing wet hair anyway, so I just left my hair as is.

Even though I was hungry, just thinking about eating

the same food as before left a nasty taste in my mouth. I might ask River to pull food out of thin air. I would rather eat a sandwich than mermaid brains or pixie-stix.

When I entered, I saw River alone on the couch.

The table to the left was void of food, and a sense of dread filled me. I was hungry.

"Where's the food?" I asked when I reached the couch.

River glanced up with a smile that brightened his face and highlighted his boyish good looks. My heart literally skipped a beat when he looked at me like that, and I felt my cheeks heat. I sucked air over my teeth and forced a nervous smile. He ran his fingers through his damp brown hair, and I wondered where he'd freshened up. He pointed at the table in front of him.

"Oh." I sat beside him and glanced at the various trays. "It looks like normal food?" I pointed at the mini-burgers, mini-pizzas, and crackers with cheese.

"I suspect the little chef who prepared the first meal may have gotten wind of your preferred tastes."

"Thank goodness. If the quiche Minotaur balls were on the table again, I was going to ask you for a sandwich."

He chuckled. "Yeah, it may surprise you to learn I'd prepared and packed the food beforehand."

That caught my attention, and I turned to face him with a mini-pizza half in my mouth. "Really, you knew about everything?" I asked while I chewed.

"He asked me to prepare the bags beforehand but didn't know the reason until we arrived at the ancient temple. Victor only shares what he feels like."

"Hmm." I leaned into the couch with the plate on my legs. I enjoyed the tasty morsels as my eyes swept across the room and at the various items against the walls. When I'd first arrived, I was so disorientated and confused I only glanced at everything. There was never time to pay proper attention to what was in the room. While I enjoyed my food, I took it in.

There was a board game atop a skeleton table that looked like rib cages fused together with femur bones as *legs*.

In the corner stood a pyramid; made of real limestone with sand dusted on and around it. One side of the pyramid was open, but I couldn't see inside—I'd have to stand up to see more.

On another table sat a large glass bowl meant for a fish but held plants and black sand. The black sand shimmered as the light caught it at various angles.

There were three portraits on the wall; the first one a jungle filled with wild leaves, a black bear near the front with a hut in the background. The next one a desert with a temple eerily similar to the one we'd visited. Another one of water with an underground maze of rocks. My brows furrowed. I set the plate down and approached the wall.

In the corner on the floor stood a skeletal table with a box and a glass lid. Inside the box was a green maze filled with flowers and tiny fountains. The bottom left-hand corner was bright and cheerful, the top left corner was white with flakes, and the top right corner was dark with passages and then the middle… I gasped and stepped back.

"What's wrong?" River stood beside me, curious for the reason for my reaction. "What the…?" He crouched and lifted the glass lid, setting it against the wall. A cacophony of wings flapping, water flowing, music and other sounds I couldn't discern drowned out my thoughts. It was like the garden maze we had been in.

Wanting to know more, I reached for the pyramid and turned it toward me, revealing rows of pharaohs leading to another room.

The board game atop the skeleton table held a bowl of rippling water.

"What the...? This is the pyramid. That's like the black sand. Over there is the water." My thoughts bounced around in confusion as I glanced at each *game*—each game we had played in. "Did you know about *this*? Did you know of these things?" I turned to River as I asked the questions.

His jaw ticked, and the vein on the side of his head throbbed. "No! I wasn't aware of this," — he pointed at everything, — "of these childish board games. This was something he used against us, to play with us." He sounded angry. "I'd been here many times and never known about them. I've never seen them here before."

A raucous laughter made me flinch, and I stepped away from River with my back to the games.

Victor steepled his index fingers and brought them to his fiendish smile.

I felt hurt, betrayed, and misled.

"Was any of it real? I mean, was the threat of you becoming human ever real?"

"Of course not." Victor stepped into the room. "But it wasn't for nothing, Scout. I did it for *your* future."

It confused me, and it must've shown on my face.

He exhaled and, in an instant, stood before me. He lifted his arms and extended his claws as he reached for my head. There was nowhere for me to go except backward as I tried desperately to avoid his touch. I didn't know what he wanted to do or why he had reached for me. I didn't want him touching me and slapped his arm away, but it didn't deter him from reaching out to me again. His large hands slipped into my tangled wet hair as he held my head. Heat poured from his dark fingertips into the base of my skull and filled my veins with fire.

And I saw...

My vision tunneled until all I saw was darkness, then struck with flashes of memories; his memories as a young boy. He had fought the same ghouls in the temple and had escaped with the golden scarab in hand with a broad, victorious smile.

That memory faded and replaced with the next one; he had battled his internal temptation in the garden and had brought down the snake and garden monster with the angel head on his own.

In the third memory he'd found his dog, Caesar, who'd followed him to the black fumes and into the watery abyss. Victor had made it out after only the second try in the creature's nest—whereas it had taken us three or four times before River had helped me to escape.

I not only saw his memories, but I felt what Victor had felt as a young boy. He'd been afraid at the beginning of his quest, but as he had won each game his confidence grew, as did his power.

With each game he had passed, he had mastered his own destiny.

And at the end of the games, he had won his birthright and rightful place within the Underworld.

It had made him what he was today.

The memories blurred as smoke and thick darkness swallowed me.

I awoke on the couch and drenched in perspiration.

The power Victor had pushed into me to view his memories had filled a gap I didn't know I had. A gaping hole within now filled me with a sense of belonging and awareness; I belonged here as my father's child, and I was aware of the possibilities... For lack of a better word, I was drunk on power and felt a smile creep on my face, and it reached my eyes. I was my father's child and had the nose to prove it.

I had passed their *tests* and overcame my weaknesses, even though I had River's help.

A stinging sensation pulsed at my fingertips. I raised my hands near my face; the blue electricity coursed between my fingertips. Power rippled throughout my body as I floated up.

The expression on River's face made me laugh.

Victor's expression held pride.

I closed my eyes and lowered myself to the ground.

"What was it all for?" I asked, keeping my eyes closed as his power poured into me, growing within. I wasn't afraid it would consume me, nor afraid of losing control. And I absorbed the power Victor offered; it was my birthright now, too. My heart swelled with love and happiness, along with a powerful bond with *Dad*. It tugged at my center, but it didn't threaten to tear me apart, instead it was a gift; a gift bonding me to the Underworld, to him, and to the dead.

"Your initiation, Scout, and to welcome you to the Underworld family. It is your Legacy."

I opened my eyes when Victor brought me in for an embrace, his dark wings closing around us.

"I'll wait right here—" River began, but then I couldn't hear what he said because we teleported.

We moved through the thickness of dark space and landed comfortably near a tree on a mountain overlooking the ocean.

I no longer felt nauseous from the trip and breathed in the fresh sea air.

"Sorry I didn't tell you before." Victor sat on the ground and leaned against the large tree. He patted the grass beside him. I sat down and beamed up at him. "If I'd told you the real reason for the games, I was afraid you wouldn't want to do it. Sometimes people don't want to risk it for themselves, but, if people they love are in trouble they often excel beyond their wildest expectations."

I leaned my head against his shoulder and for the first time felt comfortable near him. It felt like he was my father. *Dad*. Our bond had strengthened the last couple of minutes and now eternally tied to him and the Underworld. He didn't have to tell me what that meant; I knew it—I felt it deep within.

"And Seth played along?"

He chuckled lightheartedly. "Yep, he couldn't wait to play the bad guy." He nudged my shoulder with his and I sat up. He stared at me with his glacial-blue eyes that held no coldness, or hatred, only love. "You are my daughter. And you're at the age where you must take what's rightfully yours. I thought it best to introduce you to my world now instead of when you were younger. The Underworld is no place for a baby; I would know." He winked wickedly. "I knew your mom was pregnant when I left her," he said solemnly. I detected a hint of sadness in his words. "But I only did it to protect you, and her, from my family. If they had known about you, they would've wanted you in our world so they could train you. I didn't want that for you, not yet. I wanted you to have a normal childhood, then after you turned sixteen, I would come for you." His words were sincere, and it made me warm with love.

"Did Mom know about this?"

"Of course not. She would castrate me," he grinned. "And besides, you are my flesh and blood, and I did what I saw fit. And now you have more of my power and can do anything you wish."

"Can I get hurt? Uh, what I mean, am I immortal like you?"

"In the Underworld, you will live as long as any of us. But, the longer you stay on earth, you will age."

Ah, now I understood why River hadn't aged. I glanced down at my hands and felt the pulse at my fingertips.

"What can I do with these new powers? You know? Do I stay with you or Mom?" It wasn't as if there was a job directory I could browse and then pick the one I liked the most.

"There's so much for you to choose from, Scout. You can work beside me, or even River. There's so much out there. The possibilities are endless."

"Speaking of River, what about his contract?"

He sighed. "I cannot break it. I bound him by one of my best contracts. It is impossible for me to alter it."

"You lied to me."

"I did not lie. I told you I would see what I could do. And I cannot undo it."

"What must he do to reach the end of his term?"

"It's complicated."

"Tell me."

"There are people he needs to seek, items he must retrieve, and contracts he needs to gain. There's a multitude of things he must accomplish, and it will take him years to complete."

"You don't fight fair. He's been working for you for over twenty years already." I shook my head in disgust.

"Never make a deal if you don't know the consequences, Scout. You need to remember that." His tone was harsh and blood-curdling. "River understood what he was getting himself into. He didn't have to do it. His mother was ill, and it was her time, anyway. People die all the time. It didn't mean he had to put his life in my hands to save hers. But it's a business for me and right now it's booming."

I turned to him and found him smiling. "What? Are you saying more and more people are knowingly giving their souls to you?" He nodded. A wave of goosebumps bit into my flesh as I considered his words. "What are they getting out of it?"

"It differs. Some want power, others want money, while some want to get away with a crime. River's situation was the last selfless act, and that's why he works with me. His soul is safe, and I don't abuse it. The others," — he shrugged, — "are ornaments on my walls." His smile held a predatory gleam.

"Do these men continue with what they did before they gave their soul to you?"

He nodded.

"And what they did was wrong?"

Another nod.

"These men got away with their crimes."

"I know what you're thinking, Scout. The world is full of these types of men, and if I didn't take their souls and somehow keep them in line, they would've progressed into something far worse. Or they would've asked Seth for help. I'd advise anyone against going to him." Victor shuddered.

In that moment, I'd felt our newly formed bond tear. A tiny mark staining our relationship. He was righting a wrong with another wrong, and it felt awful they associated me with him. He used his contract against those who were evil, but instead of stopping them and ending their nefarious deeds; he allowed them to continue doing those evil things. All Victor did was collect souls like others collected stamps. I wanted to know who these people were; I wanted justice for those they had hurt, a punishment fitting for their crimes.

"But they're still out there doing bad things. We need to stop them." My voice raised.

"No!" he yelled. "It's not your job to stop them." He considered me, knowing what I wanted to do like I wrote it on my forehead. "It is not your job," he repeated, and I wondered if there was something he wasn't telling me.

"What if I make it my job?"

"I cannot stop you." He stood. "When these men reach their end, I will wait for them. And what waits for each is fitting for the deeds they have committed. Do not meddle in my business." He warned and held a clawed hand out for me. I ignored it and stood on my own. "Where do you want to go, Underworld or your Mom?"

"Underworld." I wanted to learn everything about Victor and even River. I wanted to understand everything about the *business*, and I needed to know who these evil men were, starting at the top.

"I know what you are thinking." He arched a dark eyebrow. "I can feel your thoughts as if they were my own. Again, I will ask you, are you sure it's the path you wish to take? It will challenge you. You will get hurt. Understand that I cannot stop you from doing it, but I can also not help."

"I don't want you to help—"

"Everybody wants my help, Scout. Whether they will admit it, but everybody comes to me."

A shudder ran through me at the sound of his voice.

"And when that day comes and you want my help, I will refuse." His eyes darkened with blue flames, then quickly settled to his usual blue.

We stood in silence for a moment. I glared up at him. I

didn't want him to see my hesitation or how afraid I was of what I had set out for myself.

The expression he held wasn't what I expected; I waited for him to be angry, to scold me, or to yell, but he didn't. I only saw love and kindness.

"Why aren't you mad at me?"

His smile crept up his face and reached his warm eyes. "I'm incredibly proud of you and you continue to amaze me."

He brought me in for an embrace; it was comforting, and I felt reassured that he was truly on my side even though I wanted to undo what he'd done.

"I'm simply overjoyed." He let go and exhaled deeply.

I wanted to smile, then remembered I was still mad at him. Instead, I cast my eyes upon the sea and wondered why we'd come here. He hadn't mentioned the reason, and we'd gone off topic.

"Before we go back, I wanted to show you this. It's all yours." He held out both hands.

"The island?"

He nodded. "All of it."

"Where are we?"

"The Bermuda Triangle."

I gasped, covering my face. "Are you serious?" I frowned. "Why here?" I pulled a face of disgust. I'd heard stories about the Bermuda Triangle, and none ended well.

He laughed. "Because no ship can ever come here. I've ensured that. You can come whenever you like, and I've built a house for you over there." He pointed at the double story mini mansion in the distance.

"Wow."

"You are the only inhabitant, but be aware that now and then a creature washes ashore. When that happens, let me know immediately." He arched an eyebrow until I nodded. "Good. Here are your keys." He handed me a set.

"How will I get here?"

"I can bring you. And when you get your wings, you can come here on your own."

"My wings?" I glanced over my shoulder, but there was nothing protruding out of my shoulder blades. I jerked my chin at his imposing dark wings. "When will I get them?"

With a knowing look he said. "I suspect very soon. I had no idea how power hungry you would be. And since you've shown you'd like to come back with me, I'll advise how you can get your wings sooner."

"I'd like that very much," I beamed, bubbling with excitement and the thought of having my own wings. The possibilities were endless with my own transportation. "And can I teleport on my own."

"Easy tiger, let's first see if you can get your wings." He grabbed my shoulders as his wings enclosed around us, and we moved through the darkness once more.

Chapter Forty-Seven

SCOUT

Victor had taken us to a part of the Underworld that was hot and the air stifling with black clouds swirling over a red sky. It reminded me of an angry fire and of a Hell I'd only read in my schoolbooks. The landscape was barren and void of anything *living*. If anything lived here, I doubted it was friendly—or really *alive*. It could be a place where hungry and angry creatures stayed. The heat would drive me absolutely nuts; I would much rather face snow than this heat.

Before, I always felt ill teleporting with Dad, and again motion sickness hadn't taken hold of me and my food had stayed in my stomach, nor was I dizzy. I was most likely getting used to these trips and hoped I could do it myself, and soon.

I stood beside Victor and watched as he did. I didn't know what we were waiting for, nor did I ask. Now was a good time to be mature and not bug him with questions or throw a tantrum.

I pulled on my armor, but it stayed tight around my

body even though I desperately wanted to climb out of it. I'd been wearing it for at least three days without having it cleaned and hoped it didn't stink.

The surrounding heat was unbearable; sweat poured down the sides of my face as I struggled for breath. Victor seemed fine, which was frustrating. I doubted anything bothered him much—he was extremely comfortable in *this* environment.

Something in the distance caught my eye. I squinted at the object, not quite understand what it was, but I knew it had moved. My eyes strained as I continued to focus on the object. Then in a split second it moved closer and continued travelling at a painstaking slow pace. I glanced up at Victor, who focused on the object too. He crossed his arms and puffed out his broad chest. His black armor rippled and reflected the red sky, making it shimmer maroon—reminding me of blood. My armor did the same, leaving a strange sensation across my skin as it rippled and hugged tighter.

I didn't know what to expect, but I knew this was a test to get my wings.

After about five or ten minutes, the object was still far from us and I was losing patience. I glanced up at Victor again, who seemed irritated himself. I couldn't help myself, I had to ask what was going on.

"Um, Victor. What are we waiting for?" I thumbed at the object, slowly edging closer. "That thing is taking forever. Is it a snail? Or a slug, perhaps."

"Have patience."

My head fell backwards as I feigned falling asleep and rolled my eyes.

By the time the creature arrived, I was sitting with my legs crossed, my elbows on my knees and my chin in my hands. The creature walked on four legs, looked like an elephant, but with two horns like a rhino. I climbed to my feet and towered over the little thing. It was adorable, a miniature elephant/rhino hybrid.

"It's so cute." I reached out to pet its head. Its gray skin was coarse like an elephant and rhino, with dark brown eyes. It was so tiny it only reached my hips.

"It's an arsinoitherium from thirty-six million years ago, a distant relative of an elephant." Victor rubbed its head, and a low trumpet sound came from the base of its throat. "Kill it."

His words rocked me backward, and I dropped my hands to my sides. "What? I can't kill it."

"Do you want your wings?"

"Yes."

"Then kill it."

I glanced between the little dinosaur, then back at Victor. "Is he the last of his kind?"

He nodded.

"I can't kill him. And besides, he's just a baby."

"What if it was something else?"

"Like what?"

"And it was attacking you." Victor raised his clawed hand. The dinosaur morphed into a dark, cloaked shadow standing twice as tall with red piercing eyes and a smile filled with sharp teeth. The demon lunged at me.

"What the—" I didn't have time to finish my sentence as it wrapped its toothy jaw around my forearm, piercing the skin and drawing blood—lots of blood. It sucked as it pushed me backward. With my free hand, I pushed against its dark forehead. But that action caused the demon to bite harder and ripped my skin. It fixed its eyes on me and glowered. Sucking sounds continued as it swallowed my blood, and I heard it drink down every drop. "Let," — I smacked its head, — "me," — I smacked it again, — "go!"

It gnawed at my bone. Pain shot through my arm like a flash of lighting had just struck me. I lowered my body to ease the pain, but it didn't help; the creature kept my forearm in its mouth like a vise grip clamping down on me.

"Do what you need to do, Scout." Victor's voice boomed around me.

I heard what he'd said, but it didn't quite register with all the pain.

"Ow," I cried out in response and tears streamed down my cheeks.

Its teeth deepened within my skin, and I hit its head again and again with my fist.

"No, Scout! Use your power," Victor ordered, making me flinch, and I yanked my arm, but all I did was tear my flesh.

I didn't understand what he meant. Should I push the creature's soul out, if it still had its soul considering where we were? But I would try anything at this moment; I pressed my palm to its forehead, and I *pushed*. A tiny spark of power flashed, then sizzled out. Nothing happened to the thing holding onto me except make it hungrier. The creature wrapped one talon around my wrist with the other one on my shoulder, digging its nails into my soft flesh, piercing the tender skin and drawing more blood.

"Use. Your. Power." Victor's voice echoed inside my head.

The red sky darkened. The warm air swirled. Dust blasted against my neck, face and in my eyes, momentarily blinding me. Pain tore through my arm. My breath caught in my throat, and I struggled to take another. The elements blasted me from all sides while the creature ripped through me. It bit down harder, cracking my bone. I knew I screamed, but I heard nothing over the sound of my heartbeat pounding in my ears.

'Use. Your. Power,' Victor whispered inside my head.

"I can't," I said through clenched teeth, followed with a scream until my voice was hoarse.

The creature pulled on my arm and bit down harder. My shoulder popped, and the creature took it as a sign to pull. I opened my eyes as it tugged and pulled, tearing flesh off my bone and snapped it in two. The creature tugged one final time, my flesh ripped apart, and my forearm separated as the creature backed away from me with my hand dangling out one side of its mouth.

I glanced down at the bloody stump before my elbow. As I saw it, I couldn't unsee it; mangled flesh, meat, and bone. I was numb, and most likely in shock. What I'd experienced before wasn't pain, that was nothing. Chunks of chewed flesh hung loosely around the broken bone and it throbbed; flames of furious fire tore through my veins as pain seared through me, threatening to eat me from the inside. The pain pounded within every cell of my body and when it struck my heart; I thought it would burst inside my chest. I collapsed to the ground, hitting my knees first against the hard dirt.

"You've failed." Victor's deep baritone made me shiver. It wasn't his voice that struck a nerve but the words he'd said; I disappointed him. What crushed the rest of my heart, he didn't care the creature had injured me. "I thought you would've done better than that, Scout," he scolded.

"My hand," I sobbed. "That creature took my hand." My throat closed as I stuttered the words, still not believing what had just happened. A creature I should've easily killed had taken a limb, shredded my flesh and started swallowing my hand. Tears flowed down my dirty cheeks, caking the sand to my skin. I cupped the stump with my other hand and lifted my head. Victor stood tall and dangerous. His wings had extended, readying to leave—without me. "Help me."

He moved his head slowly from side to side, then stared down. "You failed." He repeated.

I felt hollow.

He ripped away my life from me and quickly.

I wasn't even ready.

Another wave of pain travelled from the raw end of my arm through my shoulder until it pierced my heart once more. The sudden impact pushed me backward as I tried to keep my balance and landed on my ass as I cradled the wound to my chest. The tears stopped as I stared wide eyed at my arm, then at the creature as it finished gulping down my hand. It smacked its lips together and licked blood from its chin and claw-like fingers, staring at me as it did so. Taunting me with the fact it had won.

"That was my hand," I yelled with pent up anger and shoved the pain to one side. That thing had taken a part of me, and I'm right-handed. I'd have to learn how to do everything with my left hand. I could always get a prosthetic hand. They'd implant a chip in my brain and all I had to do was think about moving my hand and it would.

But... I didn't want that. I wanted my arm back.

"Do what is necessary, or I'll leave you to dwell here for a thousand years. I asked if you were ready and you said you were. But it looks like you were not. You have failed. And you have failed me. What are you going to do?" Victor's eyes shone crimson and his armor rippled, still reflecting that red and metallic glow. He towered over me as he morphed into his true form; red horns protruded out his forehead, his skin shone a healthy red glow, and graced me with his true demonic features.

This was what waited for me here. This would be my true form.

My arm throbbed, bringing me back to my reality; reminding me that I had failed. He was right. I had said I was ready and eager to get my wings. I wanted this, but I hesitated. I thought about how cute the creature was. But instead of treating it as the enemy, I'd lost an arm, while the creature was still alive. If only I'd killed it when I should've —before it became the demon it was now.

Victor stood like an ominous mountain of dark clouds and stormy features—an imposing figure that could smite me out of this world, and leave my soul to roam the Underworld for eternity. *Could Victor ever be nice?* As much as I wanted him to, I doubted he ever would. He was my father, my protector, and my source of strength and someone I went to when in need. I needed him now, but all he'd said was how disappointed he was that I'd failed. He wasn't trying to help me.

I winced with every slight movement and scowled at him.

What we'd learned at school was there were two different places we went to after we died: Heaven or Hell. The good guys went to Heaven, the bad ones went to Hell. So far, I'd seen both good and bad within Victor. He had already said when I'd first arrived there was no Heaven or Hell—only the in-between—only the Underworld. But it wasn't what I'd expected. In all the places I'd visited, they were a mixture of good things in evil places, or evil things in good places; The Garden of Eden with its creatures or the Ancient Temple with its ghouls. It was another realm, similar to my world, with beings and creatures that could hurt or maim. In our world it was up to Mom, Ralph, and hopefully me to eradicate the monsters forever—sending souls to Dad.

But, as much as I wanted to deny it, Victor was my father. He was a part of me, and I part of him. And I held some of his power. It was possible some of his evil was within me, too. Although I didn't feel evil. Surely, while I stayed here meant I could do things he could do; live longer, heal... recreate... reconstruct... restore... and kill.

I exhaled.

And I let go.

I let go of the hate I had for the creature and shoved it away. It had taken my hand, but I forgave it. I drowned out the sounds around me and concentrated on my heartbeat. I forgot about the sand against my body and swallowed the blood in my mouth. Then... I felt something. Whether it was my inner power, I did not know, but it was strong. It pulsed. My power blossomed bright red with flecks of white. Without using my legs to stand, I rose and floated just above the ground. My body hummed with a foreign energy; a force unto its own and I hovered higher. When I opened my eyes, Victor stared at me with a wicked grin and a twinkle in his red eyes.

The creature licked the last drop of my blood from its paws until it was clean.

An eye for an eye.

And I had a taste for blood.

My jaw ached as my fangs emerged. I ran my tongue over the points, baring them. I darted at the creature; it squealed in surprise and tried to pry itself out of my grip, but I was fast—surprisingly fast. I bit into its arm until I tasted its foul, sour blood, but I didn't stop as I chomped on its arm until I struck the bone, then I bit down harder, cracking it between my teeth. I felt the strength of my power flow through my veins as it restored what the creature had taken from me. I felt tissue pull and twist, veins extended, bones stretched as my hand grew and formed whole as if nothing had ever happened. I opened and closed my fist, feeling the tightness of my skin over my new bone and the power throbbing right there—to cause harm.

The creature shrieked from the pain I'd inflicted, then I hurt it some more by digging my now long fingernails into its neck and upper arm. I pushed my sharp nails into its soft flesh until my hands were wet and sticky, but I didn't let go, not yet. The creature tried to get away. It pushed and pushed, but I would not let go. I couldn't let go. This was war. And I wanted blood; its dirty ichor poured down my chin, in my throat, and dripped to the ground. I bit harder and tore flesh from its broken bone and scraped my nails down its skin, pulling chunks of flesh out. The creature shrilled and yanked. I let go then pounced onto it; we crashed to ground, and I went for its jugular. I ripped out its throat, silencing it once and for all.

The quiet wind whipped past me.

The creature lay limp on the ground and its black blood covered my front.

A slow clap sounded behind me, followed by a low raspy laugh. "Well done, Scout. I never thought you would bounce back so quickly. I thought you would give up and cry for me to help you, to baby you. You might only be sixteen, but you share my powers, dear child. You are mine and you will overcome your flaws in time. This was a splendid start and I'm very proud of you."

I stood, wiping my mouth clean with a part of my shirt not ruined, then doubled over when a tiny cluster of stings zapped my shoulder blades, followed by two distinct popping sounds. I glanced over my shoulder and found tiny black wings.

"What the…?" I glanced from one shoulder to the next, not quite believing what I was seeing. "Is this it? Is this how big they are?"

His raucous laughter infuriated me, and I turned cold eyes at him.

"Easy, Scout. Those are your training wings. They will grow as you master your," — he waved his hands in my direction, — "power."

"I can't do anything with these?" I grumbled, rounding my shoulders as the little wings flapped gently with tiny feathers floating around me. Victor laughed harder. "It's not funny," I yelled.

"Oh, come one. It is a little. They're cute."

"Were yours ever this small?"

He shook his head. "No." Then he quickly added, "But that's only because I'm a full blood. You're half human and if I had to guess, it was your mother's half stopping you from getting all of your powers at once. Give it a year and with enough training, they will mature."

"It's still not funny. How do I hide them?" I grumbled, folding my arms across my chest and pouted.

"Why do you want to hide them? You've just proven to me what you can do. Everyone in the Underworld needs to know who you are. So be proud of your accomplishment."

"I thought nobody could know I was your daughter."

"I don't want them knowing you're my daughter, but they must know what you can do. And those tiny wings show you wield the power to stop anyone. They will be afraid of you, Scout, believe me, you will terrify them."

"Oh?"

"Your power will grow and mature in such a way that I'm sure you mother would either be proud or afraid of you. Either way, it's a win-win."

I shrugged, and more baby feathers fell around me. "I guess." I dusted them from my face.

"Come, let's celebrate."

Chapter Forty-Eight

Léon wiped puke off his chest, then gave up when the mark didn't come out of his new silk shirt.

"I told you he'd just eaten." I handed him a wet wipe.

He clucked his tongue. "He reminds me of myself at that age. I could never sit still."

"I'm amazed you remember that far back," I smirked.

Zenon ran around us making car noises and bumped his toy truck into Léon's foot—he just stared at our son with one corner of his mouth curled slightly. He reached for Zenon, but he darted away, making the truck fly.

Sebastian chuckled from the pool where he'd been swimming lengths.

"Uppie, Mommy." Zenon ran to me with raised arms.

I picked him up and settled him on my hip. I offered him juice, but he refused. He leaned his head against my shoulder and sucked his thumb.

"Someone's finally tired." Sebastian climbed out the pool.

I licked my lips. Water droplets ran down his face and throat and over his chest. I felt my cheeks heat. He grabbed a towel to wipe the water off his honed body, teasing me as he slowly dried his sculptured cheekbones. He moved the towel over his chest and his muscles flexed and all I wanted to do was explore him with my tongue. I sucked on my bottom lip. I glanced at Léon and he wore clothes—he was no fun.

"I need to leave." Léon stood and kissed my cheek, then Zenon's.

Zenon reached out for Léon and he took him in his arms. "And he's heavy. What have you been feeding him?"

"Whatever the little monster wants to eat." I pinched his cheeks. "Which is everything."

"Well, he's only a week old, yet five years in age. He needs to eat to grow. I must add, he's aging quicker than either of us." Léon handed Zenon back to me.

"That he is, brother. Just as long as he's healthy, I don't mind how much he eats or how quickly he grows."

Léon squeezed Sebastian's shoulder. "I must tend to business at the club. I'll see you later."

I glanced down at Zenon and his eyes were closed.

"Perhaps we should see if Elena can babysit?" Sebastian said, wiggling his eyebrows.

As I leaned over to place Zenon in his cot, he gripped my top and shook his head.

"Or not," Sebastian said, sounding deflated.

Ever since Zenon's birth, I hadn't had a moment alone with either man. I'd healed completely, and my body missed Sebastian's and Léon's touch. All I wanted to do was strip them naked and ride them until we were too tired to move. But we had a newborn who grew older with each passing day. We had to keep him occupied, fed, and schooled.

Zenon was bright, and like now, got us to do what he wanted us to do.

Someone cleared their throat behind us. I turned to see Salvador standing on the steps, the moonless sky bathing him in dim light from the house behind him. Shadows played on his face, accentuating his sharp cheekbones.

"Give me the boy." Salvador floated down the steps and held out his hands. "I don't have any performances tonight. I have the time to keep him busy, while you two get busy," he whispered mischievously and took Zenon out of my arms.

"Thanks, Dad," Sebastian said, holding out his hand for me.

We barely made it to the room. Sebastian pushed me up against the wall, fumbling to get me out of my clothing. In the end, he tore it from my body along with my underwear. The next moment his board shorts lay shredded on the floor, and he pressed his hard body against me.

We just closed the bedroom door when Salvador walked past singing a lullaby.

I clung to Sebastian's neck and kissed him fiercely. He moved between my legs, moaning as his hands reached for me. I demanded more of the kiss that left no part of me untouched. My need overwhelmed me and wanted it to go on forever, even though I knew it was going to be rough and quick.

He broke the kiss leaving me gasping for air as he teased down my jaw and growled into my neck sending pleasurable vibrations throughout my body.

I cried out with the stroke of his tongue over my aroused nipple. My hands clutched his head, mussing his hair. He kissed down my stomach, leaving a trail of gooseflesh. He kissed up the other side and squeezed my other breast.

I lifted my right leg, wrapped it around his hip and drew him closer. He lifted my other leg, wrapping it around his waist, and pressed his hardness between my legs, pushing me against the wall.

I shoved my hand between us, grabbed his steel length, guiding it toward my opening.

I moaned as he nudged inside, slowly sliding into my slick heat. He eased into me, savoring every delicious touch. He grabbed my ass as I held onto his shoulders and grunted as he angled my hips to go deeper, ensuring I felt every inch of him.

He walked us to the bed, slowly dropping onto it without letting go. He pressed his hips forward, hitting deeper inside the soft wet spot that's been aching for his touch.

I crushed my lips against his, as he withdrew almost all the way out before sliding back in.

He was slow at first, then picked up the pace, slamming into me without restraint. With each hard thrust, he pushed me over the edge; and he gladly went over it with me.

He released his passionate wrath on my body, not holding back. He thrusted deeper with long sensual strokes.

In that moment, there was nothing but him moving within me, watching me, loving me.

All I could do was hold on to him as he embraced me, rocked into me, and loved me with his body, tearing grunts from me as he fought for control.

I couldn't contain myself.

My restraint shattered beneath him and I rocked into him, driving him deeper, harder, and faster.

"Christ, I can't go on for much longer," he grunted the warning.

My nerve endings ignited like fireworks, and I bit his lip. "Fuck!" I moaned.

He growled into my mouth, then buried his face into the nape of my neck, kissing and licking.

I felt his release rising as he pinned me harder, his heart beating against my chest as his honed body worshiped mine.

My body quivered around his, drawing him deeper, scalding him with my climax.

He grunted as he thrusted, filling me. His entire body shaking as heat spread throughout him.

I sagged beneath him, exhausted. As much as I wanted our first lovemaking after giving birth to go slow, it didn't. It was the raw, pent up frustration that one had to get out immediately before going for another round of that slow, delicious, sensual play.

He slowly slid out and lay beside me, pulling me into the curve of his body. His dampened skin stuck to mine, and I clung to him, savoring the moment.

"Say you'll be mine forever?" he breathed the words of honesty and love.

We linked hands; our fingers clenched together.

"I do," I smiled.

Chapter Forty-Nine

SCOUT

Victor allowed me a few moments' grace to shower again, which I used to wash away the blood of the creature I'd destroyed.

My arm was as good as new as I stretched it out and felt the area where the new met the old—it was sensitive to the touch, but it felt awesome to have my arm back. I flexed my fists and extended my hand, testing to make sure it was still there.

I sniffed my armor and amazingly it didn't smell sweaty, but it had a stainless-steel odor if there was such a thing. I pulled on the armor even though I didn't have to, I'd become accustomed to wearing it and felt naked without it. Before pulling it over my shoulders, I reached over and felt the soft feathers on my back. I moved my tiny wings, and they flapped, lifting me an inch off the floor. I giggled. It was so weird. My wings already felt a part of my body, a new limb I controlled. All I had to do was think of flying and they'd flap, and I'd float. If I wanted to hide them; I thought about it, and they automatically pressed firmly against my back, melding with my skin. If I wanted to show my wings, I thought about opening them and they'd reappear through my armor and clothing, like magic. I pulled on my armor and rolled my shoulders. The armor automatically merged with my skin, leaving a tingling sensation, then pulled on a dress. We were celebrating my graduation, from human to Princess of the Underworld.

They had filled the living room with monsters, creatures of the night, and other ghastly things. Luckily, I didn't know any well enough to speak to.

Victor sat on a chair in the corner with three women at his feet.

River stood near the couch and spoke with a bald man with one eye.

In the corner cowered a werewolf who stood in his half-man, half-wolf form like he'd gotten stuck halfway through his change. He licked his elbow and paw, then cleaned behind his ear.

Beside me on the table were trays filled with the familiar yucky food I'd never eat, except the one tray at the back with the savory vegetable balls. I grabbed a handful and ate, while I continued to watch everyone.

Beside Victor was a champagne fountain. Bright sparkly liquid with flecks of glimmering gold sprouted out lips of an angel. My mouth salivated for just a sip, but I was only sixteen. It was illegal for minors to drink alcohol.

In the closest corner, the Fountain of Souls continued its torment of rippling screams and moans as it collected fresh souls.

The Eternal Fire raged on, forever angry and wild. Flecks of blue flame tried to escape but got sucked back into the raging pit. I definitely got the feeling that it was alive and furious—a hostile soul, perhaps.

"Congratulations."

I flinched and spun around to face the person who'd spoken. Seth stood tall, dark, and broody. He chewed on a pixie-stix then licked his long fingers.

I stood with a mouth full of teeth, thinking of a response that didn't come. Instead, I narrowed my eyes and wondered what his motive was for speaking to me. I couldn't understand why, but I didn't trust him, even though he was my uncle.

"At first I didn't want the boy to help you," — he pointed at River, — "but I'm glad he did. I don't think my brother would survive your violent death," he said nonchalantly, like he didn't care whether I'd survived. "And to my surprise, you actually made it through each game. And I had fun; it was a win. Did you like my creatures?"

I nodded. "I did."

The tilt of his mouth and dark gaze told me otherwise; he knew I'd been afraid but said nothing.

"Victor said I should leave my sand serpent, but I know you sensed him. He's a bit of a wild card and I thought better to leave him be. It's hard controlling him."

"I felt him watch me. What would he have done if you allowed him out to play?"

His smile broadened. "Let's just say he's a master at flaying."

I choked on my food and coughed into my hand. "I guess I should thank you then."

"Well, I'm glad to have you in the family. At first, I didn't believe it true, but when I saw you in action," — he smiled a toothy grin, — "I just knew you were my brother's offspring."

I furrowed my brows, opened my mouth to respond when he lifted his hand to shush me.

"Not only are you his child, but you are the first female to be born within this family in," — he shrugged nonchalantly, — "centuries. Imagine my surprise when he had said he had a little girl somewhere. After all these years, he had kept you hidden like a dirty secret. And I always wondered why." He stepped closer, I was too close to the Fountain of Souls to move backward and I didn't have space to move around him. I felt his fiery breath on my face as he spoke. "When Father found out about you, he couldn't wait to test your skill." He brushed strands of loose hair out of my face, leaving behind a burning sensation against my skin. "Do you know the best part?" he asked.

A cold sliver darted down my spine, leaving me chilled to the bone. I didn't know what Seth was getting at or why he was speaking this way, but I sensed danger in bright red letters as if they were flashing on his forehead. He was someone I should never, ever trust. I couldn't respond; I stared deadpan. He smiled sinisterly.

"That your mother is a white light," he whispered.

A cascade of goosebumps bit into my flesh, like blades cutting into me. I swallowed hard.

A large hand crashed down onto Seth's shoulder, forcing the man to cower and step aside. Victor towered over his older brother and it was in that moment I sensed hesitation in Seth's demeanor; he was afraid of Victor.

"Until we meet again," Seth said as his eyes flitted from Victor's to mine, then he disappeared into the crowd of monsters.

"Don't listen to a word he says. He is a vile creature. The worst of us all. He's a skilled player though, but that's where it ends," Victor said as he watched Seth scurry away, speaking to a man with hunched shoulders, then he darted off to another monster with two heads. "Never trust him," he added in a deep tone with silent warning bells.

I nodded. "I won't."

"Good." He squeezed my shoulder reassuringly. "Are you having fun?"

"Uh-huh, thanks for doing all this."

"Have you tried the champagne?"

"I'm only sixteen."

"We don't have an age limit here." He winked. "Go on, try some." He reached for a glass, filled it and handed it to me.

I had a small sip, the bubbly liquid fresh on my tongue with hints of summer fruit. I smiled. "It's delicious."

"Have as much as you want—"

Before Victor said anything else, another voice boomed behind him. "Victor!" the man said.

Victor spun around and stepped away from me. I had sight of the person who had spoken. I glanced at the portrait above the fireplace, then back at him. The portrait had changed; the painting of my grandfather was no longer of a formidable creature but an old pale man, hunched over a walking aid with flowing white hair. The man talking to my dad was tall, with crimson eyes, skin the color of blood, and angry horns out the side of his forehead.

His meaty hand slapped Victor on the back, making him jump. He was an entire head taller than Victor.

My eyes danced from my grandfather to Victor and to the portrait. When I glanced at the portrait, the old man winked at me. I flinched and stared at the two men interact. I was so engrossed with the portrait and of my grandfather's imposing stature, I didn't hear a word discussed between them. It was only when I saw my grandfather speaking directly at me, did I pay attention.

"Finally, I get to meet my granddaughter." My grandfather placed his large hand on my shoulder, his hand was so big it covered my entire shoulder. He rubbed my little wing. During the party I'd forgotten about them and they had become visible to all. A smile flitted across his face. "I'm so proud of you, little one, you have no idea how happy it makes me to have you here with us." He brought me into an embrace; he smelled of mint and dirt. "And to think you came from Victor. I didn't know he had it in him to produce such a wonderful offspring." He stepped back but kept his hands on my shoulders as his gaze raked over me, as if trying to burn the image of me in his brain. I wanted to hide my face as I felt my cheeks burn. "She's beautiful. Are you sure she's yours?"

"Look at the nose," Victor said with a sly smile. "And she wields my powers."

"Hmm, I know, I've been watching." He let go of me but kept his eyes trained on me. "Well…" he slapped his hands together, creating a loud boom. "Let's enjoy the party." He saw someone behind me and smiled, pushed past us and draped his arm around one lady who had sat around Victor's feet, whispered into her ear and she giggled.

Victor rolled his eyes. "Well, that's Dad." He pointed at the portrait. "As you can see, his true self is in the painting now. He always hides behind his other form while he's here. Anyway, enjoy yourself while I tend to the others."

Victor disappeared down the hallway where my room was, and I sat beside River on the couch. I sipped on my champagne; the taste was fresh and tantalizing.

"Does Victor know you're drinking?" he teased.

"He's the one who gave it to me." I clinked my glass against his. "What are you doing here by yourself?"

"I like to watch the interactions among the guests. It's like watching a soapy."

I laughed. "That's for sure."

We fell into a comfortable silence as we watched all the monsters. Some had had a little too much champagne while others were happily keeping the conversations going. A pang of guilt hit, and I leaned into his shoulder.

"I'm sorry I couldn't get your contract cancelled."

"Don't worry about it. It's not your fault, it's mine."

"But I feel bad—"

"Don't, please. It's on me and my dumb actions. Thanks anyway." He bumped my shoulder and warm, amber-colored eyes met mine. "What's next?"

"What do you mean?"

"Oh."

"No, what do you mean by *oh*?"

"Victor needs to tell you. I'm not getting involved."

I punched his shoulder. "Tell me, dammit."

He stood and called Victor when he entered the room. Then River whispered into his ear.

"It's okay." He patted River's shoulder. "I will tell her." He sat beside me while River sat on the coffee table near my feet. "I wanted to wait until after your party and maybe give you a day or two to unwind. Maybe show you a few more levels. But if you want to know what I'd asked River to do, I can tell you now."

I nodded, "Sure, tell me. What is it?"

"Now, it's not like the *games*. This is real. Are you sure you still want in? I'm comfortable for River to do it on his own, but if you want to accompany him, I will allow it."

"What?" I glanced between the two men, but they were incredibly hard to read.

"Think of it as an adventure."

I listened to Victor tell me what he needed. And it was something I wanted to do. But, there was a downside, I would travel for a while. I would miss school, and probably not graduate. Mom wouldn't allow it, but my dad had given me his blessing. Now all I needed was my mom's.

Chapter Fifty

"Absolutely not." My anger swirled around me. "You spend a month with him," — I pointed at Victor, — "and when you come home, you tell me you're leaving again." I eyed the boy who would accompany my daughter on her trip and didn't trust him—he was much older than her. A boy his age had *needs*. I shuddered thinking about what could happen.

"Please, Mom. It's the chance of a lifetime."

"I don't care, Scout. The answer is no."

"Why?"

"You need to finish school—"

"You never finished school."

"I didn't have a choice, but you do."

"I want to do this," Scout groaned, folding her arms with a pout playing on her lips.

"The answer is no." I stormed out of my house and sat on the lounger near the splash pool.

"Let her do it." Sebastian sat on the lounger, forcing me to make space for him. "Allow her the freedom to make her own decision or she's going to go without your permission." He raised both eyebrows.

I glared daggers at him. He was right, and I hated him for it.

"She will have River—"

"Who I don't know at all may I remind you," I groaned. "And he is much older than her. Did you see how he looks at her."

"He isn't her boyfriend, Blaire, he is going to keep her safe, and she has her spirit animals. If you like, I can get a leopard to go with—just in case."

My hard expression softened as I mulled over his words. "You would do that for me?"

"Hell yes, and you know I would. If it will put your mind at ease, I will ask a leopard to join them. She's going to go with or without your approval. So set her free. She 'aint going too far," — he grinned, — "give her the space to grow and to learn on her own terms. Nobody learned anything by staying at home."

I hated it when he was so diplomatic. His hand moved to my other thigh, and I narrowed my eyes at him. He'd pushed some of his power into me to calm me down. I shoved his hand away.

"Don't be like that."

"I know what you just did. Whenever my opinion differs from others, you always do that."

He cupped my face, leaned over and planted a soft, delicate kiss. "I love you. You will make the right decision." He stood and held out a hand for me.

Once we were back inside, I found Scout bonding with Zenon. She sat beside him on the couch, and they played video games. Zenon was only a month old, but the size of a thirteen-year-old. Scout kept glancing at him, not quite believing her brother was catching up to her. I hid my smile.

We'd hired tutors to school Zenon every day, which he managed perfectly. In the evenings when we were at Léon's he'd teach him everything he knew about his clubs, and about vampires, and what it meant to be the Master of them all. Then every other day Sebastian took him to the Leap to learn the leopard's way.

We did not know whether Zenon would shift into a leopard or a saber, or if he was bloodthirsty. But so far, he ate normal cooked food and wanted nothing else. He had no cravings apart from carrot cake which he loved.

Every day I snapped a photo of Zenon and would make a short video once he reached full maturity to see how quickly he had changed. We suspected that by the end of the second month he would be an adult—which Scout was incredibly unhappy about.

I watched Scout and Zenon laugh over their game and who was winning, and my heart swelled with pride and overflowed with love.

Scout glanced at me as if she had felt my stare and plastered on a smile, even though she was still upset. A genuine smile crossed my face as I approached her. Her expression softened and her smile became real, as if she sensed what I was about to do.

I knew if I kept her at home, she would rebel against me and either go live with her dad in the Underworld or run away from both of us. I couldn't allow that to happen. I'd been a child living on the streets with no-one to turn to. It was only because I'd followed Marcus around like a lost puppy, did he take pity on me and had trained me. She might not be as lucky, and I'd hate to imagine what would happen to her in the same situation. It left me with few options, and I couldn't afford to push her away. She was my flesh and blood. I needed to trust her and let go. If Victor was comfortable sending River with her, then I had to trust him; if anything happened to her, I was sure Victor would skin the boy alive. And if Sebastian sent one of his leopards with, then I could take comfort both would keep Scout safe from harm.

I called Scout over. She hugged her brother, set the controller on the coffee table and sat beside me.

The room became eerily quiet, as if everyone was waiting for the bomb to drop. I smiled at the thought of playing a joke on Scout by telling her I'd grounded her. It would be cruel of me and incredibly insensitive and thought best not to tempt fate.

"You can go—"

Scout let off a high-pitched squeal, forcing me to cover my ears. Poor Sebastian almost fainted with his super hearing abilities, it was so painstakingly high he exited the house and went out back.

"Sorry," she gushed and sat back in the chair. "You've made me so happy."

"One condition—"

"Here it comes," she said, sounding deflated.

"It's not that bad. Sebastian is sending a leopard to accompany you and River." I held up my hand to stop her from interrupting me again. "If everything goes fine and you are capable, then he or she can return home and you and River may continue. It's only a precaution."

"Fine, I can live with that." She pouted, then stopped when I arched an eyebrow. "Thanks Mom." She darted out of her seat and hugged me. I felt the soft feathered wings on her back. "Stop, that tickles." She squirmed out of my embrace.

"Sorry, but they're so soft. And I'm very proud of you." I eyed Victor, who stood tall. She still hadn't told me what she had to do to get them.

"Thanks Mom."

I hugged her again, not wanting to let go. She basically had to pry herself away from me.

"When are you leaving?"

"In about a week."

"And where are you staying until then?"

She glanced at Victor, perhaps silently asking him for help on how to break the news she was going with him.

"It's okay, just stop by before you leave."

"I will," she smiled sweetly, gave me one last hug, then ruffled Zenon's hair. "See you when you're older, brat."

"Hey, aren't you still playing?" Zenon complained.

"Sorry, kid, I must go."

"I'm not a kid, you know."

"I know, but it's still weird you're aging so quickly. I can't even call you my baby brother anymore." She pinched his chubby cheeks. He smacked her hand away, glared at her with angry yellow eyes followed by a feral grunt.

"Zenon!" Sebastian chided and shook his head from where he stood.

Zenon sat back and continued playing his game, sulking.

"One last hug before you leave."

Once Scout, Victor, and River had left, I lounged outside by the pool—it wasn't as big as Léon's, but it kept us cool on hot days.

I still had a long way to go before I was back to my normal weight, but I wasn't in a hurry to slim down. I enjoyed my food, I just had to exercise a bit more and maintain a healthy balance. Although sometimes I fell off the wagon and ate two slices of pie or added an extra scoop of ice cream.

I perused the document Ralph had dropped off; it was an assassination order Slayerbody had given us. I didn't like it, but it came with a hefty price tag. I'd already told Ralph we didn't need to do this for the money anymore, but he had insisted on it. Apparently, our mark was an evil monster and needed to die.

If we did it, if I was happy for us to do it. We'd have to plan it well. Nobody would survive an assassination of someone in the new government.

Chapter Fifty-One

Three Months Later

I couldn't stop staring at Zenon. My four-month-old son was a twenty-eight-year adult.

Sebastian said something funny and Zenon laughed—the similarities between the two were striking. Zenon had yellow/golden eyes with a green sliver in each iris, where Sebastian's green eyes held that familiar golden sliver. Zenon was slightly taller than Sebastian, but not as muscular. He was training with Sebastian and Ralph to build muscle, but I'd advised him not to do too much too soon.

And one of my greatest fears...

"Hi Zenon," said one of the younger female leopards. She battered her eyelashes at Zenon and blushed.

"Hey," Zenon replied, then continued speaking to Sebastian—not overly concerned with the attention.

The poor girl looked deflated when Zenon didn't hug her or give her the attention she craved, and I couldn't help but beam with pride.

"That's Naomi," Sebastian said.

I followed his line of sight and found the three sitting near the bonfire. Sebastian had told me Kai had met his mate, and I couldn't be happier for him.

"Now we need to find someone for Lee."

"He's a big boy, he can do it himself," Sebastian said dryly.

I rolled my eyes.

"I saw that."

I smacked his ass playfully, wrapped my arms around him and pressed my face against his back. "But you love me for it."

"Gross mom, please, not in public."

"And I'm proud of you."

"Why?" Zenon furrowed his brows.

"Don't give in to the lady's charms just yet. You still have a lot to learn even though you look like that—" I waved a hand at him. "You're a quick study, but that doesn't mean you're immune to heartbreak."

"Ugh, not you as well. Dad's already given me *the speech*."

"Good, I've trained you well," I said to Sebastian, who coughed into his hands.

"Are you ready to hunt with Dad?"

"I was born ready."

I laughed. "Yes, son, that you were."

Zenon opened his mouth to say something, then closed it again. He had something on his mind.

"What? Spit it out. You know I won't stop until you tell me."

"Scout called—"

"When? What did she say?" My brows furrowed. "She didn't tell me."

"She asked if I wanted to join her." He chewed the inside of his cheek.

"What?" I pushed away from Sebastian. "When? Are you going to go?"

"I'm thinking about it."

"Now was not the right time, Zenon." Sebastian chided our son.

"You knew?" I slapped his chest.

"You have anger issues."

"Which I'm working out, thank you very much." I turned my attention back at Zenon, who looked deflated. "I'm sorry. Okay, let's try this again. What did she say? Is she in trouble?"

"No, it's nothing like that. She just asked if I wanted to come along, you know, to gain some life experience. I am twenty-eight after all."

I lifted my hand to stop him from rubbing that in my face. "You are four months old, and in my books you're still a baby." He pushed his hip out and rolled his eyes. "Don't give me that look, Zenon. I'm serious."

"We can discuss this at home." Sebastian brought me into the curve of his body and my shoulders relaxed.

"I hate it when you do that." I pushed away from him again.

"Then stop getting angry."

I exhaled a shaky breath and shook my hands out. "Fine. I'm relaxed. Is Jeremiah still there with her?"

"Yes, he says everything's fine."

"It will be the four of you?"

"Yep."

I closed my eyes and counted to ten. "Fine, you can go. But I want daily updates or I'm going there myself and I'll embarrass you."

"Thank you, Mom!" Zenon hugged me then his Dad and ran to Lee and Kai.

"I hate this." I turned to Sebastian and buried my face into his chest.

"You did fine, woman. And I love you so much." He cupped my face and lifted my head. He smiled in that luscious way that made me weak at the knees and putty in his powerful hands.

"I love you more."

Also By N Gray

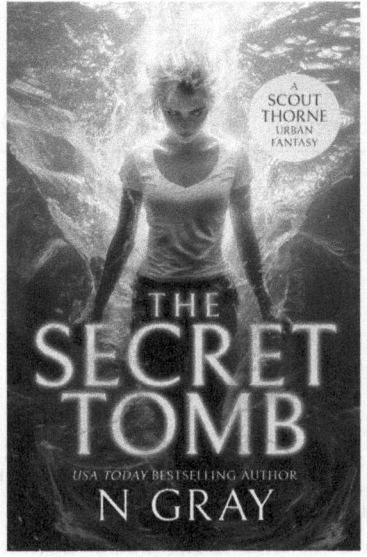

vinci-books.com/secrettomb

What price would you pay to unlock immortality—your soul, or someone else's?

Scout thought she had escaped her past, but the underworld has a way of pulling you back. When a fiery blast drags her into a dangerous hunt for the Mask of Immortality, secrets unravel, and trust becomes a gamble. Can she survive the darkness… or will it consume her?

Turn the page for a free preview…

The Secret Tomb: Chapter One

Victor stood beside his older brother and watched the madman show them how they could use the mask. But the real reason for the demonstration—they needed to determine whether it was the right mask. Harry 'Houdini' Morris pulled the cart closer so they could see clearly.

The darkness of the night never bothered Victor, he thrived in it. He did his best work at night, using the shadows to blend in, but tonight his eyes scratched, and the blackness troubled him for some unexplained reason.

Victor's older brother, Seth, was as impatient as a young child waiting anxiously for Father Christmas to deliver his presents.

"Father is going to get a kick out of this," Seth said, grinning from ear to ear. His emerald-colored eyes sparkled like jewels in the starless sky. "He's been looking for this mask for centuries."

Victor rolled his eyes. It was true, their father, the King of the Underworld, had been looking for the mask, but only because he wanted to destroy it. Their father was afraid of anything that posed a threat to his power, and their father didn't want to lose his position within the supernatural world. Which was understandable. Neither did Victor nor his brother.

Harry made an exaggerated show of draping his coat over his shoulder and crouched behind the old cart. The action reminded Victor of the good times when there was no electricity, and gaining souls for his pleasure was easier. He, too, walked around in a long black coat and top hat, enticing men and women with delicious sins for their pathetic soul. These days, it was all about the latest electronics or immediate gratification that created the shortest attention spans.

Harry coughed, gaining Victor's attention. Victor smiled knowingly; it seemed he too had a short attention span.

Harry slowly opened a large vintage wooden chest held within the cart. "My Dark Lord's, thank you for meeting me here," he said, gesturing at the ancient cemetery. "It's rare my Lord's venture out of the Underworld, but I assure you tonight will be worth your while."

"Just get on with it, human," Victor snapped, his eyes burning red. "Before I eat your soul."

"Yes, my Lord," Harry muttered and stood straighter. "We found the mask that was once lost," Harry said, pulling a never-ending cloth out of his pocket. "It wasn't easy to find, and we had casualties. When my men found this hidden in a secret tomb, I knew who the rightful owners were—"

"You weren't interested in the riches that could come with finding such an artifact?" Victor asked suspiciously. His left eye itched as he watched Harry with the cloth and wondered why the distraction. "You could've auctioned this off to the highest bidder."

"Oh, no my Lord," Harry said, sweeping his arm low and bowing down. "It is not riches I'm after." He stood up and continued pulling the never-ending cloth out of his pocket. Once done, he threw the cloth on the ground but kept the ring that was tied to it.

"Then what do you seek?" Victor asked. His tone was louder and harsher than normal, making Harry flinch.

"Only to serve," Harry said, averting his eyes. "I wish to serve the Dark Prince's in the Underworld and when it is time, you will ensure my family gets what they deserve." Harry's eyes flitted to Victor and then to Seth before staring at the ground once more.

"Why?" Victor's suspicion grew. Nobody willingly gave something away for free, along with their soul. Was this charade only so that he could exact revenge on his family? It made little sense.

"I assure you," Harry said, glancing at Victor. He stepped closer to the dark angel, whose black wings had opened and now spread wide, displaying his power over the human. "My time here has ended, and I wish to become a servant in your world. I honestly have had enough of this world," he swept his hands wide, "I'm sixty-seven and my tricks are old in these times. Nobody wishes to see an old man perform magic tricks. I can do nothing about my parents for sending me to that institute when I was a boy. They thought I was special when I was not. I only loved doing magic; that was what made me special. But my wife and kids are alive and well. I wish the worst to happen to them," Harry said maliciously as his eyes filled with hate and narrowed.

"Ah, there it is. You wish revenge on your family?" Seth asked, nodding. "They treated you unkindly?"

"Yes, my Lord. They were cruel all my life. They never

supported my shows or appreciated the life I'd given them. No matter how many hours I worked, the street corners I performed tricks on, did my family say thank you. Ever. And I think it's time they all got what they deserved."

Seth clapped his hands slowly, creating a sonic boom sound. "Deal, now let's get on with the show."

Victor glared daggers at his brother, who shrugged in response. "You're far too trusting, brother. If anything happens, it's your fault."

"Yes, yes, as it always is." Seth waved Victor away like he did when they were children and nodded curtly for Harry to continue.

Victor stared suspiciously at Seth.

Harry called someone over who had been lurking in the shadows of a tree. It surprised Victor because he hadn't seen that person until they walked across the lawn. He was usually more aware of his surroundings and could tell the difference between hidden dangers and shadows. He tugged on his shirt, glancing over his shoulder and then back at the assistant as he approached the magician.

The assistant wore a matching red coat that billowed out behind him as he walked toward Harry. The assistant was younger than Harry, but that meant nothing; some supernaturals never aged at all, and from this distance, Victor couldn't tell what he was. The assistant held open his hand, and an orb glowed blue in his palm; he was either a wizard or a warlock. When he closed his eyes and said an incantation, Victor heard and understood what was about to happen; he was going to raise the dead at their feet.

The ground vibrated, and the headstone near the necromancer toppled over. The sand dispersed, creating a hole big enough for the corpse to animate and sit up. But before the dead could rise, Harry removed the mask out of the wooden chest and slapped it on the necromancer's face.

Two things happened at once; the corpse crumpled back inside its coffin like a dirty old rag. And the necromancer's shoulders dropped when the orb disappeared, and he glared daggers at the magician.

"There we have it, my Lords; The Mask of Immortality or the opposite when used on any supernatural, rendering them powerless," Harry said. His smile widening as he removed the mask from the assistant.

Harry's eyes flitted from the brothers to the mask, and then something happened in slow motion. He raised the mask as if to praise it, then lowered it onto his face.

Harry grew twice his size, fell onto all four limbs as he shifted into something much bigger. He didn't stop growing as he morphed into a gigantic wolf-orca hybrid; a killer whale on land. He swished his large, dark tail backward and forward. His head turning toward Victor and growled hungrily like a wolf.

Victor didn't have time to transport himself back to the Underworld, and he didn't have time to call for help as Harry 'Houdini' Morris lunged for him.

The Secret Tomb: Chapter Two

Ralph ran to my right-hand side and away from the action. I stopped running and yelled, "Why are you going that way?" I shrugged when he turned to look at me. "The corpse went this way." I pointed at the nearby shed, the door banging shut.

"You go that way, I'll go this way," Ralph said sarcastically with a roll of his eyes. His wavy brown locks held tightly in a ponytail. Every couple of years, he'd either shave his hair close to his head or grew it long, reminding me of a grizzly bear; like now. "Didn't your mother teach you various maneuvers to get the dead guy?"

"Ha, funny." I rolled my eyes. "But you're going far off, buddy. The dead guy went inside the shed."

"That's what you think," he sang and continued up the stairs and into the house. "I'll flush him out," he yelled. "Be ready with those deadly palms of yours."

"Fine," I yelled. "I'll just catch him here," I grumbled to myself, pulling my gloves out of my pants pocket and slipping them on. I crept toward the shed and slowly opened the door; the sun behind me casting the small room in enough light to see. "Where did you go, you zombie?" I mumbled to myself.

"Scout!" Ralph shouted.

I spun around in time to see the animated corpse reach for me, its beady black eyes dripping pus while the rest of his body losing chunks of rotten flesh in its wake. I couldn't believe I missed him. For a dead guy, he was pretty smart and quick on his dead feet.

"Aaaaar," mumbled the corpse. His head flopping from one side to the other while he growled with lips that were no longer there. He only had a few teeth left after the fight that had put him in the grave, and those few stood in different directions.

"Not today, buddy," I said, shoving my palms into his chest.

The corpse grabbed my wrists, its slimy grip tightened.

"Ew, you're so gross." I gagged, then pulled a face when a chunk of green, rotten flesh fell on my new sneakers, which angered me. "No," I screamed as I pushed my power into his chest, pushing the corpse backward.

Heavy footsteps stomped down the stairs and approached me. The corpse's soul flew out of its body as Ralph stopped beside me, out of breath, and sprinkled salt around us. The salt wasn't always necessary, but we needed it because the animated corpse was so volatile. And to my other side, Blaire, my mother, ran up to us, whispering an incantation, keeping the soul out of its body. The incantation was necessary but sometimes I'd forget to say it. When that happened, I had to work harder, pushing their souls out of their bodies.

I whistled a specific tune. The ghostly figure of the ferryman appeared in his phantom boat, scooped up the silently screaming soul, and continued on his merry way. His eyes glaring at me from the back of his head like it did every time. I no longer shuddered or glanced away, instead I waved and smiled.

I let go of the corpse and his body crumpled to the ground, and dusted my gloved hands. After flicking off chunky pieces of the corpse, I carefully removed the gloves. "All in a day's work," I said, beaming.

"Good job, my child," Mom said, kissing my cheek. "But don't relax too much. We have another case," she thumbed behind her at Ralph's vehicle. "I suggest we grab something to eat before heading that way."

"Good," Ralph said, grinning. "I'm starving."

"You're always starving," I chortled, smacking his abdomen. "What's the other case?" I asked, slipping my gloves into a plastic bag. They'll need to be dry-cleaned before I could use them again, but I had another pair in the car.

Ever since I started working with Mom and Ralph at Ulysses Assassins, the need not to touch those we were after became greater. There was something about me shoving their souls out of their bodies that made me feel queasy, but wearing gloves seemed to remove the nausea.

"It's at the aquarium. There's an issue with their new orca," Mom said, scratching the left side of her chest until it became inflamed. "And a village in Peru just vanished," she said absentmindedly as she scrolled upward on her touch-screen phone. "Weird things are happening around the world," she rambled, still scratching her chest with her free hand.

I reached for her and stopped her from scratching. "You're about to make yourself bleed," I said, pointing at the raw skin.

"Blaire seems to be allergic to the new detergent as well," Ralph chimed in. "Come, I need food."

Lately, my mom had been struggling with allergies; first it was tomatoes, then her shampoo, and now it's her detergent.

"I'll be fine. I'm seeing Mel later," Mom said with an urgent need to scratch.

"Stop it." I chastised her like she used to do to me. "You can't see Mel now?" I asked. Mel was a werewolf and the doctor for every shifter in Sterling Meadow. She was great at what she did, and the wolves didn't seem to mind sharing her with every supernatural. Years ago, when they formed the Were-Animal Alliance—the WAA—, Sterling Meadow became one of the safest towns for shifters and supernaturals to live in. Even the vampires didn't seem to mind working with everyone.

"She's busy with the leopards," Mom said, rubbing the inflamed area with her index finger.

"You probably can't put anything on that right now? It might sting the crap out of you." I winced looking at the reddened area.

"I'll be ok," Mom said, slipping her arm through mine, and resting her head on my shoulder. We walked in silence toward Ralph's vehicle, but before I opened my door, a warm wind caressed my cheek and all the hairs on my body stood on end.

Mom let go of me and spun around with her weapons drawn, ready to use it. I unsheathed my knife, glancing around for the attacker. Unfortunately, Ralph was very human and human slow. He noticed nothing until he turned around and saw us standing like we were ready to strike an invisible force.

Tiny blue sparks flickered at my fingertips, ready to blast this creature approaching.

In the distance, a tall, dark figure approached with a dog running beside him. I eyed him narrowly and mumbled his name.

"Who?" Mom asked, ready to pull the trigger.

The blue sparks at my fingertips died down like an ice-cold bucket of water washing over me and my heart stuttered in my chest. My breath caught in my throat, and I swallowed hard.

It was River…

The Secret Tomb: Chapter Three

"What are you doing here?" I said through gritted teeth. "I told you never to seek me out ever again." My anger coursed through my body like a shot of adrenaline. "You promised never to see me." The last word came out softer than I hoped, and I swallowed hard, not trusting my voice to speak again.

Luna jumped up and down, her tail wagging, and her tongue hanging out of her mouth when she saw me. I couldn't ignore this sweet girl. This fight was between me and her owner. I crouched down and scratched behind the Mexican Mutt's ears.

River sighed heavily. "Your father needs you," he whispered.

I glared up at him, but he averted his eyes. It didn't help to show him how angry I was after our breakup if he wasn't paying me any attention. I continued scratching behind Luna's ears while she licked me, then I stood up.

Mom and Ralph climbed into the car, giving us privacy; Ralph switched on his radio, blaring country music. While

Mom tried hard to be busy, but I knew she was watching us out of the corner of her eye and most likely going into protective-Mommy-mode.

River's eyes flitted to mine; those amber-brown colored eyes held nothing but pain and sadness. The weight of his emotions was clear on his face. There was much we needed to discuss, but I couldn't do that now. I may never be ready to talk about what would never be.

My anger seeped out of my pores as we stared at each other knowingly. His sad expression matching my own. He was just as heartbroken as I was. We had separated over a year ago, but the heartache was still raw, like it had happened yesterday. And it wasn't just me. He felt the same way.

I'd been working with my father, Victor, in the Underworld until I couldn't anymore. He kept on giving bad guys free passes. These men hurt innocent humans and supernaturals alike without a care in the world because my father would always be there for them. I took it upon myself to go after these bad guys, but no matter how many I killed, more replaced them. My father won in the end when he got contracts for their souls long before he was supposed to, and he kept on getting new souls. It was never ending, and I couldn't continue any longer.

River, on the other hand, could never leave my father's side until his contract was up. He was the one soul I could never help. My father would never give up his best soul; River, no matter how hard I tried, or how much I begged. My father never relented.

I swallowed the emotional lump in my throat and wanted to understand why he was here. "Why does he want me? I told him—"

"He's in trouble," River said, interrupting me. He held

up a hand to shush me, then reached out for me. I didn't want him touching me. I couldn't. Not so soon. I stepped backward. "Please Scout," he said my name with so much emotion the back of my throat ached.

"What did he do this time, or is it like that awful game he made us play and he isn't really in trouble?" My anger had returned, and I felt better. My small black wings flared to life and stretched out behind me. I calmed down and thought hard about hiding them again.

There were things I had to do to gain my much larger wings, but I didn't feel like harming anyone, even though I wanted my fully developed wings. Sometimes being the daughter of a devil didn't sit well with me.

"You need to come home with me." He reached for my hand.

I stepped farther away. "No," I said, shaking my head. "I never want to return. He has demons to help him. Start there."

River shook his head and sank his hands into his deep pockets. "You don't understand, your father is... uh, he isn't who he used to be."

"Your words are cryptic. What do you mean?" I sounded angry again.

He shook his head slowly, his eyes never leaving mine. "Not here. You're too exposed, and I'm being vague on purpose. It's to save both of your lives," he said gravely, making my arms pebble.

I rubbed my arms and stepped closer. "I don't like this."

"Me neither. But you must come with me. It's not something I can say. I need to show you."

My eyes flitted to Mom, who remained in Ralph's car. She stared at me and shrugged as the lines between her eyes deepened.

"Give me a second," I said and approached Ralph's car. Mom wouldn't be pleased if I left without speaking with her first. She lowered her window, and some cheesy song assaulted my ears. She switched off the radio.

"I need to go with River," I said, thumbing over my shoulder. "Something is up with Dad."

"Do you need me to come with?"

"No, I should be ok."

"And you trust him?" she asked, narrowing her eyes at River.

I glanced over my shoulder at River and deep in my heart, I once trusted him with my soul. I hated him at the moment, but I still trusted him. "Yeah," I said, turning back to Mom. "I shouldn't be long." I slapped the car. "I should be home by dinnertime."

"Ok, call me if you need my help." Mom patted my hand and smiled lovingly. "And if you need Zenon, he should be back this afternoon. I'm sure he'd love to help."

"Thanks, Mom."

"Love you."

"Love you, too." I kissed her cheek and approached River.

Grab your copy...
vinci-books.com/secrettomb

About the Author

A Multi-genre author writing twisted endings...

N Gray is a USA Today Bestselling Author who lives in Cape Town, South Africa, with her daughter and adopted cat named Miss Beans.

During the day, she's an analyst and provider profiler for a medical insurance company. At night, she types on her curved keyboard, creating fictional characters some may love and others you want to kill yourself.

She writes in four genres: urban fantasy, thriller, horror, and paranormal romance.

She now writes under Natalie Michaels for her new thrillers and SD Syns for her new horrors.

Acknowledgments

Thank you to Erika, a Patreon supporter. Because of her support I included a character, Negan, into this story.

Thank you to my BETA team, Jessca and Mariel, who helped sort out any gremlins before the book went to the editor.

And *thank you* to Liz who helped with the finishing touches.

Also a shout out to my family, without you I may not have gotten this far.

Lastly, to my readers, thank you for reading!

www.ingramcontent.com/pod-product-compliance
Ingram Content Group UK Ltd.
Pitfield, Milton Keynes, MK11 3LW, UK
UKHW041953291225
466476UK00005B/3